The Vienna Trilogy

BOOK 1: ESCAPE TO THE WEST

BOOK 2: NAZIS ON THE RUN

BOOK 3: STOPPING THE RUSSIAN BEAR

by Tom Gilligan

Illustrations by Everett Walker

Intelligence e-Publishing Company
Cape Cod, Massachusetts

Intelligence Book Division

Intelligence e-Publishing Company, Cape Cod, Massachusetts

Illustrations by Everett Walker.

Book Design by Charles King (ckmm.com).

ISBN 978-0-9729659-6-5

Library of Congress Control Numbers:
Book 1: 2022912940
Book 2: 2022914020
Book 3: 2022917921

The Vienna Trilogy

The Vienna Trilogy

BOOK ONE

Escape to the West

Contents

For Bonnie

and other wives and children

whose support and sacrifices

helped win the Cold War, 1947–1989.

1

Vienna at Night

The Date: Tuesday, June 3, 1947—just 24 months after World War II ended.

The Time: Shortly before midnight—when spies go out for their own "day's work."

David Hale heard movement on the back stairs. His dad must be descending to his study, David concluded, when he heard the fourth creaking sound. Like spies, who work best in the dark, David was one of the night wanderers of Vienna. He had already learned well the *nocturnal** sounds of his newest home. Four months before, within a day of moving into the old castle, he had made plans for his late night *capers.†* He had scouted out his new home from *apex‡* to foundation and, in reverse, from cellar to tower.

The first thing David had done was to check out the back stairs. Creeping upstairs and downward from his second floor bedroom in several trips, he found three creaky stairs going up to the attic. He then counted four loose ones going down to

---

* Nocturnal: Night time.
† Capers: Adventures.
‡ Apex: The highest point in a structure or building.

the first floor where his dad had his study. Good to know, he figured, when he—or anyone else—moved about the house.

"It'll have to be the tower tonight," David whispered to no one in particular. "The cellar can wait for another time—when the coast is clear and Dad will not hear me."

David had this habit of talking to himself in a barely audible whisper. It made him feel less alone—much like the whistling a person does to *feign confidence** when sensing danger. Before summer passed, David would need every security aid he could *muster.*† By entering the world of *espionage*,‡ his life would be transformed in ways he had never imagined. In fact, he would soon be talking to himself and whistling. But, like a spy, he would be doing it ever so silently.

David was not afraid of the dark. As far back as he could recall, he fought to stay awake at night—not wasting time "going off to lullaby land," as Mom would say when he was a toddler. When David went to bed each night, he felt as if he was going to jail—he saw himself as being no different from a prisoner or caged animal. Some animals prefer daylight—they are called *diurnal.*§ Nocturnal animals, of course, hunt and roam about in the dark. David, however, liked to think of himself as the world's first *biurnal*¶—one of the few persons on the planet who can work and explore day and night.

---

*   Feign confidence: Pretending to appear self assured, safe, and free from danger.
†   Muster: Call forth or rouse.
‡   Espionage: The world of spies where secrets are stolen from other governments.
§   Diurnal: Those that roam about and hunt or eat in the daylight, such as wolves and lions.
¶   Biurnal: David created this word to mean he can operate both in daylight and in the dark.

SLEEP! David had reflected on it a great deal and finally calculated that sleep was an enormous waste of time—a waste of life, in fact! "You can't do anything worthwhile in your sleep—except lose half your younger years and a third of your older years." David declared to anyone who would listen when the subject of sleep arose in conversation. Those were the dreadful fractions—one-third and one-half—that David came up with when he first learned to divide. The eight hours most adults sleep divided by the twenty-four-hour day is one-third. The twelve hours little kids sleep divided by the twenty-four-hour day is one-half.

"That's nuts!" he blurted out to Thor, his handsome German shepherd resting peacefully on his rug in the corner. If only David could be like the inventor Thomas Edison, he estimated, the dreadful fraction could be cut down to one-sixth. "Thor, one out of every six hours ought to be the *maximum** time I am forced to lie in bed. Why, if I slept four hours a day, when I am thirty I will have gained five additional years of life. Imagine that!" The dog stared back at David with what the boy considered to be an interested look. But, just as quickly, Thor shut his eyes and dozed back to sleep.

Before *embarking*† on tonight's *trek*‡ to the attic, David thought about his dad downstairs in the study. He wondered whether the late evening visit there had anything to do with the startling conversation David had overheard in the afternoon—the talk about gunmen and spies. The spooky conversation had

---

* Maximum: The most or greatest amount. Opposite of minimum, the least amount.
† Embarking: Starting or beginning a trip or journey.
‡ Trek: A difficult journey or trip.

occurred shortly before his mom and sister Ellie had left for the airport. They were taking a flight to New York to visit relatives for the summer. David, by choice, was staying in Austria with his dad until late August when they would all meet in New York for a couple of weeks. That was the plan, at least.

His parents' words repeated in David's head. He was excited, certainly—he was *perplexed*,* also. After all, his dad was a medical doctor—nothing more. Or, was he still only a doctor?

Dr. Matthew Hale had done secret work during *World War II.*† David learned this when his dad returned home from the war after having been reported *missing in action.*‡ It turned out, in fact, that Matt Hale was not missing at all. Rather, he had been sent into Nazi Germany on a secret intelligence operation. That mission required his medical and German language skills and concerned a group of top German rocket scientists whom the United States Government wished to contact.

David long had wanted his dad to tell him all about the war—especially any secret work he had done. However, since returning safely at war's end, Matt Hale was reluctant to talk about wartime activities. The subject of the war itself, to use one of dad's favorite German words, was *verboten.*§ "Too many good people died," he said, "for us to be chatting about it idly. Maybe when you get a little older, we can really talk. When it's safe."

---

*   Perplexed: Surprised, puzzled, confused by something.
†   World War II: The greatest war in history that began in Europe in 1938, spread to Asia in 1941, and affected the whole world before ending in 1945. Sixty million people died in this war.
‡   Missing in action: Being lost in a war and believed to be dead or captured.
§   Verboten: Forbidden, in German.

Due to the afternoon's visit to the study, the boy wanted to go downstairs and ask his father directly about the new secret business. But, if he did, his dad would know that David had *eavesdropped** this afternoon. Listening in on the *cryptic*† remarks of his parents had been unintentional. David knew that. But, he knew also that his being in the study was not entirely *virtuous*† either. He was playing *hooky*§ from German class, which surely wouldn't earn him any rewards from his parents. He was in a *quandary.*¶

David now understood *implicitly*** that things were different from what he had assumed. Vienna was different—his dad was different. And maybe, just maybe, David's own life could be different, too! Or, so he hoped.

He loved his family, the new castle home and faithful Thor, who had an interesting history of his own. In the war, Thor was a U.S. Army *Patrol Dog*†† and was wounded in one of the last battles. "Why, even you, Thor, have had a more exciting life than I've had," David remarked to his *canine*‡‡ pal who showed no interest in the matter. "You may be the best secret keeper of them all, I'm afraid!"

David Hale wanted more in life than growing up *passively*§§

---

*   Eavesdropped: Listened secretly to something that is private.
†   Cryptic: Hidden, mysterious or having a secret meaning.
‡   Virtuous: Innocent or good.
§   Playing hooky: Skipping class or school.
¶   Quandary: Not knowing what to do.
** Implicitly: To understand naturally without it being pointed out or discussed.
†† Patrol Dog: Dogs used in wartime battles to search out and find enemy soldiers.
‡‡ Canine: The scientific term for dogs.
§§ Passively: Without strong purpose or goals. The opposite of actively.

and *predictably**—"like a mushroom in a cave or a dandelion in sunlight," he had muttered more than once to Thor. David craved action—something to bring life to his life. *Lo and behold,*† it would happen sooner than he could ever have imagined. He was on the *threshold*‡ of passing into the world of Vienna's spies. This transition would change his life in ways he never expected—boredom would soon be a thing of the past.

---

* Predictably: Without any surprises or sudden changes.
† Lo and behold: An expression of surprise on what comes next.
‡ Threshold: The opening or beginning, as a threshold is the entrance-way to a building or home.

2

Why David Hale

David's difficulty in understanding the talk about spies was rather simple—he did not yet grasp what really was going on in Vienna. After all, no one had told him. To this energetic youth, Austria did not seem all that special or interesting. As with an iceberg in the ocean, however, more was going on below the surface than David or most people realized or could see. Spies, naturally, work best when no one has a clue that they are at work—or even around. David soon would learn about mysterious Vienna and about spying itself—from his dad and his new secret life.

It certainly mattered that Vienna, the Austrian *capital city*,* had become the most active *stomping ground*† for spies—more so than far larger cities of the world, including Washington, Moscow, London or Tokyo. What had converted relatively small Vienna into the world's busiest spy center? Geography! Located deep within Eastern Europe, it was wide open to all major nations whose spies flocked there to steal secrets from each other.

But, how did young David Hale come to play an important role in the world of secret intelligence, or espionage? After all,

---

* Capital city: The City where the government's main offices and officials are located.
† Stomping ground: Favorite place or territory.

he was eleven years old—"going on twelve," he would quickly add. To begin with, having arrived there in 1947 when things were still *fractured** from the war, he was truly in the right place at the right time. Spies, after all, thrive when things are really messed up, or *chaotic.*[†] But, Vienna's world of spies was not only because of geography or location. In the late 1940's, many thousands of Americans passed through Vienna and had no connection to the work or the world of spies—at least, none they were aware of!

David, as it would turn out, was a natural for this kind of work. For starters, adventure was in his blood and he was itching for an adventure-filled life. From a young age, he *avidly*[‡] read the lives of earlier explorers and heroes—including Alexander the Great, Marco Polo, Daniel Boone, and George Washington. Most of his life's excitement, of course, had come from reading books—Robert Louis Stevenson's "Kidnapped" and James Fenimore Cooper's "The Deerslayer" as well as "The Spy." He read all the Zane Grey books he could get his hands on.

Not only was David Hale curious and full of energy—he also was quite *teachable.*[§] When really interested in something, he listened carefully and worked hard to improve his knowledge and sharpen his skills. This was true whether he was building a *slingshot,*[¶] reading a *compass*[**] and map, or working

---

*   Fractured: Broken apart.
†   Chaotic: When things are completed out of order, messed up, or in what we call chaos.
‡   Avidly: Eagerly or enthusiastically.
§   Teachable: Someone who listens carefully and learns what is being taught.
¶   Slingshot: A weapon used for hunting that starts with a Y-shaped stick and has rubber bands and a pocket that holds a stone that is shot at great speed.
** Compass: A tool used by sailors, explorers and hikers to find direction and location. It has a thin needle that points northward.

his father's *shortwave radio** to hear broadcasts from around the world, especially from *The States.*†

Most importantly, whenever his dad took time to teach him some subject or skill, he was an eager student. Just being with his dad made him happy—which explains why he begged and pestered his mom to let him stay in Austria for the summer. The three years Dr. Matt Hale had been off to war were the loneliest in David's young life. During the long war, the boy struggled at times to remember his father—how he looked, how he spoke, how it felt when his dad hugged him. Often, David would picture his dad on his way home and being there that very night.

Hundreds of nights came and went, with no Matt Hale coming through the front door. So, David worked his imagination even harder. At such times, he *visualized*‡ his dad as a powerful superhero, such as those in comic books he liked so much. Captain Marvel. Batman. Superman. Well, maybe not as strong as Superman, but pretty close!

Which gets to the final ingredient needed for David's growth into the shadowy world of spies—an excellent teacher. Luckily for David, his teacher would be experienced spy Matt Hale, his favorite man in the whole world. As things would develop, it did not hurt that the master spy would, in turn, require special assistance that only David could provide. An espionage

---

* Shortwave radio: This radio sends signals for hundreds and even thousands of miles and is the favorite of spies who encode their messages so they can only be read by those who have the same code book for decoding messages which means the person receiving the secret message can understand it.

† States: Americans living outside of their country usually call their home "The States," only.

‡ Visualized: Formed a picture in his mind, a mental picture stored in his brain.

partnership was about to be born—a partnering of father and son.

As a result of all four *factors**—having an adventurous spirit, being in the right place when things were really *brewing*,† possessing a strong desire to succeed, and having an excellent *mentor*‡—David had the potential to grow into a talented spy. A junior spy certainly, but a spy all the same.

When David Hale arrived in Austria less than twenty-four months after the war, Vienna itself was still recovering from the damaging combat that took place during the Battle of Vienna. When the war was over, the armies that defeated Nazi Germany soon *partitioned*§ Austria into four *sectors*.¶ Each sector was controlled by one of the four victorious powers—the United States, England, France, and their growing *adversary*,** Russia.

Vienna, with one-third of Austria's population, was deep inside the Russian Sector. That was a serious problem because the Russian authorities controlled all of the roads and trains in and out of Vienna. This gave a huge advantage to the Russian military and *spymasters*†† trying to turn Austria into their ally in an entirely new battle against *The West*.‡‡ Austria's freedom as an independent nation required huge support from the United

---

*   Factors: The things that make something happen or develop.
†   Brewing: Getting exciting and with a lot of hot things happening.
‡   Mentor: A trusted and very special teacher who guides a person wisely in life.
§   Partitioned: Divided.
¶   Sectors: Parts of a larger system, in this case the country of Austria.
**   Adversary: An opponent, foe or enemy.
††   Spymasters: The bosses who are in charge of managing a large number of spies.
‡‡   The West: Meant the free nations that the Russians and Chinese—The East—were fighting to control.

States Government. The aid came in many forms—food, clothing, medicine, as well as money and military equipment.

American spy operations were also needed to block the *subversive** actions of Russian spies who were in Vienna in great numbers. It was in this dangerous setting that young David Hale would begin his career in support of his father's *secret intelligence operations.*† In the end, David Hale's spy operations on the side of freedom would prove to be highly significant—in fact, so important that they were kept "Top Secret" by the U.S. Government for seventy-five years. Until now. Until "*The Vienna Trilogy.*"

---

* Subversive: The actions meant to weaken or destroy a free society and people.
† Secret intelligence operations: The work of spies who both steal secrets from enemies and block the actions of an enemy nation's spies.

3

A Spy Again

So, David had learned in the afternoon that his father was back in the spy business—important information he was not supposed to know and could not *readily** talk about. How had David gotten himself into such a pickle? A little before noon that day, he had slipped unnoticed into the study and crawled under dad's massive wooden desk. He had his *whittling*† knife and *sapling*‡ branch in hand. His primary goal was to skip the day's lesson in German. He *opted*§ to use the time instead to work on making a new slingshot. He thought the flexibility of a fresh tree branch would permit him to shoot much longer distances.

When he heard the study door open, he stayed still. He thought it must be his thirteen-year-old sister Ellie searching for him—the Hale family's extremely *reluctant*¶ summer student. With school vacation here, David saw no reason on earth why he should be in school—even for a final German class. Ellie did not need the class and David did not want it.

Instead of it being his sister coming into the study, however, David was surprised to hear his parents talking as they entered

---

*   Readily: Easily or comfortably.
†   Whittling knife: One used to shape wood by cutting off thin pieces.
‡   Sapling branch: Branch from a young tree.
§   Opted: Chose.
¶   Reluctant: Unwilling, not wanting to do something.

the beautiful *wood-paneled** room. Closing the door behind them, his mom and dad believed they were alone.

David's first *inclination†* was to crawl out from under the desk and make his presence known. He certainly was not trying to listen in on anything. But, neither did he have any *zeal‡* to spend the next ninety minutes in class along with *super-linguist§* Ellie and German grammar teacher Katrina. They would probably go over vocabulary words for what, to David, seemed the hundredth time. There was also the probability Katrina would drill him repeatedly on his pronunciation, which was improving but not as good as Ellie's.

Already beginning to sound like an Austrian *fräulein,¶* she would sit in class with a gleeful twinkle in her eyes as David struggled to pronounce new German words correctly. "I'll bet she can't use a slingshot," he *mused,*** "or climb to the castle tower without making a single sound. Or pick up a snake."

After the door was closed and locked, his mom spoke in a soft but determined voice. "Matt, the war has been over for two years! When millions were fighting and dying all around the world, it was one thing. You now have important medical work to do—leave the Russian problem to professional spies. I am proud of what you did in the war. Right now, however, I want a normal life for our family—and a safe one."

---

* Wood-paneled: Having nice wood on the walls of a room.
† Inclination: A natural tendency in a certain direction.
‡ Zeal: Strong interest in doing something.
§ Super-linguist: A person who is really good at learning and speaking foreign languages.
¶ Fräulein: German word for young girl.
** Mused: To think deeply about something.

David was dazed by what he was hearing. His *respiration** changed. The more he tried to control or calm his breathing, the deeper each breath became. And, when Matt Hale walked around to the rear of the desk, David could practically touch his father's shoes. So, the youth's heavy breathing worsened even more.

He knew, too, that if dad sat down he would be discovered—the family spy hiding in the *recesses*† of the old desk. In the least, he would be sent scurrying off to German class. At worst, they would be upset if they thought David had been purposely listening in on their private talk. It was now too late for an *honorable*‡ exit. And, it was too late not to hear the *intriguing*§ business about spies. So, David figured, maybe it would help if he tried not to hear any more.

He placed the knife and emerging slingshot on the rug. Then, he reached up slowly and placed a hand over each ear. In that way, if discovered, David in all honesty could say he tried not to listen. He covered his ears for several minutes. He now heard only *muffled*¶ sounds of his parents' voices—nothing he could *comprehend*.** For the moment, he felt safe. Well, if not entirely safe, at least safer. All the while, he watched his father from the knees of his pants downward, pacing back and forth.

Then David's own body betrayed him—his nose began to itch. He tried ignoring it at first by thinking of other things; for

---

*   Respiration: Breathing.
†   Recesses: Hidden part of something—usually deep inside.
‡   Honorable: Noble, good, virtuous or worthy of praise.
§   Intriguing: Fascinating or exciting—involving mystery.
¶   Muffled: Not able to be heard because something is blocking the sound.
**   Comprehend: Understand.

example, running in the park with Thor or shooting at small targets with his slingshot. Nothing helped. The bridge of his nose got itchier and itchier. He wrinkled his face with all the might of his facial muscles. He wiggled his nose like a rabbit. Nothing worked! The itch only got worse.

He felt like screaming out because the unscratched itch had become unbearable. Despite *misgivings** about again listening in on his parents, he removed his right hand from his ear. He slowly *maneuvered*† it to the front of his face in the direction of the itch. All the while, he prayed his dad would not sit down. To his surprise, David quickly found that one uncovered ear was about as good as two ears when it came to eavesdropping.

Now, he clearly heard his dad speaking. "As I said already, dear, I did not volunteer for anything. They asked if I would provide a little special assistance—no shooting this time, so no one should get hurt. They said the Russians are less reckless these days—now that three of their own gunmen have disappeared."

David reached the itchy spot and scratched ever so slowly. The relief was *exhilarating.*‡ His hand shot back up to his right ear and the parents' conversation became *unintelligible*§ again. After a few minutes passed, both parents left the study before David slipped out and climbed up the back stairs to his room. As he made his silent ascent, he heard Ellie in the kitchen speaking German as only she could after a few months of study.

---

*   Misgivings: Feeling of doubt about something.
†   Maneuvered: A careful movement.
‡   Exhilarating: To become very happy or cheerful.
§   Unintelligible: Unclear and not able to be understood.

His thoughts were not on his *sibling** or German class, however. Instead, his head *reeled*† over what he had just heard—"Spies! Russians! Gunmen!"

---

* Sibling: Brother or sister.
† Reeled: Spun or went around and around.

4

Stairwell Acrobatics

The Date: Wednesday, June 4, 1947

The Time: 12:00AM

As the chimes in the hall sounded midnight, David glided quietly across the floor of his room in stocking feet. He moved diagonally toward the front left window and around the creaky flooring which had tripped him up the first night in the castle. Stepping on those loose boards had alerted the family *sentinel** Ellie that David was roaming about the large house. She did her usual, big-sister thing and called out loudly so all could hear that David was, as she put it, on the prowl.

"What a pain!" he thought at the time—but only briefly. Because David changed his *tactics,*† she had not caught him in weeks. *Ironically*‡ as well as unintentionally, his big sister had become his ally. How? When she did NOT call out in the night, everyone assumed David must be securely in bed. In the language of spies, this now gave him the *cover*§ he needed for

---

*   Sentinel: A guard or sentry who protects things.
†   Tactics: The planned and disciplined way of doing something that requires skills.
‡   Ironically: When something unexpected or opposite happens.
§   Cover: Cover is the innocent-looking action or explanation that hides the real spy action taking place. For example, a spy looks like he has gone shopping but he really is placing a signal on a wall with chalk.

undetected nighttime exploration of the castle's chambers and passageways, as well as its countless *nooks and crannies*.*

Weeks earlier, Ellie had assisted David's nightly explorations in another unintended way. For his birthday, she gave him what became a valuable aid for exploring in the dark—a U.S. Army flashlight with six batteries. The foot-long *tubular device*† enabled him to look through old trunks and closets without turning on any overhead lights.

When he used the powerful flashlight without any covering, it *emitted*‡ a beam that seemed sunlight bright. When he needed to be more secretive, he could reduce the glow *appreciably*§ by putting a light sock over the flashlight. To expose even less light, he used a green German Army sock with a small hole in the toe. He found it in the cellar along with some other military stuff, including maps and helmets.

The flashlight and two socks became, as he called them, his trusty trio. He stored the trio in his own secret hiding place—beneath a loose floor board he found in the closet of his bedroom. Before long, David would hide more important things there, things of value and of interest to spies.

David reached the hallway and *hooked*⁹ a right onto the first stair. This one was solid and gave no hint that David was up and about. The next two stairs gave off no sound unless he pressed

---

* Nooks and crannies: Little places and hiding areas such as underneath stairs or deep parts of closets.

† Tubular device: A tool which is shaped like a tube.

‡ Emitted: To come out of; for example, the sun emits light or a horn emits a sound.

§ Appreciably: A great deal, quite a lot, considerably.

⁹ Hooked a right: Made a circular turn onto the stairs, in the shape of a hook used in fishing.

down too hard. So, he pulled with both arms on the *banister**
to support some of his weight. Then came tricky stairs four and
five, each sure to produce a *telltale*† noise if David so much as
lightly touched either one with his foot.

At first, the technique for *scaling*‡ the two stairs was awkward, even difficult. However, he practiced his stair climbing
and, within days, had become very good. He would reach up
and grab the railing with both hands and place his left foot on
the wooden *molding*§ that ran alongside the stairs. He pulled
himself up forcefully and slid two feet until he was able to place
his right foot onto stair number six.

At this point in his climb, he was off-balance. He had to
kneel onto stair seven, first with his right knee and then his
left. At this point, he could stand up and walk again toward the
summit.¶ "This is not exactly *Mount Everest*,** *Mount McKinley*,††
or the *Matterhorn*,"‡‡ he thought, "but the best thing available
at the moment."

At stair thirteen, he again had to be cautious. He could put
some weight onto the right half of the stair without making

---

*   Bannister: The hand railing in a stair case that keeps a person from
    falling.
†   Telltale: An outward sign or warning.
‡   Scaling: Climbing up and over some barrier; for example over a cliff
    or mountain.
§   Molding: Fancy wood used for decoration around windows and along
    stairways.
¶   Summit: The highest point or top of something—such as a mountain.
** Mount Everest: Highest Mountain in the world is in Asia: 29,028 feet,
    or almost 6 miles high.
†† Mount McKinley: Highest Mountain in North America is in Canada,
    20,320 feet, and 4 miles high.
‡‡ Matterhorn: Beautiful Mountain in Switzerland climbed by only the
    best mountain climbers.

a sound. But, any downward force to the left of center would surely make a noise and end his escape. It happened the third night in the castle when David developed his peculiar case of *triskai-deca-stepa-phobia**—his own created word for fear of stair thirteen. It was at that point in his ascent that Ellie detected him—ending the night's flight to freedom when she sounded the alarm. But, that was the last time he had been caught.

Now, with his sister on her way to New York, David found that he actually missed having a sentinel he could fool. Her absence took much of the challenge—and fun—out of *clandestine†* exploration.

Reaching the final stair, David waited a few seconds, letting his eyes get used to the castle's dark *garret.‡* He moved quickly into the first chamber on the right. *Blackout curtains§* left over from the war covered the windows. *Scant§* light came in, even on the brightest of nights. Tonight, there was a full moon. Compared to his earlier homes, the castle at first seemed creepy. Now, David was accustomed to moving about quietly in the dark.

For one thing, the cobwebs that *invariably*** caught his face no longer bothered him—once he learned that Austria had no

---

* Triskai-deca-<u>stepa</u>-phobia: Triskaidekaphobia is fear of the number 13; David fears step #13.
† Clandestine: Something done in secrecy so that no one else knows what is happening.
‡ Garret: The attic area just below the roof of the castle.
§ Blackout curtains: Dark black shades or curtains to keep inside lights from being seen from outside.
§ Scant: Very little.
** Invariably: Not changing, always, consistently.

deadly spiders. What David had yet to realize, though, was that the previous occupants were worse than the worst of poisonous spiders. Nazis had walked the castle halls planning and committing crimes of every sort against freedom-loving Austrians. For almost seven years, it had been a "center of evil." In time, Dr. Matt and David Hale would cleanse that terrible stain by turning the castle into a *haven** of hope and freedom—although a very secret one.

---

*   Haven: A place of safety or refuge—often called a safe haven.

5

The Midnight Visitor

The young *sleuth** drifted over to the first window and peered down at the garden below. *Stratus clouds† obscured‡* light from the moon but, generally, the rear garden seemed quite bright. Light from his dad's study—partially blocked by thick bushes that *nestled§* around the castle—was barely visible. As David glanced about the garden, he spotted movement near the study. A human figure flashed past the window, then cut across the lawn away from the house and, finally, continued in the direction of the pathway leading down to the river.

Hairs on the young night wanderer's head and neck came alive and seemed to stand on end. David's next sensation was a chill running down his spine. Clearly, he was scared. He worried not for himself, though, but for his father. Was his dad okay? Who was the *furtive¶* stranger? Had Dr. Hale spotted him, too? With questions but no answers, David immediately *resolved*** to slip downstairs to see what was occurring—and of course make sure his dad was all right.

---

* Sleuth: Detective or person that uncovers secrets.
† Stratus clouds: Flat, stretched clouds usually found between 2,000 and 7,000 feet in the air.
‡ Obscured: Hid or partly blocked.
§ Nestled: Hugged or comfortably rested—as in, "the children all nestled asleep in their beds."
¶ Furtive: Acting secretly as though one has something to hide.
** Resolved: Made a firm decision.

David *retraced** his earlier journey to the garret. With the instinct of a *predator,†* he made his way *adroitly‡* down the attic stairs to the second floor. Stair thirteen posed little problem as David, this time, used the left side of the staircase to support his weight. Stairs four and five were easily avoided in the descent as his foot—with the help of gravity—slid effortlessly down the wooden molding. With help of the banister, he reduced the downward pressure on stairs two and three.

He used the tricks of his practiced routine to get to the first floor—this time *eluding§* four squeaky stairs on the way. Thanks to his training and practice, his anxiety to find his dad did not interfere with his agility. He descended from the garret to second floor and on to the first floor in less than seven seconds—without making a sound. *Disciplined¶* practice worked, after all. A panther in the jungle or a wolf pack on the hunt all move about their own *turf*** with remarkably similar stealth.

Reaching the study, David saw his dad working calmly at his desk where the boy had hidden earlier in the day. David felt tremendous relief. "Someone's out in the garden, Dad. I saw a big guy dashing into the woods, heading for the river," he exclaimed.

For a brief *interval,††* Matt Hale looked at his son, *grimaced,‡‡* and told David to sit down so they might have a brief chat.

---

*   Retraced: Go in the opposite way or direction.
†   Predator: An animal that hunts or preys on other animals.
‡   Adroitly: Skillfully or cleverly.
§   Eluding: Skillfully avoiding; like the mice eluded the trap set to catch them.
¶   Disciplined: Hard work that made him a skilled staircase acrobat.
** Turf: The land where an animal roams around.
†† Interval: Period of time between two events or happenings.
‡‡ Grimaced: Twisted his face in a way that showed he was annoyed.

"Son, that 'big guy' was visiting me. But, I am curious—how could you possibly see the garden from your bedroom—on the other side of the castle? Unless, of course, you were prowling in the upper chambers again."

David wondered how his dad correctly concluded that he may have been in the garret. Had he known all along about David's middle-of-the-night trips? The young fellow at first was stunned—then he was embarrassed.

Hoping to change the subject—and take attention off his own secret movements—he said, "I was wide awake, Dad. Was out exploring. Found some neat German medals and military stuff I'd like to show you, when you have some time."

His father spoke not a word, but continued to stare at him. So, David tried to avoid answering by, instead, asking his own questions. "Who visited you at midnight, Dad? Why would he leave through the rear garden and the river—not through the front entrance and the roadway?"

For a moment, Matt Hale hesitated and then spoke slowly in a serious tone. "Son, there are some specific things we can discuss later—not tonight. It's late. But, from our chats, you should know that a major struggle is *underway** here in Austria. In fact, all across Europe. No one knows whether the Russians will take over Austria—just as they already have taken over most of Eastern Europe. Russia's powerful *Red Army*† is certainly strong enough to do it. I am hearing that the Russians, in fact, will be in full control of neighboring Czechoslovakia in

---

*　Underway: Happening or taking place.
†　Red Army: Red is the chosen color for Communism.

a matter of months. So, Son, if they *prevail** here in Vienna—
and if they eventually control all of Western Europe—the very
freedoms so many fought and died for in World War II will be
entirely lost."

His dad continued. "*Communism*† is a very poor substitute
for the murderous system of the Nazis. 'Visitor' is working to
ensure‡ that the Russians do not succeed. I have been asked—
and have agreed—to give him a hand. Without *elaborating*§
right now, I may need some help. You can start by keeping
tonight's discussion—and 'Visitor''s being here confidential.
Between us, only! No mention of this to Ellie in any short
wave messages or letters. Nor can you speak about any of this
to Katrina or her husband. They're good people—but, they
have no *need to know*."¶

David's eyes widened—he was about to ask a *slew*** of
questions when his dad whisked him out of the study. The
doctor-spy repeated to him that the middle of the night was
no time to talk. "By the way, son, please *refrain from*†† whittling
under my desk. I have a hard enough time keeping the study

---

* Prevail: Win or gain victory.
† Communism: An evil system of government that takes freedoms away
from the citizens and gives all important decision making and power
to a small unelected group—The Communist Party. Communist
Governments in Russia, China, North Korea and Cuba have killed
more than one hundred million people in the past hundred years.
Most of the murder victims were their own citizens!
‡ Ensure: To guarantee or make happen.
§ Elaborating: Telling all of the facts.
¶ Need to know: This is one of the most important or basic rules in the
world of spies—you tell someone only what he or she must know to
do an intelligence operation.
** Slew: A large number.
†† Refrain from: Stop doing something.

clean." The remark caught David by surprise—but his dad's smile, before sending him upstairs, reassured him he was not in trouble.

The final surprise of the evening came when Matt Hale winked and said, "Be careful with stairs three, five, seven and twelve on the way to your room—don't want to awaken the castle goblins." Then and there, he *grasped** the reality that his dad was more aware than he had imagined—about Austria, about the castle and about David himself. As he entered his room, Thor looked up and wagged his tail. Suspiciously, David stared at his *lethargic*† pet and wondered whether Thor too might have secrets he wasn't revealing. "Naw, my imagination is running wild from all this spy stuff," he murmured. "Have to settle down."

David Hale lay wide awake for another hour, recalling the day's events. He could hardly wait until dawn—once the sun came up, no one would keep him in bed.

---

* Grasped: Understood immediately.
† Lethargic: Lazy, without energy, tired.

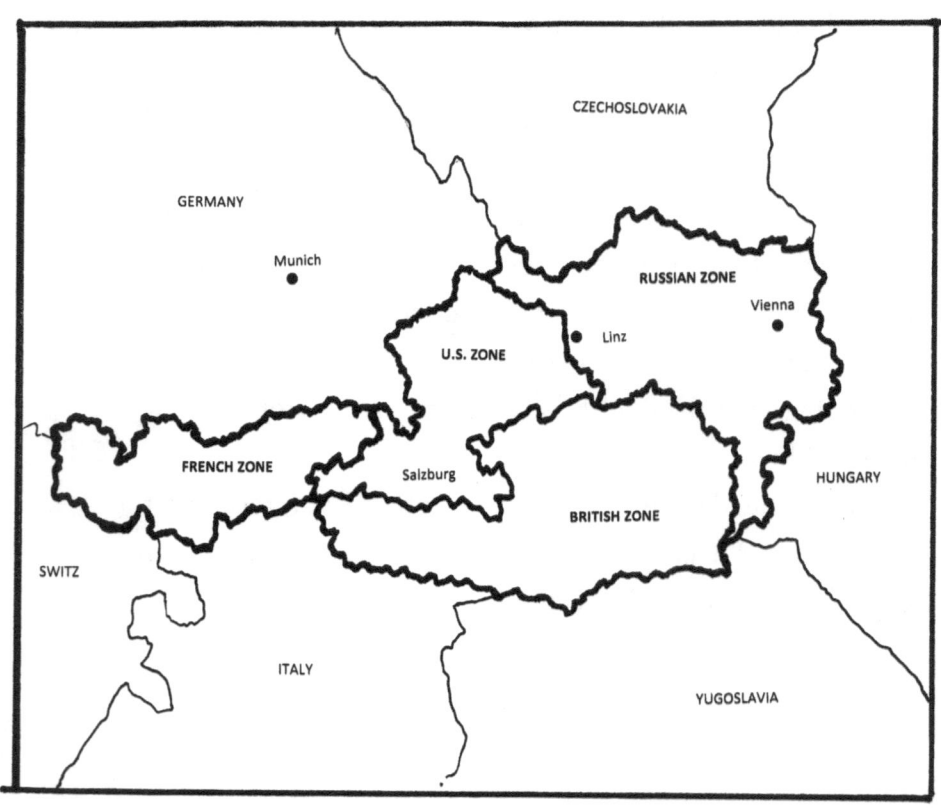

6

The Russians Are Here

The Date: Wednesday, June 4, 1947.

The Time: 8:00AM

Instead of rising before sunrise as usual, however, David slept late—until well after the roosters stopped crowing down at the chicken coop. When he did awaken, he jumped out of bed, threw on his clothes and ran down the corridor to his dad's room. Not finding him there, he headed for the kitchen.

Matt Hale was having Turkish coffee, which was popular in Vienna's old coffee houses. Thor, on the floor next to dad, was getting a back rub. In the war, the old Patrol Dog was hit by a bullet that left him with some muscle damage and stiffness. He never grew tired of a good *massage*.*

"Hey, Dad, a good time to have that talk?"

"Sure, son, let's take a walk—but, first, grab yourself a little breakfast. Thor has had his fill."

David had a quick breakfast and the two strolled out through the kitchen door, with Matt Hale in the lead. They headed in the direction of the river. They could see Katrina working in the garden next to her cottage at the entrance to the castle grounds.

---

* Massage: Rubbing sore, damaged or stiff muscles to reduce pain and improve recovery.

She was planting seedlings for vegetables because food was scarce and prices had *soared** in the post-war period. This was an unfortunate result from the fact that most of Austria's farms were in the east—in the Russian Sector.

After the war, from mid-1945 through mid-1947, the Americans had been bringing *massive*† amounts of food into the country to feed both Austrians as well as the tens of thousands of *Displaced Persons*‡ in the camps for *refugees*.§ While the Americans brought in food, the Russians were doing the opposite—they were stealing Austrian-grown food and sending it out of the country and on to Russia.

The Russians were doing the same thing with the machinery and *heavy equipment*⁋ which they stole from the factories in their sector of Austria—that too was shipped out of Austria and on to Russia. *In light of all this*,** Matt Hale would comment, only *half in jest*,†† "Countries that lose a war to Russia will starve, lose their warm clothing—and even be left without toilets."

When they reached the river bank, Matt Hale sat on a log and waited until David was equally settled and ready to chat. He looked down at his son and said "Look, sorry I cut you off last night—I had to do some planning and thinking about how to

---

*   Soared: Rose or increased to a very high level.

†   Massive: Great or enormous quantities.

‡   Displaced Persons: Also called, D.P.'s for short, these were the hundreds of thousands of refugees mainly from Eastern Europe who did not want to return to their home countries that had been taken over by the Communists and the Russian Army.

§   Refugees: People who left or were thrown out of their country during war and have no country of their own.

⁋   Heavy equipment: Tractors, plows, railroad engines and cars, automobiles and trucks.

**   In light of this: Because of this.

††   Half in jest: In sort of a funny way, but really a serious matter.

go about a rescue operation. I have to help a man escape from the Russian Sector—very soon, or it could be too late for him. Before discussing *how* this might be done, let's take some time and talk about *why* this must be done. After all, the *why* tells us how important or *crucial** it is to take risks to get this man out of the Russian Sector and to freedom."

"I know why I agreed to help—I want you to understand as well. To begin with, let's be sure you don't think the intelligence or spy business is some sort of game—just a fun thing to do. It is, in fact, serious and *critically†* important. Can we agree on that?"

"Sure thing, Dad!" was David's instant response. He was already beginning to feel he was on his Dad's team.

Matt Hale continued. "There are things about this you need to *comprehend‡* as clearly as any adult can. *Maturity§* comes to different individuals at different ages. I am confident you are both serious and grown up enough to handle this information. I have seen too many adults in my life who continue to act and think like children—they get stuck more or less as lifelong *adolescents."¶* They make very poor doctors and equally bad spies.

"By contrast, in the war, I saw *firsthand*** that boys your age grasped what was *at stake††* and did very brave things when their

---

* Crucial: How important or urgent something is.
† Critically: Severely or dangerously urgent.
‡ Comprehend: Understand and to know.
§ Maturity: How serious and responsible a person is—the opposite of childishness.
¶ Adolescents: The time between childhood and adulthood.
** Firsthand: Directly and in person—not merely from the gossip or reports of other people.
†† What is at stake: The importance of something.

country was attacked. Many Polish youngsters at the time even fought the foreign *invaders**—first, the Nazis from the west and, then, the Russians from the east. Unfortunately, Poland was caught between two armies of invading *barbarians.*† But, for starters, let's talk about Austria, and specifically Vienna. Do you know why this city is so important?"

Initially, David was at a loss for words. He was accustomed to being asked history questions by his mom—not his dad. David thought a moment and said the first thing that came into his mind. "Don't know a lot about Vienna yet, Dad. But, I am curious—we were once an ally of the Russians and that was only a couple of years ago. Why are we against each other now?"

Matt looked at David and responded carefully. "Excellent question—one that is important as well as complex. Without turning this into a boring history class, let me explain. You're a little sick of school, I hear. Well, I will have to back up a bit, Son, and cover some recent history—things that led up to the war itself."

"Yes, the United States and the British started helping the Russians. That was in 1941, after they were attacked by Nazi Germany. Ours was an *alliance of convenience*‡—it did not mean the Russian Communists had become our permanent ally, much less great friends. Only two years earlier, these same

---

* Invaders: Those armies that attack other countries.
† Barbarians: A brutal uncivilized people who act cruelly and without a sense of decency.
‡ Alliance of convenience: A partnership between countries that was useful in practical terms but not because the nations had the same ideas about how people should be treated and governed.

Russians partnered with Hitler and the Nazis in a secret *pact**
or deal to conquer peaceful Poland and divide that country and
most of Eastern Europe between them!"

"Only because Hitler was the greater evil and threat to
America and England in the war, did we decide to support
Russia. Was it because we trusted them? Not at all! Rather, it
was the surest and quickest way to defeat the Nazis and win a
war that, if we lost it, would have cost all of us our freedoms."

"How could we be certain that Russia never became our true
partner? It gets back to spying—our secret agents in Russia
reported in 1943 that Russia's Communist leader, *Joseph Stalin,*†
had told his intelligence organizations that America was Russia's
main enemy‡—'*glavni vrag*' is the Russian term for it. Stalin gave
orders to his spies to go after America at the time we Americans
were sending Russia thousands of shipments of military equipment as well as food and clothing! So, it is absolutely certain
that we never had a true partner in the Russians."

"Time after time, they have shown themselves willing to
betray allies and break agreements whenever it is in their interest to do so. The Red Army repeatedly showed they had no
interest in liberating or truly freeing other countries from Nazi
control. Instead, their plan was and is to turn the countries of
Europe into Communist nations and destroy their freedoms."

---

* Pact: An agreement between nations to work together as allies.

† Joseph Stalin: The evil leader of Soviet Russia for more than twenty
 years. The number of people he had murdered is somewhere around
 forty million—making him one of the greatest killers in human
 history.

‡ Main Enemy: The Russian term is *glavni vrag*. This meant that, while
 Stalin was supposedly an ally of the United States, he was secretly call-
 ing America the most important enemy of Soviet Russia.

David listened *intently** to all that his father was saying. He then returned to the first subject his dad had raised earlier: "What about Vienna, Dad? Why is this place so important?"

Matt smiled, impressed that David was asking the most *immediate*† question. After all, it was just outside Vienna where he faced the challenge of rescuing a person from the Russian Secret Police. This rescue operation would take place in Austria's Russian Sector where the Russian Army and Secret Police controlled much of the *landscape*‡ and all the means of *transportation.*§ It was also where Russian kidnappings and murders had recently become an *epidemic*¶ of sorts.

Matt Hale responded. "VIENNA! This is indeed an important place. It is a *strategic*** city—it has been one since the ancient Romans built a military camp and fortress here to protect themselves from Germanic tribes to their north. That was 2,000 years ago! The Romans stayed here for five hundred years— until Rome itself fell to Germanic invaders who effectively ended one of the great empires in human history."

He continued: "Ever since, Vienna has been a key *cross-roads*†† in European history. After all, one of the world's great waterways—the Danube River—flows through Vienna and ten countries on its eighteen hundred mile journey. It runs from

---

*   Intently: With great interest and seriousness.
†   Immediate: The first matter of importance or timing.
‡   Landscape: The physical geography of roads and highways, hills and valleys.
§   Means of transportation: The trains, bridges, airports, and highways in and out of Vienna.
¶   Epidemic: A bad disease affecting a population or region at the same time.
**   Strategic: Of great importance to plans and goals.
†† Crossroads: A place where great roads from many lands meet

high in the Black Forest of Germany down to the Black Sea that separates Europe from Asia."

"And, Son, the Russians—who are among the best *chess** players in the world—know the strategic value of Vienna. In March 1945, the Red Army captured the city—they have no intention now of just walking away from what they consider theirs. They see Vienna as a place where their spies can steal lots of secrets from lots of nations."

Matt Hale waited a bit till this information sunk in and David had a little time to think about things he was hearing for the first time—the things of spies.

"My job," he continued, "is to do something that would be extremely difficult for American intelligence officers to do. American officials drive cars with US Government markings on them—my car does not! They are known to the Russians who suspect all of them to be spies. Instead, the Russians probably see me as merely a doctor trying to stop the spread of deadly *typhus†* around the refugee camps. They probably think I am too busy fighting disease to be working also as a spy. That is our *ace in the hole‡*—our advantage."

Father and son finished their chat and headed back up the hill to the castle. Matt Hale told David to remember the "need-to-know" principle—the boy must *refrain§* from discussing these things with anyone else. "Right now, I've got some work

---

* Chess: A board game that requires great skill and thinking several moves ahead.

† Typhus: A deadly disease spread by lice bites that infect people living in overcrowded camps.

‡ Ace in the hole: Edge or advantage—as in poker where the aces have the highest value.

§ Refrain from: Hold one back from doing something.

to do in the study. Maybe we can play *cribbage** after dinner. Better still, since we're going against the Russians, maybe we should play some chess."

David gave a wide smile—he loved playing his dad in games of any kind. Except for shooting a slingshot, the youngster lost to his dad much of the time—but his attitude was "So what! Dad's all mine when we're playing anything."

---

*   Cribbage: A card game played usually by two people and using a board to keep score.

7

Ping, Ping, Ping

The Date: Thursday, June 5, 1947

The Time: 6:45AM

Early the next morning, Dr. Matt Hale was back at his desk in the study when David took Thor out to the garden for exercise and for a little target practice with the newest home-made slingshot. This was not the *excessively** flexible one he had whittled while hiding under his father's oak desk. That one, it turned out, did indeed shoot rocks and *horse chestnuts†* an extremely long distance.

David discovered, however, that the *whippyness‡* of the sapling branch made his shooting far less accurate. With slingshots, David was learning, it was most important to hit what he was aiming at—in fact, the single most important quality of a good slingshot is its *accuracy.§* Having learned this lesson, he had whittled yet another slingshot but, this time, from a *sturdy¶* branch.

---

* Excessively: More than is necessary or wanted.
† Horse chestnuts: They look like other chestnuts but are poisonous to humans.
‡ Whippyness: Like a whip, the ability of the material to snap back after it is bent or pulled.
§ Accuracy: The ability to hit a target time after time.
¶ Sturdy: Solid, stronger and less whippy.

39

As Dr. Matt Hale tried to concentrate on the problem at hand, the sounds "ping, ping, ping" drifted through the open window. David was shooting pebbles at empty Coca Cola bottles resting on top of the garden wall. More often than not, he wasn't missing as this was the best shooting device he had yet whittled. Its accuracy was clear from the *incessant*[*] sounds of stone striking glass—ping-ping-ping. Satisfied with the results he was getting with his new device, the younger Hale was feeling pretty good.

"Ten in a row! Fifteen in a row! I wonder whether anyone has ever shot a hundred straight." All this was going through the boy's mind as he went about his practice.

Matt Hale, *on the contrary,*[†] was becoming annoyed that his son had picked that spot and that time to target practice. It made it harder for him to focus on the secret mission which could turn out to be *exceedingly*[‡] difficult, mainly because it had to be carried out so soon. But, whether in a hurry or not, his operational planning still had to be *flawless.*[§] Any mistake in timing or performance could cost a good man his freedom—permanently!

'Visitor' had *outlined*[¶] the problem *succinctly*[**]—an important scientist had to be *evacuated*[††] secretly from the Russian Sector in Austria—the sooner the better! The urgent and risky assignment was given to the person with the best chance to

---

* Incessant: Unending, not stopping.
† On the contrary: Quite the opposite.
‡ Exceedingly: Very.
§ Flawless: Without any mistakes or errors—foolproof.
¶ Outlined: Described generally without all of the details.
** Succinctly: Briefly and to the point.
†† Evacuated: Removed or taken away from.

accomplish the operation—Dr. Matthew Hale. In his medical work in the refugee camps and in the hospitals surrounding Vienna, he was *uniquely** able to move about more or less freely. And, he knew very well the streets in the Russian Sector where he would have to rescue the scientist.

Like all Western travelers, Matt Hale was at times *harassed*[†] by Russian Border Guards—at other times, even by the murderous Russian Secret Police. But, his medical work gave him the *justification*[‡] needed to drive from sector to sector throughout Austria. That, in turn, would give him also the operational cover to do secret intelligence tasks with less risk of being detected.

American Intelligence[§] officials had learned from a recently-arrived refugee that a famous Polish scientist, Dr. Stanislaw Kaminski, was hiding in the Russian Sector under a *false identity*.[¶] The refugee reported that Dr. Kaminski wanted to go to the United States to continue his *nuclear research*.[**] His specific field of expertise—nuclear safety—was important in medical research, nuclear power plants and in building nuclear bombs. If the Russians found him, he knew, they would certainly make him work in building bombs. But, Kaminski was tired of war. It was *vital*[††] that he be moved out of Austria before the Russian Secret Police discovered his real identity and loca-

---

*   Uniquely: Being the only one.
†   Harassed: Bothered, disturbed or hassled.
‡   Justification: A good reason for doing something.
§   American Intelligence: The spy organization that worked against the Nazis and then the Russians.
¶   False identity: Using a name different from one's real name.
**   Nuclear research: Studying what is possible in the field of atomic energy. This includes everything from making bombs to finding ways to fight cancer.
††   Vital: Extremely important.

tion. If they did, they would *kidnap** him and send him off to Russia—or kill him if he gave them too much trouble.

Since the war, hundreds of scientists—as well as hundreds of thousands of Eastern European refugees and *prisoners of war*[†]—had been *spirited*[‡] off to Russia. Tens of thousands never returned to their homeland—nor were they seen or heard from again. Why did the Russians want all these foreign prisoners?

Back during the war, a half million of Russia's own *forced laborers*[§] died in *Siberia*[¶] from overwork, freezing temperatures as well as from starvation and beatings. To replace the dead Russian prisoners, the Russian Government decided to kidnap German and other prisoners of war—as well as simple homeless refugees—not letting them leave Siberia for their own countries when the war was over.

Laborers[**] were sent to mines and forests where, again, hundreds of thousands of them were worked to death in terribly harsh conditions. The Communist authorities did not care when these uneducated people were killed by their Secret Police or died in other ways. As far as they were concerned, that was how their system of *terror*[††] worked best.

---

*   Kidnap: To take a person away by force.

†   Prisoners of war: These were foreign soldiers captured by the Soviet Red Army.

‡   Spirited off: To make people disappear mysteriously—as though by ghosts.

§   Forced laborers: These were prisoners sent by the Communists to work camps—for life!

¶   Siberia: The huge northern part of Russia that is mainly cold, forested and lonely and where Communist Governments sent millions of political prisoners to be worked to death in mining and tree cutting.

**   Laborers: Men who work with their hands building roads, bridges and tunnels as well as cutting trees.

††   Terror: The use of murder and violence to make people so scared that they do what they are told.

Scientists, however, were extremely valuable to the Russians, and they were sent to research centers near Russia's capital, Moscow. Most of these educated and highly trained experts were forced to work in military weapons programs.

So far, Dr. Kaminski had barely avoided being captured within the Russian Sector. He now believed it was only a matter of days before his true identity would be discovered by the Russians. So, he asked his refugee friend to contact the Americans. He saw this as his very last chance to escape.

In Poland, after the war, Dr. Kaminski saw that living under Communism was little different from living under the Nazis. In each case, there were none of the freedoms available in Poland before the war or now in the West. He was aware also that the Russian Secret Police had murdered more than 20,000 Polish prisoners of war. The secret executions took place in 1940 in the Katyn Forest, a short distance from the city of Smolensk in Soviet Russia. Kaminski personally knew many of these victims from his own student and teaching days in the university.

Why did Russia's Secret Police *execute** so many of Poland's military officers and educated leaders? The reason was *political†*—after the killings, it would be easier for Russia to turn Poland into part of the growing Communist empire. By these *brutal‡* acts of murder, the Russian Communists were making sure that, at war's end, many of the leading Polish opponents of Communism would already be dead.

---

* Executed: Murdered or killed on orders—in this case, from the Soviet Government in Moscow.

† Political: For reasons of government power and control, in this case of the Polish population.

‡ Brutal: Cruel, barbaric, evil.

Matt Hale's first task tomorrow was to get a message to Kaminski. Escape instructions had to be delivered to him without alerting the Russians. Matt Hale could not risk having a *face-to-face** meeting with the Polish scientist before the escape itself. That would be dangerous. If the Secret Police—or any of their *informants*†—saw Dr. Kaminski meeting with a foreigner, especially an American, they would investigate and quickly discover the scientist's *true identity*.‡

Neither could Matt Hale make a simple telephone call to contact Dr. Kaminski. The Russians *tapped*§ the phone lines in all of Vienna—any phone call could *endanger*⁋ the scientist and lead to his arrest. A basic rule for every spy—do not use telephones to make contact—instead, find another safer way!

*Initially,*** Matt Hale thought about doing a night-time *black pajama operation*†† to get the escape plan to Dr. Kaminski. In such a *ploy*,‡‡ the doctor-spy would dress in dark clothing and sneak on foot into the Russian Sector. However, the full moon this week was too bright for that. With so much moonlight, it would be too risky to try to move *surreptitiously*§§ on foot around the Russian Sector—he might be spotted by Russian Border

---

*   Face to face meeting: When two people meet personally, not by telephone for example.
†   Informants: People who work secretly for the police in Communist and Nazi countries and report on other citizens—especially on those who would like to escape.
‡   True identity: Who a person really is.
§   Tapped: Secretly listening in on the telephone calls of other people.
⁋   Endanger: To place in a risky or dangerous situation.
** Initially: At first or in the beginning.
†† Black Pajama Operation: Dressing entirely in black clothes to be able to sneak around in the dark of night without being seen.
‡‡ Ploy: A trick, move or action designed to fool an opponent or enemy to gain advantage.
§§ Surreptitiously: Sneaking around without being seen.

Guards. The *new moon** that gives off little light would not be for another two weeks—on June 18. But, with the Russians *screening†* refugees more carefully these days, Kaminski could be arrested by then. Another way had to be found!

While Matt Hale studied his street map of the Austrian Russian Sector, he couldn't ignore the *vexing†* sounds as David continued shooting at Coke bottles. Finding it hard to think through the rescue operation while his son ping–ping–ping'd in the garden, Matt Hale was ready to *dispatch§* David to another part of the castle grounds. Then, like a bolt of lightning, it struck him. The message could be delivered *airborne¶* after all—by slingshot! In a heartbeat, ping–ping–ping took on the air of a *sonata.*** Instantly, the irritating noise of stones hitting glass had been transformed into *melody.††*

Matt Hale bounded out the study door and into the garden. He exclaimed, "David, it's time we work on our *joint venture.‡‡* We're going for a ride—bring your slingshot and plenty of *ammo.§§* Horse chestnuts will be just fine." A partnership in *clandestinity¶¶* was born—senior-spy needed junior-spy. As they

---

* New Moon: Unlike a bright Full Moon, the New Moon gives off little light—a good time to sneak across borders between countries because the Border Guards cannot see you.

† Screening: Carefully examining identity papers by police.

‡ Vexing: Bothersome. Irritating or distracting.

§ Dispatch: To send away.

¶ Airborne: Through the air.

** Sonata: A musical piece written for instruments.

†† Melody: A succession of sweet musical notes.

‡‡ Joint venture: A deal or agreement between two or more people to do something.

§§ Ammo: This is short for ammunition such as bullets or stones used in war.

¶¶ Clandestinity: The world of spies and spying where secrecy is used to hide from the enemy.

entered the study, Matt Hale's face was serious. *By contrast,**
David Hale was grinning from ear to ear.

---

*   By contrast: Instead of; compared to.

8

Practice Makes Perfect

Matt Hale opened the door of his Mercedes sedan and got into the driver's seat. He directed David, who was followed by Thor, to ride in the rear, with the right rear window rolled down all the way. "You've done well so far against *stationary** Coke bottles, Son. Now, for a genuine challenge—let's see how well you can hit a target when we're going 20 miles an hour. If you can do it, my first problem tomorrow night might be solved."

The Hale car started down a long winding road that led off into the farm country several miles from the castle. David felt the breeze coming in the window and streaming past his face. It was somewhat cool this June afternoon and, ordinarily, he might have felt chilled. But, right then, he felt more alive than ever. The coolness of the day seemed absolutely perfect. After all, he was *on fire†*—as never before.

The sack of old chestnuts lay on the floor between his feet. His newest slingshot rested in his lap. *Committed‡* to following the Boy Scout motto—'Be Prepared'—he had placed a second slingshot on the seat. David was more than ready for the *trial run.§* He had been thinking ahead like a good chess player— very much like a good spy.

---

*   Stationary: Not moving; staying in one place.
†   On fire: Feeling wonderfully energetic, alive and well.
‡   Committed: Having his mind set on doing something.
§   Trial run: A test to see whether a plan will work.

Thor, meanwhile, was doing what dogs naturally do—he was trying to push his way past David to get his snout through the open window. He loved the many smells that came to him as the family car moved *briskly** past farms in the area. Needing that window to himself, David reached over and rolled the left window down for Thor. Now, each could do what he did best—the junior spy could target practice and the Patrol Dog could happily sniff the *aromas[†]* of the Austrian countryside.

Dr. Matt Hale pulled the car over to the side and came to a stop at a bend in the road. He selected a bush some hundred feet from the road and told David that the bush would be his target area in this practice session. The plan, he explained, was to have David sling one chestnut toward the bush as he rode past in the car. Matt Hale told David that his *objective[‡]* was not merely to hit the bush—it would actually be harder than that. The goal was to have the chestnut hit the ground so that it would come to rest just before the bush. In that way, a message could be delivered to Dr. Kaminski who said he would be waiting in a specific spot for contact from the Americans.

They began their practice runs at ten miles an hour. If that worked out, Matt Hale explained, he would increase to the *mandatory[§]* driving speed for the next evening's operation. Twenty miles an hour was his normal driving speed in the Russian Sector of Austria. He knew that if he slowed down to give David a better shot, it could be noticed by the ever-watchful Russians. They sometimes followed him *aggressively[¶]* in one or

---

*   Briskly: Quickly or lively action.
†   Aromas: Smells which are usually pleasant.
‡   Objective: Goal or intended result.
§   Mandatory: Required or absolutely necessary.
¶   Aggressively: In a forceful, active way.

more cars when he drove in their sector of Austria. His goal tomorrow evening was to alert only Dr. Kaminski—certainly not the Russians!

He mentioned to David, another *ground rule** for successful spies—when you are carrying out a secret task, do nothing that appears or seems *out of the ordinary.*† Because Matt Hale always drove at 20 MPH‡ through the Russian Sector, he would drive the same way tomorrow evening—no faster and no slower than normal.

The practice session began. In his first few attempts, David's shots missed the target by a wide margin—as much as thirty feet. He had to get used to shooting the *projectiles*§ well before the car reached the bush. Why? Because the *forward momentum*⁹ of the car itself caused the chestnuts to leave the vehicle at the car's own forward speed of ten miles an hour—even when David shot straight out the window. After two dozen tries, David got the hang of it. He was able to have chestnuts land and stop near the bush four times *in succession.*** His dad was impressed—so far at least.

Then Matt Hale increased the driving speed to twenty miles an hour—David began missing again badly. At the faster speed, shooting turned out to be far more difficult than David had expected. In fact, he found he had to shoot as soon as the bush

---

* Ground rule: A basic principle of action.
† Out of the ordinary: Different from what one usually does.
‡ MPH: Abbreviation or short form for Miles Per Hour.
§ Projectiles: The things being sent through the air—in this case the chestnuts.
⁹ Forward momentum: The force that keeps a thing moving in one direction.
** In succession: In a row, one after the other.

came into view. If he waited even a *fraction of a second** after spotting the bush, it was too late—he would *overshoot*† the target bush and miss again *considerably*.‡

This was not going to be easy—nothing at all like shooting at motionless Coke bottles on the garden wall—just as his dad had predicted.

At first, David was frustrated. His dad was counting on him and the youth was afraid to let him down. But with practice things gradually got better. Within another dozen practice runs, he again was able to shoot the chestnut close to the target area—and do so *consistently*.§ The rescue operation was *falling into place*.¶ When the chestnuts landed in the bush zone for the fifth straight time, father, son and Thor headed toward home.

Before taking the road back to the castle, Matt Hale drove into a farm. He bought six large sacks of potatoes that he put in the trunk. He often bought fresh vegetables to take to the refugee camps—never this many potatoes. With the rest of the family gone to the States, David knew the potatoes were not for the family. Maybe, he thought, they have something to do with the operation. His dad had bought a dozen eggs. "These will come in handy tomorrow night," he remarked with no further explanation.

---

*   Fraction of a second: Less than a second in time.
†   Overshoot: Shoot too far beyond the target.
‡   Considerably: By a large distance or a wide margin.
§   Consistently: Time after time, repeatedly, over and over.
¶   Falling into place: When good things happen that help get a job done successfully.

9

Preparing the Message

It was four o'clock in the afternoon when they pulled up to the castle. Being June, the sun was reaching its *zenith**—but a few more hours of daylight remained. Matt Hale led David out back to the tool shop and put him to work. The rescue mission was set to begin in twenty-eight hours.

Matt Hale had been told that tomorrow evening at eight o'clock *precisely*,† Dr. Kaminski would be sitting on an old park bench in the Russian part of the city of Linz. That was a little over one hundred miles drive from Vienna. In 1945, Linz was divided into two zones separated by the Danube River that ran through the middle of the city. On the north side of the river was the Russian Sector—the American Sector was to the south. A bridge with border stations connected Communist-controlled Linz to the free part of the city. Unfortunately for Dr. Kaminski, at least so far, he was stuck on the wrong or Russian side of the Danube in a part of Linz known as Urfahr.

According to his refugee friend, Dr. Kaminski told him that he would sit in the park for fifteen minutes—from 8:00 to 8:15PM—every third night beginning on June 6. He would do this until contacted by someone who could assist his escape,

---

* Zenith: The highest point in the sky which for the sun occurs on the first day of summer.

† Precisely: Exactly—not more or less and not before or after.

unless he was arrested by the Russians. The friend said the Polish scientist was praying that the Americans would make contact with him soon. Well, tomorrow night his luck could change. He would indeed be contacted—not as he might expect, but by *airborne delivery** from America's junior spy!

David's first or immediate task this afternoon was to take one of the drier horse chestnuts and drill in it a one-quarter inch *diameter†* tunnel that would be a little over an inch deep. He was told not to drill all the way through the chestnut. The escape message would be rolled up and slipped into the chestnut tunnel. The carving tool he was given to break the tough skin of the nut was an *awl.‡* Once he had made a tiny hole, he would use a hand drill left behind by the previous castle occupants. He would soon find he was not as naturally *adept§* at this task as he was at making slingshots.

David punctured the skin of one chestnut, then another. Each time he tore away too much of the chestnut shell—this was more difficult than he *anticipated.¶* To achieve some stability, David slipped the third chestnut into a *vise.*** Slowly and carefully, he *excavated††* a narrow *chasm‡‡* in the chestnut, just as his dad had instructed. After thirty minutes of *painstaking§§* work, he was just about done.

---

*   Airborne delivery: Through the air, in this instance by slingshot.
†   Diameter: The longest line across a circle, its widest point.
‡   Awl: A hand tool used to punch holes in leather.
§   Adept: Skillful or talented.
¶   Anticipated: Expected or foresaw.
** Vise: A heavy iron tool attached to a work bench and used for holding things steady between the two jaws of the tool.
†† Excavated: Dug out or made hollow by digging a hole.
‡‡ Chasm: An opening shaped like a cave.
§§ Painstaking: Very careful.

David removed the chestnut from the vise and began admiring his own handiwork. Then, holding the chestnut up to the light, he spotted a little of the nut's loose core deep inside the tunnel. Wanting to impress his father with a perfect job, he placed the nut back into the vise and tightened it again.

As he did, he heard a sharp cracking sound. He watched helplessly as his work of art—under the powerful force of the vise—collapsed and split along its surface. In perfect German this time, David grumbled a couple of nasty words.

David had, of course, *violated** and was learning the hard way another important rule for spies—*perfectionism*[†] is a true enemy of success. In other words, once he had accomplished his task and produced a usable chestnut for tomorrow night's operation—he should have stopped messing with it. Now, he had to begin again and was lucky he had *time to spare.*[‡]

As David labored with chestnuts out back in the tool shop, Matt Hale was in the study carefully preparing the written message. He wrote it in German on very thin paper, the kind used by spies. On the first line of the message he wrote this warning, "Swallow this message immediately after reading it." The *water-soluble*[§] paper would instantly *dissolve*[¶] in Kaminski's mouth.

Matt Hale's message contained further guidance for Dr. Kaminski.

---

* Violated: Broke a rule or did something wrong.
† Perfectionism: Trying to do things too well, too perfectly and beyond what is needed.
‡ Time to spare: Extra time available to finish the job.
§ Water-soluble: Able to break apart or be dissolved in water.
¶ Dissolve: Become a watery mixture—in this case, one that can be swallowed.

"Walk in a northerly direction on the right hand side of the *Linz Underpass** tonight at eleven o'clock—precisely! If no one is following you, carry your hat in your left hand and I will know it is safe. If no other person or car is in sight, I will stop. I am driving a Mercedes Four Door sedan and will have a boy with me. I will open and get you into the trunk. If I do not get you this evening, I will be back three evenings from now, Nine (9) June, at 10:00 PM (Repeat 10:00 PM). A friend of *Chopin*."†

"Friend of Chopin" was the *safety signal*‡ which Dr. Kaminski had passed through his refugee friend to the Americans—anyone who said he was a "friend of Chopin" would be *trustworthy*.§

When the message was complete, Matt Hale went out to the workshop. He found David putting the finishing touches on chestnut number four. The father examined it carefully and then lit a candle. David assumed it was to see inside the narrow tunnel that David had excavated. Instead, Matt Hale let some of the candle wax drip into the tunnel and harden. "This will keep the chestnut oil from bleeding into the message, Son. It creates a hard wall that will protect the rice paper from getting wet and *disintegrating*¶ before it is read by its *intended recipient***— Dr. Kaminski, of course."

---

* Linz Underpass: Where a road passes under a bridge in the City of Linz.
† Chopin: Kaminski is Polish and Friedrich Chopin is the most famous Polish composer.
‡ Safety Signal: Carefully chosen words of action that tells a spy that he is being contacted by the right people, and not the enemy.
§ Trustworthy: Able to be trusted and relied on.
¶ Disintegrating: Falling apart or being damaged.
** Intended recipient: The person who is supposed to receive something.

Using a pair of *tweezers,** from his medical bag, Matt Hale carefully inserted the rice paper message into the core of the chestnut. Finally, he dripped a cap of brown candle wax over the opening to the chestnut tunnel. This was to make certain that, to any *casual observer,*† the chestnut would appear no different from any other chestnut under the tree. Yet another rule for spies—make the tools of espionage seem as natural and ordinary as possible to avoid *arousing suspicion.*‡

---

*   Tweezers: Small metal instrument held between a thumb and finger and used to pick up and hold things too small for the human hand and fingers.
†   Casual observer: One who is not looking, but just happens to see the chestnut.
‡   Arousing suspicion: Making people curious.

Margot and Anne Frank

10

Amsterdam Remembered

When David headed upstairs to his bedroom, it was late. In addition to his natural *aversion** to sleep, his young mind was spinning with all that had taken place this day—and what he would face tomorrow. He thought for a while about the *tangible*[†] parts of the operation—slingshots, horse chestnuts, the Mercedes sedan, potatoes, the secret message, Russian Guards, and the Russian Sector road map his dad had been studying.

He stayed awake longest this night, however, *reflecting*[‡] on the rescue operation's *intangibles*[§]—things David could not see, touch or shoot with his slingshot. Never having lived any way but free, he could only *speculate*[¶] what the Polish scientist must have gone through to get from Poland to Austria on foot and to have been hiding for months from the Russians. This, the boy concluded, was all about a man's freedom.

David's mind flashed back several weeks when the Hale family had passed through *The Netherlands*[**] on their way to

---

*   Aversion: Very strong dislike or repugnance to something—in this case, sleep.
†   Tangible: Things that can be seen and touched.
‡   Reflecting: Thinking very deeply on something, not just giving it a passing thought.
§   Intangibles: Things that cannot be seen or touched—such as ideas, thoughts and feelings.
¶   Speculate: Imagine or guess.
**   The Netherlands: A small country on the North Sea next to Germany and Belgium; also called Holland.

Vienna. The Hales spent a few days in Amsterdam, the capital city, where Dr. Hale met with international doctors and nurses to discuss the problems he would be facing in the refugee camps.

While there a family friend—like Matt Hale, a medical doctor—read the Hales a 1946 Dutch newspaper article titled "A Child's Voice." It told of a special young Jewish girl who, just before the war with Germany ended in 1945, died in the Nazi Bergen-Belsen *Concentration Camp*.* Of the hundreds of thousands of such innocent and *tragic*† victims of the Nazis, what made her special was that she left behind a wartime diary— one that many people around Europe were talking about.

The fifteen year old girl—ANNE FRANK—spent two years hiding in an attic as her family tried to escape capture by the Nazis after Germany invaded Holland in May 1940. The invasion took place just days before Anne's eleventh birthday—David's present age. Soon, the Germans began sending Dutch Jews off to concentration camps—at least the Jews they could find. Brave Dutch citizens successfully hid from the Nazis some 16,000 Jews who were able to survive the Nazi *occupation*‡ and the war.

The *time line*§ for Anne Frank's difficult struggle to try to stay alive was brief. She went into hiding with her family in

---

* Concentration camp: A large prison camp where Nazis sent millions of innocent people to work and to die in savage conditions. This included men, women and children who were Jews, political opponents, homosexuals, Gypsies, handicapped people, and Christians opposed to the Nazi government and ideas.
† Tragic: Extremely sad, painful and unnatural.
‡ Occupation: When a foreign enemy invades and takes control over another country.
§ Time line: A listing of important dates and events, in this case in Anne Frank's short life.

July 1942—she was thirteen years old. The Nazis *stormed** their secret hiding place two years later and arrested the whole Frank family—it was then August 1944. Within six months she died a death camp prisoner along with her older sister Margot— young Anne Frank was barely sixteen when she *perished.*[†]

What struck David the hardest was that the Frank sisters had died from typhus—Dr. Matt Hale's medical specialty. David *pondered*[‡] the sad *irony*[§] that the Frank family had purposely moved in the 1930s to Amsterdam to get away from Germany, away from the Nazis, and away from Adolph Hitler. Going to Holland turned out to have been a *disastrous*[¶] choice—of the millions of European Jews to die at the hands of the Nazis, the highest percentage in any country were those, like the Franks, who found themselves in Amsterdam in 1940. Despite the several thousand that survived the war, three out of every four such Jews in Holland were killed—seventy-five percent in all!

Adding to the story's tragedy was what happened to the girl's mother, also in the early months of 1945. Edith Frank died at *Auschwitz,*[**] a *notorious*[††] Nazi death camp in Poland built by the Germans to complete their evil and secret plan to murder all of

---

* Stormed: Made a military or police raid on the building where the Franks were in hiding—breaking down doors and aiming guns at these peaceful, innocent and unarmed people.
† Perished: Died in a horrible way from violence or, as in this case, lack of food and medical care.
‡ Pondered: To weigh in the mind carefully and thoroughly.
§ Irony: When something happens or is said that is the opposite of what one would expect.
¶ Disastrous: The worst possible thing that could have happened, in this case resulting in death.
** Auschwitz: A group of death camps in Poland where the Nazis murdered over one million innocent human beings, including woman and children.
†† Notorious: Famous, not for good things but for doing things that are evil.

Europe's Jews. Separated by hundreds of miles from her children—and with no idea where they were imprisoned—Mrs.
Frank had saved and hidden food for her daughters. Unable to
bring herself to eat that food, Edith Frank died of starvation.

With all these things swirling in his head about the night in
Amsterdam, David had a hard time getting to sleep. When he
tried to sleep he kept wondering "Oh, God, why couldn't Dad
and the American Army or British Army have arrived in time
to save them?" As tears fell from his eyes, he thought of Anne
as well as her sister and mother—he thought also of just how
wonderful his own life had been compared to theirs.

David's mother, especially, had taught him it was a bad thing
to hate people—but then and there, he really hated Nazis.
For a moment he wished he had been an American soldier in
the war. "Too bad I wasn't born ten years earlier," he mused.
"Maybe I could have done something—to save a family or save
at least someone."

There was no direct link, of course, between the Frank
family tragedy and Dr. Kaminski. The Franks lived in The
Netherlands in the early 1940s and the Polish scientist was living in Poland and then Austria in 1947. In David's young mind,
however, it was *uncomplicated**—he saw all of them as innocent
victims of *monstrous*[†] people. In the case of the Franks, it had
been German Nazis who took their freedom and then their
lives. In Kaminski's case, Russian Communists were trying to
take away his freedom for the rest of his life. This *connectivity*[‡]

---

*   Uncomplicated: Clear, direct, plain and uncluttered.

†   Monstrous: Behaving like monsters or savage animals, not decent hu-
     man beings.

‡   Connectivity: Being closely associated with another person or thing.

made David Hale deeply *committed** to help save at least one innocent person from such capture—Dr. Kaminski would be that person.

To do his part in the rescue, David had to be absolutely certain that his slingshot would work at the *critical moment.†* He promised himself he would do it right.

He felt a sudden need to *reassure‡* his dad—and maybe even himself. So, he walked downstairs to the study where Matt Hale was examining and measuring distances on the city map of Linz. The boy looked at his dad and, without further discussion, said simply, "Dad, remember Amsterdam and the news article about the young Jewish girls? Well, now I know why you do what you are doing—I really want to help—and I will!" Then he went upstairs and fell into a deep, restful sleep.

---

*   Committed: Totally intending to do something—no matter what!

†   Critical moment: The exact time when it would be most needed.

‡   Reassure: Tell someone that things will work out fine, that things are okay; in this case, that David will do what has to be done to make the rescue operation successful.

11

D-Day*

Date: Thursday, June 6, 1947

The Time: 5:45AM

Just as the sun was coming up the next morning, David arose, fed Thor, skipped breakfast and headed out to the garden. He was determined to test his slingshots to be sure he was equipped tonight with his very best one—and had a good backup, or spare. Within an hour, he broke one of the less *robust*[†] slingshots he had carved from the branch of a maple tree. It turned out not to be strong enough for the job.

The one he preferred for the night's work was an unfinished slingshot he had been making from ash—the hard wood used in the United States in the *legendary*[‡] Louisville Slugger bats used in professional baseball. Ash proved to be harder and more difficult for David to whittle. But, it promised to produce a more *durable*[§] slingshot. David would ordinarily

---

* D-Day: The target day for the rescue operation of Dr. Kaminski. The most famous D-Day in history was three years earlier on June 6, 1944 when Allied Troops landed in France to begin the land war against Nazi Germany and that ended World War II in Europe.

† Less robust: Not as strong or well constructed.

‡ Legendary: Famous for a very long time, in some cases for centuries.

§ Durable: Stronger, tougher and longer lasting.

have *procrastinated** some days or even weeks before getting it finished. With Dr. Kaminski's freedom *at stake*,[†] he was now committed to getting it finished and tested. If he was satisfied by the target shooting results in the garden, he would ask his dad to make additional practice runs in the car that afternoon.

As Matt Hale had taught him weeks earlier, David built his slingshot in three stages. His dad told him to begin by selecting the proper tree branch which, he said, is the *key*[‡] part of any good slingshot. "Son, you can always replace or repair the other parts," he advised, "but, if the central handle or *structure*[§] is not right, you may as well throw away the *device*[¶]—in fact, just start over again *from scratch*."**

After a strong storm with high winds had swept through Vienna one weekend back in May, David and his dad—with Thor strolling along—wandered around the castle grounds before heading out to the *Vienna Woods*.[††] They were searching for fallen tree branches that might be used to make a new slingshot or two.

Thor, of course, had seemed to think they were out looking for sticks to throw and that he could chase. To keep the

---

*   Procrastinated: To delay or put off doing something which should be done now.

†   At stake: At risk or on the line.

‡   Key: Most important or essential thing.

§   Structure: The main or strongest part that gives the sling its shape and power.

¶   Device: A tool for doing something, in this case slinging a shot a long way.

** From scratch: All over again, from the beginning.

†† Vienna Woods: The famous hilly and forested land in and around Vienna. It stretches over an area that is 27 miles by 13 miles. It has historically been an area for hunting and hiking and for the past 150 years has been preserved to protect its trees, wildlife and flowers.

*rambunctious** dog satisfied, David spent half his time doing just that. Within a couple of hours, they had found several seemingly good branches—*Y-forked†* shape, about a foot long, and at least ¾ of an inch thick. They examined each one to see if it was strong enough and without *blemish.‡* If a branch had a crack or was rotted in any way, it could not take the stress and would eventually break—possibly at the worst possible time.

Once they had brought all the selected branches into the castle tool shop, David used his *Swiss Army pocket knife§* to strip the bark from each branch and look for cracks or *imperfections.¶* When he found a sturdy branch, he began the second stage— cutting rubber strands that, when stretched, would produce enough power or force to send a rock, metal ball or chestnut flying through the air. From the inner tubes of an old bicycle tire left at the castle by the Germans, he went about cutting two rubber strips—each about a foot long and a half inch wide. *Pre-war*** inner tubes made from *genuine rubber††* proved to be consistently stronger and last longer than if he used wartime *synthetic rubber.‡‡*

---

*   Rambunctious: Out of control excitable behavior.
†   Y-forked branch: A part of a branch that forms two smaller branches and looks like the letter Y.
‡   Blemish: Some weakness or imperfection in the wood.
§   Swiss Army Knife: The most famous military knife made since 1870 in Switzerland. It has several tools, including a small and large blade, a can opener, a cork screw, two kinds of screwdrivers and more.
¶   Imperfections: Things that are wrong and, simply, less than perfect such as worm holes.
** Pre-war: Before 1938 when World War II began in Europe.
†† Genuine rubber: Real or original and made from the rubber plant; not fake or artificial.
‡‡ Synthetic rubber: A material developed in the 1940s by chemists as a substitute for real rubber.

David had learned the hard way to use sharp scissors to cut the strips. Weeks earlier, he tried using his pocket knife to cut the rubber—the blade slipped and almost chopped off the tip of a finger. By the time the bleeding stopped, David had learned another important lesson, for spies or anyone working with his hands—using the correct tools to do a job is both safer and gets better results.

The final step for David was finding and cutting a piece of leather three inches square. It would serve as the pocket or pouch to hold the chestnut while the slingshot was pulled back and re-leased. The source for the leather pouch was an old Army boot. It was so difficult to cut that David had his dad do it so he would avoid any more bleeding fingers. Another good rule for spies—get expert help when you need it! Everyone cannot do everything.

As David was putting on the *finishing touches*,* Matt Hale came into the workshop to see how the boy was doing. The father liked the idea of having a stronger slingshot and agreed it needed to be tested before tonight's operation. "When carrying out an intelligence operation," he said, "no one likes surprises—surprises usually mean something bad will happen—in fact, last-minute surprises are almost never helpful."

Father and son got into the car and left the castle grounds for a final field test with the newest slingshot. They drove out into the country to the same quiet road and target bush they used the previous day. To make the test realistic, the driving speed would be the same as the required *operational speed*†—20 mph.

---

* Finishing touches: The last thing needed to complete a job—in this case, wrapping some strong fishing line around the rubber strands and the wooden structure to give added strength.

† Operational speed: The required driving speed when the airborne de-livery will take place.

Fortunately, there were no surprises. After three tries, David was able to get the chestnut to land in the target zone. Matt Hale went through the test ten more times before he was entirely satisfied. Confident now that David could get the chestnut to the target zone with accuracy, Matt Hale headed for home. They still had time to re-examine all materials needed for tonight's mission.

David then got to see his dad in action as a senior spy—Matt Hale reached into his shirt pocket and took out an *operational checklist** he had put together for the rescue operation.

As he handed it to his son, he said, "David, an airplane pilot who wants to live a long life doesn't take his aircraft skyward without going first through a complete *pre-flight*† review or checklist. Well, David, it is the same with intelligence operations. We don't *initiate*‡ this evening's action until we have gone *methodically*§ through the checklist I prepared. Everything must be done correctly—in the right order and at the right time."

Matt Hale started by *thoroughly*¶ checking out the Mercedes. He began with the tires and lights to be sure there were no problems there. He checked the gas gauge as well as the oil level. He made certain the car had water in the radiator. He got down on the ground and examined the car underneath from front to back. He had to be certain there was no gas, oil or water leak that could cause problems later in the evening.

---

*   Checklist: A careful written listing of things that are needed as well as actions that need to be taken.

†   Pre-flight: Taking place before an airplane flight occurs.

‡   Initiate: Start or begin.

§   Methodically: Going step by step through a number of things needed for success.

¶   Thoroughly: Completely and without forgetting or leaving anything out.

He then placed the horse chestnut with the message into an empty pocket in his medical bag and put the bag itself on the front passenger seat, so he could reach it later on. Then he had David pretend to be Dr. Kaminski and crawl deep inside the trunk to see how many potato sacks he would need to conceal the Polish scientist. He had bought six—after the test with David inside, he decided he would need only five.

Matt Hale then pulled out, first, the Austrian country map and showed David the road they would be taking to get to the city of Linz which, late in the war, was bombed *intensively** by the Americans. It was Adolph Hitler who selected Linz, his childhood home, to be one of the so-called 'Five Cities of the Fuehrer.'† To increase the importance of Linz, he ordered that military equipment factories be *dismantled*‡ and moved there from other Nazi-occupied areas—especially from Czechoslovakia which is barely twenty miles away. Things did not work out at all as the Fuehrer had intended—by making his home town an important factory center, Hitler in the end made Linz a target for twenty-two large-scale American and British *bombing raids*§ during the war.

Matt Hale then took out a Linz city map showing the roads that would take the Hales first to the park where Dr. Kaminski would be waiting and then to the Austrian medical buildings they would visit during the evening. Next, he pointed to the

---

* Intensely: In a repeated, concentrated way.
† Fuehrer: Leader or guide in German—was the title for Adolph Hitler as head of Nazi Germany.
‡ Dismantled: To be taken apart.
§ Bombing raids: In 1944, hundreds of American and British airplanes dropped bombs on Linz.

Linz Underpass where they would pick up the Polish scientist at 11:00PM—if things went as planned.

The last road of importance on the rescue map, Matt Hale pointed out, led directly from the *pickup point** to the *Nibelungen Bridge†* that crossed from the Russian Sector to the American Sector. The Danube River flows directly under this bridge.

For the Hale father–son spy team, the *stakes* in this operation *were high.‡* It was not only a question of whether they could carry out the rescue successfully. They had to do it without the Russians ever knowing or even suspecting in the future that they had been involved. Otherwise, this rescue operation would be a one-time event and their future spy roles would be over. Secrecy, after all, is at the heart of this special work.

For Dr. Kaminski, the stakes were obviously, and personally, so much higher—he had everything to gain or lose—it all depended on which side of the Danube he would find himself when Austrian clocks struck midnight and the night came to an end. If the Hales managed to get him safely across that bridge, his life would forever be changed—from prisoner to free man. Assuming he did get free, he could then travel to America or anywhere in the *Free World.§* If he did not make it to freedom,

---

* Pickup point: The place where a person is waiting to be picked up by car in a spy operation.

† Nibelungen Bridge: Hitler ordered building this bridge when he arrived in his "home town" of Linz in 1938. It was completed in 1943. The American Army arrived and captured the bridge in 1945, before the German Army was able to blow it up. In 1947, the Russians controlled the eastern half of the bridge and the Americans controlled the western half. The bridge was 400 yards long, or the length of four U.S. football fields.

‡ Stakes were high: There were high risks involved in the operation.

§ Free World: During the Cold War, this meant all the countries not controlled by the Communists.

he would be forced to spend the rest of his life as a prisoner of the Russian Communists.

After having David trace with his finger the entire route they would be taking to and around Linz, Matt Hale suggested they go to the kitchen for a bite to eat—something to give them strength for the evening's work. David finished the bowl of his favorite beef stew that mom had cooked and left for them in the *ice box*.*

Finally, his father broke and dropped several eggs into a *thermos bottle*.† He added some milk and a dash of salt. "This *magic potion*‡ will be useful tonight," Matt Hale remarked. When he explained how the potion would be used, David's eyes widened like those of a barn owl. This was a part of the escape operation he would have liked to avoid. But, if that would be needed, he made it clear that he was *fully aboard*.§ This operation was not about David Hale's *short-term*⁋ comfort or discomfort—it was about the Polish scientist's lifelong freedom.

---

*   Ice box: Before refrigerators, people used ice boxes or cabinets to keep food cold.

†   Thermos bottle: It is a bottle that keeps hot liquids hot and cold liquids cold for a few hours.

‡   Potion: A liquid mixture that usually has some medical or even magical powers.

§   Fully aboard: Totally committed and without any objections or complaints.

⁋   Short-term: Not lasting a long time.

12

Entering the Russian Sector

The Date: Saturday, June 7, 1947

The Time: Early afternoon

Matt Hale drove out of Vienna and into Austria's Russian Sector at the usual *checkpoint.** He came to a stop as the Russian Guard approached the car. David felt some anxiety as the Guard inspected dad's *passport†* and then the car. Dr. Hale had been through this checkpoint regularly. The Guards knew him *on sight.‡*

Tellingly,§ the Russian paid no attention to David. This *disinterest¶* in children would prove helpful in the future—the younger Hale would be able to see and do operational things without getting or attracting the attention an adult would normally receive from the *paranoid*** Russians. His dad told him

---

* Checkpoint: A guarded place in the road where cars are stopped and searched before they are permitted to enter or leave the Russian Sector of Vienna.

† Passport: A booklet used to travel from one country to another.

‡ On sight: As soon as they saw him.

§ Tellingly: Importantly revealing a way of thinking and acting.

¶ Disinterest: Not caring about or noticing.

** Paranoid: Extremely suspicious and untrusting; in their case, because the Russians for many years were in fear of government and Communist Party terror against their own citizens.

later this made David "operationally invisible." He became *thereafter** "The Invisible Spy of Vienna!"

The Guard peered into the trunk filled with potatoes and remarked that Dr. Hale was supposed to have an *official permit†* to transport food through the Russian Sector. Matt Hale produced the necessary document which the Guard examined. The Russian had to be sure it had the correct date and the required signatures. This process took five minutes—to David, it seemed longer. In this, his first secret operation, time seemed to be moving quite slowly.

Dr. Hale, meanwhile, looked and acted as *cool as a cucumber.‡* In time, Dave would develop the ability to stay *cool under pressure§*—a good thing too, because nervous spies do not survive. As he crossed into the Russian Sector, David had *embarked¶* on his career in intelligence—America's youngest spy. There was no turning back. Flashing through his own mind was a simple, logical question—would he stay cool and calm when the operation got heated?

The Hale sedan pulled away from the checkpoint and David felt better. He let out a deep breath of air. His sense of *well-being*** was *short-lived††*—it came to an *abrupt‡‡* end when he noticed a Russian Military car following closely behind. Matt

---

*   Thereafter: From that time on.
†   Official permit: A paper signed by government officials that allowed him to transport potatoes.
‡   Cool as a cucumber: To remain nice and relaxed or cool, not nervous.
§   Cool under pressure: Being able to be calm when difficult things are happening.
¶   Embark: Starting out or beginning.
** Sense of well-being: Feeling good and at peace.
†† Short-lived: Lasted a very short time; brief.
‡‡ Abrupt: Sudden.

Hale, of course, had *spied** the Russian car as soon as he drove away from the checkpoint. He was highly pleased that there was only one *surveillance*† vehicle—not two, as *occasionally*‡ was the case. If two surveillance cars were following him this evening, the pickup *phase*§ of the operation would have to be *postponed*ᵍ to another night. Matt Hale knew he could fool one surveillance team—but maybe not two.

He told David to relax, act normally and not look back as though he were doing anything suspicious. "Keep the slingshot and vacuum bottle out of sight, Son. As we talked about, the more natural you act, the better. We want to make these two Russians relax—to become so completely bored that they lose interest in us and what we are doing. Bored *surveillants*** can be fooled just about every time."

It was now 3:25PM—four hours and thirty-five minutes before the expected *initial contact*†† with Dr. Kaminski.

They drove away from Vienna along the Danube River for almost 100 miles and approached the outskirts of Linz—they were, of course, still on the north or Russian side of the river. The Russian car tailed closely behind. As they approached the park where the scientist said he would be waiting, Matt Hale told David to look for the bench in the northeast corner—just as he had shown him on the map. This was where David would

---

*   Spied: Noticed or spotted them.
†   Surveillance: Following someone who is doing secret things.
‡   Occasionally: Once in a while, or sometimes.
§   Phase: Part of a plan, in this case the rescue operation.
ᵍ   Postponed: Put off until another time.
**   Surveillant: A person who is following another person and trying to discover secrets about that person and what he is doing.
††   Initial contact: The first interaction.

have to launch the secret message, if his dad gave the command to shoot.

"Do you see it, son?"

"Got it, Dad."

The doctor kept moving past the bench and away from the park at 20 miles an hour—all part of his plan to keep the Russian surveillants off Guard.

Thirty minutes later they pulled up in front of an old hospital now serving as an Austrian Government headquarters for *medical relief** programs in the area. Matt Hale went inside. One of the Russian surveillants followed and saw him speaking with Austrian officials and doctors. They were discussing the *dysentery*[†] that was making many refugees sick since spring. Hale examined patient medical records, taking his time while the *sullen*[‡] Russian Secret Policeman waited near the front door.

Keeping his mind on the time, Dr. Hale suddenly got David and returned to his car, started it up, and turned back in the direction of the park. The Russian surveillant who had gone inside was using a toilet. As a result, he was a little late getting back to his own vehicle where his driver was waiting—very impatiently!

By design,[§] Matt Hale and David had drunk no fluids for three hours. The older spy knew that their not having to use a toilet would prove helpful. So, the Russian car with its two

---

*   Relief: Aid given to people, like refugees, who need assistance. Because refugees had left their homes and all of their belongings during the war, they needed help.

†   Dysentery: Being sick in the stomach and intestines, causing diarrhea and loss of fluids.

‡   Sullen: Gloomy and silent, even appearing to be angry.

§   By design: As planned.

burly* men in the front seat was well behind the Hales' car as Matt Hale had expected and planned. With the Russians far behind, but driving fast to catch up, the Hales' Mercedes again approached the park. Matt and David both *peered†* into the darkening park and spotted Dr. Kaminski seated on the bench. Matt's watch showed 7:59PM and then turned to 8:00PM. *Zero hour‡* had arrived!

---

* Burly: Big, strong, rough looking.
† Peered: Looked with some difficulty, in this case because it was getting darker as the sun went down.
‡ Zero Hour: The exact moment when a military or spy operation begins.

13

Bull's Eye

The Date: June 7, 1947

Time: 8:00PM

The doctor-spy gave a quick glance backwards through his rear view mirror and *confirmed** that the Russians were not in view. "Get ready son and I will begin the count down, just as we agreed—seven, six, five, four, three, two, one, FIRE!"

David launched the chestnut high in the air in the direction of the park bench and Dr. Kaminski. The Russian car now came into view, but too late to see anything unusual taking place. Too late to see David and his ash wood slingshot go into action. The launch itself had taken less than a half a second. As planned, once the launch was made, neither father nor son had his head turned toward the bench—or even the park itself. Both stared straight ahead as though watching the road.

The Russians, now having caught up, became relaxed again. They did not want to have to report that they had fallen behind. They especially did not want to lose their *prey*.† Their *Officer-in-Charge*‡ would punish them for certain if they even briefly lost

---

* Confirmed: To make sure that something is true.

† Prey: An animal or person that is hunted—in this case, the Hales are being hunted by the Russians.

‡ Officer-in-Charge: The Military or Secret Police Officer who commanded these surveillants.

sight of Hale. The surveillants now felt comfortable—which was exactly how Matt Hale wanted to keep them. It would then be easier to *lull** them *back to sleep*† later in the evening when he had to pick up the scientist—again without being seen.

Dr. Kaminski, meanwhile, had spotted the Hale car and noticed a child's head in the rear window as the sedan pulled past. Then it happened—a brown horse chestnut rolled across the path and came to rest less than thirty-six inches from his feet. Just then, the Russian surveillance car came into view. It was still speeding to catch up with the Hale car which now was departing the area at its normal 20 miles-per-hour speed.

Kaminski sat calmly for a couple of minutes to be certain no one was watching him. He then bent over, seeming to re-tie his boots. In a *graceful motion*†, he reached out a few inches and picked up the chestnut. He got up and headed out of the park in the direction of his war-damaged apartment building, not far from the center of Linz.

As the old scientist reached the corner of his road, he spot-ted a Russian Red Army truck parked directly in front of his building. He had no way of knowing whether the Russians were there looking for him or only doing a *routine*§ check of *identity papers.*⁕ Dr. Kaminski decided not to take any chances. He

---

*   Lull: Fool them into relaxing.

†   Back to sleep: Not a real sleep—but in a relaxed unwatchful condition.

‡   Graceful motion: Smooth, natural movement that would not attract attention.

§   Routine check: An unscheduled examination or inspection that is conducted without warning.

⁕   Identity papers: Documents such as passport, driver's license, birth certificate that prove that a person is who he claims to be or has per-mission to be in a country or cross a border.

stepped into a doorway where he took this strange little horse chestnut out of his pocket and examined it carefully.

Having lived in Poland first under the Nazis, and more recently under the Communists, Dr. Kaminski had learned to think and act in secret ways, too. Feeling the small *defect** in the chestnut's surface, he pressed hard against the nut until the wax cap over David's hidden tunnel fell off. He spotted the paper note inside. He carefully *extracted*† the note with the help of a wooden match and read its contents. "Three hours to freedom," he thought. "Three hours to freedom," he prayed.

For a brief moment, tears of joy almost came to his eyes. But that emotion quickly passed. Fear returned as Kaminski's mind got back to reality. He was not free of the Russians—at least not yet! The sight of the Red Army truck had *jarred*‡ his nerves a bit. Being free, and being close to freedom, are two entirely different things—worlds apart, in fact. It seems that the closer he got to escaping, the more worried Dr. Kaminski was becoming—a natural and normal thing for men in his situation.

The scientist read the note again to be sure he had not missed anything. He rolled it into a ball. He put it in his mouth where it *dissolved*§ instantly as it turned into a pasty mixture. It had the taste of rice and salt. To Dr. Kaminski, it tasted as wonderful as *strudel*.¶ It was, after all, his ticket to freedom. He

---

* Defect: a rough spot or imperfection, in this case where the tunnel was covered by the brown wax.

† Extracted: Removed or taken out.

‡ Jarred: Shaken or upset.

§ Dissolved: Mixing with a liquid, in this case saliva—or as David would call it, spit.

¶ Strudel: A fruit-filled pastry, usually apple, found in Germany and Austria.

swallowed and left the doorway, turning away from his apartment and away from the Russian search team going through his building. They were inside looking for someone, possibly Kaminski himself—he would never know.

He cut across the corner of the park and walked deliberately under a horse chestnut tree where he let the secret chestnut, the *concealment device,** slide down the inside of his pant leg and onto the ground. It came to rest among old leaves and worn chestnuts which had been through the cold hard winter and the heavy spring rains. This was one time Kaminski was glad to have holes in his pockets. Anyone watching him, even closely, would not have noticed a thing.

Eight kilometers away, the Hale and Russian cars were moving in the direction of another Austrian medical center where doctor and son would spend the next two hours.

While his dad conducted examinations of typhus patients, David sat in the *lobby*† trying to read an adventure story about the Amazon River. South America is a long way from Austria, David mused. As his mind wandered a bit, he asked himself which was more dangerous, an Anaconda snake on the Amazon or a Russian Secret Policeman along the Danube. At that moment, he concluded, it had to be the Russian!

David Hale continued to turn the pages of the book he thought he was reading. Then, it occurred to him—he had gone on for three full chapters, but could not recall a word. His mind and inner thoughts had remained entirely focused on

---

*   Concealment device: A hiding place used by spies to hold messages or other secret things.

†   Lobby: The usually large entrance area in a building where people wait to make a visit.

tonight's rescue operation—an adventure that was not a thing of *fiction** or *fantasy.*† This was as real as life can get—eleven year old David Hale understood that perfectly well.

As he reflected on the night's events so far, three images flooded the young sleuth's active thoughts—the shot in the park as he released the chestnut toward the target—then, the almost *irresistible*‡ urge to look back and see how it came out—finally, the two *gruesome*§ Russians waiting for Matt Hale's next move and quite ready to capture a Polish scientist who wished only to be free.

David too was unsure what exactly would happen next. His dad had not discussed the rest of the plan in great detail. The boy knew that the pickup was supposed to take place in less than three hours. David wondered how his dad would get Dr. Kaminski secretly into the trunk of their car. The Russians were staying close behind—they could see practically everything the Hales were doing. Well, practically everything.

They had not seen the slingshot or the vacuum bottle resting on the floor of the car. Both were hidden under Thor's blanket. They had not seen his launch of the horse chestnut in the park. David felt better when it *struck him*¶ that the Russians were seeing only what Matt Hale wanted them to see.

"Ha, they think they are in control," David thought, "when, in truth, they are really mere puppets in dad's stage production.

---

* Fiction: A creation of the mind and imagination; an invented story.
† Fantasy: Wild and unrealistic creation of the imagination; a tale of space creatures, for example.
‡ Irresistible: Unable to be avoided.
§ Gruesome: Frightening and fearfully dangerous.
¶ Struck him: Occurred to him, became suddenly clear to him.

Dad is pulling all the strings—they are dancing to his tune!"
The boy was suddenly feeling a great deal better.

At 10:30PM, Dr. Hale returned to the reception area and told
David that it was time to get going. As the Hale car departed
the medical center, this time the Russians were ready. They
followed close behind as Hale drove in the direction of the
Linz Underpass.

Dr. Matt Hale, like a trained stage actor, switched roles
again. He was no longer simply the infectious disease doctor
doing medical examinations, treating sick patients and writing
reports. He was now the intelligence operative on a secret mission. He had studied the Linz map intensely—he had measured
exactly the distances he would travel from point to point. He
knew each of the roads as well as the men who had designed
and built them.

He also had been studying the Russian driver who Matt Hale
expected to play his part in the rescue operation—although not
intentionally. Having driven for several hours with the Secret
Policeman *in close pursuit,** Matt Hale had developed a clear
understanding of the personal driving habits of the Russian.
He could tell that the guy was getting increasingly impatient
and probably *anxious*† to get back to Vienna. He figured that
was why the Russian was driving so closely behind—which is
exactly what Matt Hale needed to mislead him at the right time.

Matt Hale's mind was on the upcoming *maneuver*‡ that he
was confident would free him of the Russians for the three or

---

*   In close pursuit: Following closely and aggressively behind.
†   Anxious: A feeling of not being at peace or at ease; worrisome;
     uncomfortable.
‡   Maneuver: A planned, tricky move designed to gain an advantage.

four minutes he needed to get Kaminski into the trunk unseen. He looked back through his rear view mirror at the Russian driver and whispered, "Stay real close behind us, *Ivan*,* stay really close."

---

* Ivan: Ivan the Terrible was a brutal Russian leader five hundred years ago, and is still remembered for murdering his own son in a rage. To Matt Hale, Russian Secret Policemen were all Ivans of sorts.

14

The Linz Underpass

Just before 11:00PM, the Linz Underpass was *tranquil**—empty of cars or people as the Polish scientist walked into the tunnel from the south. He had not spotted anyone following him, so he held his hat in his left hand, as the rice paper note had instructed.

Meanwhile, four miles away from the pickup spot, Matt Hale got his three minute *window of opportunity.*† He did this by driving *abruptly*‡ to the right at a fork in the road where the main highway *veers*§ left towards Vienna. 'Ivan' had been following close behind and was right *on his tail.*¶ So, when Matt Hale swung his car to the right, the weary surveillance driver was unable to follow—instead, he found himself heading down the wrong road and with no easy way to turn around.

As the Russian took the time to find a safe place to change directions, Hale was heading *vigorously*** toward the Linz Underpass—slightly increasing his speed to gain precious seconds free of the Russians. He entered the underpass from

---

* Tranquil: Nice and quiet, peaceful and sleepy.
† Window of opportunity: A brief period of time in which to get something done—in this case, pick up the scientist without the Russians seeing what is going on.
‡ Abruptly: Suddenly; without notice or warning.
§ Veers: Turns or changes direction slightly.
¶ On his tail: Directly behind and extremely close.
** Vigorously: With lots of energy and power.

the north and spotted Kaminski. Hat in his left hand, the old scientist was walking ever so slowly in Hale's direction. The Russian *chase car** was nowhere in sight.

Matt Hale pulled over to the side and jumped out. He went immediately to the trunk and pulled out the bags of potatoes. Kaminski followed Matt Hale's directions in German and climbed into the trunk as far as he could squeeze. As he helped Kaminski into the trunk, Dr. Hale noticed that the scientist was obviously and seriously *under-nourished.*† "Just skin and bones," Matt Hale thought, "exactly like so many of my refugees."

Hale pushed the potatoes back in and Kaminski was now fully covered and hidden from view. Matt Hale got back into the car and resumed his drive towards the Nibelungen Bridge.

As Hale drove out of the Linz Underpass, the Russian Secret Police car came back into view. The scowling Russians *resumed*‡ their surveillance. They talked about the incident and agreed not to report their *omission*§ at the Russian checkpoint or when they got back to Vienna—that would only get both of them in trouble. "After all," one said, "the American was out of sight only for a couple of minutes."

"After all," the other *rationalized,*⁋ "this guy is only a doctor who treats typhus. He is not one of the American Embassy or

---

*   Chase car: The surveillance vehicle that was closely following behind.
†   Under-nourished: Being much too thin due to lack of food, and dangerously so.
‡   Resumed: Began again.
§   Omission: A mistake or failure involving leaving something out or skipping something.
⁋   Rationalized: Using reasons to support their conclusion—in this case, faulty reasons that they should not report losing Matt Hale for five minutes.

Military spies we have to watch every second. My guess is he was weary, got lost for a moment, and made that crazy turn. You report nothing when we get back to Vienna and neither will I. Agreed, *Comrade*?"*

"Agreed!"

When they saw that the Hale Mercedes was approaching the bridge leading only to the American Sector of Linz, the Russian surveillants turned their car around. They were glad their work was over for the day—especially since they had a hundred mile drive back to Vienna. They chatted about what a waste of their time it had been. "Why they have us follow a doctor and his kid around Austria makes no sense at all," one remarked.

"What kid?" asked the driver?

Yes, David really could be operationally invisible!

---

* Comrade: A Communist term meaning ally or friend. The Russian word is Tovarich.

15

Checkpoint Diversion*

Meanwhile, Matt Hale pulled up to the Russian checkpoint. He got out of the Mercedes and headed towards the Russian Guard shack. David stared down at the vacuum bottle at his feet. He lifted up the *concoction*,† held his nose, and quickly swallowed the whole solution.

And, just as quickly, he switched his thoughts from stomach to baseball—musing about the Red Sox and Yankees. He wondered whether, in 1947, the Sox might repeat last year's victory in winning the American League Pennant for the first time since 1918. His heart said Red Sox—his brain said Yankees! As things developed in September, his brain would prove correct.

To David, the voices coming from the Guard shack were *incomprehensible*.‡ He tried to understand what was being said. He wished he had been a better student of German, which his father was speaking. The Russian Guard Officer was speaking a mixture of Russian and very poor German.

In fact, Matt Hale understood all that the Russian was saying and trying to say in his own language. Hale spoke Russian *fluently*§ although he never let the Russians in Austria know. He

---

* Diversion: An action meant to confuse or fool another person by taking their eye or mind away from the business at hand.
† Concoction: A weird mixture of things—in this case, raw eggs and milk.
‡ Incomprehensible: Could not be heard clearly.
§ Fluently: Just like a Russian would speak.

preferred they assume he had no idea what they were talking about—this gave him an advantage in his medical work but, especially, now in spy operations.

If the Russians knew, or even suspected, that he spoke and understood their language, they would start looking at him quite differently. To begin with, medical doctor or not, they would assume immediately that he might be an intelligence officer. The Russians would take some practical steps, *for starters.**

They would double the number of surveillance teams they had following him around Vienna as well as in the Russian Sector. They would start *recording*[†] his comings and goings very *thoroughly*[‡]—in the same way they were already doing for the American Military and Embassy Officers. In other words, rather than view or think of Matt Hale as 'probably not a spy,' they would think of him as 'MOST PROBABLY A SPY.' In sum, Matt Hale could listen in on Russians and understand what they were saying—but he had to be careful to speak to them only in English or German. Such was the care he had to take to protect his cover and protect his intelligence operations.

David, meanwhile, was feeling the *effects*[§] of the potion. The internal changes involved three organs—his stomach, his lungs and his brain. Naturally, he felt a great deal of *increased activity*[¶] in his stomach. He was also beginning to breathe more deeply. Finally, he started feeling *woozy.***

---

*   For starters: To begin with.
†   Recording: Writing down in a careful and systematic way when and where he was going when he entered the Russian Sector.
‡   Thoroughly: Completely.
§   Effects: What happens as a result of some cause, in this case the "magic potion?"
¶   Increased activity: More things going on at once than before.
** Woozy: Sickish and confused.

He was determined, however, not to let the potion control him or the situation. The young spy thought of the 'guest' in the trunk and covered with sacks of potatoes—an older man who was probably trying to breathe as quietly as humanly possible. "I absolutely will not do it!" David whispered to himself, "not until the time is exactly right—as Dad said."

Dr. Kaminski and David had spoken not a word to each other back there in the Linz Underpass. However, as the scientist approached the car, he had glanced into the back seat and given David a wonderful grin and a wink of the eye. It had reminded the boy of Grandfather Hale—he liked the man instantly.

The voices from the Guard shack suddenly got louder and David's mind got back to his work. He was paying close attention as he never had before. He had noticed, when observing adults, that their voices get louder when they are about to end a conversation—whether on the telephone, in a meeting, or completing official business in a Guard shack. Sure enough, Matt Hale and the Guard *emerged** from the shack and moved in the direction of the Hale car—towards the *secret cargo*[†] hidden in the trunk. Young David Hale, of course, had a part in his dad's stage play this night—he was in the back seat and ready with a surprise *distraction*[‡] of his own.

As the two men approached the sedan, David got ready to do his special part in the rescue plan. His dad was walking in front—behind him was the Russian Guard with his rifle clearly

---

*   Emerged: To come out from.
†   Cargo: A shipment, in this case the Polish scientist.
‡   Distraction: Used by magicians, it gets a person to look in the wrong direction at a key time.

in view. Matt Hale gave David a slight nod and that *reassuring look** that seemed to say, "You can do it, Son—we're partners in this."

The Guard came nearer to the car—no smile, no hello, and none of the pleasant greeting adults usually give young-sters when they meet. "These Russians are *sour pusses,†*" David thought.

The youth lowered the car window slowly. The Guard was now five feet away. "Wait until you can see the whites of his eyes,"—the order given at *Breed's Hill‡* in the American Revolutionary War—was Matt Hale's way of describing the timing of the 'shot.' David waited, lowered the window fur-ther—the Guard was coming ever closer.

The boy was now leaning slightly out the window and this narrowed the gap to a mere three feet between boy spy and Russian Guard. The boy turned away for half a second and put his index finger deep into his mouth. His finger went past the tongue to the back wall where his tonsils once were—before his *tonsillectomy.§* His finger found the *soft palate,¶* as his father called it, and the boy knew something was about to happen. He turned back towards the clueless Guard.

From that point on, everything progressed in what appeared to David to be ultra-slow motion—even the Guard seemed to be moving at a *snail's pace.*** Also, things now seemed to be

---

*   Reassuring look: A facial expression that conveys or gives confidence.
†   Sour pusses: Gloomy people with a grouchy look on their faces.
‡   Breed's Hill: A small hill just north of Boston where an early battle of the Revolutionary War took place.
§   Tonsillectomy: A surgical operation to remove infected tonsils in the throat.
¶   Soft palate: The soft roof of the mouth in the back.
**   Snail's pace: The speed of a small snail which is very slow indeed.

happening to David without his even trying. From a medical standpoint, David's *autonomic nervous system** completely took over.

David gagged once, and then again. The potion started its ascent. David thought of *Mount Vesuvius†*—and of his own internal *eruption‡* as milk, egg whites, egg yolks and particles of beef stew exited the stomach in a sudden explosion. The mess exited his mouth and sailed through the air like a *Ted Williams§* home run. The vomit, which David called "the puke," hit the Guard in the chest—right on the buttons with the Red Stars.¶ The mess dripped quickly down the front of the coat, onto the pants, and all over the military boots of the startled Russian.

The *commotion*** was total. The Guard did not immediately *fathom††* what had just occurred. When he grasped what just happened to him, he screamed at Matt Hale some Russian swears. He pointed the rifle and yelled again, this time in German, "Get this miserable kid out of here before I shoot you both—I have six hours more on Guard Duty and will stink all night because of you!"

There would be no searching of the car trunk that evening.

---

* Autonomic nervous system: Centered in the brain, this is what keeps a person breathing when he is sound asleep, or the heart beating, or any other important action that happens in our bodies without our having to think about it or make decision.
† Mount Vesuvius: The volcano in Italy that exploded and buried the Roman City of Pompeii.
‡ Eruption: Explosion of a mountain volcano.
§ Ted Williams: A great baseball hitter for David's favorite team, the Boston Red Sox, and who batted .406 in 1941 before going off to fight as a U.S. Marine Corps pilot in World War II.
¶ Red Stars: The symbol of the Russian Army.
** Commotion: A loud, confusing situation.
†† Fathom: To understand something deeply and completely.

The 'potato man' would make it to safety. Matt's plan had worked. David too had hit a home run.

When he drove away from the checkpoint, Matt Hale banged three times on the floor boards—a signal that let Dr. Kaminski know that he was finally safe. Buried behind a wall of potatoes, the Polish scientist closed his eyes and said a private prayer of thanks. To all three occupants of the Hale car, the drive across the Nibelungen Bridge was one of pure *jubilation*.* Matt Hale smiled at David and said "Well done, Son." The junior spy responded, "Thanks Dad. But, next time, maybe you will think of something else—I'm afraid I have eaten my last eggs for quite a long while."

---

*   Jubilation: Complete joy, happiness and celebration.

16

Polish Farewell

The Date: June 8, 1947

The Hales' Mercedes headed for a meeting that had been *pre-arranged** with the 'Midnight Visitor.' It was just west of Linz in a place that would provide maximum protection to Dr. Kaminski. Just because they had succeeded in getting him out of the Russian Sector did not mean that security arrangements would *diminish*.†

The Russians were kidnapping innocent people from all Sectors of Austria with *regularity*.‡ The kidnappers sometimes wore stolen American Military Uniforms when doing their dirty work. At times, they even *recruited*§ American Military Policemen to kidnap people for them—a crime for which some American soldiers were arrested, kicked out of the U.S Army, and sent to the military prison at *Fort Leavenworth, Kansas*.¶

By the time a kidnapped person realized he had not been arrested by the Americans, it was too late. The Russians had

---

* Pre-arranged: Agreed to ahead of time.
† Diminish: Become less strict or serious.
‡ Regularity: Happening quite often.
§ Recruited: To get someone to join the Military, work secretly for an intelligence organization, or become an agent for the Secret Police—in this case, the Russians.
¶ Fort Leavenworth in Kansas is where the Army has its most important Military Prison.

him. If it turned out that the kidnapped person was the one
the Russian Secret Police were really after, he would be sent to
Russia for life—forever! When the Russians made a mistake
and found out they had kidnapped the wrong person, at times
they would simply release him and at times they would drown
him in the Danube. In any case, it would be *foolhardy** not to
continue taking all available security *precautions†* to protect a
brave man like Dr. Kaminski until he was safely out of Austria.

Matt Hale drove into a U.S. Army Base that, during the war,
had been an airbase of the German Air Force. The Americans
renamed it Camp McCauley. He pulled the car into an airplane
hangar‡ in a quiet part of the base. The large hangar doors were
closed behind them. No one outside could see who was inside
the car or who got out.

Waiting in the hangar to greet Dr. Kaminski was 'Visitor.' To
David, 'Visitor' appeared even bigger and more powerful than the
night he was seen running in the castle garden towards the river.
He gave David a nice greeting and got *down to business§* with Matt
Hale. They pulled the potato sacks from the trunk and helped
the Polish scientist get out of the car and onto his feet. He had
been tightly squeezed deep in the trunk for well over an hour—
he *emerged,⁋* however, with a wonderful smile on his face.

The first thing he did was nod his head in a respectful way
to Dr. Hale and then to 'Visitor,' who later introduced himself

---

*   Foolhardy: A foolish and careless way of acting.
†   Precautions: All of the wise security steps needed to be safe.
‡   Hangar: A very large, open spaced building where airplanes are kept
     or worked on.
§   Got down to business: Turned his attention to his work, which
     involved Dr. Kaminski.
⁋   Emerged: Came out of a hidden place.

as "Walt Perkins." This was not his true name—it was an operational *alias** 'Visitor' was using in this operation only. Using an alias is a *standard*[+] way to protect one's own security as well as other current operations against the Russians in Austria. 'Visitor' was wearing a disguise which, in this case, was a false moustache and some over-sized black rimmed eyeglasses that changed his general appearance.

Dr. Kaminski saved his first handshake for David Hale to whom the scientist owed so much in making possible his escape. Earlier in the evening, he saw the boy's head in the back seat of the sedan. Later, as he sat alone in the park, the secret-message chestnut suddenly came rolling towards his feet. At that point, he knew that this young fellow had done something very special. Dr. Kaminski was grateful and wanted David to know it. He had escaped the Russian Sector with only the clothes on his back and had no gift for the boy—except to express in Polish how grateful he was for what David had done. "*Dziekuje bardzo*,"[‡] he whispered, which means "thank you, very much."

Although the hour was late, a room in the hangar had been prepared with food and hot drinks for the late-night guests. David's stomach was now aching in hunger—he had left his last meal with the Guard at the Russian checkpoint. He was pleased to have a drink and some popular Austrian dessert, *Linzer Torte*.[§]

---

*   Alias: A false name used to protect his security and identity.
†   Standard: Common, usual or ordinary way an intelligence officer works to protect his operations.
‡   Dziekuje bardzo: Pronounced zed-ku-yeh bard-zo, is Polish for "Thank you very much."
§   Linzer Torte: A tasty crumbly pastry usually filled with fruit jam on top and named for the City of Linz.

When he was offered a hot dinner, he *declined** with a bit of a scowl on his face. Matt Hale laughed and explained why David did not accept the hot meal the U.S. Military team had cooked for them—scrambled eggs with chipped beef was the last thing David wanted to eat!

As it was now after midnight, Matt Hale accepted the American Military's offer to stay for the night and sleep in the hangar building. 'Visitor' earlier had *informed†* Matt Hale that Dr. Kaminski was well-known to U.S. Intelligence agencies for the underground work he had done—first against the Nazi invaders, and then against the Russian so-called '*liberators*.'‡

Kaminski, it turns out, had run a clandestine *network§* of programs in the 'Secret University' that the Poles set up after the invading Germans had closed all the schools in Poland in 1940. The Nazi plan was that the Poles—and all other *Slavic¶* people of Eastern Europe—would be given almost no education. If Germany won the war, Polish children would go to school only for four years and learn to count to no more than 500. They would not be taught to read at all! The Germans, clearly, were trying to destroy the Polish people and nation.

With the war over and Germany defeated, the situation got much worse for the Poles. It was now Russian Secret Police

---

*   Declined: Said no, or did not accept.
†   Informed: Told or advised.
‡   Liberators: Those who free people from a terrible invader or enemy. It is placed in quotation marks because the Russians called themselves liberators but, in fact, were freeing no one at all.
§   Network: A countrywide system that included many people from many places in Poland.
¶   Slavic people: Besides the Poles, includes the Russians, Ukrainians, Bulgarians, Slovaks, Serbians, Croatians, Slovenes, and Bosnians all of whom total in the hundreds of millions of people.

who were hunting down and arresting leaders of Poland's Secret University system. They did this for the same reason they had murdered tens of thousands of Polish Army Officers and educated Poles in the Katyn Forest *massacre.**

When Dr. Kaminski learned he was being hunted by the Russians, therefore, he had no choice but to leave his beloved homeland. He had been betrayed to the Russian Secret Police by one of their secret informants in Warsaw and was placed on their *Most Wanted List.*†

He was able to get out of Poland by taking and using the identity papers of a Polish worker who had died of typhus. He walked 450 miles from Warsaw, Poland and got as far as Linz, Austria. To reach Austria, he had crossed the whole of Czechoslovakia and had to sneak across two national borders without being captured or shot. What helped him get as far as he did was that, in 1946 when he left, hundreds of thousands of homeless war refugees were still walking *aimlessly*‡ around Eastern Europe. He was able to join the wave of Displaced Persons without being identified and caught by the Russians.

But, even when he got to Austria, he still was not safe—he was stuck inside the Russian Sector. That was when he started trying to contact the Americans—he knew he could not escape without outside *assistance*§. His good fortune was that he met

---

* Massacre: Killing a large number of helpless individuals and doing so with great cruelty.

† Most Wanted List: This includes the names of people most wanted by the police. In the case of the Soviet Russians, a person was usually not on the list because he was a real criminal but, instead, because he did not support the Communist Government.

‡ Aimlessly: Without any real plan, sense of direction, or goal.

§ Assistance: Help or support.

a former student from Poland who was in the same *bind** as
Kaminski. The younger man had managed to get only as far as
Austria and was trapped too. But, because he was strong and
athletic,[†] he decided to try swimming across the Danube—his
'river to freedom' was what he called it. He did it one night
during a terrible rain storm when the Russian Border Guards
did not have good *visibility*[‡] on the river.

After the young Polish patriot got across to the American
side, he was *interviewed*[§] by U.S. Military Intelligence. That was
when they learned from him of Dr. Kaminski's *whereabouts.*[¶]
As soon as they knew that this important Polish scientist was
living secretly in the Russian Sector of Linz, the operation to
rescue him was *set in motion.*[**]

The rescue operation turned out to be a triple success—an
operational *hat trick.*[††] It happens rarely but, when it does, it is
a cause for real *satisfaction.*[‡‡] Not only did it get Dr. Kaminski to
the West and out of danger of being kidnapped by the Russians.
It also got Dr. Matt Hale back in the spy business. This, in turn,
had set the stage for young David Hale's entry into the world
of secret intelligence operations.

The following morning, the two Hales—senior spy and
junior spy—headed for home. They stopped in the city and

---

*   In the same bind: Caught in the same mess or situation.
†   Athletic: In good physical condition because of exercise and sports.
‡   Visibility: The ability to see things clearly, for example, as one would
    see in bright daylight.
§   Interviewed: Careful questioning of a person.
¶   Whereabouts: The general location of a person.
** Set in motion: To get something started, in this case a rescue.
†† Hat Trick: Originally from the game of cricket—and used in ice hockey
    when a skater scores three goals in a game—a hat trick describes any
    difficult achievement that happens three times in a single event.
‡‡ Satisfaction: Happiness with a situation or results.

took a ride on Vienna's *Giant Ferris Wheel** that was working again after being badly damaged in the war.

As Matt and David Hale reached the *pinnacle*[†] of the famous ride some 212 feet in the air, they could see *virtually*[‡] all of Vienna and across the Danube into the Russian Sector as well. When they got to the top in the final *revolution*[§] of their ride, David said to his father, "Funny thing, Dad, but from up this high you can't tell the Russian Sector from the rest of Austria—or East from West—or Communism from Freedom."

Matt Hale nodded in agreement and said "That's why America needs spies on the ground, Son. From a distance, important things may appear the same but be entirely different. America's leaders need to know what is really happening around the world."

Father and son drove back into the hills to their castle home. Each felt good about their recent adventure. David, in his memory, would forever keep the smile and grateful handshake of a man whom he had helped live the life of freedom called for in our Declaration of Independence—"All men are created equal—they are *endowed*[§] by their Creator with certain *inalienable*[**] rights—among these are Life, Liberty, and the *Pursuit of Happiness*."[††]

---

* Vienna Giant Ferris Wheel: In 1947, it was the tallest in the world and called the Riesenrad.
† Pinnacle: The highest point.
‡ Virtually: Almost or nearly.
§ Revolution: The circular motion of the Ferris Wheel.
¶ Endowed: To be given or supplied with a gift or gifts.
** Inalienable rights: Rights that are permanent and cannot be taken away.
†† Pursuit of happiness: The right to choose the way you live your life in freedom.

Before this week, these had been mere printed words on a page in David's history book. He had read them but, given his limited *life experience** so far, his understanding of their *significance*[†] had been limited as well. No longer, however! For the young Hale, the words of America's *Founding Fathers*[‡] took on human meaning in the person of Dr. Kaminski. David was now a *motivated*[§] junior spy with one very good success to his credit and looking forward to his next adventure—his next intelligence operation. "Heck," he thought before falling off to *well-deserved*[¶] sleep that night, "I'd swallow two dozen raw eggs to get one more person to freedom."

---

*   Life experience: The full picture of what a person has heard, seen, and done in life so far.
†   Significance: What they really mean to a nation and to its people.
‡   Founding Fathers: Thomas Jefferson and the other American patriots who risked their lives for the sake of freedom and expressed their intentions for America in this document.
§   Motivated: Having strong intention and determination to do what was right.
¶   Well-deserved: One that he had earned.

17

H.I.S.S.

The Date: Monday, June 16, 1947—Third week of vacation for David Hale.

The Place: The Castle, Vienna, Austria.

The Time: 6:00AM

David Hale awoke this Monday morning just as the first rays of sunlight slipped through his bedroom window in the southeast corner of the castle. With his summer vacation barely started, he let out a *chuckle** as he *calculated*[†] that he still had ten weeks before his new school year would begin in early September.

The Hale children did not attend an *ordinary*[‡] school. However, their quite-demanding teacher—their mother—kept David and sister Ellie on a strict 180-day *academic*[§] program that she ran in the castle library. They used the same books and tests found in New England schools. Mrs. Hale ordered also the new 1947 edition of the Junior Encyclopedia Britannica which

---

*   Chuckle: To laugh inwardly or quietly.
†   Calculated: Figured out in his mind using simple arithmetic.
‡   Ordinary: Regularly or normally found.
§   Academic: The subject matter taught in advanced educational institutions, including Math, Science, Literature, World History, and Foreign Languages.

gave the children excellent *background** information on many hundreds of subjects that came up in class.

Before she married Dr. Hale in the mid-1930s, Margaret Hale taught English and History. Arriving in Vienna, Austria, she decided to teach the children at home rather than send them away to private school. She *drafted†* her husband, Dr. Matt Hale, to teach classes in Math, Geography, and Science. His classes were usually taught on Saturday mornings when he was not traveling around the countryside of Eastern Austria doing his medical work. *Characteristically,‡* David *bargained§* successfully to have Wednesday afternoons off from school. This was to make up for the Saturday classes and, as he claimed, "would give other children a chance to catch up."

Having *negotiated¶* the half-day of classes on Wednesdays, David at first felt great—then he had second thoughts and kicked himself for not having been bolder by shooting to get Wednesdays off altogether. After all, he now *reasoned,*** under the new arrangement he had just agreed to, Sunday was the only day they had no school. Once his parents and he agreed to the half-day-off deal, he didn't like the *prospects††* he had of getting off

---

*   Background: This is the basic or elementary information about a subject and that does not change from month to month; for example, maps of a country, kinds of animals in Africa, names of famous people who helped build a nation—not the kind of thing found in a daily newspaper or on the radio.

†   Drafted: To select someone to do a certain job.

‡   Characteristically: That which is special or noticeable about someone.

§   Bargained: Traded or exchanged; in this case, he traded Saturday morning for Wednesday afternoon.

¶   Negotiated: Bargained or worked out an agreement with others, in this case his parents.

**   Reasoned: Thought through carefully.

††   Prospects: The possibility or chances.

Wednesday mornings, too. In all this *dickering,** Ellie had been no help whatsoever. Unlike David, she liked school—enjoyed classes—heck, she even welcomed homework! "Sometimes I feel like an only child," he *groused*[†] to his pal Thor, but the German shepherd just responded with a yawn.

Because the castle school had merely two students—*eager*[‡] Ellie and *dubious*[§] David—there was no way of escaping the teacher's attention. Privately, David and Ellie labeled it the Hale Institute for Suffering *Siblings*"[¶]—known only to them as HISS. But, in all this HISS business, Ellie was really fooling—David really meant it!

All the order and close *monitoring*[**] at HISS made young David Hale absolutely *ecstatic*[††] when school was finally out for holidays and the summer break. By the end of the school year in late May, he wished he never had to go to school again. "Classrooms were NOT designed for boys," he proclaimed to his Father. "I can hardly stand sitting one hour let alone six hours in a chair," he announced with his usual deep emotion.

Recalling his own boyhood school days—and weather *permitting*[‡‡]—Dr. Hale conducted some classes out in the woods or in nearby fields, especially when teaching Science and Geography. When teaching Math, he tried to use realistic problems so the children would learn more than just basic

---

*   Dickering: Bargaining back and forth, as in "I'll give you this for that."
†   Groused: Whiny complaining.
‡   Eager: Enthusiastic and happy to be there.
§   Dubious: Doubtful or unsure he wanted even to be there.
¶   Siblings: Children of the same parents.
** Monitoring: Keeping track of class work and homework done.
†† Ecstatic: Happy and thrilled beyond anything ordinary or normal.
‡‡ Weather permitting: As long as it was not too wet or cold outside.

arithmetic problem solving. He made sure they learned how to read a map, use a *compass** and *slide rule,*† exchange American dollars for Austrian money, locate the stars and planets, and design a strong *arch*‡ or bridge that would not fall down. He too found it *confining*§ to stay inside. He was, therefore, often the first to suggest they go out for a stroll and discuss trees and plants—and bring Thor, who got restless when stuck in the castle library very long.

Dr. Hale made use of the *flora*¶ and *fauna*** of Austria to teach Ellie and David the *principles*†† of *Taxonomy*‡‡—the scientific *classification*§§ of plants and animals. He used it to illustrate order in the world of living things as found in both the animal and plant kingdoms. David was delighted to learn that Thor had a more impressive scientific name than just 'dog'." A dog's scientific name—*Canis Familiaris*—pleased David enormously when he learned that the awesome wolf is known scientifically as Canis Lupus. "Ha, they really are cousins!" he exclaimed, when he saw how close the dog and wolf are on the Taxonomy charts.

Taxonomy uses Latin—the language of the ancient Roman

---

*   Compass: A tool or device for showing north, south, east, west and to help a traveler during a journey.

†   Slide rule: A device with a ruler and a sliding piece used to multiply and divide and do other mathematical calculations similar to what a computer does today.

‡   Arch: A curved structure over an open space that supports the weight above it such as a ceiling or roof.

§   Confining: Sense of being squeezed in, enclosed or smothered.

¶   Flora: The plant life in a certain area.

**   Fauna: The animal life in a certain area.

††   Principles: Ordinary accepted rules and beliefs about a subject.

‡‡   Taxonomy: The scientific way animal and plant life are arranged in a highly organized way according to the things that make them alike or different.

§§   Classification: Arrangement of things by the way they are made, shaped, act, or are connected.

Empire and now called a *dead language.** Why dead? Because it is no longer spoken, it never changes. Because it is unchanging, Latin is used by scientists as a common *international†* language. Several important languages spoken today are *derived‡* from Latin—including French, Portuguese, Spanish, Romanian and the language spoken by modern Romans—Italian. The *gypsies§* of Europe speak a *Romance language¶* called Roma.

David was glad to learn the scientific name of Horse Chestnuts—*Aesculus Hippocastamon*—that wonderful nut that played such a *pivotal*** role in helping rescue the Polish scientist, Dr. Kaminski. The Horse Chestnut took on greater significance for David when his dad read to him an entry made in the diary of Anne Frank. The girl who died in a Nazi concentration camp had touched David's heart. She wrote:

> *Nearly every morning I go to the attic to blow the stuffy air out of my lungs, from my favorite spot on the floor I look up at the blue sky and the bare chestnut tree, on whose branches little raindrops shine, appearing like silver, and at the seagulls and other birds as they glide on the wind.—As long as this exists, I thought, and I may live to see it, this sunshine, the cloudless skies, while this lasts, I cannot be unhappy.††*

---

*   Dead language: A language no longer spoken and, therefore, does not change over the years.

†   International: Involving more than one country.

‡   Derived: To come from or grow out of something else.

§   Gypsies: People who move around on old wagons and do not stay in one place.

¶   Romance language: Any of the several languages that have their origin in Latin.

**   Pivotal: Important or central.

†† From the *Diary of Anne Frank*.

To this young Jewish girl hiding from Nazis near the end of World War II, the leafless Horse Chestnut or *Aesculus Hippocastamon* tree behind the house formed part of the winter beauty she treasured in her final two years of life. David never again looked at such a tree, whether it was bursting with *foliage** in summer or entirely *barren*† in winter, without thinking of Annelies Marie Frank, the girl he *regretted*‡ being too late to save.

---

* Foliage: The leaves, buds, flowers and nuts that appear on trees or bushes.
† Barren: Bare, without leaves or foliage.
‡ Regretted: Was sorry for.

18

Awaiting More Adventure

The whole Frank tragedy had focused his young mind on the existence of genuine evil in the world—in David's view, that of "Nazis back then" and "Russians right now." Where young David was not entirely accurate was in thinking that because the Nazis had lost the war, they were a *thing of the past*.* Within days, right here in Vienna, he would learn *first-hand*† that the 1945 defeat of Hitler's Germany did not mean there were no more Nazis to worry about—no more Nazis to deal with.

In fact in mid-1947, the same *brutes*‡ who had sent millions of innocent families to die in concentration camps during the war right then and with great *stealth*,§ were highly active in both Germany and Austria. In *Vienna* itself, one dangerous Nazi group had hidden a special *cache*⁹ of counterfeit money along with travel documents and gold. It was from Vienna that they were *orchestrating*** the escape of top Nazi *war criminals*†† to *sanctuaries*‡‡ in other parts of the world.

---

*   Thing of the past: No longer existing or important.
†   First-hand: Directly and personally.
‡   Brutes: Men who are cruel and behave more like wild beasts than human beings.
§   Stealth: The act of moving and acting in a covert, quiet or sneaky way.
⁹   Cache: A hidden treasure of value (pronounced like "cash").
**   Orchestrating: Arranging and managing, as when directing and coordinating instruments in an orchestra.
†† War criminals: Evil men who broke the normal rules and practices of war by murdering innocent people who were not fighting or in any army.
‡‡ Sanctuaries: Places of safety where they would be protected.

Now, with David Hale barely three weeks into his summer vacation, this Nazi group was *setting its sights** on the Hale castle which held the keys to their escape. Their only *obstacles*† would be a brave boy and his fearless dog which, *coincidentally*,‡ was a "German" Shepherd, one who served in the U.S. Army and fought the Nazis in the war.

On this bright morning, David was *unaware*§ of what he would soon be facing. He might, after all, get his chance to strike a blow against those who had killed many thousands of innocent people—like the Frank family. This could not bring Anne Frank back to life. But, if he succeeded, it could help David Hale deal with the pain he felt in his *soul*¶ when he thought of her family and other victims of the war.

For an American boy of eleven who had arrived only a few months earlier from the safety of the United States, he had learned already quite a bit about war. After all, as he and his dad drove around Vienna, he saw sections of the city still in ruins from the Allied bombings and the Russian Red Army *artillery*** *barrage*†† during the *Battle of Vienna*.‡‡ Beyond the physical damage one could easily see in the buildings and roads, he knew some of the *human cost*§§ of war—which he learned

---

*   Setting its sights: Planning to approach or attack.
†   Obstacles: Barriers in their way.
‡   Coincidentally: Happening without any plan or decision.
§   Unaware: Not knowing.
¶   Soul: The inner heart, mind, or voice of a person that helps them know what is right or wrong.
**   Artillery: Large guns that shoot big explosive shells many miles.
††   Barrage: A heavy and continuous shooting of big guns during a battle.
‡‡   Battle of Vienna: The Russian Red Army attack on the Austrian capital in early 1945.
§§   Human cost: People killed or wounded.

mainly from stories Dr. Hale told of the *Displaced Persons** in the Austrian camps.

Dr. Hale worked with *refugees*[†] who came from *war-torn*[‡] Eastern Europe. These poor people had the *misfortune*[§] of seeing their countries invaded and *occupied*[¶] by brutal armies of both the German Nazis and then the Russian Communists. Some of the innocent and *wretched*[**] victims of war, especially those who came from Poland, had suffered military invasion three times in the course of five years! Many had spent months or years in harsh concentration camps. They had no money or *possessions*[††] other than the clothes on their backs and shoes on their feet. The *majority*[‡‡] of the refugees had lost family members and friends in the war itself or, later, in the terror campaigns of the Russian Secret Police.

Well, summer was here, school was out, and David was *resolute*[§§] to make the most of what he called his short *parole*[¶¶]

---

* Displaced Persons: Also knows as "DPs" these were people driven out of their homelands and with no place to call home. Millions of them eventually went to live in America, England and other countries where they could have the freedoms people need to live happy lives and raise children.

† Refugees: People driven out of their homelands. Another name for Displaced Persons.

‡ War-torn: Damaged by the battles of war.

§ Misfortune: Very bad luck with poor results or outcome.

¶ Occupied: When an army takes over a city or country after winning a battle or war.

** Wretched: Poor, helpless and suffering people with no way to defend or protect themselves.

†† Possessions: Things people and families own, such as homes and furniture, family photos and clothing.

‡‡ Majority: More than half.

§§ Resolute: Firmly decided.

¶¶ Parole: Usually a release from jail or prison requiring the prisoner to behave and act a certain way.

from HISS. To him, summer vacation had gotten off to a *spectacular** start. Even in his wildest dreams—and young David Hale had a *vivid†* imagination—he never would have dreamt he might become involved in the world of spies. A battle between good and evil. A struggle between innocents like Anne Frank and *vicious†* war criminals now hiding in *post-war§* Europe—including one such dangerous group within a few miles of the castle itself.

The young Hale had joined the fight and, in helping rescue the Polish scientist, had enjoyed his first *taste of victory¶*— *furthermore,*** he wanted more of it! Yet, even though he was delighted to have become Dad's junior partner in secret operations, he was becoming increasingly afraid that the adventure might end and never happen again. "That," David thought, "would be the worst possible thing! After all who will help the next Anne Frank or Dr. Kaminski if Dad and I don't?"

So, before he got out of bed this Monday, he lay a while and *reflected††* on things. He had no *concrete‡‡* plans for the day; nor did he look forward to anything especially important or thrilling. He did not understand the science of his earlier excitement—the *surge of energy§§* and life he felt during his first

---

*   Spectacular: Fantastic and beyond the ordinary.
†   Vivid: Lively, intense, and strong.
‡   Vicious: Evil, brutal, enjoys hurting other people or animals.
§   Post-war: The period of time after a war, in this case right after World War II.
¶   Taste of victory: The feeling one gets when he wins a competition, contest or battle.
** Furthermore: In addition to.
†† Reflected: Thought about deeply.
‡‡ Concrete: Exacting or clear.
§§ Surge of energy: Like lightning, a sudden and strong lively feeling.

spy *caper.** It had been caused by a rush of *adrenalin*† through his body. That chemical, which the human body produces naturally, had boosted his energy level and made him feel alive, ALIVE, ALIVE! Now, however, with no such excitement or important purpose in sight, he was feeling a little down. He had little enthusiasm for anything else. Ordinary life seemed too *routine*‡—in fact, downright boring!

For the first few days after Dr. Kaminski had been *evacuated*§ safely out of Austria, David awoke each morning hoping, in fact *anticipating,*¶ that his dad would soon need him and his slingshot skills. More than a whole week had passed but, so far, nothing! Then David began practicing more than ever to *perfect*** his shooting skills. He set as his goal to reach a level of skill with the slingshot that might equal that of one of his *legendary*†† heroes, *William Tell.*‡‡

Five hundred years earlier, skill with the *crossbow*§§ had en-abled¶¶ that Swiss patriot to save his son's life when a *wicked****

---

*   Caper: A mystery or spy adventure.
†   Adrenalin: A chemical produced in the body when one needs a boost of energy—as in a fight, dangerous or other exciting event.
‡   Routine: Ordinary, regular and without anything special happening.
§   Spirited: To be carried away secretly without anyone seeing or knowing—as with ghosts.
¶   Anticipating: Strongly and eagerly expecting.
**   Perfect: To make absolutely correct and excellent.
†† Legendary: So heroic that people will be talking about the person for many years, even centuries.
‡‡ William Tell: A Swiss national hero who was so skilled with the bow and arrow that he was able to shoot an apple off the head of his son from 300 yards away.
§§ Crossbow: A more accurate and powerful weapon than the regular bow and arrow.
¶¶ Enabled: Helped or allowed.
*** Wicked: Deeply evil person who enjoys hurting or killing innocent defenseless people.

official made him shoot an apple off the boy's head. If he missed the apple, both he and his son would be *executed*.* The tale goes on to say that William Tell succeeded—he did it by making a perfect arrow shot that split the apple from over three hundred yards away. After saving his son's life, William Tell eventually helped free Switzerland from the evil foreign rule.

With that heroic *role-model*† in mind, David had practiced with the slingshot several times a day until his arms and hands ached. He wore out two *hand-crafted*‡ slingshots. When Matt Hale took notice of his son's regular presence in the garden, he nodded approvingly at David's display of *diligence*.§ He gave the boy a *crisp*⸗ *military salute*** that young David found quite pleasing—it made him feel part of Dad's team. Like Robin would be to Batman.

But, David wanted more than membership on a team. What he craved was direct action where he could do something adventurous and make a contribution—another rescue operation would be just fine as far as he was concerned. He wanted things to happen soon to relieve his own itchiness. But, the world obviously turns at its own pace, not always the way David or anyone else may wish. At times, as in any profession, spies just have to be patient. Patience, however, was not one of this eleven year old's *natural virtues*.†† The good news for this Junior Spy was that he would not have to wait too long to get back in the hunt.

---

*   Executed: Killed or put to death.
†   Role-model: Good example.
‡   Hand-crafted: Made by hand and usually of high quality.
§   Diligence: Hard work and determination.
⸗   Crisp: Sharp, rapid and well done.
**   Military salute: A hand signal that shows respect to another soldier.
††   Natural Virtues: The good things or permanent qualities of a person's character and life, such as courage, loyalty, honesty, hard work and, of course, patience.

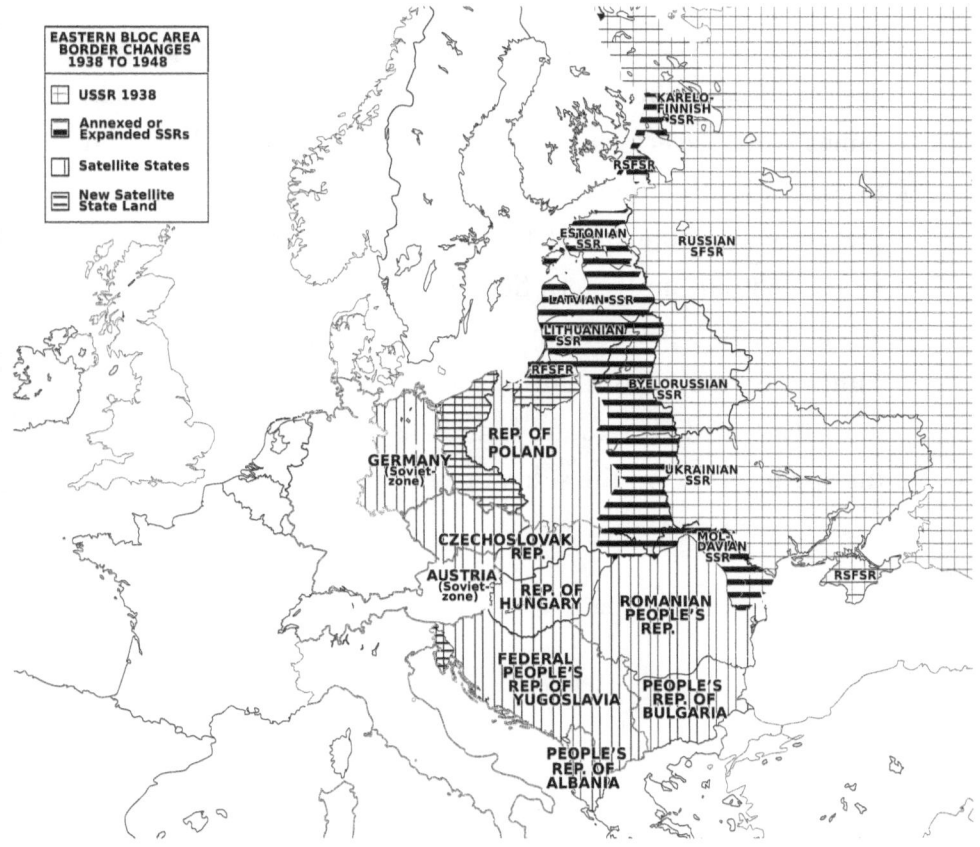

EASTERN BLOC AREA
BORDER CHANGES
1938 TO 1948

USSR 1938

Annexed or
Expanded SSRs

Satellite States

New Satellite
State Land

Former Eastern Bloc area border changes between 1938 and 1948.
(https://commons.wikimedia.org/wiki/File:EasternBloc_BorderChange38-48.svg
Author: Mosedschurte, June 1, 2009)

The double tragedy for Austria from 1938 to the late 1940's had come to them first from Nazi Germany to the north and then from Soviet Russia to the east. By the time the Hales had reached Vienna, the Austrians had been through a decade of threats, invasions, bombings and open warfare* not to ignore the loss of several hundred thousand soldiers and civilians who were killed in that period. In sum, both the cities and the

---

* Open Warfare: A fight were people are actively doing organized violence to each other, as opposed to the "cold" warfare of threats and maneuvering in secret.

countryside were a mess; it would take over a dozen years to get the Russian Soviet Army to leave the country. To make things worse, everywhere to the east of Austria—all the way to Russia itself—the countries of Eastern Europe were under the guns and controls of the Soviet Army and their Secret Police. Within the Eastern Sector of Austria, Russian soldiers and attack dogs patrolled the streets and fields—night and day, summer or winter, sunshine or snow. This then was the reality* in which David Hale found himself as he was just getting into the spy business on the side of freedom.

---

*   Reality: The actual situation or conditions existing in that time and place.

The Vienna Trilogy

BOOK TWO

Nazis on the Run

Contents

Prologue

World War II had come to an end in late summer 1945 when both Germany and Japan surrendered to the Allied Armies led by the United States and Great Britain who had entered into a treaty with Soviet Russia. It is believed that as many as 50 million people were killed in what became the greatest war in human history. The first two years after the war were a time of both great suffering and modest recovery from seven years of destruction and death. The first two years were also especially confusing, as Communists in both Europe and Asia, rather than seeking peaceful ways, launched their own programs of world conquest.

By mid-summer of 1947—as many European nations and millions of wandering refugees were still struggling to recover from World War II—eleven year old David Hale had just completed his first mission as a junior spy. He had recently helped his father rescue an important Polish scientist who was on the wrong side of the Danube River that separated East from West—the Soviet Russian from the American zone of Austria (*The Vienna Trilogy, Book One: Escape to the West*). At the time of this book, there were Nazi war criminals who wanted to escape to Latin America to pursue once again Adolf Hitler's dream of world conquest.

What could one boy do in the face of such dangerous enemies? Nazis, on the run, would soon find out.

Dedication

To all innocent souls who lost their freedom
to Nazism, Fascism and Imperialism
in World War II
—especially women, children
and the most vulnerable
unable to escape or fight back.

1

The Vogels

After trying without success to think of ways to get his dad to put his medical duties aside and get back to spying, David rolled out of bed. He descended to the first floor in his usual way—acrobatically, swiftly but silently. As he almost glided down the stairwell, he felt that, with a little more effort and practice, he might actually be able to fly. Dr. Matt Hale, David's dad, under no false *illusions*,* was busy writing medical reports on his examination of Displaced Persons in the camps. Typhoid fever was becoming again a major problem. It was his job to get the problem *resolved*.†

The boy went into the study, made *eye contact*‡ with his father, said he had been thinking about things and had an idea. "What if I use some of my free time to improve my German, Dad? I admit that I have been *indifferent*,§ even lazy, when it comes to studying the language. That was BEFORE. However SINCE the rescue operation, I now see things differently."

His father did not respond right away, but let David go on— he could see the boy had something important on his mind.

"Dad, you know what I realized when you were in the Russian guard shack the other night? You know, when we had

---

*   Illusions: Fantasies or unrealistic dreams.
†   Resolved: Fixed, cured, taken care of.
‡   Eye contact: When two people are looking at each other at the same time.
§   Indifferent: Having no real desire or motivation.

Dr. Kaminski hidden in the trunk—hanging in there between a new life of freedom and getting captured by the Russians?" Without waiting for a response, David continued. "I could tell, Dad, it was your excellent German and Russian language skills that made all the difference in getting us away from there and getting Dr. Kaminski to safety. Well, I want to understand and speak German much, much better—so I can help in the future—so I won't mess things up because my German stinks."

"Darn good idea, Son, and I have a suggestion—why not spend some time each day studying and speaking German with Katrina? You have lots of free time, especially with Ellie away. As you have probably found already, it is not easy to *master** German. It is one of the more difficult languages to learn and to speak really well. *Frau*[+] Vogel would be happy to help. Because you're on vacation, let's not call it a class—maybe we'll just call it a *tutorial.*[‡] It'll be entirely up to you and Katrina when you work on your German."

David liked what he was hearing—"That is how school ought to be," he thought. Later that morning, Matt Hale spoke with Katrina Vogel and her husband, Konrad, an old friend of Matt's from the war. Konrad had been in the anti-Nazi Austrian Underground Army that fought against Hitler starting in 1938, when the Germans invaded Austria. He found himself *eventually* being hunted by the Nazi Secret Police and *Herr*[§] Vogel

---

* Master: To learn something at a high skill level. In the case of language learning, it would mean being able to speak as well as a person born and raised in Austria or Germany.
† Frau: Mrs., in German.
‡ Tutorial: A private class with one teacher and one student.
§ Herr Vogel: Means Mr. Vogel in German.

managed to escape to London where some 30,000 Austrian refugees were organizing to fight against Nazi Germany. Having been trained by the U.S. Army Intelligence in England, Konrad Vogel in 1943 was dropped by *parachute** into Western Austria, not far from Salzburg. This was also not far from Adolf Hitler's mountain homes in nearby Bavaria, Germany.

Hitler's mountain home, known as 'The Berghof,' was bought with money he received for the book he wrote while in prison in the 1920's—it was named *Mein Kampf,* or *My Struggle.*[†] Naturally, every Nazi had bought one or more copies of the Fuehrer's book so Hitler's book earned him a lot of money.

For his 50th birthday—April 20, 1939—the German Nazi Party built and gave Hitler an entirely separate and *breathtaking*[‡] mile-high mountaintop *retreat.*[§] They called it "Eagle's Nest." *Ironically,*[¶] the Nazi leader seldom visited his Eagle's Nest for a simple reason, which was one of Nazi Germany's best kept secrets. Unlike those *majestic*** eagles that soared high above the *Alps,*[††] Adolf Hitler was afraid of high places.

---

* Parachute: A silk or cloth umbrella-like device for jumping safely from a flying airplane to the ground.
† *Mein Kampf (My Struggle)*: Hitler's own hate-filled explanation for his Nazi plan to restore Germany's lost powers from their defeat in World War I.
‡ Breathtaking: Something so striking that it would be said to take one's breath away with its beauty.
§ Retreat: A place for rest and relaxation.
¶ Ironically: Where reality goes against the words used to describe it— the Nazis saw Hitler as an "eagle" but he was, in reality, *afraid of high places.* Irony is often used in a humorous way.
** Majestic: Considered grand and noble, the eagle is king of the bird world just as the lion is king of the jungle due to its great strength.
†† Alps: European mountain range that runs through Germany, Switzerland, Austria, France and Italy.

In the closing two years of the war, Konrad Vogel was kept busy fighting the German Army. He communicated, or sent back his secret messages to the U.S. Military Headquarters that were located outside London. Using a *shortwave radio,** Vogel reported on Nazi *troop movements.*† He engaged in *sabotage operations*‡—blowing up bridges, roads and electric power stations. Konrad in the war was a genuine Austrian war hero—but a silent and secret one known only to the American Military. After the war ended, he returned to Vienna and to having the simple life as a carpenter and furniture maker. Except for Matt Hale, none of his neighbors in Vienna knew of Konrad Vogel's anti-Nazi wartime activities.

Besides improving David's German language skills, Matt Hale saw an added benefit in his son spending time each day with the Vogels—it might help the boy stay out of trouble. When Dr. Hale left the castle to visit and treat sick refugees throughout Eastern Austria, he could not take David along. He did not want to expose his son to any of the *communicable diseases*§ that existed among the foreign refugees. To keep from catching and spreading diseases, the doctors and nurses working in the camps had to wear *protective sanitary garments.*¶

---

*   Shortwave radio: A machine that sends and receives messages over long distances, thousands of miles in fact because of the kind of radio wave it uses. It is, really, a perfect machine for spies working far away in enemy areas.

†   Troop movements: The movement of soldiers and equipment to fight battles.

‡   Sabotage operations: Blowing up and destroying tunnels and bridges, cutting electric power lines, and destroying German Army military equipment and supplies.

§   Communicable diseases: Diseases easily passed on to other people by contact, such as typhoid fever, pneumonia, tuberculosis, and the worst post-war disease—typhus.

¶   Protective sanitary garments: Working clothes and uniforms that were free of germs and diseases.

Dr. Hale also wore this equipment, for he had no intention of becoming another *Typhoid Mary*.*

It was agreed, then, that David would spend part of his mornings with Katrina. After lunch, however, David and Thor would be entirely free to explore the castle itself as well as the castle *grounds*† until the doctor returned in the late afternoon or early evening. It would be during this free time in the afternoon that he would encounter the *intelligence trove*‡ at the center of his second spy operation.

David's German teacher Katrina was quite pleased that the boy was finally taking learning the language seriously. Katrina Vogel was a remarkable woman—more so than her *humble*§ manner would suggest. During the war, this very proper woman was a member of the secret 'O5 Austrian Resistance Organization'¶ which fought bravely against the Nazi *occupiers*.** Late in the war, Katrina had assisted *downed*†† American pilots and *flight crews*‡‡ to escape being captured by the Nazis and

---

* Typhoid Mary: A cook in the first part of the 20th century in the States, she is believed to have infected hundreds of people with typhoid fever that she carried in her body but which did not make her sick.
† Grounds: The land all around the castle.
‡ Trove: A treasure or valuable collection that is found hidden somewhere.
§ Humble manner: Acting in a simple way that does not call attention to oneself.
¶ O5 Resistance Organization: Of the 100,000 Austrians who fought in the underground or resistance, O5 was the main group opposing German Nazi occupation.
** Occupiers: The people who invade and take over a country.
†† Downed: Those who had been shot down in the airplanes over Austria.
‡‡ Flight crews: On every Allied four-engine bomber there were as many as ten men who were all crew members, including the pilot who flew the airplane. There was a co-pilot, a navigator who chose the flight route they would take, a bombardier who dropped the bombs on enemy factories, dams and military targets, and men who fired the machine guns at attacking enemy fighter airplanes.

helped them work their way back to England, usually through Italy or Switzerland.

As with so many who risked their lives to help others live in freedom, Katrina Vogel never spoke of her wartime *exploits.** She never got a medal for her bravery. There were no parades for those like her and Konrad who worked in the shadows against the German invaders. This *heroic†* couple did what was dangerous and right for a simple reason and a simple *code of conduct‡*—fighting against the German Nazis was the correct thing for any *patriotic§* Austrian to do.

---

*   Exploits: Adventuresome achievements.
†   Heroic: Men and women who do extremely brave things, often in wartime.
‡   Code of conduct: The rules in life that a person lives by.
§   Patriotic: Acting out of love for one's country.

2

Doctor Hale Is Away

Date and Time: June 16, 1947—Noon

Dr. Hale pulled out of the driveway and headed towards downtown Vienna. Most of the refugee camps were off to the North and West. This afternoon, he was on his way to the Displaced Persons Hospital. David took his usual position off to the side of the castle gate and waved with his right hand, all the while gripping Thor's collar firmly with his left. Ever since Thor had his first ride in the Hale's Mercedes, he was continually anxious to jump aboard for another ride in the country.

As trained as Thor had been in the war, two years of *civilian life** seemed to have *undermined*† a bit his *military bearing*‡ and discipline. This was especially evident whenever he went out to play with David only. When alone with the boy, he generally acted like other dogs unless David gave him a *command signal.*§

By contrast, when his real *master*¶ Matt Hale was present,

* Civilian life: No longer in the Army, Thor was now a civilian.

† Undermined: Weakened or softened the strict habits he had learned in the Army.

‡ Military bearing: The serious behavior of someone in military service.

§ Command signal: A hand signal that silently told the dog to be alert or take an action.

¶ Master: A dog's master is the person to whom the dog looks for direction and guidance. Back in the Army, Thor had a trained handler who used Thor as a Patrol Dog to find enemy soldiers in battle.

Thor reverted back to Patrol Dog behavior. At those times he was neither *inclined** to be playful nor what humans might call, *carefree.*† This ability to *compartment*‡ his *dual personality*§ meant that Patrol Dog Thor, when the war ended, adapted smoothly to his role as the Hale family pet. After two years of tough military training and several months of harsh warfare, not all K-9s were able to make this transition to peacetime or to family life. As will be seen, even when alone with his pal David, Thor retained the alertness he had developed and shown in warfare. Thor was, after all, no ordinary family pet.

At the moment, David's mind was focused on his dad. For an instant, David's eyes and thoughts followed his father as he maneuvered the sturdy Mercedes down the long and winding road leading away from the castle. "How great it must be," David thought, "to be in Dad's shoes, fully grown up and able to come and go as one may like—no school, no homework, and no one telling him when to go to bed." Young David never considered that Dr. Matt Hale obviously had gone many years to school to become a medical doctor. He also had gone through *extensive*§ military training during the war to become a senior intelligence officer—or what some people called a spy.

---

*   Inclined: To have a natural tendency towards something.
†   Carefree: Relaxed and seemingly without a worry in the world.
‡   Compartment: Maintain a distinction or separation between his role as family dog and Army K-9.
§   Dual personality: Thor is two things—a family pet and a Patrol Dog and has both personalities.
¶   Extensive: Long training lasting several months of 18 hour workdays, physical exercises, long marches with heavy backpacks, explosives and weapons exercises where they fired pistols and rifles as well as blowing up bridges and dams. There also were countless hours of classes and studying, so it was not all action stuff that the young warriors were undertaking.

*Overly-simplifying** life was, of course, David's natural tendency—he saw and examined things through his eleven-year-old eyes and mind. Clearly, he could judge only things by what he had seen, had experienced or had been taught. So far, his life experience had been quite limited as well as *structured.*† Now, entering the world of spies, his life would change *decisive-ly.*‡ To be effective in the *amorphous*§ world of *spooks,*⁋ David needed to alter his view of many things. At this point—barely ten days into spy stuff—it is fair to say that David was still very much a *neophyte.*** He still saw most things in much the same way as other eleven year olds. That would soon change.

Dr. Hale caught the image of David in his rear view mirror and he was having *parallel thoughts*††. He, however, was peering through the telescope of life from the opposite end—in his case, as a mature man thinking about his eleven year old son and about youth itself. For an instant, Matt Hale longed to be a boy again—free from the burdens of the world and able to explore the castle and Vienna with faithful Thor.

After all, life as a doctor, and then in the war as a doctor-spy, had been *jam-packed*‡‡ with demanding work that needed to be

---

*   Overly-simplifying: Thinking about complicated or unclear things in too simple a way.

†   Structured: Organized and controlled; in this case by his parents, especially his mom who had raised the children alone when Matt Hale had been off to war.

‡   Decisively: In a major or important way.

§   Amorphous: Without a fixed or firm shape or form.

⁋   Spooks: Another name for spies, who can be ghostlike in their actions.

**   Neophyte: A beginner or someone who is new to an activity; in this case, to the world of spies.

††   Parallel thoughts: Thinking along the same lines such as two train tracks going along side by side.

‡‡   Jam-packed: As tightly packed as possible.

done and problems that needed to be solved. In fact, Dr. Matt Hale had not had a real vacation in seven years. "Can you imagine having a whole summer just to yourself," he wondered. He let his mind *linger** a bit, reliving in his mind the Dr. Kaminski adventure in which his son played a key role. "David performed rather well," Matt Hale thought. "Maybe he can help me again real soon—so long as his mother doesn't *get wind of it*.† She would not be too pleased if I let him get too close to any really dangerous spy stuff. But, David did show a lot of toughness. That is good; life can be tough."

Sometimes, though, even if one does not seek out danger, it comes to that person—unannounced and unanticipated. And that, precisely, was what was about to happen to David Hale. He had no idea what was coming his way—Nazi *Swastika*‡ and all.

---

*   Linger: To remain in place for a while.

†   Get wind of it/catch wind of it: Find out about something hidden, in this case David's spy work with his dad.

‡   Swastika: The spider-like symbol the Nazis used on their flags, uniforms and military equipment.

3

David Will Play

As soon as the big black sedan disappeared from view, David made a *beeline** for the kitchen. Katrina was cleaning up from breakfast and was getting ready to head down the hill to her cottage. David asked her if he could get started right away on his German language tutorial and Katrina was delighted. She immediately sensed the change in the boy's attitude which previously had been anything but positive. Katrina had no idea why David suddenly wanted to improve his German. She was pleased *nonetheless.*†

What surprised her the most was that David was eager—even smiling—as they went through vocabulary drills. To make it more interesting for him, she had him read aloud an Austrian newspaper story in German. It was about a young American who had driven his bicycle throughout the whole Russian zone of Austria without permission. Of course, being a *perfectionist,*‡ Katrina had him read the same German article ten times until he pronounced each word as well as he could. For a moment, David started wondering why he was punishing himself like this in the beginning of summer. But, he *persisted.*§

---

* Beeline: A direct and straight course or path.
† Nonetheless: Anyway, regardless, in any case, no matter what.
‡ Perfectionist: One who does and expects that others will do things exactly right.
§ Persisted: Kept at it and did not quit.

"Well, you still sound a lot like an American boy reading German," Katrina said with a stern face. "But, let's see if we can work hard enough to make you sound more like an Austrian. That would be a nice surprise for Mom and Ellie when they get back in September."

David did not react, but her comment made him think. "Hey, if I get good enough to sound like an Austrian, maybe I could be a better spy. Like Dad." That, of course, had become his own *unspoken** goal in taking the German tutorial in the first place. David asked Frau Vogel if she had a little more time and suggested she let him repeat the news article a few more times—just to see if he might get it exactly right.

The surprised woman was pleased by his request but did not show it. She had not thought he would show up for the first lesson, let alone be asking for more. They spent the next half hour working on his *pronunciation.*† When he got to the point where she seemed satisfied, he told her he would like to hold on to the newspaper for a day and surprise Dad on how he was doing.

By this time, it was Thor who was getting quite itchy—he had heard David tell Katrina that he was going exploring "outside." Once Katrina departed, the dog ran for the door with David following right behind. The bright, cloudless day was as clear as David could remember since his arrival in Austria. He told Thor to stay while he ran back into the kitchen and made his way up the back castle stairs to his bedroom. He grabbed

---

* Unspoken: A private or secret idea that stays in a person's mind and is not mentioned.
† Pronunciation: The way he person speaks a language and makes the correct sounds.

his binoculars and slung the strap around his neck to free his hands for his downward descent.

To make the staircase more challenging, he had begun making the plunge with eyes closed as though he was either blind or it was the *dead of night.** In any case, it gave him a bigger thrill than doing it the ordinary way. He grinned as he imagined his mom looking on in horror should she see him taking chances that might possibly get him hurt. "Heck," he thought, "if she saw how high I go when I climb the enormous pine tree out back, she would have a *conniption,*† I am sure."

He spent the next hour with Thor running the trails that led away from the castle and down the hill towards the river. It seemed to David that no matter how hard he tried, he simply was incapable of wearing out Thor. When he occasionally stopped to rest a bit, Thor would *invariably*‡ find the nearest stick or branch to try to get the boy to run and chase him more and more.

Finally, David decided to make the woodland time more realistic. He looked at his canine pal and gave him a hand signal that stopped Thor right in his tracks. No words were used—none were required. Thor had been trained in wartime to respond to silent signals. That had been necessary whenever he was on combat patrol and German soldiers were trying to kill both him and his handler.

So, when David gave the cue, Thor stopped, perked up his ears, and waited for the next command. Thor lifted his snout,

---

* Dead of night: Late at night when everyone is asleep and things are still or quiet.
† Conniption: A sudden outburst of surprise or fear.
‡ Invariably: Always, without fail.

looked all around, and started pulling in more air which he seemed to be testing and evaluating.

This practice was deeply rooted in his Shepherd *instinct** which had been further sharpened during Patrol Dog training days. Upon arriving in France in early June 1944 to begin combat operations, Thor and his handler—an American cowboy from Montana named Mike Walker—*perfected†* Thor's alertness during what was some of the heaviest fighting of the war. Working as a team, Walker and Thor managed to keep each other and their fellow soldiers alive in battle after battle. Thus, when David *reverted‡* to using hand signals, it told this war dog that the playing around was over and his new handler, David Hale, was now in charge. At that point, the dog's character seemed to change and he was, mentally at least, back in the battle zone—fighting Nazis.

Of course, neither David nor Thor had any idea there were any real Nazis around. *Regardless,§* they carefully moved through the woods as though they might come across enemy soldiers at any moment. David had placed the *spyglasses¶* inside his carrying bag which hung from a strap over his shoulder. Together, they moved low to the ground through the *thicket.*** When they reached the *crest††* of a ridge or hill, they proceeded to crawl on their hands, knees and stomachs to see what lay beyond.

---

*   Instinct: The natural capabilities and habits of an animal, usually having to do with survival.
†   Perfected: To develop to the highest level of skill.
‡   Reverted: To change back to a previous way.
§   Regardless: Even though.
¶   Spyglasses: Also called binoculars, they let a person see things more clearly from a long distance.
** Thicket: Crowded or dense bushes and grass.
†† Crest: The top.

Thor, of course, played his part and moved with the stealth of a wolf hunting a herd of caribou for dinner—even though he had eaten a full meal barely an hour earlier. After all, if David was willing to play soldier, Thor was okay playing the Patrol Dog role in these afternoon *skirmishes.** Anything was better than sitting quietly in the castle library.

Not coming upon any make-believe enemy troops by the time they reached the river, David decided to head back to the castle and climb the tower. He had no *inclination*† to stay inside on a day that felt so *refreshing.*‡ The tower would give him a fuller view of the surrounding landscape and he would be able to spot any enemy forces approaching from a distance in this mid-June *drama.*§

As boy and dog made their way homeward through the woods, several miles away two vehicles were heading in the direction of the castle. The *occupants*¶ had been there before. They, in fact, knew the castle and grounds quite well. Better even than the Hales! These were Nazi *goons*** who had lived there during the war and were secret members of the most evil organization in Germany—the *Gestapo.*†† They were not there for *sentimental*‡‡ reasons! They had been planning all this for two full years since the war was lost and they had gone into hiding.

---

* Skirmishes: A brief battle between enemy forces.

† Inclination: A feeling that one should do something.

‡ Refreshing: Wholesome and making one feel energetic.

§ Drama: A story with excitement and surprises.

¶ Occupants: People who are inside a room, house, or car or truck.

** Goons: Dangerous, brutal men who do evil things.

†† GESTAPO: The Secret State Police. The name is an abbreviation for **GE**heime **STA**ats **PO**lizei.

‡‡ Sentimental: Warm feelings that come from happy memories.

4

The Castle Parapet

As the *duo** at mid-afternoon climbed the last mound before the castle tower, David was feeling adventurous. However, he had nothing for or against which to apply his fighting spirit. No dragons to slay, no invading army to *vanquish*†, and no scientist to rescue. So, drawing on one of his favorite books and movies—*The Adventures of Robin Hood*—David pretended he was a warrior *knight*‡ and that an enemy force was encircling and preparing to attack the castle.

Staying low to the ground he reached the narrow passageway leading up to the highest point in the castle, the *parapet*.§ Thor moved with equal stealth as he had done so many times in the war. Today, he again had become the hunter—a role he played as well as any animal in the wild.

The tower had been built in the *Late Middle Ages*¶ for defense of the castle. Its high protected area enabled those defending the castle to fire arrows down on any attacking enemy. To get outside, the boy climbed through a narrow window onto the

---

*   Duo: Two of them, as in a team.
†   Vanquish: To conquer or beat in battle.
‡   Knight: A warrior who fought bravely in battle and was honored by a king with knighthood.
§   Parapet: The highest defensive place in a castle and important in defending against attack. Often a wall behind which defenders can be protected from arrows or other weapons fired from below.
¶   Late Middle Ages: The years between 1300 and 1500.

sloping roof. He then worked his way upward to the parapet itself which crowned the tower and made it a genuine *fortress.**
Thor followed right behind. This tower high point gave any defending warrior a complete view of the surrounding countryside. He would therefore have an enormous advantage over an invading force—in ancient times or even now.

The sky was clear and the sun was still relatively high in the sky. David could see several miles in all directions. On one side, to his south, David's eyes fell upon the small stream that led down the valley and connected with the mighty Danube River, eight miles away.

David felt this waterway gave him a path to all the kingdoms of the world because the Danube River flowed directly into the Black Sea. That sea in turn meant he could reach the Atlantic and eventually all seven oceans as well as the other six continents. Faraway China could be within reach so, in some ways, he could be another Marco Polo—he just needed to be a little older, have a better boat, and pack plenty of supplies to begin his global trek.

Using his spyglasses, he looked over the woods and fields leading up to the castle. He imagined he was on *guard duty*†
and was searching for the invading force, one that was probably coming his way on horseback. He was glad he had worked to overcome an earlier fear he had of high places, something he had accomplished on his own in two steps.

First, when no one was watching, he climbed the highest

---

*   Fortress: A heavily protected building, castle or fort.
†   Guard duty: The time a soldier is protecting a camp or fort from attack.

tree in the woods nearby, up behind the castle. He spent a few hours swinging from branch to branch. This was followed by his second and final test—he had climbed alone up to the parapet where he sat on the castle wall and let his legs and body hang over the side. He sat and ate a candy bar and let the sense of fear he had just disappear.

At that point, he was about 90 feet above the ground, high enough to kill him if he slipped and fell. What helped him in the end was realizing that, once he got higher than thirty feet above the rocky ground below, gravity itself presented no greater danger to him than it would at either 200 or 300 feet. A fall from any of these heights would probably be deadly. Reading in his dad's medical book had helped him decide he had to do something about what Dad told him was a bit of *acrophobia*.* Dr. Hale said most people when they are young fear heights—and with good reason.

Reading always seemed to help the boy figure out the world as well as himself. One afternoon, David read an article in the *National Geographic* magazine. It showed Mohawk Indians working to build *skyscrapers*† over sixty floors and many hundreds of feet above the ground. These *ironworkers*‡ walked and worked on the buildings skeleton or steel *girders*§—in the open air with neither nets below nor safety ropes of any kind.

David mused, as he became more accustomed to high places, that he might possibly be American Indian. After all, mom's

---

* Acrophobia: A fear of heights.
† Skyscrapers: Tall buildings usually 50 or more floors or stories high.
‡ Ironworkers: Men who build the strong steel skeletons of high structures or buildings.
§ Girders: These are the strong steel skeletons that hold buildings up.

family came from *upstate New York*.* That was the home area to tribes of the *Iroquois Nation*,† including the *daredevil*‡ Mohawks who a *decade*§ earlier helped to build the mighty Empire State Building in New York City.

As David scanned the countryside to the North, he spotted a car in the distance moving slowly along the road that led up to the castle. It came to a stop by the side of the road alongside a meadow. That was where the Vogels *grazed*¶ their two cows. Coming up behind the car was a motorcycle with an attached *sidecar*,** the kind used by all armies in the war. The German motorcycle with sidecar (the BMW R75) was made by Bavarian Motor Works and was the best such machine in the war. David's heart seemed to skip a beat as he recalled seeing this particular model in *Life* magazine photos of the war in the North African desert—between the Germans and the tank armies of the British and the Americans.

He squinted a bit to get a better view. He could not tell much from the distance of over a mile, but the motorcycle was clearly yellow. That was the color of the military vehicles used by the German Army in desert warfare. He also had read that in *Life* magazine. Few cars ever came up this road. So, David was instantly interested—especially since his mind was on the day's

---

*   Upstate New York: The northern lake region of the State going up towards Canada.

†   Iroquois Nation: The six tribes in upstate New York that agreed to not fight each other.

‡   Daredevil: People who do dangerous or risky things such as skydiving, climbing mountains, or working outside on skyscrapers.

§   Decade: Ten years.

¶   Grazed: Letting animals eat grass in a field or meadow.

**   Sidecar: A small wagon with a seat that is on the right or left side of a motorcycle.

make-believe adventure and *intrigue*,* the imaginary invading army, and defense of the castle by him, the loyal knight. That was, of course, make-believe stuff.

In David's real world, however, since working on the rescue operation in Linz, he had become somewhat suspicious of strangers. He had been wondering, for example, whether the Russians might somehow *trace*† the Polish scientist's escape back to the Hales. Less than two weeks into the spy business, David Hale was beginning to think like an intelligence officer—aware of the threats, risks and dangers that can happen to spies.

David crouched behind the parapet wall and occasionally took a peek. Two men got out of the car and one got off the motorcycle. The side car was empty. All three seemed to be looking in the direction of the castle. One seemed to be pointing directly at the tower—directly at David! Or so it seemed. They were too far away for him to know for certain.

Peering through his spyglasses, David was surprised by what happened next. The tall man pointed back at the car and seemed to be ordering one of the men to fetch something. That man in turn seemed to salute and off he walked to the trunk of the car to take out a canvas carrying case.

The next thing really caught David's attention—the man was holding in his hand a rifle and removing something from it. He placed the rifle and carrying case back in the car trunk and hurried back to the tall man, handing him what turned out to be a single lens *sniper scope*.‡ The tall man held it up to his eye for

---

* Intrigue: Mysterious adventure often involving spies, criminals or murder.
† Trace: To track someone.
‡ Sniper scope: A telescope that is used on a rifle to get a better look at a target.

quite some time as he scanned the whole castle. All this time, young David Hale was stooped down but occasionally looked out through a gap in the wall. He was not sure whether or not he had been seen or could be seen by these men.

For more than a half hour, David continued to do what soldiers and spies do when necessary—he kept his head down. Thor, soldiering again, stayed down as well. After a few minutes, the motorcycle driver and the tall man now seated in the sidecar drove around the far side of the meadow. They were clearly taking a tour of the area. Each time they stopped, however, they could be seen looking in the direction of the castle—and nowhere else! By this time David knew these were not ordinary tourists. He wondered whether they too could be spies and was curious why they were there. Then, just as abruptly as they had appeared in David's world, they were gone. Both the car and the motorcycle drove away, one to the north and the other to the south. David could hardly wait until his dad got back from Vienna to tell him what he had observed.

When Matt Hale pulled into the driveway at *dusk*,* David was eagerly waiting. The doctor had a number of things running through his head. After all, he had a lot to get done before *crunch time*†which was this coming weekend when an international medical meeting on refugees would be taking place in Vienna. In addition to his medical reports he needed to prepare for the meeting, he also figured he may have some spying to

---

* Dusk: Late afternoon when the sun has just gone down and night has not yet fully arrived.
† Crunch time: An especially busy period when many important things are happening at once.

do. Such a conference would likely include a number of *hostile targets** in whom Visitor would have an interest.

David did not realize his dad had a lot on his mind. Nevertheless, the boy had something to say about the afternoon strangers who showed a special, in fact unusual, interest in the castle. That was certainly how it seemed to David as he recounted for his father what he had seen that day from the parapet *observation post.*†

"These are not ordinary people, Dad. I can tell you that for sure. They acted like a bunch of burglars or spies looking for a way to break into the castle." With a lot on his mind, Matt Hale told David he would chat more about it in the morning. Right now, his mind was on his next meeting with Visitor which seemed more urgent than three guys driving in the *outskirts*‡ of the castle grounds. After all, they could have been hunters.

David talked his father into playing a couple of hands of *cribbage*§ and then headed off to bed just as the moon came over the tree tops and shone a brilliant glow into the boy's room. "Okay, Thor, let's catch hold of Dad in the morning. He is, after all, a morning person—he always gets started well before the local roosters. Good night, Thor. Happy dreams, old boy. I'm sure things will be even more interesting tomorrow—for both of us I hope."

---

*   Hostile targets: In the world of Intelligence Operations in the late 1940s, hostile targets meant individuals from the Communist world, especially Russians, and working with the Russians.

†   Observation post: a high spot where one can see clearly in all directions.

‡   Outskirts: Surrounding area.

§   Cribbage: A card game where each player's score is recorded on a board with pegs in rows of holes.

Thor, exhausted from the day, was already asleep. Without realizing it, David was in fact really talking to himself.

5

A Secret *Rendezvous**

Date and Time: Tuesday, June 17, 1947—6:00AM

Bright and early, David went sliding down the stairwell and reached the kitchen just as Matt Hale was drinking his coffee. "Come on in, Son, and sit down. Now, tell me all about the strangers. I have some time before I have to leave for the day. Breakfast?" The boy said he would postpone eating, but was glad he could now tell the tale in greater detail. He really felt that he had *witnessed*† something important. David then proceeded to tell his father everything that he had seen.

"Dad, I was up in the tower parapet when these men pulled into the field where the Vogels keep their cows. Three men, one big car, and a motorcycle with a side car just like the ones I saw in *Life* magazine—you know, the ones used by the Germans in the desert war. The three men got out of their car and were looking around. One of them returned to the big car, opened the trunk and came back with telescope in hand. It looked like the kind the Germans used to attach with their Mauser rifles—as we saw at the War Museum. He was looking over the castle from top to bottom. Carefully. From many angles."

---

* Rendezvous: A mysterious meeting place.
† Witnessed: To see something happening, usually something important.

Matt Hale first listened carefully to the facts. Then he heard David's *opinion** and *speculation*[†] on why the boy thought these were in fact bad guys up to no good. "At times like this, David, it is important to trust your instinct and your gut. Nature has given us these *defense mechanisms*[‡] for a reason—to keep us alive in this dangerous world. I will stop on the way out and tell Herr Vogel to keep his eye on things today—in case these guys show up again."

As David was engaged the day earlier in his make-believe *foray*[§] around the castle grounds, Dr. Matt Hale was actually this Tuesday morning back in Intelligence Operations as he stopped for an inspection at the Russian Guard shack. He was entering the Russian Sector surrounding Vienna and on his way to an *operational meeting.*[¶] The stop at the guard shack this time took around 15 minutes as the Russian Guard examined his travel documents, his *International Medical Credentials,*** and the one place they searched most often and most closely—the trunk of his car. Only a week earlier, that same trunk was crammed with potatoes—and an escaping Polish scientist who was being hunted by the Russian Secret Police. Today, Matt Hale had filled the trunk with medical supplies for testing and treating

---

* Opinion: What a person thinks about a subject, a person or an event and that may be different from someone else's viewpoint.

† Speculation: This is what a person guesses has taken place or will occur. It is also an opinion.

‡ Defense mechanisms: Nature's way of letting a person know, sense and feel when situations or people may be dangerous. It alerts a person and animals in general to danger.

§ Foray: A sudden attack into enemy territory.

¶ Operational meeting: A secret meeting between spies.

** International Medical Credentials: Papers with his photo, name and identification as a medical doctor with permission to travel throughout all of Austria for treatment of Displaced Persons, or refugees.

refugees at a camp that had an outbreak of yet another deadly disease—*cholera*.*

His trip was taking him in a northwesterly direction towards the Displaced Person Camp in Linz—the city where he and David had concluded their successful *escapade*† only the week before. On the way to Linz, he planned to stop by the U.S. Army Airbase at Tulln—some 21 miles outside Vienna but still within the Russian Sector. He had agreed to meet there with the Midnight Visitor who had sent him a message saying he wanted to discuss a few matters of importance—to Matt Hale this meant more spy stuff.

Driving in the direction of the American Airbase, Matt Hale watched for signs he possibly was being *tailed*‡ by the Russians. If he found that he was under *active surveillance*,§ he would by-pass the air base altogether and continue on his way to Linz. Later on, once he crossed the Nibelungen Bridge into the American Sector, he and Visitor could then meet *securely*⁋ at a different U.S. Army Base.

This morning, as things developed, the Russian Secret Police had their hands full dealing with food riots that had begun breaking out in May throughout the Russian Sector of

---

* Cholera: A deadly disease where a person loses so much fluid he dies what is called *blue death*.

† Escapade: Adventure, with some danger.

‡ Tailed: Followed by mobile surveillance, probably the Russian Military or Secret Police.

§ Active surveillance: Where the Russians would have surveillance cars and men following him all day or part of a day. *Passive surveillance* is when they would have someone in a fixed place (such as a guard post) who reports that foreigners have traveled their way.

⁋ Securely: Safely, without anyone else seeing or knowing they were meeting or working together.

Austria. Russia had been taking Austrian-grown food back to Moscow and leaving the Austrians without enough to eat.

With no sign of any Russian surveillance cars in front or behind him, and confident he was not being followed, Matt Hale drove into the Tulln Airbase. He pulled his Mercedes into one of the empty aircraft hangars. The big hangar doors closed behind him. Visitor was waiting for him. The two men exchanged greetings and went to a small conference room where they could be alone and speak privately.

Visitor began by expressing once again his appreciation for Matt Hale's assistance in last week's rescue operation. He relayed to Matt Hale that everything had worked out well in getting Dr. Kaminski to safety outside Austria. "Most of the operational success, of course, was from your *exceptional** ability to move freely around the Russian Sector— so much better than we American Military or Embassy officials are able to do. Maybe, Matt, we can make more and better use of your special *mobility*[†]—if you are willing, I have an idea that may help us."

"Matt, I don't need to emphasize that what you have done is really important—Dr. Kaminski already has provided us with *considerable*[‡] information on the political and security *situation*[§] in Poland. The Russians have been tightening their grip on the country. It turns out that Dr. Kaminski has a close childhood

---

* Exceptional: Very special and unusually good.
† Mobility: Ability to move around from one place to another.
‡ Considerable: Quite a bit.
§ Situation: What is going on in a place; in this case, Poland. *Security situation* would include what the Secret Police are doing to destroy freedom in the country.

friend in the Polish Government—this is the same fellow who privately warned him months back to get out of Poland because the Russian Secret Police were in fact *closing in** on him."

Visitor continued, "Kaminski believes this friend *deep down*† is a patriotic Pole and might even be *recruitable*‡—may even be willing to spy for us. His friend, according to Dr. Kaminski, is disgusted by the way the Russians have taken over all important *internal security*§ responsibilities. It reminds him more and more of the wartime Nazi *occupation*."¶

Visitor ceased talking for a moment and let Matt Hale think about what he had just been told. Clearly, this was important information he had shared. As a former intelligence professional, Dr. Hale knew immediately he was being told all this for an important reason. It was not because Visitor was trying to make him feel good—Visitor wanted and was looking for more help from him.

In the world of spies, the 'need to know' rule has both a positive and a negative side to it—much like car or flashlight batteries have both positive and negative *poles*** if you wish to start a car engine or light a bulb. As a negative rule, 'need to know' means you do not tell people secret things they have no good reason to know about or understand. The positive side of

---

* Closing in: Close to arresting him.

† Deep down: Inside his heart and mind.

‡ Recruitable: Able to be persuaded to work secretly with U.S. Intelligence as a spy.

§ Internal security: The protection of a nation from harm by its enemies.

¶ Occupation: The period of time after the Germans invaded and were in control of Poland.

** Poles: These are the two contact points on a battery, one with a positive electrical charge and the other with a negative electrical charge.

the 'need to know' *security principle** is that people working in spy operations must be given 'all the information needed' to be able to perform a mission or operation successfully. Knowing how much—or how little—information to reveal or share separates the good from the bad intelligence officers.

Matt Hale smiled and said, "I suppose you have heard that a medical *delegation*[†] from Poland will be here in Vienna this weekend for meetings on infectious diseases and other refugee issues. I assume that is why you're telling me all of this."

Visitor smiled back and said he assumed Dr. Hale would be attending those meetings. Matt Hale nodded. Visitor added, "Dr. Kaminski's friend will be here with the Polish Government group. In fact, he is in charge of Security for the Polish delegation—but still under the *watchful eyes*[‡] of the Russian Secret Police. As you know, Matt, even the watchdogs are closely watched in the Communist world!"

"Matt, we are not asking that you personally try to *recruit*[§] him. Of course! Your own medical work and excellent operational cover are too important to be risked in that way. We just need to find a way to get a message to him *discreetly*[¶]—without anyone else and especially the Russians knowing he has been secretly contacted by us. If you can find a way that we can do

---

* Security principle: A general rule to protect spies and governments from enemy agents and actions.
† Delegation: A group of people from the same country attending a meeting or conference.
‡ Watchful eyes: The Russian Secret Police are always looking; they do not trust anyone.
§ Recruit: Get him to agree to spy for the Americans.
¶ Discreetly: Privately, quietly and without anyone else seeing what is happening.

this securely—without Dr. Kaminski's Polish friend knowing you had any role in it; that would be perfect."

Matt Hale said he would see what could be done. "The first meetings will take place on Friday at one of the Austrian government buildings. I do not know where the visitors from Poland will be staying, but I know it certainly will not be the Vienna Grand Hotel—far too expensive for them. I will see what I can find out and get back to you. If this fellow is *recruitable** by us, then Dr. Kaminski will have repaid us quite well for helping him escape. Sounds good—will send you a message if I learn something."

---

* Recruitable: Able to be recruited and willing to spy, in this case for the United States against the Russians.

6

A Twin Is Born

Visitor had another proposal he wished to discuss. "For start-ers, Matt, how would you like to have a twin?" The twinkle in Visitor's eye and his *sly** way of asking made it clear there was some intentional humor in what he was asking. Matt Hale sat quietly—without responding— waiting for Visitor *to show his cards.*† As a trained doctor and intelligence officer, Dr. Matt Hale understood that one often can learn more by listening than by speaking. So, he waited for Visitor to continue.

"Getting back to last week's rescue operation and your *relatively free*‡ mobility in and through the Russian Sector," Visitor began, "what if you had another Mercedes sedan, Matt? A twin of sorts. This second one would look just like the one you're driving but it would have another secret purpose altogether?"

Still not responding, Matt waited to hear more. Visitor continued, "I read in your report how in Linz you hid Dr. Kaminski in the trunk—deep inside and behind some sacks of potatoes. It worked out fine that time. But, certainly, for the long run we need a better hiding place than that. The Russians are going to start to realize that something is *fishy*§ in your transporting

---

*   Sly: Clever and playful.
†   Show his cards: Explain what is really happening—in this case, what he means by "have a twin."
‡   Relatively free: Compared to others, such as U.S. officials, he had bet-ter freedom of movement.
§   Fishy: Funny or not right.

potatoes too often through their sector—especially now with the shortage of food and with the food riots around Austria."

Matt Hale agreed, and said he had no intention of doing that precise type of rescue operation again. "How many times can I ask David to throw up on a Russian Border Guard? Heck, if we do that over and over we might start another war." Both men had a good laugh and Visitor told Dr. Hale that he wished he had seen the expression on the face of the Russian Guard when he got doused in vomit.

"Good for David," said Visitor, who smiled and closed his eyes trying to *visualize** how surprised the Russian Border Guard must have been. Visitor went on, "A combination of raw eggs and stew, if I recall correctly. Oh yes, *Wunderbar.*"[†]

Visitor went back to business and brought up the twin again. "Matt, we have an exact *replica*[‡] of your 1935 Mercedes 200 W21. It looks like yours, but with a terrific additional feature that might prove helpful *down the road,*[§] so to speak. We have constructed a man-sized concealment chamber underneath the rear seats. The way into this *cavern*[¶] is through a spring-loaded *trap door*** in the interior back wall of the trunk—the person can just seem to disappear. When border guards examine the trunk, they will not see anything unusual or different."

---

*   Visualize: To picture mentally.
†   Wunderbar: Pronounced "Voon-der-bar" in German. It means 'wonderful' in English.
‡   Replica: A copy of something.
§   Down the road: Sometime in the future.
¶   Cavern: A space large enough to hold a man, usually underground, but in this case in the lower part of the Mercedes.
**   Trap door: A secret, hidden door that opens and closes in a way that makes discovery impossible.

Visitor continued, "You know how am I so sure? We actually ran a series of border-crossing tests at various Russian Sector checkpoints, both in Austria and up in Germany. In fact, we both entered and departed the Russian Sector several times— and not once did they show any signs of curiosity or suspicion. Of course, we are fortunate they are not using guard dogs at the borders to sniff around our cars passing their way—at least not yet. When and if they start doing that, we are ready with some special chemicals that will confuse their dogs."

Visitor said that during his nighttime visit up from the river two weeks ago, he had spotted an old *carriage house** behind the Hale castle. He wondered whether there would be room inside there for a second Mercedes.

Matt Hale explained there would be plenty of room. He added, "*Furthermore,*† that building is not visible from the front gate or the road up to the castle. I could drive my car into the carriage house, drive out a short time later in the twin and no one outside will be able to tell the difference. Of course, that is true only if the cars not only appear similar, but in fact seem *identical*‡—the same car."

Then Matt Hale became serious. "I would need to go over this new vehicle personally with a *fine tooth comb*§ to be totally certain the twin really can appear to be my own car. After

---

* Carriage house: An old garage or barn where carriages were stored before there were automobiles.
† Furthermore: In addition, besides.
‡ Identical: The same in all ways and looking just alike.
§ Fine tooth comb: This is a comb with such fine teeth that it is used to remove tiny bugs from children's hair, especially in the Displaced Persons camps. Here it means to examine so carefully that any tiny difference between the two Mercedes sedans can be found and corrected.

all, the Russians—both their Border Guards and surveillance teams—are quite used to mine. They have seen and inspected my automobile countless times. I am quite certain they would readily notice any difference—if there were one."

Visitor nodded and agreed with all Matt Hale had said. And he had some good news. While they were chatting this morning, a team of American *concealment technicians** were in the hangar. They were going over both cars—Dr. Hale's and the twin—to be certain the two vehicles appeared the same. This meant tires, paint, seats, antenna, door handles, and even the sound of the engine as well as the weight of each vehicle. The only difference between the cars was that one had an invisible hiding place which was built so carefully that no one looking under the car would see anything *out of line*.† "That is accurate even if they stand right behind and peer into the open trunk," he said.

"It's really quite magical," he added with a big wide grin. "Matt, we even had one of the German technicians from the Mercedes-Benz factory work on the twin's engine, clean out the trunk, and replace the tires the other day—the man didn't notice or mention a thing about anything unusual with the trunk. It was in this fellow's factory where all Mercedes W21 models were built before the war—the factory in *Stuttgart*."‡

Matt Hale took the next hour and checked out each sedan

---

* Concealment technicians: Men in the spy business who hide things in cars, furniture, lamps, clothing, magazines and other innocent-looking things to fool the enemy.

† Out of line: Unusual or different. in this case, the changes that were made to the twin could not be seen from behind, from underneath, or from the inside of the open trunk. Magic!

‡ Stuttgart: A major manufacturing German city.

before driving away from the Airbase in his own car. He was very satisfied and even he could not tell the difference. He smiled as he thought about how Visitor was so careful in his spy work, but also enjoyed it so much that he was unafraid to inject some humor into things.

Matt Hale thought, "Yes, at times it's difficult enough dealing with all the poor refugees who with good reason are *depressed** about their situation. After all, they had to *flee*[†] their own countries. Friends and family members have been killed or are missing. And, what makes the job tougher is that I have to deal with the *dour*[‡] Russians who never smile or laugh at anything in life—except when they get *roaring drunk*.[§] It sure is nice spending some time with Visitor whose sense of humor by contrast is so *refreshing*."[¶]

The doctor-spy continued northward towards Linz, satisfied by the way the meeting with Visitor had gone. Unlike his son David, though, it was not the thrill of the spy game that attracted him—Matt Hale had seen enough action in the war for two or three lifetimes. What he currently missed most in his wartime intelligence work was being able to do something to help defeat an evil nation that was trying to conquer the entire world.

"Unfortunately," he thought, "no sooner had the Nazi butchers been defeated, then from the East came the new

---

*   Depressed: Deeply saddened and sorrowful.
†   Flee: Run away from.
‡   Dour: Sour, harsh and often threatening.
§   Roaring drunk: Getting so drunk that they become loud and impolite.
¶   Refreshing: Makes one feel good.

*barbarians,**—the Russians. This new group, the Russian Communists, are as bad as the Nazis when it comes to *suffocating*[†] freedom and murdering millions of innocent human beings."

Since he arrived in Vienna, Dr. Matt Hale had been feeling increasingly like a helpless *spectator.*[‡] He had a *front-row seat*[§] on what the Russian Communists were doing in Austria itself and in neighboring Czechoslovakia. He also was hearing horror stories of Russian *brutality*[¶] as told by refugees from all parts of Eastern Europe. But, 'knowing something' and 'doing something about it' are entirely different. And, in his heart, Matt Hale knew that we was a doer and not a dreamer—he could not just stand aside and let evil men conquer other people, take away their freedom and, in many cases, their lives.

Simply put, Matt Hale despised bullies—whether they wore a Nazi Swastika or a Communist *Hammer and Sickle*** on their uniforms—or inside their *blackened hearts.*[††] When it came to wearing his own U.S. Army uniform in the war, Lt. Colonel Matt Hale wore his proudly—at least when he was not op-

---

*   Barbarians: Wild, murderous and uncivilized tribes that make war on peaceful nations and people.

†   Suffocating: Choking off.

‡   Spectator: One who watches things happen, such as at a sporting event.

§   Front row seat: Being so close to the action that he could see all the bad things that were happening.

¶   Brutality: The vicious treatment and torture by barbarians such as the Nazis and the Communists.

**   Hammer and Sickle: The Russian Communist symbol for their Revolution—the hammer used by factory workers and the sickle used to cut grains by farm workers.

††   Blackened hearts: Without kind or decent feelings for other people. Especially the weak and the poor.

erating under cover as a spy. Now, working against Russian Communists, he again would be putting on the unseen uniform of spies—the *cloak and dagger*.* He also would have the assistance of his 'invisible assistant,' David, who looked like any other kid. But, this 'kid' would prove to be a powerful adversary against Austria's *leftover*† Nazis and against the *hoard*‡ of spies coming to Austria out of Communist Russia.

In 1947 Vienna, both of these evil forces of Nazis and Communists were at work. A handful of wartime Germany's most senior Nazis—including Adolf Hitler—were no longer in the game because they were dead. Before he could be captured by the Russians, the Fuehrer committed suicide by gunshot. That was on April 30, 1945. Ten of the most senior Nazis were hanged eighteen months later. That was on October 16, 1946, after they had been tried in an international criminal court and found guilty of *war crimes*.§ By 1947, two years after the war, the *majority*⁋ of Nazi war criminals had not yet been caught. The worst of them were still in hiding and trying to escape the *hangman's noose*** by moving out of Austria and Germany to other parts of the world. But, they could not get very far without travel documents—and they needed money, plenty of it!

---

*   Cloak and dagger: The two symbols for spies—the cloak to hide him and the dagger to represent a silent weapon that makes no sound.
†   Leftover: Those who had not been killed in the war or run away to other countries.
‡   Hoard: A stampeding or uncivilized army of barbarians.
§   War crimes: Evil actions such as murdering women, children, sick people, and innocent prisoners.
⁋   Majority: More than half.
** Hangman's noose: The rope used to hang and kill a person.

As Matt Hale drove closer to Linz, his mind was on the Russians. He had no idea that, at that same moment, the previous Nazi Gestapo residents of the castle were planning their return visit to his very home! It would not be a *social call*.* They were going there to retrieve things they badly needed for their *getaway*† to South America. Before the war, the Gestapo had chosen the Vienna castle carefully to hide things from public view. The Nazi *ruse*‡ had worked completely—outsiders paid no real attention to the castle.

---

*   Social call: When a friend comes by a home in a friendly way.
†   Getaway: Escape from people who are hunting for them.
‡   Ruse: Tricky maneuver to avoid capture.

7

The Castle's Secret Past

Date and Place: Early 1940's—Secret Police Headquarters, Berlin, Germany

With the takeover of Austria by the German Army in March 1938, another German organization came to Vienna—the *dreaded** Gestapo. Its chief was the *infamous†* Heinrich Himmler, one of Nazi Germany's most *despicable‡* leaders. Over the next seven years, he personally would order the murder of millions of human beings.

The first order of business in Vienna was to recruit Austrian Nazis to work in the Gestapo in downtown Vienna. Most of the new Gestapo members had been Vienna policemen before Austria was invaded and *forcibly§* became part of the Nazi Third Reich.

Himmler next ordered the takeover of one of Vienna's major downtown buildings—the beautiful four-story Metropole Hotel. This historic building would serve as the *principal¶* Gestapo-Austria headquarters during the war. From here, the

---

* Dreaded: Feared, scary.
† Infamous: Known to be evil and vicious. Famous for a bad reason.
‡ Despicable: Worthy of disgust and scorn, a person who has nothing good or decent about him.
§ Forcibly: Not freely but, instead, under pressure from the invading German Army.
¶ Principal: The main or best known building.

Nazi Secret Police ran a terror campaign that in time sent tens of thousands of innocent Austrians to concentration camps either to be worked to death or murdered. From the Gestapo's own records, it is *estimated** that 50,000 Austrians were tortured in the Gestapo-Austria headquarters before being sent to their deaths.

As Himmler anticipated, the Metropole building was eventually identified to the Allies as the center for Nazi terror in the country. On March 12, 1945, it was bombed and destroyed by Allied bombers. This was late in the war when American planes were able to reach Vienna from bomber airbases in northern Italy. March 12 was an important date for Austrians— it had been on that day back in 1938 that the Germany Army invaded and forcibly made Austria a part of the Third Reich. The bombed-out Metropole Hotel was never rebuilt. After the war, however, a memorial stone was placed on the *site†* and rests there today for tourists and Austrians to see and remember. The English translation of the memorial reads as follows:

> *Here stood the House of the Gestapo. To those who believed in Austria it was hell. To many, it was the gateway to death. It sank into ruins just like the 'Thousand Year Empire.' But Austria was resurrected and with her our dead, the immortal victims.*

Gestapo Chief Himmler was *shrewd‡* like a good chess player—he was always thinking several moves or steps ahead.

---

*   Estimated: Guessed or calculated without exact proof.
†   Site: A piece of land.
‡   Shrewd: Clever, and wise like a fox.

Realizing the downtown headquarters would eventually become well known, he ordered the creation of an entirely separate but 'most secret' operations post away from downtown Vienna. This secret base would be for a private terror operation that Himmler personally would direct. No one else in Berlin even knew of its existence.

He soon found precisely the two things he wanted. First, for this special operation he used only pure-blooded Germans which is all he absolutely trusted—not local Austrian Nazis such as those who worked downtown at the former Metropole Hotel. The special castle group he assembled were chosen and sent by him directly from Berlin. He selected every member of this team, including its leader.

Himmler's second *requirement** was that the building must be *isolated*.† His choice turned out to be the very castle that, nine years later, would become the Hale's Vienna home. Back in 1938, the castle owners and *residents*‡ were an elderly Austrian Jewish couple that somehow just seemed to disappear. Most people believed they left the country immediately after the German invasion, as tens of thousands of Austrians had done. In a *typical*§ Gestapo way of doing things, however, it was Himmler who had the couple secretly arrested and sent to a Nazi concentration camp. Like so many victims of the Gestapo, they were never heard from again! With the real owners out of the way, the castle was now Himmler's. He got it without

---

*   Requirement: Something that is demanded and necessary.
†   Isolated: Far away from the busy part of a city, off in the woods.
‡   Residents: The people who lived there.
§   Typical: The normal or usual way they did things.

paying a single German *Reichsmark.**—in his mind he *only* had to murder two old people.

The *seclusion†* of the castle in the hilly *outskirts‡* of Vienna gave it the privacy the Gestapo Chief required for the special work that he wanted to go unnoticed—even by Gestapo-Vienna! The castle was to house a *deep-cover operation§* controlled entirely by Himmler's headquarters in Berlin. The castle's *cover story¶* was that it was a quiet office for studying *human evolution*** and *genealogy.††* It would be made to appear as if it had nothing to do with Secret Police activities of any kind. To avoid attracting outside attention, the selected cover story was purposely meant to seem *academic,‡‡* even boring. It worked! For seven years of the war, the operational cover of Himmler's castle operation was never *compromised.§§*

---

*   Reichsmark: The German money then equal to about two dollars and fifty cents.

†   Seclusion: Isolated or away from other homes or buildings.

‡   Outskirts: An area surrounding a town or city, usually a few miles from the city center and not having many buildings or houses.

§   Deep-cover operation: An activity that is so secret that it is kept entirely away from publicly known buildings or sites.

¶   Cover story: This is the false story that is told to people to protect security and, in this case, to lead people to believe that nothing evil was taking place at the castle during the war.

**   Human evolution: How man may have developed from other animals. The Nazis believed the Germans—who descended from the Aryan tribe—had reached the highest level of human development and had a right to conquer and destroy other non-Aryan people who were inferior or not as heroic as them.

††   Genealogy: The study of family history in terms of a person's parents, grandparents, great grandparents etc. which for the Nazis was a way to learn whether a person was a pure Aryan German or may even have forbidden Jewish blood in their family history.

‡‡   Academic: Related to education and learning.

§§   Compromised: Revealed or found out.

Heinrich Himmler's brilliant criminal mind and *ruthless**
ways in time enabled him to become head of all Police and
Security organizations in Nazi Germany—beating out highly
important Nazis competing against him for power. By the middle of the war, he had become the second most powerful Nazi
in all of the Third Reich—right behind Adolf Hitler himself.
As head of both the German State Police—the infamous SS—
as well as the Gestapo, Heinrich Himmler was personally feared
as was no other Nazi. He also ran all the concentration or death
camps and was in charge of murdering the Jews and other
groups who were considered enemies of Hitler, the Third Reich
and Himmler himself.

Besides having high intelligence, Himmler paid attention to
details. Under his direct orders, the windows were covered in
order to keep secret the evil activities at the castle that included
torture and murder. Late in the war, the dark curtains prevented
Allied pilots from spotting any castle lights as they flew night-
time bombing *raids*† over Vienna. Had the Allies known what
was going on within this center of death, they would surely
have bombed the castle to *smithereens*.‡ But, the old building
survived the war *intact*§—its *brutal*¶ secrets remained entirely
undiscovered.

The only people in the war years to *emerge*** alive from
the castle were the Nazi killers—the small group of Gestapo

---

*   Ruthless: Cruel and without mercy.
†   Raids: Bombing attacks in which large numbers of airplanes dropped
    bombs.
‡   Smithereens: Small or tiny pieces.
§   Intact: In one piece, with no damage.
¶   Brutal: Cruel, wicked, violent.
** Emerge: Come out of.

officers pretending to be academic *researchers.** Their *victims*[†]
were brought out always at night for burial or were thrown in
the surrounding rivers. Whether or not they had opposed the
Nazis or had been arrested by mistake, if they had even set foot
one time inside the castle they were murdered. Once they were
caught in the web of this Gestapo group, the result was certain
and the outcome the same—death! Every time. Every one.

Even two years after the war, there were no signs the Gestapo
had been there. It was David who had found some simple
German military materials both in the basement tunnels and in
the upper chambers of the castle. It was regular Army stuff the
Gestapo had left behind in their haste during their departure
from Vienna. Their flight from capture took place just before
Russia's Red Army began its *assault*[‡] on the Austrian capital
city—the 2nd of April, 1945. Within two weeks of heavy fighting,
the Russian Army captured the capital city. But just a few miles
from downtown Vienna, the castle sat empty. The Gestapo had
in fact made a clean escape—well, except for one thing.

In their rush to leave, they made a mistake—they left a trail
that Thor and young David Hale would eventually follow to the
secret cache that rested in one of the castle's distant tunnels.
With all the *precision*[§] that the Gestapo was so famous for in
all their evil work, how could they have *erred*[¶] so badly? What
had gone wrong?

---

*   Researchers: Men who study science and other subjects and write
     studies.
†   Victims: The people who were tortured and murdered.
‡   Assault: The attack.
§   Precision: Exactness, the habit of doing things correctly without er-
     rors or mistakes.
¶   Erred: From the word error – they made a mistake.

1883–1938 Metropol Hotel Vienna, which became Gestapo Austria headquarters from 1938 until destroyed by Allied bombing during the war.

8

As the War Ended in Europe

Date and Place: Spring, 1945
The Place: Gestapo Castle, Vienna

In March 1945, as the Russian Red Army approached the Austrian capital, the senior Gestapo Officer at the castle received a most secret two-part message from Berlin. The first part of the *coded** message to SS Colonel Kurt Schmidt explained that a truck would arrive at the castle that very night from Berlin with an important shipment. The message directed that ALL OTHER SECRET MATERIAL BE IMMEDIATELY BURNED so that nothing remaining would show that the Gestapo had ever been there.

The second part of the message from Gestapo headquarters was truly *sinister*[†]—even for Nazis known for doing horrible things. It came from Gestapo Chief Himmler himself and was addressed personally to Colonel Schmidt for *his eyes only*. It was *double-encoded*[‡] and, because Schmidt alone had the

---

* Coded: Written in a secret code or form that other people cannot understand until the message is decoded. For example, using numbers instead of letters so that the message looks like a bunch of numbers and nothing more.
† Sinister: Suggesting a most evil action.
‡ Double-encoded: Means that the message is written in a code and then the message is encoded a second time so that the first code breaker cannot read the final message.

second code book, only he could decode it. It was brief and *to the point.**

"Colonel Schmidt: First, you will hide the shipment from Berlin in one of the castle *subterranean*† tunnels and seal off that tunnel so no one else can find it. Second, you will *execute*‡ anyone under your Gestapo command who helps hide the shipment and who you believe is not "100 percent loyal to you." Third, you will meet me on my way southward out of Germany. I will meet you at '*The Spa*'§ near Salzburg. We will return to the castle at a later date to retrieve the shipment and make our final voyage together. Heil Hitler."

It was no simple coincidence that Schmidt had been stationed at the castle. His distant cousin—SS and Gestapo Chief Heinrich Himmler—sent him to Vienna early in the war for two reasons. First, Himmler wanted to make certain that cousin Kurt was not sent to fight against the Russians on the bloody *Eastern Front.*¶ It was on that battle front where Germany suffered its greatest losses and where some 30 million people would be killed in combat between June 1941 and May 1945.

The second reason Kurt Schmidt was in Vienna was because the Gestapo Chief wanted someone he totally trusted for his castle operation. He needed a Nazi absolutely loyal to him and

---

*   To the point: Not wasting words but directly giving directions.

†   Subterranean: Underground, in the castle cellar.

‡   Execute: Murder.

§   The Spa: A code meeting place known only to both men. They had met there before.

¶   Eastern (or Russian) Front: This was the battle line where the Russians and Germans had been fighting for four years since Germany attacked Russia in June 1941. Of the 3.4 million German soldiers killed in the War, 80% of them died on the Eastern Front. It was the most dangerous place to be fighting in all wars in human history.

to him alone—one who would keep the castle secret from the other top Nazis in both Vienna and in Berlin. Himmler's initial goal for the Vienna castle was to use it for a private program to steal valuable artworks that were not already taken by the two biggest art thieves in the Nazi regime*—Adolf Hitler and his Air Force Minister, Hermann Goering.

Hitler's intention, 'after he won the war,' had been to build a 'Fuehrer Art Museum' in his home city of Linz—dedicated, of course, to himself. Thus, as the German Army marched victoriously across Europe in the early years of the war, he had his armies collecting or stealing great paintings and other art works for his Linz museum.

Why was Hitler so interested in art? Even though he had political victories later in life, Hitler in his younger years had been an extremely frustrated and failed artist. After the First World War, he twice had applied and twice was rejected for admission to the Academy of Fine Arts in Vienna. Although he considered himself talented, the Fine Arts Academy did not. Why? Well, because all of Hitler's sketches were only of things—buildings and monuments 'that had no people in them'—the Fine Art Academy suggested to Hitler that he forget trying to be an artist and instead study to be an *architect*.[†]

Hitler's fellow grand art thief, *Reichsmarschall*[‡] Hermann Goering, loved both power and great wealth—including stolen paintings. A heroic German fighter pilot in the First World War,

---

*   Regime: A particular government, and usually unlawful or undemocratic.
†   Architect: A person who designs building, bridges, and monuments.
‡   Reichsmarschall: The highest rank in the German Army—above all of the other Generals.

he was famous throughout all of Germany—at times more popular than Hitler himself. As head of the German Air Force, he
was given enormous powers by Hitler. Thus, Goering was able
to control Nazi art theft which totaled hundreds of thousands
of valuable works of art found in conquered territories. His
orders to the German Army were simple—they were to divide
stolen art equally between Hitler and himself.

That *fifty-fifty split** meant, of course, that there would be
nothing left for other top Nazis such as Heinrich Himmler.
So, the Gestapo Chief decided he would have to do something
about it. And he did—he set up his own personal art theft
program and based it at the Vienna castle.

By early 1945, though, it was clear Nazi Germany would
soon lose the war. The Gestapo Chief by then realized—a little late to do him any good—that he needed a backup escape
plan. At his Berlin headquarters, Himmler made certain that
the shipment to the Vienna castle was assembled with great
care. He included *forged†* travel documents such as passports
and birth certificates as well as *counterfeit‡* British money. He
added four bricks of pure gold, each weighing 25 pounds. The
gold, of course, was stolen—it came from melted-down jewelry taken from Jewish prisoners murdered in concentration
camps under Himmler's command. Himmler had been hiding
it away for months, because he knew things were going badly
for Germany in the war.

---

* Fifty-fifty split: One for you and one for me, one for you and one for
  me.
† Forged: Fake or falsified papers such as birth certificates, passports,
  and drivers licenses.
‡ Counterfeit: Completely fake money so well made that it will fool
  most people into accepting it as real.

The Gestapo Chief added two sets of Swiss *identity documents**—a set for himself and a set for cousin Kurt. These were in false names. Himmler, the man who ordered the murder of millions of innocent men, women and children turned out not to be so brave after all. Instead, as the Nazi empire was falling apart, he was busily putting together an emergency plan and personal *escape route*† in case they were needed. Clearly, Heinrich Himmler was not inclined to fight to the death for the Nazi cause, as Hitler had ordered his soldiers to do.

Cleverly evil and *calculating*‡ as he was in so many ways, Himmler completely misjudged his own situation with regard to his Western enemies—the British and the Americans. As a result of this *miscalculation*,§ he wasted several weeks trying to make a deal to surrender to the British and avoid punishment for his war crimes. In March 1945, when it was already too late for him to get away safely, he received word that British Prime Minister Winston Churchill had turned him down entirely. The British leader responded through an *intermediary*¶ that Hitler and Himmler—if they survived the war—were going to be tried and hanged for *crimes against humanity*.**

How was it that this Nazi *true-believer*†† did not fight to his

---

* Identity documents: Papers such as driver's license, passport, birth certificate, credit cards and school records that are used to prove a person is who he claims to be. In spy operations, they are always fake.
† Escape Route: A path or way to avoid capture.
‡ Calculating: Carefully analyzing or thinking about a situation step by step.
§ Miscalculation: The wrong conclusion, decision or judgment.
¶ Intermediary: A person who serves as a messenger between two people.
** Crimes Against Humanity: These are quite different from the usual fighting of soldiers in war. These are murders of innocent people who are not soldiers and include women and children.
†† True-believer: One who is completely, and crazily, committed to a radical cause.

death like some legendary and heroic Germanic warrior—
instead, sneaking away from Hitler himself and the Third
Reich? It so happened that Heinrich Himmler—a chicken
farmer before joining the Nazi Party in 1927—was in some
ways a practical man. After all, raising chickens is the business
for a practical *realist** and not a dreamy *idealist.*[†]

Knowing by late 1944 that he was fast running out of time
and options, Himmler tried to give himself flexibility and a
position of power[‡] to deal with other Nazi war criminals also
on the run.[§] In his secret cache, therefore, he included travel
documents for other leading Nazis trying to escape capture. In
the shipment, he included travel papers for one hundred of the
most *notorious*[¶] German Nazi leaders—including Lt. Colonel
*Adolf Eichmann*** who organized all of the railroad shipments
of Jews to concentration death camps, and to Nazi Party head
Martin Bormann,[††] who was Hitler's private assistant for most
of the war and had been no friend to Himmler.

Many members of the SS and the Gestapo were included
in the collection. These identity and travel documents—some

---

* Realist: A person who deals with the world as it is—that is, he is not a
dreamer.

† Idealist: A person who creates an imaginary world or reality in his
mind, making him not practical in many ways.

‡ Position of power: Having the strongest position in a group, in his
case among the other leading Nazis.

§ On the run: A person who is trying to avoid being captured by going
to another town or country.

¶ Notorious: Most famous and most evil of men.

** Adolf Eichmann: This Nazi did escape after the war and was eventually captured by an Israeli Intelligence team in Argentina, brought
secretly back to Israel for trial, and hanged.

†† Martin Bormann: For many years he too was believed to have escaped
from Germany but is now believed to have been killed by Russian soldiers as he tried to get away from Berlin.

Swiss and most from Argentina, Paraguay, Bolivia, Chile and Brazil in South America—were the *equivalent** of a *Who's Who†* of Nazi war criminals. Himmler also included some *Nansen Passports‡* that were created back in the 1920s for refugees driven out of their homelands as a result of war. They were not by any means supposed to be issued to war criminals—ever!

Why did Himmler, at such a *perilous§* time near war's end, go to such trouble to pull all these documents together—even for men who opposed him during much of the Nazi period? Well, you cannot raise chickens as Himmler had done unless you are willing to do some of the detailed tasks of feeding and managing a flock of birds—animals that have small brains and few natural *survival skills.¶* Although Himmler was never a successful chicken farmer, he was an expert when it came to surviving in the brutal world of Nazi politics and war. During the dozen years of the Third Reich, Heinrich Himmler showed himself to be the ultimate survivor. For him, the Vienna castle was meant to play a crucial role. Right then, as Germany crumbled, Himmler needed help wherever he could get it—at that moment, the shipment sent from Berlin to the castle was it.

It made little difference to Himmler at this perilous time that Hitler's personal secretary, Martin Bormann, had long been his main enemy within the Nazi leadership. With the war almost

---

* Equivalent: The same as or equal to.
† Who's Who: Books that list important people in a country.
‡ Nansen Passports: After World War I, this travel pass allowed 450,000 refugees from Russia and Armenia to look for a place to live and work after losing citizenship due to the Communist Revolution.
§ Perilous: Extremely dangerous or hazardous.
¶ Survival skills: Being able to protect themselves from danger or dangerous enemies.

lost, the Gestapo Chief would have made a deal with the Devil himself in order to escape being captured by Germany's worst enemies from the East—the Russians. The massive Red Army was right then close to capturing Vienna before moving on to capture the German capital, Berlin. Like most Nazi leaders, Himmler was far more frightened of facing Russian Communist brutality than the American-British *systems of justice*.*

Yet, despite all of Himmler's shrewd planning, sometimes a man's luck just runs out. After Adolf Hitler's suicide in Berlin in April of 1945, Himmler decided to make his escape. He drove in Germany southward towards *Bavaria*,† hoping to get to Salzburg in Austria to meet up with cousin Kurt. But, this once-powerful Gestapo and SS Chief never made it out of Germany.

Dressed in the disguise and uniform of a simple German Army soldier, Himmler was captured by alert British soldiers in Bremervorde in May 1945. What caught their attention were his false identity documents. Here is where Himmler's escape story becomes amusing. It was not that there was anything *technically*‡ wrong with his travel documents. Ironically, his travel papers just looked 'too bloody good' as far as the British soldiers were concerned. They looked perfect—and this time, Himmler's perfectionism *did him in*.§

So, as it went, Heinrich Himmler never did *hook up*¶ with

---

* Systems of Justice: The courts, legal rules, judges and lawyers who are supposed to give citizens or prisoners fair and honest trials.
† Bavaria: The beautiful mountainous section of Southern Germany that borders Austria and Switzerland.
‡ Technically: In the details of the documents: the kind of paper, ink, printing, signatures.
§ Did him in: Was responsible for getting him caught.
¶ Hook up: Meet or connect with.

cousin Kurt. Although not nearly as clever as his evil Gestapo Chief relative, SS Colonel Schmidt was just as vicious. After all, Gestapo Chief Himmler, the butcher who ordered millions of murders without hesitation, used to *feel faint** at the sight of blood.

On the other hand, Cousin Kurt, was not at all *squeamish.*† He had already murdered many times to keep the castle secrets and, in fact, personally enjoyed killing people! When his famous cousin was alive and in charge of the Gestapo, Schmidt *indirectly*‡ had more power than other SS Colonels in Nazi Germany. He used that power to keep other Nazis in line as well as making them quite fearful of him. Those who knew him were very afraid to get on his bad side—otherwise, they would find themselves on the way to the Russian Front to an almost certain death.

Once captured by the British, Gestapo Chief Heinrich Himmler knew he would soon be correctly identified for the monster that he was. So, on May 23, 1945, before he could be tried and hanged for war crimes, he committed suicide. He did this by biting into a glass *capsule*§ which released *cyanide poison.*¶ He died violently in ten minutes, but not so terribly as did millions of his wartime victims.

His art-thief *competitor,*** Hermann Goering, would later be captured, tried for war crimes, and sentenced to death by the

---

*   Feel faint: When a person's head gets woozy and they begin to lose consciousness or pass out.
†   Squeamish: Easily shocked or sickened.
‡   Indirectly: Through someone else, not on his own.
§   Capsule: An inch long tube.
¶   Cyanide poison: A quick-acting poison that the Nazis used in their concentration camp murders. Adolf Hitler was given cyanide capsules that he first tested on his dog, who died right away, before giving it to his wife, Eva Braun, and taking it before shooting himself in the head.
** Competitor: One who works against or competes against another person.

International War Crimes Court at Nuremburg, Germany. But in October 1946—the day before his scheduled hanging—he too bit into a hidden cyanide capsule and died in a matter of minutes. Where had the cyanide come from? Well, the poison capsules had been developed by Himmler's own Gestapo during the war—they were part of his program to use poison gas to kill millions of prisoners. At war's end, however, it was then used by leading Nazis to die a quick but horrible death—by suicide.

In mid-1947, after two years of hiding out in Bavaria, Kurt Schmidt was now back in Vienna. He was preparing for his return to the castle to recover what he felt was his. There was, after all, everything to be gained by taking the risk to get his hands on the hidden trunks. With his Gestapo Chief cousin long dead, Kurt needed more money. The castle gold, money, and documents would help him escape to South America.

The trove also would establish for him a strong position among those *die-hard** Nazis hoping to build a new German *Fourth Reich.*† The hidden cache was Kurt's *ace-in-the-hole.*‡ If he used the documents to help top Nazis escape justice, his own power and *prestige*§ would rise as well. So, he had no intention of letting anyone or anything stand in the way of his getting hold of the trunks he personally had hidden—and for which he had already committed two murders. The gold that once

---

*   Die-hard: Those who never quit.

†   Fourth Reich: The dream of Nazis whose *Third Reich* had just been lost in the war.

‡   Ace-in-the-hole: Taken from the world of poker, a special power or advantage over other people.

§   Prestige: Good reputation and respect from others, in this case from genuine Nazi monsters.

belonged to innocent people caught in the brutal web of the Third Reich would now be his. He would just have to eliminate or get around one more *obstacle**—the American family and dog now living in the castle.

---

* Obstacle: Something or someone in the way.

9

Trip to the Castle Cellar

The Date and Time: Wednesday—June 18, 1947
—Mid-afternoon
The Place: The Vienna Castle—North Tunnel

At this point, everyone seemed to be at, or moving in the direction of the castle—known as the Hale Castle to young American David Hale and as the Gestapo Castle to Nazi Lt. Colonel Kurt Schmidt. Dr. Matt Hale, on his return trip from Linz, was expected home by late afternoon. David decided, after his morning's German tutorial, to head for the cellar—with Thor of course—to see what he could find or dig up. It was raining pretty heavily outside, so being in the damp basement tunnels was more appealing than being outdoors.

And the Nazi Three? They were collecting shovels and *pick-axes** to dig their way into the Northern tunnel. It was there, in March 1945, that they had buried their trunks of counterfeit British money, international travel documents and the five solid-gold bars. And, oh, the two dead Nazis. They did not know whether they would be able to start the actual digging in the next few days. They had to be sure they would not be discovered while they went about the *excavation.*† Schmidt estimated

---

* Pickaxes: Heavy sharp metal tools with handles and used to crack stones and dig huge holes.
† Excavation: Digging large holes and removing all the stones and dirt.

that they would need at least six and as many as twelve hours to break through the outside wall, get inside the tunnel, carry away the valuable trove, and re-seal the tunnel so no one would know they had been there.

Schmidt was especially interested in getting in and out of there unnoticed. He wanted to depart the Vienna region— in fact, get away from Austria altogether without Allied or Austrian government officials becoming aware that his group of Nazis had come back to retrieve buried treasure. By 1947, searching for stolen artwork and valuables had become an *industry of sorts** throughout Austria—people were searching everywhere for *loot*† the Nazis buried before the Russian at- tack. If word got out that former Nazi SS *thugs*‡ were actively searching in Vienna itself for valuables, the roads and border crossing points would tighten and motor vehicles would be searched more aggressively.

Schmidt told his two *henchmen*§ that, once they had the valuables in hand, they all would need to disappear into thin air—like steam from a tea kettle. He added, "Superior secrecy and perfect discipline are everything. This is a military opera- tion—one of the first in support of the Fourth Reich. We are soldiers still. We must not fail. Germany needs us."

David, meanwhile, was fully equipped for his own trip to the basement. He was wearing waterproof boots and a warm

---

*   Industry of sorts: A kind of business, in this case one where men made money by finding valuables stolen by the Nazis.
†   Loot: Stolen money and other goods.
‡   Thugs: Tough, cruel and dangerous men who use violence to get what they want.
§   Henchmen: Thugs and rough bullies who work for criminal organizations.

woolen sweater Katrina had knitted him for his birthday. He also carried his Army flashlight, Swiss Army Knife as well as an empty sack to haul whatever interesting stuff he might come across. Thor, naturally, was going along to the castle *under-world** just as he was. Nature already had equipped him with everything he needed—a sharp sense of smell, excellent hearing and the hunting skills of his cousin, the wolf. It also turned out that Thor could dig quite well.

Once he got to the bottom of the long cellar stairway, David decided to head this time in a new direction—northward to a part of the *subterranean†* basement he had not fully searched before. During his first trek in that area a few weeks earlier, he found there must have been an explosion of sorts some time ago. *Rubble‡* from a cave-in blocked the tunnel itself and prevented him from traveling the full length of that passageway. Every other castle tunnel eventually led to the outside—but not the North Tunnel. All medieval castles had various escape routes—that was so people could get away from an enemy force about to *overrun§* the fortification.

When David had scouted outside along the *periphery¶* of the castle, he found a blocked entranceway that he guessed once connected and met up with the North Tunnel. He later confirmed his *hunch*** by use of his compass. It showed him that the blocked tunnel in the interior and the blocked wall

---

* Underworld: The basement area of the castle. Can also mean all the evil people who commit crimes.
† Subterranean: Below ground level.
‡ Rubble: Rocks, stones, sand and dirt.
§ Overrun: An enemy force completely conquering a fort, city, or army.
¶ Periphery: The complete or entire wall surrounding the castle.
** Hunch: A guess.

portal* on the exterior were close to the same castle wall at the Northern-most point of the castle.

As David and Thor *slogged†* along the new pathway, mostly in the dark, the sounds of rats broke the eerie silence. It made the boy glad he had along an impressive *canine‡* to send the rodents scurrying for hiding places within and under the tunnel walls. The rats, like the Nazis, considered the castle to be theirs. As a result, anything edible under the castle became breakfast, lunch and dinner to them until any food was entirely gone. And so it had begun many hundreds of meals ago when two hefty Nazis took their *final resting place§* in the North Tunnel—alongside the shipment from Berlin.

The last *directive¶* from Gestapo Chief Heinrich Himmler to cousin Kurt was quite clear—any Nazis who knew of the treasure trove BUT WERE NOT 100% LOYAL TO THE HIMMLERS were to be *disposed of.*** Two of the German SS soldiers fit that description in Kurt Schmidt's mind. He once heard them telling a joke about Fuehrer Adolf Hitler, and Gestapo Chief Himmler. That had taken place more than a year earlier when they had been drinking too much beer and telling jokes. But, Schmidt never forgot.

So, he made certain that these two brutes carried the last of the trunks from Berlin down to the North Tunnel. Once the explosive charges had been put in place to seal off the

---

*   Portal: Doorway or entry way.
†   Slogged: Moved slowly with some difficulty
‡   Canine: A member the dog genus of animals.
§   Final resting place: The place where someone is buried or left after they die.
¶   Directive: Orders to be followed carefully.
** Disposed of: Got rid of, eliminated or murdered.

passageway, Schmidt personally shot both of the unfortunate joke-telling Nazis. He then set the *delay timer** for the explosion and got out of there as quickly as he could.

The local rodent population living in the North Tunnel was stunned when the explosion occurred. The blasts shook their *dank,*† rocky world and made the biggest noise that they had ever heard. So they retreated a couple of hundred feet and were frozen in fear for close to half a day—until something got their attention. They smelled food. Actually, they smelled dead Nazis. And so it happened that, for weeks afterwards, the North Tunnel became the scene of rodent rats feasting on dead Nazis. Some rats even moved there from other tunnels under the castle. That process continued until there was nothing left except bones, uniforms and, of course, the Berlin shipment.

The *gruesome*‡ business of the murders turned out to be "the" *telltale*§ mistake the Nazis made in trying to hide the secret shipment.

Two years later, as David and Thor moved along the North Tunnel close to the area blocked by the explosions, Thor suddenly became alert. It was too dark to see, but his *hackles*¶ stood up. He quickly moved ahead of David just as he had done when on patrol in the war—when he smelled enemy soldiers. Thor sensed danger for which he had been trained—trained to get out in front to protect his master. Dog and boy soon found

---

* Delay timer: This is a clocklike device that gives the person time to get far away before the explosion happens.

† Dank: Cold, wet, uncomfortable.

‡ Gruesome: Terrible, evil, disgusting.

§ Telltale: Something that gives away a secret.

¶ Hackles: Hair on the top of his neck that are raised when a dog gets nervous or frightened.

themselves facing the huge pile of material that blocked any further progress. David's immediate conclusion was to stop and go back. Thor, on the other hand, had something else in mind—he started digging. And dig he did!

For some minutes, David just stood there shining his flashlight on the mound of stones and dirt that Thor was attacking. Whatever it was that got the dog's attention, he intended to get to it. Seeing the determination being shown by Thor, the boy decided to help. He was soon on his hands and knees digging away. He placed both shining flashlights on a large rock and aimed them in the direction of their work site. This now had become a team effort and in this instance the Patrol Dog was leading the team. David was better able to roll away large stones—Thor excelled when it came to dealing with the dirt.

For well over an hour, they dug and pushed and rolled this material or that. David stopped from time to time to get a closer look with his trusty flashlight. They were *progressing** just fine. He concluded they would eventually make a *breakthrough*† to the other side—the tunnel ahead and whatever was over there. David had no idea what to expect—Thor seemed to have a pretty good idea! Well, at least what he could tell from his keenest sense—his sense of smell.

By this time it was getting a bit late as far as David was concerned. He was hungry and thirsty—he was dirty and tired. He reflected a bit on the world of miners and was grateful he did not have to grow up to be a coal miner. Just as quickly, he

---

* Progressing: Getting the job done and moving forward.
† Breakthrough: Getting past an obstacle, in this case the pile of rocks and stones blocking their way.

thought it would not be so bad mining for gold or precious stones, such as rubies and diamonds. But so far, all he had seen was worthless stuff—rocks and dirt of no value whatsoever. Not even any war souvenirs! He would have given anything to get his hands on a *German Luger,** the really neat pistol he had seen in so many war and mystery movies before he left the States for Austria. Right then, however, his stomach growled for food. If he had a choice between a Luger and a cheeseburger, he would no doubt have asked for salt, ketchup and certainly for a burger.

The boy started putting away his backup flashlight and getting ready to quit for the day when he heard a new sound—rocks and stones went crashing downward on the other side of the wall of material. They had in fact broken through. Or better, Thor had. David crawled as high as he could onto the pile and held his flashlight up close to the stone ceiling. He could not tell for sure, but he got the feeling that they could actually get to the other side if he pushed really hard on the remaining blocking material. He figured he at least might as well see if he could create a hole to get a look.

At the highest point on the pile he started to push—little by little he could feel and hear rocks falling on the other side. This went on for maybe fifteen minutes by which time he had made a small clear opening about the size of a basketball. He then took his prize Army flashlight and peered into the darkness of what initially seemed to be an *abyss.*† Gradually, however,

---

* German Luger: An automatic pistol used by the German Army in both World War I and II as well as the Swiss and other armies throughout the world because of its accuracy and reliability.
† Abyss: A bottomless pit or hole in the earth.

as his eyes got used to the dim light in the tunnel beyond, he could see some things that looked familiar—shapes that made sense to him.

He saw three trunks seemingly no different than the regular German Army foot lockers he had found in other parts of the castle basement. And, no more than six feet away, he saw what shocked him as nothing else had ever done—he saw two German Army uniforms that seemed to be draped around a pair of skeletons. One was resting on a chair. The other was on the floor in a corner. Each one looked like something out of a horror movie.

"Oh, 'that' is what got your attention, old boy," he whispered to Thor. "Now I understand." Why he was whispering surprised even himself. He thought it just seemed appropriate under the circumstances of two dead people down there in the dark!

The skeletons alone did not shock David as they might have startled other boys his age—or even adults. His dad had a skeleton he used in the medical classes he taught before taking the Austria *assignment*.* David had gotten to the point where he could name close to a hundred and fifty human bones with little difficulty. He used to compete with Ellie to see which of them knew the most bones by name and by sight. Sister, of course, was a few thousand miles away vacationing in the *serene*† lake region of Upstate New York. At that moment, David would not have changed places with her for anything—dead Germans and all. If this was what spying is about, he was all for it!

---

* Assignment: A job that would send him to another country to work, in this case Austria.

† Serene: Quiet and peaceful.

But what made the skeletons weird was finding them down here in the pitch black darkness of a sealed-off *tomb**—as though they had been murdered. "What a place to die," he thought. "What a way to have your life come to an end. Scary!"

At this point two strong emotions were raging in David's body. He was still hungry, thirsty and dirty as—well—a sewer rat. At the same time, he was exploding with curiosity to get a look inside the trunks neatly stacked along one of the walls, but covered with rocks and dust from the 1945 explosion. Several questions raced through his mind.

Did the trunks hold only a bunch of Army junk? Were they empty or full? Why were the two soldiers murdered and left there before the explosion? Why was the tunnel blocked in the first place? Question after question came flashing through his mind. Each question *bred†* more questions—none of which could be answered so long as he stayed on his side of the pile of rubble and the trunks remained on the other.

"Maybe I should just wait for Dad to get home," he thought. "Or, instead, run down the hill and get Herr Vogel. But, no, Dad must be told first and he is due back home in a few hours. I'll tell him then. But, maybe I should just take a quick peek. Then, at least, I can present him with a full report—and not only a confusing mystery."

As things went, David would not be first in getting a close look at what little remained of the dead Germans, at the trunks, or the burial tomb in the North Tunnel. As the boy was starting up the pile again, flashlight in hand and getting ready to crawl

---

*   Tomb: A burial place such as one would find in a cemetery.
†   Bred: Created or made.

headfirst towards the other side, he felt himself being dragged backwards. The next thing he knew he was being yanked down the rubble pile to where he began. Thor, it turned out, had grabbed him by the seat of his pants and resumed his role as excavation team leader.

David was just picking himself off the ground when Thor shot up the pile and headed into the opening to the other side. All David could do was crawl back up to the top and shine his light into the chamber. Thor was all business and busily sniffing around—quite alert and looking like a dog at war.

With Thor clearly taking charge, the boy crawled through the opening and joined his buddy on the other side. And, with his sense of humor still *intact*,* David looked at the two uni-formed skeletons and murmured to Thor, "Now that there are four of us, Old Boy, maybe we can play some cards. Bridge or poker?" At that point, the only one chuckling in the cold damp death chamber was David Hale—he thought his own joke was as funny as any he had heard at the movies. Thor looked as though he had heard it all before.

---

*   Intact: Whole, complete, undamaged.

10

The Treasure Trove in Hand

David wanted more light so he scooted quickly back through the hole and got his hands on the second flashlight. Then he went back into the burial chamber yet again. The boy went quickly to the trunks that had been *security sealed** before leaving Berlin back in 1945. Back then prior to setting off *dynamite*† charges in the North Tunnel, Col. Schmidt had opened the trunks to get a look. He wanted to be certain of exactly what his cousin was asking him to protect. He looked and he liked what he saw—it was exactly what David Hale would be seeing in 1947, twenty-five months later.

With the security seals broken, all David had to do was lift the latches and open the lids. Everything was in plain view for anyone to see. One trunk was stacked to the brim with *Five Pound British Bank Notes*‡—not real, of course, but counterfeit money that had been printed under Himmler's orders at the Nazi concentration camp at Sachsenhausen, Germany. Bundled in stacks the size of a small loaf of bread, there obviously was a *king's ransom*§ worth of English money—but only if it all were genuine and not fake.

---

* Security sealed: Wrapped with special materials and markings that would show whether anyone had opened the trunks.

† Dynamite: Explosive material that is used to blow up rocks to build highways or buildings.

‡ Five Pound British Bank Notes: British money came in denominations of 5, 10, 20 and 50 Pounds.

§ King's ransom: This means a huge amount of money, enough to pay to rescue a king who may have been taken prisoner by an enemy.

The huge pile of British Notes gave David a pretty good idea why the North Tunnel had been sealed off. It became clearer still when he reached into trunk number one and tried to lift a heavy object wrapped in a leather pouch—it turned out to be solid gold. It was the heaviest material he had ever tried to lift. The German Eagle design stamped into the bar made it seem like it could be the real thing. All he could say was "Wow" and then "Holy Moses." If this were really gold, David now understood why the murders had occurred.

The third trunk didn't look special to him. When he lifted the lid, all he saw was a bunch of papers and photographs. It would turn out that the third trunk was in fact the *jackpot*.* More valuable than the gold or paper money? Absolutely! These were documents assembled personally by Heinrich Himmler to assist escaping senior Nazis—men who could not get far traveling with their own passports or identity papers. The top Nazi leaders of the German Third Reich were *infamous*† far and wide. At war's end, Intelligences Services, Armies of the world and victims of Nazi brutality were trying to find them—not to honor them but to hang them.

Looking once again into each of the three trunks, he saw three more leather pouches, each holding a gold brick. David weighed his next move. He certainly could not carry much of the buried loot on his first trip. He had only brought one carrying sack—it was a fairly long distance through the tunnel just to get back to the stairs. Then he would have to haul it up the extremely long stairway to Dad's study which he decided would be his first destination.

---

*   Jackpot: The biggest prize of all.
†   Infamous: Famous for being evil men or criminals and murderers.

He didn't waste any time *mulling things over**. He grabbed the first heavy gold bar, scooped up a bundle of the British money, and he added four packets of travel documents with photographs. All of it went into his carrying sack. He then recovered both flashlights and said to Thor, "We're getting out of here, old fella. We're not passing 'Go' and we're not collecting two hundred dollars." Obviously, the language of his favorite board game—*Monopoly*—had come to mind in his excitement. Right now, he was dying to get the stuff and the news to his father. "Sure hope he is home pretty soon. He'll know what this is all about—if anyone does."

Ten minutes later, huffing and puffing as the dirt-covered boy opened the door to Dad's study, his *heart sank*†—all he saw was the empty desk and his father nowhere in sight. Nor was there any sign he had even arrived home. David then slid the carrying sack under the great desk and headed for the door to the yard.

He glanced down the hill to the Vogel house, hoping Dad had stopped there on the way home. No sign of him there, either. Then, with Thor in close pursuit, he headed for the parapet. If his dad were fairly close to the castle, David would spot him several miles away. As he got to the *pinnacle*‡ and searched the road from the west, he saw no sign of Matt Hale. Just as he was about to descend to ground level, he took a last westward look—a familiar car was coming in his direction. It was a Mercedes all right, but not the Hale car—it was the same Mercedes he had spotted earlier in the week. The strangers had

---

*   Mulling things over: Thinking carefully and thoroughly about all the possibilities.

†   Heart sank: He felt let down and disappointed.

‡   Pinnacle: Highest point, the top.

returned! This time, though, the large sedan did not stop in the field or make a turn away from the castle. It drove straight up the hill to the castle gate, pulled to a stop and a tall man got out. He looked around while the driver stayed in the car.

"Son of a gun," David muttered, "they could be here for the trunks!" Feeling suddenly a bit unsteady on his legs, he sat down against the wall and tried to calm down his heavy breathing. The next thought that entered his mind was as *logical** as it could be, "If they are in fact interested in the trunks, then these guys could be the murderers! Oh, *shucks,*†where's Dad? Have to think. What would Dad do if he were in my position?"

The boy decided that the best thing he could do is find out what was going on with the strangers. As Dad had taught him when giving the boy target lessons with his pellet gun, he first had to breathe properly if he was going to get good results in anything. So, while Schmidt stood by the closed gate and looked impatiently all around, young David Hale sat a couple of minutes with his back against the parapet wall and took in slow deep breaths—"in through the nose and out through the mouth," was what Dr. Hale taught him.

By the time he got up and headed for the stairs, the junior spy was calm—and ready for action. If David could have described how he felt at the moment, he would have said "excited, not fearful."

He was pleased with how he had recovered from his sudden fright. "Darn adrenalin," he muttered. As he descended the

---

* Logical: Clear thinking that makes perfect sense.
† Shucks: An exclamation or word used to express sudden disappointment or unwelcome surprise.

tower stairway to go down the hill to the front gate, he whispered to his partner Thor, "Listen, my pal! The good thing is we know some things about these strangers—they will think I am just a kid who knows next to nothing—and you are just any old dog. Let's go and see what's up. Let's try to do what Dad would do."

By the time David reached the gate, Herr Vogel was already there and speaking with the tall stranger who was chatting away in German. The Nazi paid no particular attention to the boy as he and the dog approached. He did however cast a wary glance at Thor who stayed close to David and was neither wagging his tail nor showing any obvious signs of *aggression**—or friendliness. Thor kept his eyes focused entirely on the stranger. To Schmidt, it was clear that Thor was quite alert and likely to stay that way. "This is not your average pet," he thought. And Schmidt was correct—Thor was on patrol.

Herr Vogel—who had been *forewarned*† by Matt Hale about visitors roaming around the fields—told the tall stranger that the castle was now occupied by an international medical family and that they had been there for several months. "Nice family. The father fixes sick people; lots of them" was how he put it.

Schmidt asked about the family that owned the castle and lived there before the war. He, of course, was quite aware that his cousin had sent the old man and woman to their deaths at the Mauthausen-Gusen Concentration Camp. Schmidt falsely claimed to have been an old friend of that family. He lied even further that he was hoping to see whether they had returned to

---

*   Aggression: Being unfriendly and willing to attack.
†   Forewarned: Told before or in advance.

their beautiful castle home. He went on to *claim** that he used to visit the family in the 1930s and "hoped they had survived the war okay." To make it seem true that he and the old couple were friends, Schmidt added that he had some old photographs to give them—Schmidt, obviously, had merely found them in the castle during the war.

Well, if Thor had a good nose for danger, Herr Vogel had a superior nose for Nazis—no matter how they tried to mask their *true selves.*[†] He had gotten through the war alive precisely because he could tell the difference between a patriotic Austrian and a secret member or *informer*[‡] of the Gestapo. And, in this tall German stranger, Konrad Vogel smelled Gestapo. Schmidt's *arrogance*[§] was crystal clear. So, when the tall stranger asked David why he looked like he had been working in a coal mine or river bed, Herr Vogel spoke up to protect the boy from any suspicion—"been digging potatoes for me and doing a great job—mud and all."

Vogel then told the tall stranger he did not know the family who lived there in the 1930s. He suggested that Schmidt call Dr. Hale when he gets back later today as he might have some information. He gave Schmidt the Hale telephone number at the castle. At that point, the stranger thanked Vogel, glared back at Thor, got back in the car, and left. As the tall stranger left, the hackles on Thor's back fell back into place.

---

*   Claim: To state something new that may or may not be true. In this case, it is a lie.
†   True selves: The real person, not the one he might try pretending or appear to be.
‡   Informer: A person who secretly reports to the police, usually against his own countrymen.
§   Arrogance: A bad, mean attitude of a person who thinks he is better than other people.

The strangers had no sooner gotten out of sight than Matt Hale came driving in from the opposite direction. He was surprised to find David down near the gate with Herr Vogel. He was *chagrined** to find his son looking absolutely filthy from head to toe. "What on earth have you been up to, Son? Fall in the river? Jump in the car and go take a bath before dinner. You must have a lot to tell."

Not wanting to speak freely about the North Tunnel caper in front of Herr Vogel without his father's permission, David just mumbled an "okay" and got in the car for the short ride up the hill. Thor had already reached the kitchen door when they arrived—he too was looking dirty, *famished*† and anxious for a meal. Matt Hale glanced at Thor and said, "You too? What a mess! You guys have been quite busy I see. I hope you have something good to show for it."

"Have a lot to tell and show you, Dad. Has been an interesting day. You may not believe what we—Thor and I—*came across*."‡ Few things surprised Matt Hale any more—he had seen enough to fill a dozen books on medicine, war, spying and refugees. This time, however, would be different. He would be indeed surprised when he learned what David had been up to—and particularly by what he had found.

---

* Chagrined: Completely surprised, in fact stunned.
† Famished: Deeply hungry as though he had no eaten in a long time.
‡ Came across: To find by accident.

11

Baiting the Trap

The Date and Time: June 18, 1947—Early Evening into Night

Dr. Matt Hale had returned from seeing Visitor and visiting the Linz refugee camp with the firm intention of using this evening to prepare for a quick trip into downtown Vienna in the morning. He had to *case** the meeting site of the international medical conference. He was a bit *pressed for time*[†] because the Polish Security Official whom Visitor wanted to meet—Dr. Kaminski's friend—would be in Vienna for only four or five days—six at the most. "Not a lot of time to contact, get to know and recruit someone," Matt Hale was thinking—"and then train him in *tradecraft*[‡]—if he says Yes."

Matt Hale was *intimately*[§] familiar with recruiting and had accomplished it in far less time—under far more dangerous conditions—in war time. In one case, he recruited a leading German rocket scientist at a *resort spa*[¶] near Salzburg that was used by Third Reich leaders and their families. In that operation—in disguise, using an *alias*** and playing the role of a Swiss

---

*   Case: Check out or have a good look at.
†   Pressed for time: In a hurry.
‡   Tradecraft: The secret tricks and ways a spy carries out his work and keeps from getting caught.
§   Intimately: Closely and deeply.
¶   Resort spa: A vacation area with warm water springs where people rest and often recover from illness or to get back in good shape physically.
**   Alias: False name.

wartime banker—Lt. Col. Hale made his *recruitment pitch.**
He knew he would be hanged as a spy if the rocket scientist,
rather than saying "Yes," had instead called in the Gestapo.
That scientist did say "Yes" and, in turn, soon played a major
role recruiting other German rocket engineers to go with him
to the United States after the war.

The Americans first helped scientists avoid being kidnapped
by the Russians. Dr. Hale's medical skills came in handy also
in helping this scientist stay in Salzburg several weeks to avoid
returning to his job—his German rocket center was scheduled
in the following weeks for massive bombing by the British and
the Americans. So, there was a pretty good chance the scientist
would be killed if he went back to work.

How could this healthy young German scientist avoid returning to the rocket center? Hale gave him a crash course
in *malingering.*† Hale, the doctor-spy, made it seem that the
scientist was suddenly quite sick—even though he was not. To
bolster‡ the case, he gave the scientist some medications that
made it seem as though he suddenly had serious heart disease
and could not travel at all.

When it came to the business of recruiting, therefore, Matt
Hale had done it before and done it well. Furthermore, while
helping the scientist remain in Salzburg, Hale was able to
collect from him valuable information and sketches on the

---

*   Recruitment pitch: That is the moment a person is asked to cooper-
      ate with an intelligence service in secret operations, in other words,
      spying.

†   Malingering: When a healthy person pretends to be seriously sick so
      he can get out of work, school, a test or travel—and succeeds in fool-
      ing other people—even doctors.

‡   Bolster: Make stronger, strengthen.

leading German rocket scientists as well as the latest German rocket program—*critical** intelligence reporting that Hale sent by shortwave radio back to U.S. Army Headquarters in London and Washington. Assisting him in this operation was his wartime contact, Herr Vogel, who was with the Austrian Underground Army active in the Salzburg area at that same time.

Well, after David had taken a bath and eaten a quick dinner, father and son went into the study to talk. As he went behind his desk, Matt Hale spotted the sack David had deposited underneath. "What have we here, Son? Let's take a look." What he felt when he lifted the heavy sack got his interest. He smiled and asked if David had begun collecting rocks and boulders, or something. "Not a lot of precious jewels in this part of Austria—so it must be something else, right?"

"Better look Dad. I think even *you* could never guess."

Matt Hale emptied the contents of the sack onto the rug and got one of the shocks of his life. He recognized the Third Reich Gold Bar for what it was. He saw the packet of British money and guessed correctly that it was counterfeit. And he was familiar with two of the Nazi leaders whose photos appeared with false names on the travel documents—Adolf Eichmann and Aribert Heim—each of whom was wanted far and wide for war crimes.

Adolf Eichmann had been the Gestapo Chief in charge of transporting millions of Jews and other civilian victims of the

---

* Critical: Highly important; in this case, of significance to the American military, scientific, and political leaders at the White House and the Pentagon.

Third Reich to death camps across Eastern Europe. Aribert Heim was the Nazi monster who conducted deadly and gruesome medical experiments at the Mauthausen death camp in Austria. A member of the Nazi SS, Dr. Heim was known in the death camps as "Doctor Death" for all the murders he committed.

Matt Hale let out a low whistle and said, "Son, what have you been doing? Tell me how you came across all this. And where—the tunnel?"

The boy explained the afternoon adventure in great detail. Over dinner, he had mentioned to his father about the two skeletons and the German Army uniforms. He now told his father that he had brought up from the North Tunnel only a small fraction of what Thor and he had discovered. "Three full trunks, Dad. FULL! Looks like there are four gold bars in all. Also, a whole trunk with nothing but money. And the third trunk? It is stuffed with papers and photographs."

Leaping ahead, the boy continued: "But Dad, I am afraid the strangers who were sneaking around here the other day—and who came by here again this afternoon—may be after the same stuff. Just guessing, but I have a funny feeling that is the case."

He told his father about the conversation Herr Vogel had with the tall stranger at the gate and explained that his dad may be getting a phone call. "The tall guy in the Mercedes said he was an old friend of the family living here before the war. He said he wants to find them. I could tell that Thor did not like him one bit."

The pieces of this complicated puzzle fell into place pretty rapidly for Matt Hale. Since the war ended, he may have mainly been doctoring—his instinct as an Intelligence Officer, however, had not disappeared. He knew some things from Visitor and from his own wartime experience that *shed light** on the three items David had carried up from the tunnel and were now resting on the rug in his study.

He could tell by its weight and *look*[†] that the bar was indeed gold. He knew also the background story on Sachsenhausen Concentration Camp and *Operation Bernhard*[‡]—the Gestapo's secret program to print counterfeit British Notes or money. At Sachsenhausen, the Nazis used Jewish prisoners—men who had been *engravers*[§] and in some cases *forgers*[¶] before the war—to do the difficult printing. These Jewish prisoners had been kept alive by the Gestapo only because the Nazis needed them to print millions of fake British Pounds. Otherwise, they would have been put to death much earlier.

That fake money, though not perfect, looked and felt much like real British Bank Notes. The original Nazi plan had been to drop millions of the bills from German airplanes all across England as a way of creating *turmoil*[**] in all of England—possibly breaking or ruining their *economy*.[††] By the time the money

---

*   Shed light: Made it clear or understandable.

†   Look: The way it appeared or seemed to be.

‡   Operation Bernhard: The secret German program to hurt England by printing and distributing fake English money.

§   Engravers: They make the printing plates used by governments to print money. Most engravers are honest and work for governments—others are criminals who print counterfeit money for themselves.

¶   Forgers: Skilled artists and printers who are criminals and can print money that looks real, but is not.

**   Turmoil: Chaos and confusion.

††   Economy: The whole system of businesses, workers and governments that make, buy and sell things and use money to pay people for work, pay their taxes, or put extra money in banks as savings.

was all printed and ready, however, it was too late—the war was just about lost. So that Nazi plan was canceled.

Then, it so happened, Himmler found another use for the Sachsenhausen fake British Bank Notes—he began paying spies around the world with the counterfeit money. Himmler was so pleased to have the additional *funds** that he decided to keep his printing operation forever secret. To protect the secrecy of Operation Bernhard itself, he ordered that all 142 prisoners who worked on the printing operation be murdered. But, by sheer luck and *chaos*† as the war was ending, those prisoners were transferred away from the Sachsenhausen death camp. They were then *liberated*‡ in Austria by soldiers of the U.S. Army. As a result, the Gestapo's secret counterfeit money operation was *exposed*§ to the Allies.

After the war was over, the British and American Governments were able to find and recover much of this counterfeit money—that which had been dumped by the Nazis into Austrian lakes in waterproof containers. But, no one had caught up with the trunk of Five Pound Notes hidden in the North Tunnel of the Hale Vienna castle.

"The North Tunnel, you say, David? Let's have a look." They headed for the basement and brought along more carrying sacks—and a shovel. Thor went too and took up his patrol position as they got close to the *remains*¶ of the two dead Germans. He knew they were not alive—he was being

---

*   Funds: Money.
†   Chaos: Total confusion and mess.
‡   Liberated: Freed, set free.
§   Exposed: Revealed or found out.
¶   Remains: The body and bones of a dead person.

*prudent** and, yes, making certain. For Matt Hale to get into the burial chamber, he had to widen the hole. This time, he did the digging which went pretty quickly. They also had better light because he had brought along two *paraffin*† lanterns that let off a pretty bright glow.

Once inside the chamber, it did not take long for Matt Hale to examine the three trunks. He told David to prepare for a long night. They were going to be taking some pictures—the boy would be playing an important role. They loaded the carrying sacks with the travel documents and photographs for what Matt Hale now called "The Nazi 100." They left behind the two other trunks as they were—one with the gold and the other with the British Bank Notes.

David, a bit surprised, asked, "Hey Dad, why are we not taking it all? Why just the papers and photographs?"

"Well, Son, I have a plan and right now we first have to make sure we make a record of all these photographs and travel documents—before we give them back to the Nazis who put them here." It was David's turn to be shocked—he was shaking his head as he asked, "Why in the blazes would we ever do that? Whoever did this are murderers, Dad. Nazi murderers!"

"And that is why we want them to get their loot out of here and to never come back—to the castle—to our home. I need to keep you, Ellie and Mom safe from these monsters. The best way to do that is let them think they got away with everything. We have no idea how many other Nazis these three strangers

---

* Prudent: Using good judgment; being careful; cautiously wise.

† Paraffin: An oil used around the world in lamps and lanterns where electricity is not available. In the United States and Canada it is called kerosene.

may have told. I have no desire to let this castle become a target of those looking for treasure and travel papers—especially gold! But, first, we have to *bait the trap** in such a way that they will get stuck in their own mess."

After getting the stuffed sacks of documents to the stairway and upstairs to his study, Matt Hale suggested that David go to the kitchen and make himself a sandwich. When the boy had left the study, the senior spy opened his *concealment device*† built into a closet. He pulled out the hidden radio he used to send a coded message to "Visitor." Hale called for an emergency meeting that night at midnight and suggested Visitor come up from the river "in case the castle is being watched."

He had no sooner sent the secret message and received an answer back that Visitor would be there as requested, when the telephone rang.

Matt Hale picked up the phone and answered in German, "Doctor Hale, Good evening." As expected, it was Schmidt who then identified himself falsely as Manfred Becker, an old friend of the unfortunate Glasser family who lived at the castle before the war. Schmidt repeated his lie that he was looking for the Glasser couple and had some photographs to give them—just as he had told Herr Vogel in the afternoon.

At that point, David strolled into the study and his dad put his finger over his lips so the boy would know enough to sit down and say nothing. After a couple of minutes of hearing Schmidt telling other meaningless lies about "his old friends, the Glassers," Matt Hale abruptly told Schmidt he was

---

* Bait the trap: Putting something attractive in a trap to catch the prey you are after.
† Concealment device: Anything built to hold a spy's equipment or radio; in this case, a false ceiling where the radio equipment was hidden.

busy—too busy—to chat right then and that he was preparing to leave town for a week. "Call again or come by here after the 25th of June—when we return. In fact, July would be better. In a rush. Have to go. Good bye."

At this point, with the phone call ended by Matt Hale, Schmidt was *fuming**—almost in a rage. As a former senior Gestapo officer and Nazi, he was not used to having anyone *dismiss*† him—as though Schmidt were some *low-level*‡ private in the Army. He had a *crazed*§ look in his eyes and let out a string of curses that not only shocked his two Nazi *underlings*⁋—but terrified the pair.

Then, just as quickly, he let out a roaring laugh. "What am I saying? This is good news—very good news—wonderful news! While this stupid Doctor Hale is away, we will go in and get our stuff. Hale can then wait for my phone call *until Hell freezes over.*** By next week we will be in France. In the great city of crime—my kind of city—Marseille!††"

In the study back at the castle, Matt Hale was smiling as well. He looked at his totally-confused son and said, "David, there are *many ways to skin a cat,*‡‡ as the saying goes. But right now, we are about to skin some Nazi skunks—or make sure others skin them before this is all over. That will be perfect. Okay, partner, let's get photographing."

---

* Fuming: Exceedingly angry though trying not to show it.
† Dismiss: Send away, told to leave or go away.
‡ Low-level: Unimportant.
§ Crazed: The look of a crazy person or wild animal.
⁋ Underlings: Those who were lower in rank or power.
** Until Hell freezes over: An expression that means forever and ever.
†† Marseille: Pronounced "mar-SAY," an important French city on the coast of the Mediterranean Sea.
‡‡ Many ways to skin a cat: To get something done or finished.

12

Poisoning the Well*

Matt Hale was glad that he had recently received a *considerable*[†] supply of *35 millimeter film*[‡]—photographing as many as a dozen pages for each of 'The Nazi 100' would take a lot of that film and most of the night. The good news was that the chore of *developing*[§] the film would belong to Visitor's staff back at the Embassy.

So, the father got David organized to *tackle*[¶] each packet of documents *individually*[**] and keep them from getting all mixed up. The boy would have to make a list of each Nazi's name and make sure that the documents were put back together in the same order as they were found. Once David started working with the system, he found it wasn't hard to follow. However he could not read what he was copying—it was all in German. After a while, he got a bit tense looking at the *sullen*[††] faces of some of the world's worst murderers. In a way, each had the same scary look as the tall stranger did.

---

* Poisoning the Well: Making sure that the thieves get away—not with something useful—but with a poison of sorts.
† Considerable: A large amount or supply.
‡ 35 Millimeter Film: Also called 35MM Film, the most popular Black and White photographic film in the 1940s.
§ Developing: Taking photographing film and turning it into paper photographs by use of chemicals.
¶ Tackle: Handle.
** Individually: One at a time.
†† Sullen: Lifeless, expressionless, without a good expression.

While the junior spy went about his *assignment*,* he was feeling energized—he had not slept in close to 20 hours, but he was as wide awake as he could ever be. It would never have occurred to him to take a rest or go to bed—not with all this stuff going on! His dad had said this was important—that was all he really needed to hear.

Matt Hale, meanwhile, had returned to the North Tunnel and brought up the other three leather pouches holding the remaining Third Reich Gold Bars—all seventy-five pounds of it. The fourth 25-pound bar was in the study. He wanted them on hand when Visitor showed up. As the big Swiss clock in the hall struck midnight, Matt Hale heard a tapping sound at the study door leading in from the garden. Visitor of course had arrived as scheduled, also looking as bright and wide awake as the boy in the study working the camera all evening.

Matt Hale took Visitor to the kitchen for a coffee and made a cup of hot cocoa for David to whom Visitor gave a warm greeting. He thanked the boy for all he was doing. Visitor again referred to the recent rescue operation in Linz and congratulated David for what he had helped achieve. "And now, I see, tonight you are one of the most important photographers in all of Austria. Your dad must be real proud of you. I am."

David grimaced, took the chocolate drink and headed back into the study to continue with his work. He was not, at this point, interested in standing around being praised—or losing time chatting about the past. He knew he had to keep his mind on what was going on right now. The hot drink gave him the energy boost he needed—he was glad for that.

---

*   Assignment: The task or duty he had been given.

Seated at the kitchen table, coffees in hand, Matt Hale outlined what had been found, how much there was of it, and what he thought was the best way to *turn the tables** on these Nazis—brutes who so cleverly had buried a treasure trove that would serve their purposes in other parts of the world for years to come. His proposal to Visitor was in some ways simple—in other ways quite challenging.

First, Matt proposed that they let the Nazis get away with their loot—and do nothing that would let them know the Americans were aware of what was going on. He said, "Right now, David is photographing each and every document and picture of 'The Nazi 100.' These were top leaders in the Nazi SS, the Gestapo and in the Nazi Party of Germany. I have examined the British Bank Notes and want you to *verify*† what I think is the case—that all these Five Pound Notes are Nazi counterfeits—probably came from Operation Bernhard."

Matt Hale continued, "Finally, I am sure no one would want to just give the Nazis four Third Reich Gold Bars. That would be worth a great deal of money to them. So, if it is possible, I suggest we 'poison the well' in such a way that the Nazis will do poorly with their stock of gold—gold bars just as fake as their Bank Notes. Simply put, within 24 hours, can you get me some replacement bars that are real heavy, have a gold outer layer but are solid lead on the inside? And, of course, each bar will need the Third Reich design stamped into it—exactly like the real ones I am giving you to take along. And tonight, can you haul away this 100 pounds of real gold? You sure look strong enough for that."

---

* Turn the tables: To change things around so they are the opposite of what they were.

† Verify: To say whether my conclusion is correct or not.

Visitor laughed and said he had never carried 100 pounds of gold before, but was sure he could make it. "Matt, is that all you will need from us?"

"Not entirely. I need to make the inside of the tunnel look more or less like it was before David and I dug our way in. So, after we *restore** the three trunks with their earlier contents, I need to make a small explosion to scatter rocks and dirt all around. Then, if the Nazis try to dig their way in from the blocked outside entrance—as I expect they will do—they will not think anyone else had been there since they blew it up. That was in early 1945 I would guess. Can you get your hands on a smallish explosive device that will do the job—but not destroy the trunks or blow the castle off its foundation?"

Visitor said he would certainly do his part—the following night he would be back at midnight with the things Matt Hale requested. "You know, Matt, lead-filled bars the same size as the solid gold bars will not weigh as much. As heavy as lead happens to be, gold is almost twice as heavy. Let's hope these Nazis cannot tell the difference. By the way, our *craftsmen*[†] will probably use a small part of the gold from the Third Reich bars to make our fake bars look real, just enough for a good coating. The great thing about gold it is that is just about the most *malleable*[‡] of metals—it can be shaped and will easily coat or cover a solid chunk of lead. When we are done, they will look just like solid gold bars."

---

*   Restore: To put back in the original, initial or beginning condition.

†   Craftsmen: Men who work with their hands and are able to build things with wood, metal, cement and any other materials needed in an intelligence operation.

‡   Malleable: Able to be shaped in many different ways, even in thin layers.

Visitor then handed Matt Hale a packet of information and a photograph of the Polish Official due to arrive in Vienna for the medical conference. "I hope, Matt, you will still have some time to help us on this one, too. This darn Nazi stuff is really a *time-consuming** step backwards—into the ugly past. These days, we worry more about the Russians, frankly. But, former Nazis are a threat also—many of them will be working in the future for America's enemies around the world."

Visitor continued, "The Polish Official we need to get to is Major Otto Gorski. He was married, according to Dr. Kaminski, but his wife was killed in the war. Gorski has two children who are currently being raised by his sister who lives outside of Warsaw. According to Dr. Kaminski, Gorski would probably not return to Poland from Vienna except for his children. He said he cannot think of leaving his kids behind to grow up alone under Communism which is the way Poland is going. He got into the security field with the help of an uncle who is close to the Russian authorities. Major Gorski, however, is a Polish *nationalist*[†]—but these days a secret one. It was only through the help of his uncle that he too was not executed during the war by the Russians in the Katyn Forest *massacre*.[‡] Gorski took great personal risk in warning Dr. Kaminski that the Russian Secret Police were after him. For that reason, we think he may be happy to talk to the Americans—if it can be done securely."

Matt Hale *reassured*[§] Visitor that he would be quite involved

---

*   Time-consuming: A project or job that takes a great deal of time.
†   Nationalist: A person who is very loyal to his country, in this case to Poland.
‡   Massacre: The murder of a great many people.
§   Reassured: Telling him that things will be fine and that things will work out.

in that conference and be looking for Gorski. He said he was taking David to Vienna for the weekend as part of his plan to mess up the gold-hungry Nazis. "Yes, I have to leave this place empty so they come back and, well, steal back their stuff. The timing of the conference in fact is perfect for me."

As Visitor got ready to leave, he said he had better take a look at the tunnel to make sure he brings back the right amount of explosive material—maybe just one stick of dynamite or enough plastic explosive for a tiny "boom." Visitor then smiled and said, "Sorry, but the rules say the leftover* gold will have to go into the *U.S. Treasury.*† Too bad! Almost 100 pounds of gold could make you rich, Doctor Hale. Very rich. And, by the way, I have to get approval from the Intelligence Group for how we are dealing with these Nazis. But, I don't believe it will be a problem."

---

*   Leftover: That which was remaining.
†   U.S. Treasury: The department of the American Government that prints our money.

13

Leaving Open the Trap Door

The Date: Thursday – June 19, 1947

The first thing Matt Hale did in the morning was walk down the hill to have a brief chat with the Vogels. They discussed the Nazi strangers. Matt Hale explained the general background of what David had found, where it had been buried, and why he wanted the Nazis both to get their treasure back and leave the area for good. Herr Vogel said he would move the cows to another farm and do their own *disappearing act** by leaving town today. They would drive out to Salzburg for a few days. "If the Nazis are watching the castle, Dr. Hale, they will see us leave town."

Matt Hale grinned and said, "The only thing more we could do is put out a large sign in German saying 'Hey, Nazis: The Place is empty—Come back in and get your stuff.'"

Schmidt, meanwhile, had indeed put his two goons to work keeping track of the *comings and goings*† at the castle. He ordered that the gated entrance be watched for all of the daytime hours—which meant each of the two Nazi goons had to be sitting up in the woods for about seven hours at a time. He had them dress in dark green hunting gear so they would be

---

* Disappearing Act: As in a magic show, just seeming to disappear.
† Comings and goings: The people who visit, stay at, and leave a place.

more difficult to see. Schmidt made them climb a ridge to the steep hilltop spot he had selected. Almost a mile away from the castle, the site gave them *line-of-sight** *coverage*† of the gate as well as the fronts of both the castle and the Vogels' cottage.

When the Vogels packed their old Volkswagen later in the day and drove away towards the west in the direction of Salzburg, Schmidt soon received the goons' report of their departure—this meant that half of his problem was solved. Schmidt now had to be concerned only about the Hales.

"Now it is a question of whether that *impolite*† Dr. Hale and his dirty, potato-picking son and dog are going to be leaving as well. If so, we are much luckier than I would have thought possible. Maybe, after all, the coast will be *clear*.§ And maybe I will not have to bother hurting or shooting anybody. I would not mind hurting Dr. Hale—in fact, if this were 1943 again, I would have shot him already. But, for now, I would rather we just get in and out of the castle without anyone seeing us, hearing us or knowing anything. The Fourth Reich depends on this!"

The second Nazi goon listened, eagerly nodded his head in agreement—as always—and said, "*Jawohl,*¶ Colonel"—as each Nazi goon always did.

The war had, of course, ended very badly for Nazi Germany which had not merely lost but had been crushed by the Allies.

---

* Line-of-sight: A direct look at or view of the gate, not blocked by any trees.
† Coverage: View.
‡ Impolite: Not polite, crude.
§ Coast will be clear: No one will be nearby and looking.
¶ Jawohl: Pronounced 'Ya-vole' it means Yes Sir in the German military. It is a strong 'YES'.

The Fuehrer had killed himself as had SS Chief Heinrich Himmler and Marshall of the Reich Hermann Goering. Those were the most powerful monsters in Nazi Germany. The dreaded Russian Red Army now occupied much of Germany as well as a large chunk of Austria—the armies of the Americans and British occupied the rest. To make matters even worse, surviving SS and Gestapo officers like themselves were being hunted down like animals.

But, like the *fanatical** Nazis that they were, the former Gestapo and SS members pretended they were still in charge and dreamt of launching a Fourth Reich. Schmidt was getting restless to get back to the castle. The sun went down Thursday night, but there was still no *evidence*[†] that the Hales were going anywhere. All Schmidt had to *rely on*[‡] was Dr. Hale's claim on the telephone that he would be leaving town. "What if he was lying just to get rid of me?" Schmidt mumbled. Impatient as ever, Schmidt grumbled again and yelled at his two goons to make sure they were back on the hillside at *daylight*[§]—"Early! If Hale leaves, you cannot miss it—or else."

As the Swiss clock in Matt Hale's study struck mid-night, Visitor tapped on the garden door. When Matt Hale welcomed him in, Visitor made his entrance *toting*[¶] a heavy carrying case. He was looking somewhat weary this time because he had not been to bed since getting the emergency meeting call the night

---

*   Fanatical: Extremely devoted to a level most normal people would consider crazy.

†   Evidence: Proof or facts to show that something is true.

‡   Rely on: Depend on.

§   Daylight: When the sun comes over the horizon and the area begins to brighten enough for one to see.

¶   Toting: Carrying or hauling.

before. Since that time, he had been quite busy—the way intelligence officers *routinely** work. He not only had to get a hold of the correct explosive materials, but also *oversee*[†] creation of the *bogus*[‡] gold-lead bars.

And most importantly, he had received approval for this *deception operation*[§] that he and the Hales were putting together. At first, not everyone in the Intelligence Group *favored*[¶] the idea of letting the Nazis get away—much less do so with all the loot, fake or not. Some preferred setting a trap and arresting these monsters for murder. When Visitor pointed out that Dr. Hale's usefulness in intelligence operations would be all over—*kaput*[**]—if the Nazis were arrested at his castle home, approval was given to go ahead with the plan proposed by Visitor and Dr. Hale. The Group agreed to let the Nazis go—but stick them with worthless lead bars, the fake British notes and travel documents with a *fatal*[††] weakness.

Why fatal? Because David Hale was photographing each and every one of them. In fact, these travel documents would prove useful to American Intelligence in tracking Nazi war criminals—for years to come—everywhere in the world! 'The Nazi 100' would become *marked men*[‡‡]—they would be *leaving footprints,*[§§] so to speak, when they used the fake names and

---

*   Routinely: Usually, on a regular basis, constantly.
†   Oversee: Manage and direct.
‡   Bogus: Fake or unreal.
§   Deception operation: A plan to fool an enemy by trickery.
¶   Favored: Liked.
** Kaput: Finished, all over, hopelessly lost. From German 'kaputt'.
†† Fatal: Deadly.
‡‡ Marked men: Criminals well known to police around the world.
§§ Leaving their footprints: Like tracks in the snow, their travel documents would leave tracks that could be found and followed.

alias documents that Gestapo Chief Himmler had prepared for them. And such was the *genius** of the Hale plan that convinced the Intelligence Group to approve Matt Hale's plan of poisoning the well for almost 100 of the worst men on the planet—or at least those not already captured or dead.

Before Visitor left and took his usual path down to the river, Matt Hale told him he had come across something else in the lining of one of the trunks. He had found it only today. It was an old pre-war map of Austria from the 1930s. At first glance, it looked like any old country road map—but this one had some *discreet*† marks here and there that could mean something. He told Visitor he would photograph it after David finished copying the last of the travel documents. He added that he would have to reset the camera and lighting to copy the large map. The map itself would be going back into the trunk along with all the original Himmler materials—in case these *local*‡ Nazis were expecting it to be there.

Finally, Matt said to Visitor that he was pleased at how well the gold-plated bars had come out. He said also he would probably not have noticed the reduced weight of the new mostly-lead bars if he had not recently handled the all-gold bars.

Visitor replied, "Maybe, Matt, we should go into gold mining some day—when the *Russian Bear*§ has been caged. You know,

---

* Genius: Extremely smart, clever or intelligent.
† Discreet: Not too noticeable.
‡ Local: Near or close by; in this case, the three Nazis who have come sniffing around the castle.
§ Russian Bear: As the USA has the Bald Eagle as its national symbol, for Russia it has become the Brown Bear—although for much of the past century it was Russia's enemies who were using the Bear to show how big, slow to change, and brutal the Russians have been historically.

pure gold is indeed truly beautiful—like no other metal. Well, see you in Vienna on the weekend. Looks like we have a lot to do in that case too. *Gute nacht.*"*

David had earlier finished up the photocopying of all the Nazi top-100 documents and pictures as Visitor headed out into the night. His dad was half expecting David to be physically drained and suggested the boy go upstairs and get some sleep "while I get the trunks and North Tunnel back into their original condition. Also, I need to set off this small bomb to blow some *debris*† around—so it looks normal to the Nazis when they come back."

As soon as David heard the word 'bomb,' he was *jolted*‡ wide awake. He now had no desire to *hit the sack*§ for some sleep. "Really, Dad, a bomb? That is fantastic. Can't wait. I'm not tired—not a bit!"

Dr. Matt Hale admitted he could use some help. So, again he led the boy to the kitchen and said, "Let's have a snack and a hot drink. It will take a while to close things up in the tunnel so it looks perfectly fine to the strangers when they dig their way in from outside—as I am pretty sure they will do. Breaking in through the outside wall will be quicker and more *secure*⁹ for them—less risky than getting trapped inside the castle." For the next hour, father and son—senior spy and junior spy—hauled the mass of materials back to the basement. All the while, Thor

---

*   Gute nacht: Good night in German.
†   Debris: Wreckage, ruins, litter or waste left after a storm, shipwreck or, as in this case, a bombing.
‡   Jolted: Shocked, shaken or stunned.
§   Hit the sack: Go to bed.
⁹   Secure: Safe.

kept watch just outside the burial chamber where Matt Hale had told him to stay.

Once everything was *in position,*[*] Matt Hale restored the trunks and the burial chamber—with David's very active help. It turned out that the boy was pretty gifted when it came to recalling the contents of each trunk—how it all looked earlier in the week when Thor had 'struck gold' in the castle tunnel. As the last trunk was shut, David turned to his pal and said, "Well Thor, as soon as we get done, I'm giving you a big chunk of beef. After all, without your great nose and without your digging, I would have walked away from all this. Good dog. Good boy. You're the best."

Still on duty and on patrol, Thor kept his eyes on the two skeletons—*reacting*[†] not at all to anything David was saying. Matt Hale was there and, to Thor, the father was obviously in charge. Matt Hale then re-blocked the tunnel. Within an hour, the explosion took place. It had the power only of a couple of *hand grenades.*[‡] The blast was enough to scatter a fair amount of dirt, rocks and dust—too little to damage the trunks or re-open the tunnel. Visitor, it seems, had been a *demolition expert*[§] in the war and knew just how much of an explosion was needed for this small task.

David and Thor were not deep in the tunnel, and David begged to sit on the cellar stairs so he could hear the blast.

---

[*] In position: In the correct or proper place.
[†] Reacting: Responding or showing some emotion when spoken to by the boy.
[‡] Hand grenades: Small explosive devices the size of a baseball and used in wartime combat.
[§] Demolition expert: Men who blow up bridges and other structures.

When he heard it explode, David chuckled—all he could say was "Holy smoke, Batman!"

Matt Hale waited a while to let the dust settle before he went back to see how things looked. He wore *surgical** glasses and a mask and carried David's two flashlights to be sure he could find his way back to the stairs in case one of the bulbs went out. After they *emerged*† from the cellar, Matt Hale said, "Let's get some sleep. The sun will be up in two hours and we have to pack. We're off to Vienna for a long, busy weekend. Well done, David, both you and Thor."

When the bomb went off, the North Tunnel rat population was stunned for the second time in two years. They again put several hundred feet between themselves and the explosion—between themselves and the bones of the Nazis who had fed them so well—once upon a time near the end of the war.

---

*   Surgical: The kind used by surgeons in a hospital when they are performing a medical operation.
†   Emerged: Came up from or out of.

14

Nazis Heading West

The Date: June 20, 1947—Friday.

The Hales packed the car in the morning for the drive into Vienna. Thor was going, too. David said to his dad that he was *itching** to sneak up to the parapet instead and keep an eye on things. "Too bad we can't see what happens," he added. "I wonder, Dad, if they will blow a big hole in the North Wall."

Matt Hale smiled at the boy and said, "I doubt they will explode anything. They probably just want to *retrieve*[†] their stuff and make a clean *getaway*.[‡] But you're really thinking, Son. Anyway, things are under control—Visitor's team is taking care of that with some *long-distance*[§] surveillance and photography. We will know who comes here, what car or cars they are driving, and when they have left Vienna. The three Hales including Thor, however, need to make a highly visible *departure*[¶] that shows the Nazis that the castle is absolutely empty—so they can make their break-in. So, let's get going."

As Matt Hale drove away from the castle, he kept his eyes on

---

* Itching: Anxious or badly wanting.
† Retrieve: Get back or recover.
‡ Getaway: An escape by criminals who want to avoid being captured by the police.
§ Long-distance: From quite far away, in this case a few hundred yards or maybe as much as a mile.
¶ Departure: Exiting or leaving.

the road and made sure he and David avoided looking up into the hills where the Nazi's *O.P.** was located. The father knew the goons were in position to see him drive off in the direction of downtown Vienna. He wanted to leave the strangers feeling *smug*[†] and believing quite wrongly that they were in command of things. In fact, these leftover Nazis were *being played*[‡] and that gave Matt Hale some partial satisfaction.

Why only partial? Well, he too would like to have seen them captured breaking into the castle where the two murdered German soldiers lay buried inside the tunnel. This would have gotten them long prison sentences which they certainly deserved. But, arresting them would also bring public attention to Matt Hale, to his family, and to the castle—all that would serve no good purpose. Operating in the shadows—in the secret world of spies—was where he preferred to be as well as precisely where U.S. Intelligence officials in Vienna wanted him to remain. For it was there in clandestine operations that he could cause greater damage to old enemies—the Nazis—and to new enemies—the Russians. For *the time being*,[§] therefore, he would have to *settle for*[¶] giving this group of Nazi thugs false confidence that things were breaking their way.

And that was exactly how Schmidt later reacted when he received the team report that the castle was empty and that Dr. Hale and son had left. He was especially relieved to learn

---

*   O.P. : Observation Post. Any high point or hidden spot that is used to watch the enemy.

†   Smug: A feeling of too much or exaggerated confidence.

‡   Being played: When a person is being made the fool by those who are acting smarter.

§   The time being: For now or meanwhile; presently.

¶   Settle for: Accept and be satisfied with.

that the dog was gone, too. "Something about that animal really bothers me—didn't like him from the moment I first saw him."

Thor, for his part, had shown in their meeting at the castle gate how he felt about Schmidt. To the Hale's Patrol Dog, this Nazi was just like the enemy soldiers his handler Mike and he had fought and defeated on the battlefields of France and then Germany itself. Thor also had been shot by one of them. So, one might say, the bad feelings were *mutual** between Schmidt the German Nazi and Thor the German Shepherd. And, as is said about elephants, dogs too never forget—something Schmidt one day would find out.

David, meanwhile, had gone along with all of Dad's rules of the game this Friday morning. As much as he was itching to, he never once looked up into the hills where his father said the goons were hiding. He had also resisted the temptation to sneak up into the parapet and use his spyglasses to watch the Nazi watchers. Instead, he would follow Dad's orders and depart the castle without probably ever knowing how things turned out. It was the same, he thought, as reading through a Jack London adventure—*White Fang* for example—only to find deep into the story that someone had ripped the last chapter out of the book.

A slight breeze from the northwest drifted down the hillside to the road below. It carried the scent of the two former Nazi SS soldiers. As the Hale car slowly made its way along the curved bumpy road, Thor was in his favorite position—his head hanging out the rear window while he sniffed and pulled aromas in his usual canine way. Then, abruptly, he *converted†* from family

---

*   Mutual: The same for each of them.
†   Converted: Changed in an important way.

pet to the *stellar** Patrol Dog whose skills had taken him all the way from the beaches of Normandy in the great war. Thor came to attention and let out a low growl—he had picked up and recognized the familiar—but unpleasant—*whiff*[†] of nearby enemy troops. Knowing that Thor had picked up on the presence of *hostile*[‡] strangers, Matt Hale reached over to the back and stroked Thor's head, saying, "Okay, old boy, you can relax. This situation is under control."

When the goons saw the Hales leave, they returned to the hideaway where Schmidt was anxiously waiting. He was ready to get on with the dig. He had his goons load up the trunk of the Mercedes with the following: two shovels, two pickaxes, two sledge hammers, two sets of work gloves, and two wheelbarrows as well as paraffin lanterns. The two sets of this and that were for the goons—Schmidt had no intention of getting his hands dirty doing either the digging or the heavy lifting. After all, in his own mind he still was a senior Nazi SS Officer—war or no war—1943 or 1947!

As he drove up the road that led to the castle, Schmidt pulled into the field where Herr Vogel usually kept his cows. Driving deep into the *lush*[§] meadow, the Nazi came upon the small trail that would take them around to the north side of the castle. Arriving at the castle north wall, the goons unloaded the tools and began to dig. They could not be seen from the front road—they began working away believing wrongly that they could not be seen at all.

---

*   Stellar: Better than any other; a star animal; the best.
†   Whiff: A slight smell.
‡   Hostile: Enemy.
§   Lush: Rich and with a growth of new Spring grass.

Off in the distance, in fact, they were under *constant** surveillance as they had been from the moment they reached the
castle. Visitor had arranged with the U.S. Army to send two
special operations soldiers outfitted in *camouflage*† gear that
blended in with the *shrubbery*.‡ The two American soldiers were
posted on a hilltop off to the northeast of the castle. As the
Nazi digging got underway, so did the US Army photography.

It was mid-morning when the digging got started. By noon,
they had made excellent progress. By mid-afternoon, they broke
through the outer stone wall to the inner chamber holding
two skeletons and the three-trunk treasure trove—the cache
that once held the prospect of getting these Nazis away from
Europe. They were eager to get away to a new part of the world
so they might start their evil Nazi business all over again. Junior
spy Hale, of course, took all those document photographs to
make the Nazis' prospects less promising and less likely to
succeed.

Once the wall was *breached*,§ removing the trunks from the
tunnel took less time than Schmidt expected. By five o'clock
they were putting the dirt and stone back in place. All three
trunks were now in the back of the Mercedes. Because Schmidt
was too *arrogant*¶ to lift the trunks himself, he was never in a
position to detect whether the trunk with the fake 'gold bars'
felt heavy enough to be 'the real thing.' Within a few days he

---

* Constant: Steady or non-stop.
† Camouflage: Designs and markings on cloths, equipment and even
buildings that makes a person or thing seem to not be there because
the designs mix in with the trees and background.
‡ Shrubbery: Bushes, small trees and plant life.
§ Breached: Broken through.
¶ Arrogant: Self-important; full of himself.

would wish he had not merely lifted that particular trunk but examined the 'gold bars' thoroughly.

Schmidt was feeling pretty good about things—humming a favorite SS marching song, in fact, as he drove away from 'his' wartime castle. He felt he had everything a runaway Nazi SS Officer and war criminal could dream of or hope for—a *documented** false identity and a Swiss passport to take him far away from Austria—far away from the hangman's noose. He now had plenty of money and 'gold' as well as a trunk filled with travel documents for former SS and Gestapo brutes who hoped to form the *nucleus†* of a Fourth Reich down in South America. All he had to do was get away from Vienna and follow the path to famously-*corrupt‡* Marseille—a French *port city§* barely seven hundred miles to the west of the Austrian capital. Schmidt could drive there in two days, three at the most.

The plan was then to get into Italy—that would not be difficult. All he would need to do was pay a *modest¶ bribe*** at the Italian border—by paying a bribe he would be warmly received by the *crooked††* border guard—"*Benvenuto en Italia.*"‡‡ He would cross into Italy at night when there was little traffic and less likelihood he would be spotted by anyone who knew

---

* Documented: With birth certificates and official papers that support a person's identification.
† Nucleus: In science it is the center of the atom; in this case, it means the center or heart of the new Nazi movement.
‡ Corrupt: Controlled by criminals.
§ Port city: A city from which ships travel to and from other cities around the world.
¶ Modest: Not too large and not too small.
** Bribe: A payment in money to get a person to let you do something dishonest or illegal.
†† Crooked: Dishonest.
‡‡ Benvenuto en Italia: "Welcome to Italy."

him or either of his two goons. They all would then drive down to the port city of Livorno and board an ocean *freighter** for Argentina. *Scores*† of wanted Nazi war criminals had gone there secretly since the war. Schmidt had also heard that the U.S. Military had recently closed its own Army base in Livorno which made him feel safer. Rather than a large city such as Marseille or even Rome, he had decided to leave Europe by boat from a small Italian port—he would be less likely to be caught there by American Nazi hunters who were a danger to war criminals like himself. Once he got into South America, he knew he would be protected.

---

*   Freighter: An ocean-going ship that delivers goods all around the
    world and has a few passengers only.
†   Scores: Many (literally groups of twenty), in this case hundreds.

15

Stopover in Salzburg—
Misery in Marseille

The Date: June 21–22, 1947

First, however, Schmidt had to take care of a few things. On the way westward towards Marseille, he would make a brief *stopover*.* He had arranged to meet with a *Neo-Nazi*† leader in the Salzburg area, a little less than 200 miles west of Vienna. Schmidt was anxious to *unload*‡ the trunk stuffed with travel documents for the 'Nazi 100.' He also would pass along most of the counterfeit British Five Pound Notes. It was not that he was feeling generous. With the castle now occupied by an American, he had no immediate safe place to hide anything so bulky. He and his two goons could carry only so much *booty*§ with them on their trip out of Europe.

He was hopeful that the Neo-Nazis in Salzburg, in exchange for the fake money and 'Nazi 100' travel documents, would do something for him—maybe put him in contact with Marseille criminals with whom he could deal safely and who'd be willing

---

* Stopover: Staying for a day or so in a place during a longer journey.
† Neo-Nazi: After the war, some wartime Nazis tried to create a secret Nazi movement and were called Neo-Nazis, or "New Nazis," although they were the same group of murderers who had just lost the war.
‡ Unload: Get rid of; pass on or transfer to.
§ Booty: Treasure.

to exchange *authentic** British money for the 'gold bars.' For Schmidt did not want to get stuck with 'Operation Bernard' bills or any other fake stuff. He was far too cautious for that.

At this point, Schmidt still believed his 'gold bars' were genuine. After all, the trunk with the four 'gold bars' though mainly lead—was pretty heavy. The bars had the Nazi Eagle stamped on them, and the entire shipment had been sent to him by SS Chief Heinrich Himmler himself. And, if he could not trust his dead Nazi cousin, who could Schmidt ever trust? So, he felt no urge to weigh or examine the bars carefully. The meeting with the Neo-Nazi leader in Salzburg went smoothly. It took place at the same spa where Schmidt was supposed to meet up with cousin Himmler two years earlier. That was when the Nazi empire was in collapse and the Fuehrer committed suicide in Berlin while the Russian Army closed in on his *bunker.*† The spa was owned and run by an old Nazi couple who were providing support to former war criminals on the run.

A *model*‡ of German *efficiency,*§ the Salzburg area Neo-Nazi leader—who called himself 'Karl' only—got immediately down to business. He was pleased to get hold of the fake British bank notes. What he really wanted and most gladly received, however, were the passports and travel documents for the 'Nazi 100.' Some of the top Nazi war criminals had been killed and others had been captured by the Allies and sentenced to death or prison. The least fortunate Nazis had been captured by

---

*   Authentic: Real, legitimate, not counterfeit.
†   Bunker: An underground hiding place that was strongly built.
‡   Model: Example.
§   Efficiency: Getting things done quickly and well; doing tasks effectively.

the Russians and executed immediately. It was done the usual Russian way—brutally, and with neither trials nor *witnesses*.* More than half of the fake travel documents were for escaped Nazis still hiding in Germany or Austria itself. Now, in control of these *precious*[†] papers, Karl's personal power within the Austria-Germany Neo-Nazi community was sure to increase. He was certain of that, for he knew that he alone now possessed the special ability to get leading Nazis safely away from Europe altogether.

The document review process took only an hour. They sat in a quiet, shady section of the garden enjoying a delicious Austrian meal that the proud Nazi innkeeper's wife had prepared for her 'important guests.' To an *uninformed*[‡] observer watching from afar, they would have appeared to be a fine Austrian family and friends enjoying a simple social visit in the countryside. The difference between such a *serene*[§] but false image and the violent monsters seated at that table could not have been greater. All had innocent blood on their hands and hatred in their hearts—wartime victims of this group numbered in the thousands.

When 'Karl' had finished his meal, he wrote out instructions and drew a map showing SS Col. Schmidt how and where to contact the Marseille criminals—most of them wartime Nazis now in the business of illegal drug trafficking. Drug dealing was a cash business, so it was expected that they would have

---

* Witnesses: Outsiders who knew of the killings.
† Precious: Valuable.
‡ Uninformed: Someone who did not know who these people really were.
§ Serene: Peaceful, quiet, friendly, harmless.

money *on hand** to exchange genuine British bank notes for 'gold.' They would not pay as high of an *exchange rate*† as a bank normally would pay—neither would they report Schmidt to the Allied officials who were always interested in catching former Nazi war criminals.

This was the safety Schmidt was seeking and would have gotten if the 'gold bars' had in fact been genuine. Criminal life, however, is quite often a dangerous road with many turns and unexpected changes of direction. As it turned out, Schmidt and his two goons drove after the lunch on to Marseille and contacted the criminals that 'Karl' had recommended. Everything seemed to be *on track*‡ and Schmidt was sure he would succeed in his escape.

The actual exchange for British money was set to occur alongside an old seaside lighthouse, not far from downtown Marseille. Being his usual cautious self, Schmidt ordered his goons to make the 'gold' delivery—he observed it all from a safe distant shore peering through his sniper scope. Schmidt kept his distance mainly because he did not want any of the criminals to be able to describe or identify him to the police later on.

He watched anxiously as his goons drove up to the lighthouse where a small truck and motorcycle were parked alongside. He watched as the waiting criminals removed the trunk from the back of Schmidt's car. This he expected. But, their next moves left him stunned. They quickly carried the

---

*   On hand: Available.

†   Exchange rate: The number of dollars or British pounds that one gets for another country's money.

‡   On track: Going according to plan.

trunk over to their own truck—a meat cutter's *scale** had been set up in the back. They then appeared to Schmidt to be weighing each of the four 'gold' bars. This got Schmidt's full attention—but did not concern him. After all, it occurred to him that this was a reasonable thing for them to do before paying for the 'gold' with real British money. Schmidt was still very much relaxed.

The next thing Schmidt witnessed, though, gave him an incredible surprise he was unprepared for and could hardly believe. His two goons were knocked to the ground by the thugs from Marseille. Each of Schmidt's men was then thrown into the back of the truck. He could see a hood being tied over the head of each man. Just as abruptly, the truck pulled away from the lighthouse and raced away from the harbor at full speed. All the *commotion*† took place in less than a minute—more like forty-five seconds—enough time for Schmidt's jaw to drop open—not long enough for him to even let out a sound.

Schmidt's first thought was not for the safety of his goons— instead, he was alarmed that he may have just lost 'his gold.' Fearful he too might be in danger, he immediately drove away by motorcycle and headed back to his small rented room. He needed to get hold of his travel documents and suitcase. *Momentarily,*‡ his thinking became *jumbled§*—he was alone—he was in shock. He frankly did not know what to do next. All through the war years, he and his castle goons had terrorized others. Now, in Marseille and with his goons gone, it was

---

* Scale: A machine used to weigh things.
† Commotion: Upset and violence.
‡ Momentarily: Briefly, for a short period of time.
§ Jumbled: All mixed up.

Schmidt who was terrified. He had also just lost his car—his favorite possession from the Third Reich!

Back in Vienna the following morning, American Embassy officials received a report that the bodies of two unidentified foreigners had washed ashore early that morning near Marseille. What made the news report so unusual—and *intriguing**—was that each drowning victim had a large melted chunk of lead in his mouth and throat. The police assumed they were Germans—each had the *Nazi SS Tattoo†* showing *blood type‡* on his left arm. Rumors soon spread around criminal circles in Marseille that they had tried to sell lead-filled bars as though

---

*   Intriguing: Mysterious and unusual.

†   Nazi SS Tattoo: The 'Blutgruppentatowierung' was used in the German Nazi SS to show a soldier's blood type in case he was wounded in war and needed to be given a blood transfusion.

‡   Blood type: The particular kind of blood each person has—whether "A", "B", "AB", or "O".

they were solid gold. No one knew then, or would ever know, who they were. The castle goons had met the same *fate** as did tens of thousands of innocent Europeans whom the Nazis had made disappear in the war.

There was no mention in the news reports of a third person—it was the Embassy Intelligence Group's conclusion that Schmidt had probably escaped. If not, his body also would have been found. The Embassy felt they would *eventually*[†] know whether he had left for South America or remained in Europe. After all, the group was holding photos and passport numbers of all the travel documents David had photographed in the wee hours of the night—including Schmidt's.

Back in Marseille, it was Schmidt's turn to begin *analyzing*[‡] what happened—and why. He tried to contact 'Karl' in Salzburg by phone. The response he got was that 'Karl' was not available. 'Karl' had heard there was a problem with the "delivery" and now in fact, he too was being accused of trying to *pull a fast one*[§] on the Marseille gangsters. So, Neo-Nazi leader 'Karl' went into hiding and left a message for Schmidt not to contact him again any time soon.

Schmidt *re-read*[¶] the newspaper police report on the two drownings and rumors about 'fake gold.' This got Schmidt wondering—had Schmidt's own cousin shipped fake gold bars along with counterfeit British Bank Notes and false identity

---

*   Fate: Outcome, ending or result.
†   Eventually: Not right away but over the course of weeks or months.
‡   Analyzing: Thinking carefully and step by step about what may have happened with the Marseille gang.
§   Pull a fast one: Try to trick or fool someone with a clever move or deception.
¶   Re-read: Read over and over.

papers? If so, why hadn't SS Chief Himmler warned him in his 'most secret' message? And, if it was not Himmler, then who had done this to him? The Americans? Dr. Matt Hale?

Schmidt at this point was screaming in his hotel room like a *mad-man**—as he often had done in the war when things went badly. This time, however, there were no goons around to say "Jawohl, Colonel, Jawohl." The unlucky goons were gone.

Meanwhile, Visitor called for an emergency *safe-house*† meeting with Dr. Hale in downtown Vienna to tell him what was known about the drownings in Marseille. Matt Hale knew Schmidt might present a problem, but the doctor-spy was at the moment focused on pulling off an intelligence operation right under the noses of the Russian Secret Police. He had some casing to complete and little time to think—much less worry—about Schmidt or whether they would meet again. If he were to reappear, Matt Hale would deal with it. Like a solid chess master—in fact like a good spy. Matt Hale was always prepared to face unexpected things. He was quite *content*‡ to let the future work itself out. David, by contrast, had difficulty accepting the fact that—unlike the adventures he had read about in books—all things are not immediately knowable in the world of spies.

David was only beginning to see that occasionally spies quickly learn how matters work out—sometimes it takes a while—sometimes they never know. That is the *nature*§ of the spy world where secrecy and the unexpected play a larger role

---

*   Mad-man: An insane or crazy person.
†   Safe-house: A secret hideout where spies can meet without being seen or heard.
‡   Content: Happy or satisfied.
§   Nature: The way it is; how it really works.

than in most other fields or professions. It is, in fact, a major difference between *fiction** and *non-fiction,*† the make-believe and the real.

The boy looked over at Thor and whispered, "I have to become more like you, Old Boy. You don't seem to *fret*‡ about yesterday things—I doubt you worry much about tomorrow. Heck, in some ways, you're more like Dad than I am. Imagine that, and I'm his son!"

The senior spy returned to the room and told David they were heading back to the castle for a few days. He said the Austrian *authorities*§ and the Russians were *postponing*⁅ the conference a week as they argued about who was going to pay for and provide the food needed to run the event for five full days. The Russians had been continuing to remove great quantities of *produce*** from the local farms in their sector to feed the Red Army occupying most of Eastern Europe. Regardless of the change of schedule, Matt Hale by now knew where the Polish delegation would be staying. So, he would be ready to track down and *isolate*†† Gorski to set him up for recruitment while the Polish officer was in Vienna. Now, the doctor spy could turn his attention back to the Nazi on the run, SS Col Schmidt and his family's security back at the castle.

---

*   Fiction: Make believe stories or tales.

†   Non-fiction: Real life stories or events.

‡   Fret: Be sorrowful or regretful.

§   Authorities: The Austrians who were in charge of running the country.

⁅   Postponing: Making people delay or wait because things are not ready.

**   Produce: Things grown on farms—vegetables, fruit, eggs and chickens, for example.

†† Isolate: Get Major Gorski alone so Visitor could speak with him privately without the Russians knowing.

16

Schmidt Chooses Revenge

The Date: June 23, 1947

As young David Hale—eleven going on twelve—sat high in the branches of the tall tree at the rear of the castle, he was feeling both content and *antsy*.* He was certainly happy that the Nazi plan to escape with all the loot had gone badly for them. But, he was not satisfied he had heard the end of it all. "Two down; one more to go" was how he put it in baseball terms to Thor, resting way down on the ground below. "Yeah, I am pitching in Yankee Stadium and have just struck out the first two batters— ninth inning—American League 1947 Pennant on the line. But I still have to face 'Jolting Joe' DiMaggio. Now everything is *at stake*.† So I ask my catcher, 'Thor, do I throw him fast balls or curves? Inside or out? High or low?'" Well this time 'coach' Thor was no help at all—he was too busy scratching himself.

David, of course, was trying to figure things out here in Vienna if the tall German returned—not what to do in an imaginary game on the baseball diamond back in New York. What the young spy was doing was thinking ahead and preparing himself in case Schmidt actually returned. David looked long and hard at Thor, finally smiled and said, "Heck, Thor, I

---

*   Antsy: A little worried or concerned.
†   At stake: On the line and at risk.

have my answer—you are my *ace in the hole** and with you at my side, I have a special partner and ally. I feel better already."

The day had gotten started early. Dr. Hale had to drive north a hundred miles to the refugee hospital in Linz and spend the entire day there. The late-night call he had received concerned another outbreak of cholera as well as typhus—both probably caused by a new wave of displaced persons arriving from nearby Czechoslovakia. Before leaving the castle gate this morning, the senior spy had spoken with both Konrad and Katrina Vogel to be on the lookout for Schmidt. He gave them a *summary†* of the events in Marseille and that two of the recent castle visitors had been drowned; the third was probably very much alive and quite dangerous. The Vogels said they would be ready if he indeed showed up at the gate with any more fake stories about old friends and such. Both Vogels, husband and wife—with their wartime secret service in the Underground Army—were quite experienced with guns and dealing with Nazis. They assured Dr. Hale that they would be ready and keep David safe as if he were their own son.

SS Col. Schmidt, *unemployed‡* since Germany lost the war, had just arrived back in Vienna from Marseille. This was the first time in a *decade§* that he was operating entirely alone now that his two goons were not only unemployed, but dead. So, there was no one to ask Schmidt why he had not just boarded the boat leaving Livorno, Italy for South America within a

---

* Ace in the hole: An extra card in a game of poker and in this case an extra ally or partner.
† Summary: A brief explanation.
‡ Unemployed: Out of work.
§ Decade: Ten year period.

week. He still had his Swiss passport, enough money and his ticket for the voyage. He likely would reach Argentina before British or American authorities learn he had left Europe. Once away from the Nazi-hunters around Europe, war criminals had hundreds of places in the Andes Mountain range to hide as Nazis had been doing since 1944. Schmidt had heard very good things about Chile and Peru—he liked the mountains.

As he sat on his motorcycle-with-sidecar and, looking up at the castle from a distance, he finally asked himself the same question. "Hey, Schmidt, why not just drive away, head back to Italy and get on the ship? Our SS network in South America is strong and will help you while building the foundation for our new 'Fourth Reich.' The new Reich will be *enormously** advanced in super weapons this time. The Americans are not the only ones who can design atomic bombs and we Germans are very far ahead in missiles."

But, Schmidt found none of these good enough reasons for him to leave Austria immediately. He now realized it was personal *revenge*[†] he wanted most of all. He ached inside to strike back at the Americans—especially at Dr. Hale who had left him hanging on to a silent or dead telephone a couple of weeks earlier. Even his goons had *smirked*[‡] as he stood there burning in anger. "It has to be Hale," he grumbled. "He stole my gold—he stuck me with the lead-filled junk. And, he is going to pay for this. Yes, I will shoot the boy and dog first—then Dr. Hale. Revenge is funny—just thinking about it feels good."

---

*   Enormously: Greatly.
†   Revenge: Getting even with an enemy by doing something bad to them.
‡   Smirked: Smiling when trying not to.

He moved in nearer to the castle, to the same hill and spot his goons had used days before. It was almost dusk and the old Nazi decided to enter the castle and get both his revenge and his gold by midnight. He would sail, after all, to South America a rich not a poor Nazi, a happy not a miserable one. Though he did not personally miss his goons, he did miss having soldiers to boss around and who could do any heavy lifting.

By nine o'clock that evening, Schmidt was already up behind the castle on the north side, which brought him in close to the tower. He had a flashlight and his Luger in case they were needed. For former SS Colonel Schmidt, this was indeed a military operation. He even wore his old *combat boots** and the *Nazi Iron Cross*† his cousin awarded him for stealing so much Austrian artwork. In Schmidt's mind, the evening would end with either him or Hale victorious. He was not interested in doing this half way or any other way. "Kill or be killed."

The *aging*‡ Nazi did not look like any *historic*§ German warrior. He was breathing heavily after crawling and climbing through so much underbrush on the castle hillside. Two years of sitting around drinking beer and eating rich Bavarian food since the war had turned him into an overweight, *inflated*⁋ copy of himself. He had barely been able to squeeze into his combat gear. Schmidt looked as though he was wearing another man's uniform. He felt that way, too. All the same, his heart was as

---

*   Combat boots: Heavy footwear worn by soldiers fighting out in fields and streams.

†   Nazi Iron Cross: A German medal given to soldiers for bravery in battle.

‡   Aging: Getting older for a soldier.

§   Historic: Famous from history.

⁋   Inflated: Swollen and looking like he was filled with air.

fiery as ever—despite the extra fifty pounds of weight, he had fourteen years of Nazi hate running through his veins.

Yes, from the day in 1933 when Adolf Hitler became Chancellor and leader of Germany, Schmidt awoke each day and fell asleep each night with one thing in mind—conquer our enemies so that Germany alone would rule the world. "Yes," he thought, "with superweapons and hideouts in the mountains of South America, we Nazis could destroy America-England-Russia. Yes, we can still win the war and have our final victory."

Right now, of course, he had a job to do—recover the gold! Even that much gold would not be enough, but Schmidt also had the secret map his cousin had hidden in the lining of the last trunk. It was a map of Austria with marks showing in which salt mines the SS had hidden the artworks and jewelry Himmler had *assembled** through the Vienna Castle group. Himmler's stolen art was as good and valuable as Hitler's and Goering's stolen collections *combined.†* Schmidt and his men began hiding it on June 7, 1944—a day after the Allies landed on the beaches in Normandy, France.

Under Himmler's orders, while the entire Nazi Army fought for ten long months to defend Germany from the invading Allies—Americans, British, Polish, Canadians and French attacking from the West—the Russian Red Army attacking from the East—Himmler's Gestapo was busy hiding stolen art treasure for their own survival after the war. Much of the stolen art had—like the castle itself—been taken from murdered Jews.

---

* Assembled: Gathered or pulled together after stealing them from innocent people and museums.
† Combined: All together.

Back to the job at hand, Schmidt came alongside the small door leading to the castle kitchen and backstairs. He reached down to a bush to the right of the door and picked up a rock the size of a large potato. Turning it over, he was glad to see in the hollowed-out rock the brass key he had placed there two years earlier. It was still encased in *putty** and as good as new—once he scraped away the dried-out putty. He inserted the key in the old back door. The lock turned freely.

Schmidt chuckled thinking that the careless American Dr. Hale had not yet changed every lock in the castle—especially the lock on this old kitchen door. Well, Hale indeed had found that key—he left it there to be sure he and David would know which door the German would use if he tried to get back inside. As far as Hale's emergency *evacuation*[†] plan was *designed*,[‡] SS Col. Schmidt was coming in the correct way. David could, therefore, use a different way out—through the third floor window and roof leading out to the Parapet. The senior Hale knew from experience that David and Thor often departed that way when in a great hurry or if the boy did not want to be seen on the castle stairs.

Konrad Vogel was told about this plan and was prepared to see that, if the uninvited German got inside the castle again, it would be the last time—the only time. For Matt Hale and the Vogels, this was a leftover chapter in the Second World War and Schmidt was just another leftover Nazi killer and war criminal.

---

*   Putty: Soft wet material like clay used in building homes and putting glass in windows.

†   Evacuation: An escape path for leaving a building or place to avoid danger.

‡   Designed: Built in a careful, detailed way.

David, meanwhile, was as wide awake as Schmidt. His dad had telephoned on the drive back from Linz to say he would be late getting home. There had been a traffic accident a few miles south of Linz and, as the only doctor driving that way, he stopped to help those hurt in the crash. Fortunately, it was in the American and not the Russian Sector so a U.S. Army ambulance was on its way. But, Dr. Hale knew, he would not arrive back in Vienna till after mid-night. He reminded David to stay alert and follow the plan if anything unusual took place. The boy assured his dad he would.

Schmidt was sneaking awkwardly around the kitchen area and back stairs. He had spent little time in that part of the castle during the war. He once was, after all, Commander of that SS Unit—not one of the foot soldiers like his goons. Having concluded that there were no Hales on the ground floor, Schmidt started climbing the back stairs, on his way to the second floor.

When the German's heavy boot pressed down on the creaky third stair, David knew what was going on—what he had to do. He dropped out of bed and *scooted** over to Thor and whispered, "Old Boy, time to go—up and out." The two very *practiced†* night-time wanderers glided into the front hall and started silently up the staircase leading to the third floor and window out to the roof and Parapet beyond. The original *expectation‡* was that the doctor-spy would be home and inside the castle if Schmidt made his visit—in that case Senior Spy Matt Hale would be there to greet and deal with him. But,

---

*   Scooted: Moved quickly.
†   Practiced: Trained after having done it many times before.
‡   Expectation: What they believed would happen.

with the doctor stuck on the road back from Linz, the *back-up plan** was that Konrad Vogel would go into action—do what had to be done.

Schmidt meanwhile was ascending the back stairs ever so slowly—his feet hurt, he was not used to the dark, his over-stuffed belly meant he could barely fit on the narrow staircase designed centuries earlier for smaller, *leaner†* people. By the time Schmidt reached David's bedroom, the boy and Patrol Dog were already out the third floor window onto the roof. They quickly but carefully made their way over to the Parapet where David crouched down low behind the tower wall. He then removed from his carrying sack the Army flashlight and old army sock to signal Konrad Vogel.

The old Austrian freedom fighter was in position on an *elevated‡* hunting stand that gave him a clear moonlit view of the parapet as well as the entire south side of the castle—including the hallway window next to David's room. He spotted David's signal. Vogel had gone there earlier in the evening when Dr. Hale called to say he would be late. Vogel was holding his freshly-cleaned *Mauser K98§* which was one of the best infantry rifles of the war and a real favorite of the German Army—especially its *snipers.¶*

At precisely ten o'clock the Nazi made his move. He climbed

---

*   Back-up Plan: What would be done if the situation changed.
†   Leaner: Thinner.
‡   Elevated: Several feet off the ground; up in the air.
§   Mauser K98: A bolt-action rifle adopted in 1935 as the standard service rifle by the Germans. It remained their primary service rifle until the end of the war in 1945.
¶   Snipers: Soldiers who are extremely good at shooting enemy from long distances.

the stairs up to the third floor. He saw the open window leading out onto the roof. Just as Matt Hale had expected and planned for, Schmidt began climbing out onto the roof, hoping to catch the boy and dog in the parapet. He had figured out by then that Dr. Hale was not there. So he decided he would get his revenge on the American doctor by shooting the boy and his dog. He took his Luger in his right hand as he climbed out the window. Maybe, he thought, he would shoot his victims and get out of there so he could catch that ship heading for South America. After all, he would have gotten his revenge—but right now he was more than a little afraid.

Suddenly, things went quite badly for Schmidt—he lost his grip on the window sill and went *cascading** down and off the roof like a walrus falling off an iceberg. The Luger flew through the air. To the old Nazi, it seemed that his *plunge*† through the bright Vienna night sky lasted forever—a lifetime, really. But, later on, the laws of *physics*‡ told David that, at thirty-two feet per second, the fall itself lasted maybe three, no more than four seconds, before Schmidt crashed hard on the rocks below. This Nazi who had terrorized others in the war screamed all the way down—louder than any of his many wartime Austrian victims.

What would have happened if he had not fallen to his death? Konrad Vogel, in keeping with the plan, was a couple of seconds away from firing off a *round*§ from his Mauser K98. He had

---

* Cascading: Tumbling out of control.
† Plunge: An awkward fall through the air or into deep water.
‡ Physics: The science and laws of motion, heat, light and forces that control the planets and the universe.
§ Round: A bullet or shot from a rifle or pistol.

Schmidt in his sights—Konrad was ready to *pull the trigger** as he had done in combat against the Nazis many times in the war. Now, with Schmidt as dead as the two goons found floating in Marseille, Vogel had only to clean up the Schmidt mess, put him on a raft, and float him *downstream*† to the Danube River that would take him on to the Black Sea, hundreds of miles to the south.

Before pushing Schmidt away from shore, Vogel unclipped the Iron Cross and SS stripe from the Nazi's uniform, placed them in Schmidt's mouth, and sent him on his way. Anyone finding the body would thereby know what they had found— one of the German monsters who had cost the Austrians 250,000 soldiers and over 100,000 *civilians*‡ killed in WWII.

Schmidt, of course, never would get to Argentina, the Andes Mountains of South America, or to any more pleasant meals with Neo-Nazis around Salzburg. Nor would he be able to support the Fourth Reich *fantasy*§ that he and other German war criminals thought they could build. In many ways, the leftover Nazis were quite like the rats *scurrying*⁅ around the dark cellar tunnels of the Vienna castle. They were not going to recover. They were going nowhere. The very good *outcome*** was that David Hale was safe, castle Security and Cover had been *maintained*†† and Austria was rid of another Nazi who brought only pain and death to this beautiful nation.

---

*   Pull the Trigger: Fire the rifle and shoot a bullet.
†   Downstream: The direction toward which a river or stream flows. Opposite of upstream.
‡   Civilians: People not serving in the military.
§   Fantasy: A foolish or not realistic dream or wish.
⁅   Scurrying: Running without any clear goal.
**   Outcome: Result or what happened.
††   Maintained: Kept or protected.

By the time Dr. Hale arrived back to the castle it was shortly after midnight and everything was *tranquil** as it was when he had left for Linz twenty hours earlier. He was surprised at this late hour to see so many lights were still on and to find David chatting with Konrad Vogel down at the castle gate. Thor was there as well. It didn't take long for Vogel to fill in the doctor on how things had developed that evening—Schmidt was *no more*[†] and that was what interested Matt Hale the most. The trap set for Nazi Colonel Schmidt did not *unfold*[‡] exactly as he had expected it would. Schmidt, after all, had fallen to his death. But, as far as Hale was concerned, and as Shakespeare wrote, *"All's well that ends well."*[§] With Schmidt floating miles away from the Vienna castle, the Hales were no longer in danger.

David and Thor finally climbed the stairs back up to bed. David looked over at Thor and said, "Well, old pal, that was Strike Three!" Yes, the last Nazi was now dead. Before dozing off, the boy tried to decide which adventure made him feel better—getting the Polish scientist to freedom in the West, or blocking the escape to South America by Nazis with the documents, money and gold? When he couldn't *reach a conclusion,*[¶] David Hale just drifted off into a deep and peaceful night's sleep. More adventure lay just ahead. Next time, again, it would be against the Russians.

---

*   Tranquil: Peaceful and quiet.
†   No More: Dead.
‡   Unfold: Happen.
§   All's Well That Ends Well: A play written by English writer and poet William Shakespeare. It means that what really matters is how things finish up, the final result.
¶   Reach a conclusion: Decide or come up with an answer that made sense to him.

The Vienna Trilogy

BOOK THREE

Stopping the Russian Bear

Contents

Prologue

As junior spy David Hale became actively involved in the Cold War in 1947, he had no way of knowing just how pivotal Austria—and especially its capital city, Vienna—was becoming in the upcoming struggle between East and West. To the east of Austria, everything in Europe had already fallen under the brutal Russian Communist control of the Red Army and the Soviet Secret Police. To Austria's west, every European nation was struggling to retain its freedom and independence.

Out in faraway Asia, the Chinese Communist Army—with Soviet Russian support and encouragement—was on the brink of conquering all of mainland China, which it would accomplish by 1949.

Eleven-year-old David Hale, barely two years after World War II, had joined an important struggle for freedom at a dangerous time and place. Vienna, Austria—and David himself—were at the forefront of the upcoming global battle that would be fought—not by armies dropping bombs and a world in a fighting "hot" war—but rather, by diplomats and secret spies who would engage in a different kind of contest—a "cold" war that would last almost 50 years.

Dedication

To the people of Ukraine
valiantly fighting for freedom and independence
against the criminal invasion
of the brutal Russians
whose military and Secret Police
have produced an uninterrupted
and sordid history
dating back to the Russian Revolution.

Glory to Ukraine! Glory to Heroes!

Post-War Chaos across Europe

1

Post-War Chaos

The Date: Monday, July 7, 1947
Downtown Vienna, Austria

Even though the Hales had managed to rid themselves of the Nazi trio, there was still some urgent work that needed to be done to support the Intelligence Group. The following morning, a Monday, David Hale, his father, and Thor headed for downtown Vienna. *Living conditions** were far from normal and the city was still a mess from all the wartime bombing. The Austrian *capital city*† itself was being run by the military *authorities*‡ of four different countries: the United States, England, France, and Russia. To make things even more difficult, one of these four *occupying*§ countries was making things worse. The Russians, rather than helping Austria recover from the war, were doing their best to see that Austria would never be an *autonomous*¶ or free country again. So far, the Americans and British had been able to prevent the Russians, who had already

---

* Living Conditions: The kinds and quality of buildings, homes, trains, food supply, and health care.
† Capital City: Most important city in a state or country where the government has its main offices.
‡ Authorities: Top or most important leaders or officials.
§ Occupying: Living in a country.
¶ Autonomous: Ruling your own country and making your own rules and laws.

conquered the countries east of Austria and Germany, from pushing any further across Western Europe.

As things turned out, however, America would need to be both patient and strong over several decades to solve the 'Soviet Russia Problem.' It would take the next eight years—until 1955—before the Red Army was *pressured** enough to leave Vienna and the rest of Austria. It would require another 35 years—until 1990—before the Russian-led Empire known as the Soviet Union or *USSR*,† would itself *collapse*.‡ Only then would the countries and the people of Eastern Europe have a chance to be *genuinely*§ free.

The victories in the years ahead by the *Western Powers*¶ over Communist Russia were made possible *primarily*** because of both the strong United States and British Military Forces in Europe, as well as the good work of the U.S. Embassies—their diplomats and their secret spies—operating in key cities such as Vienna, Berlin, Warsaw, and Moscow. It was in Vienna where young David Hale had recently joined the battle on the side of freedom-loving people everywhere. He was at the right place—Vienna, Austria—at the right time—1947. And, as it would turn out, he was just the right kid for the secret and dangerous work that lay ahead.

---

*   Pressured: Being tough with the Russians and not letting them have their way.

†   USSR: Union of Soviet Socialist Republics included Russia and all the countries in Eastern Europe that had been conquered by the Red Army and the Communist political leaders in Moscow.

‡   Collapse: Fall apart or come crashing down.

§   Genuinely: Really or truly.

¶   Western Powers: Led by the United State of America, included England, France, Canada, Italy, and the nations of Scandinavia.

** Primarily: Mainly, principally, and mostly.

His father—medical doctor and senior spy Matt Hale—was mighty proud of what David had done so far. After all, it was the boy's *superb** slingshot skill that had made it possible for Dr. Hale to safely contact the Polish scientist, Dr. Kaminski, and rescue him from the Russian zone up in Linz, Austria. In addition, it was David and his German Shepherd Thor who had found the gold, counterfeit money, and the false travel documents that had been hidden late in the war to help important Nazi war criminals escape to South America. The Hale team of boy and dog also found a secret Nazi treasure map in the lining of one of the trunks and that would become quite important to the Americans for learning where the Gestapo had hidden Chief Himmler's stolen art.

Now, father and son were in downtown Vienna in support of another intelligence operation—this one designed to give the Americans a secret agent in Warsaw, the important capital of Poland, which both the German and the Russian Red Army had attacked in 1939. Warsaw lies 350 miles to the east of Vienna and about a third of the way to Moscow, Russia's capital city.

In Poland, as well as in the dozen other *unfortunate*[†] Eastern European nations that remained occupied by the Red Army after World War II, the Russian Secret Police had begun to tighten their *chokehold*[‡] on the local government and on the citizens. The Russians *essentially*[§] followed the same program

---

* Superb: Wonderful, excellent unusually good.
† Unfortunate: Unlucky.
‡ Chokehold: Complete control as when a wrestler places his hands around the other guy's throat.
§ Essentially: In most important ways.

that the German Nazis had *imposed** early in the war—after all, Nazis and Communists in fact are similar when it comes to limiting freedom. Each of their *systems*† requires their leaders to have total control over its citizens, who are important only as long as they support the goals and programs of the government. This horrible way of thinking explains why Nazis and Communists murdered and imprisoned so many millions of their own people. It is also why so many of their own citizens tried every possible way to escape to *The West*.‡

As father and son settled into their *lodging*,§ they did not at first discuss the larger problems facing Europe or Austria. They had to get busy—they had work to do. They reviewed their day's tasks and discussed what they needed to accomplish over the next few days. To begin with, Matt Hale had to go over to the conference center where the international medical meetings were scheduled to begin the next morning. He had to find the location of the Polish Officer in charge of security for the visiting Polish *delegation*.¶ His name: Major Piotr Gorski—he was the American Embassy's *recruitment target*.** (During the German occupation, Gorski had used his middle name, Otto, but that was too Germanic for him to use once the Russians took over Poland.)

Matt Hale's first job was to find a way for his U.S. Embassy friend, Visitor, to meet Major Gorski—alone and safely. Visitor

---

*   Imposed: To force on a person, group of people or nation.
†   Systems: The kinds of government they had.
‡   The West: The countries of Western Europe, America and nations living in freedom.
§   Lodging: The place where a person is staying, in this case a hotel.
¶   Delegation: The group attending the conference from the same country, in this case Poland.
**   Recruitment Target: A person whom an intelligence service wants to recruit as a spy.

spoke *fluent** Polish which he had learned as a child from his parents when they moved from Poland to the U.S. in the 1920s.

The American Intelligence Group was fairly confident from what they had been told by an earlier Polish *defector*† that Major Gorski was likely recruitable. First, however, the Americans needed to meet and speak privately with Gorski. The American goal in this operation was not to get the Major to defect and go to the United States. Instead, the American plan was to re-cruit and train him right there in Vienna—starting this week if possible. If the recruitment and spy training went well, Gorski would return from Vienna to his security position back in Poland. From then on, he would be operating as a secret spy for the Americans.

What made this operation more difficult and dangerous was the risk it involved. If the Russians in *Warsaw*‡ were to catch Gorski spying for the Americans and reporting secretly to them, either now or in the future, they would do what they always do when they catch such a spy—they would torture and shoot him.

Recalling the rescue operation of the Polish scientist—Dr. Kaminski—David was thinking that the Mercedes twin, with its secret hiding place, would be used to sneak Major Gorski out of Vienna. So, he asked his dad whether he would have to do the egg *diversion trick*§ all over again. He *assured*⁹ his dad that he was ready to do it again if that was what was needed.

---

* Fluent: Speaking and understanding a foreign language very well.
† Defector: One who runs away from his country and helps his coun-try's enemies.
‡ Warsaw: Capital city of Poland at the time under control of the Red Army.
§ Diversion Trick: A way of fooling the Russian guard.
⁹ Assured: Promised or guaranteed.

Matt Hale smiled and said, "Not at all, Son, but thanks. No eggs—this time, we do not plan to use the twin car but, instead, want this fellow to return to Poland and from then on report to us secretly. But, that would be true only if he looks like he could be a good spy—and not get caught by the Russians. If he can do all that, his secret reporting could keep us *informed**on what the Russian Red Army and Secret Police are doing. Being so informed, in turn, will help us make sure the Russians are not successful in their program to conquer all of Western Europe. Unfortunately, most of Eastern Europe is already under the control of the Red Army and Russian Secret Police."

Dr. Hale went on, "America needs spies reporting to us in Warsaw, the Polish capital, more than we need another Polish refugee going on to live in the United States. Keep in mind son, if America and England had recruited and trained spies inside Germany back in the 1930s—before World War II—we might very well have dealt with Hitler and the Nazi *madness*† earlier. Who knows, we might have been able to avoid World War II altogether. Just think of how many millions of innocent lives would have been saved if America—*before the war*—had good reporting spies in Germany, in Japan, or both."

David listened intently to his father's words and was beginning to understand the *big picture*.‡ The West, led by America and England, had only recently decided to be part of a *joint program*§ to contain the Russians and keep them from conquering other lands and countries. That program and *policy*⁋ to defend

---

*   Informed: Knowing or fully advised.
†   Madness: Insane, as Adolph Hitler clearly was.
‡   Big Picture: The background and broad understanding of what was going on all across Europe as well as in Austria.
§   Joint Program: Something done as partners working together.
⁋   Policy: The decisions and goals of a country in dealing with other nations.

Western Europe, in fact, came to be known as *Containment.*[*] By 1947, when the Hales joined the fight on the side of freedom, the Russians in Eastern Europe had already conquered much territory, including Albania, Armenia, Byelorussia, Bulgaria, Czechoslovakia, Estonia, Georgia, Hungary, Latvia, Lithuania, Romania, Ukraine and the eastern regions of Germany and Austria. In addition, Russia controlled the nations of Uzbekistan, Azerbaijan, Kazakhstan, Kyrgyzstan, Tajikistan and Turkmenistan. Communists were in control of Yugoslavia and Chinese Communists would soon win the civil war in China. Meanwhile, local Communists were gaining strength in France and Italy and were becoming more powerful in Greece as well as Turkey. So, anyone looking at the map of the world in mid-1947 would surely conclude that Communists were taking control of much of the world.

To succeed in stopping the Russians from making even more gains, therefore, the Western Powers needed intelligence reporting from spies in the right places. The week's attempted recruitment operation of Major Gorski in Vienna—if successful—could help do just that, because Poland borders Germany, Soviet Russia, Byelorussia, Lithuania, Czechoslovakia, and Ukraine.

The Hales were spending the week in *temporary quarters*[†] behind the Rothschild "Displaced Persons" (DP's)[‡] Hospital.

---

[*] Containment: The name for the policy or game plan of America, England and the Western Powers for dealing with the Russian Communists and the Red Army—not letting them conquer Western Europe.

[†] Temporary Quarters: Housing for a short period of time.

[‡] Displaced Persons (DP's): These were the millions of refugees who had lost everything in the war and wandered around the continent for weeks, months, or years until they were able to find a new home— assuming they were able to escape the Russians who kidnapped many hundreds of thousands to work in their prisons, factories, and mines.

This *clinic** since the war ended had been taking care of refugees who could not return to their native lands all across Eastern Europe. It had been a little over two years since the Russian Army *stormed*† into Austria, capturing Vienna before going on to capture the Nazi capital of Berlin. All across Europe when WWII ended in May 1945, 16 million refugees were left scattered hundreds and in some cases thousands of miles from the towns and villages where they had lived before the war. During 1945 and 1946, train-loads, bus-loads and wagon-loads of displaced refugees were sent back to their homelands—many not *voluntarily*.‡ In fact, hundreds of thousands of them were sent back forcibly, especially to Soviet Russia.

The Eastern European refugees in Austria who knew too well the horror of Communism—and what living under the brutal Russians would mean to them and their families—had no desire whatsoever to go back to their *pre-war*§ homes. For people living in normal times and places, returning to their homeland is usually welcomed as a great blessing. For those forcibly sent to Poland and other Eastern European nations in the grip of the Russians Secret Police, going back home was a horrible curse. Many thousands of refugees instead chose to *commit suicide*.¶

Dr. Matt Hale, in his medical work since arriving in Austria, was deeply involved in giving *humanitarian*** support to these

---

*   Clinic: A small hospital.
†   Stormed: Violently attacked or invaded.
‡   Voluntarily: By free choice and decision.
§   Pre-War: Before the war, back in the 1930s.
¶   Commit Suicide: To kill oneself.
** Humanitarian: Caring for and helping people who are poor, helpless and sick.

poor, displaced peoples. He treated and cured infectious diseases affecting a high *percentage** of the refugee population—most of whom had not received medical or dental care for the whole period of the war. Rather than helping them, however, the Russians were instead stealing food from Austrian farms. *As* a result, over half of the hospital patients in Vienna in 1946 and 1947—foreign refugees as well as Austrians—were suffering from extreme *malnutrition.*† A good part of the population was on the verge of starving to death.

When he was not doing medical work and wearing his doctor's *garb,*‡ senior spy Matt Hale was fighting another deadly infection of sorts—that of the *murderous*§ Russian Secret Police. These evil *brutes*¶ used kidnappings, terror campaigns and even murders to try to conquer The West. In 1945 and 1946 alone, the Russians kidnapped around 130,000 refugees and sent them from Austria to *slave camps*** as far away as the frozen region of Siberia, in northern Russia.

Among the permanent refugees who escaped from Eastern Europe and Russia was a sizeable group of displaced persons who no longer had a homeland—they had nowhere really to go. In the early 1940's, the German Army had destroyed their homes and villages, stole their belongings and killed most

---

* Percentage: A share of something such as a quarter, a half or all; usually written 25%, 50% or 100%.

† Malnutrition: Starvation.

‡ Garb: Clothing or dress.

§ Murderous: People who kill many people, usually those who are completely innocent of doing anything wrong.

¶ Brutes: People who behave like wild animals.

** Slave Camps: The Communist Government sent prisoners to camps in the far north and worked them to death cutting trees and mining.

of their families. The German Army, and especially the SS/ Gestapo, did this in every country they invaded. In Austria alone, the Nazis sent around 65,000 Austrian Jews to death camps between 1938 and 1945.

When the war was over, the Russians did not want this group of refugees back. The Jewish people of Europe found at war's end that they had no safe place to go. They had been robbed entirely of their European *roots*.* They knew that their former *countrymen*† across Europe would not let them return to their lifelong homes.

As a result, homeless Jews stuck after the war in Austria— even more so in Germany itself—were trying to find a way to depart for England, Canada, Australia, and the United States—to any country where they might be able to rebuild their lives in freedom. Many Jews went southward through Italy and then to the *Middle East*† where they would build the Jewish State of Israel. Yes, the Jewish people of Europe who had suffered millions of dead under the Nazis had to get away from the European *continent*§ altogether when the war was over. *Ironically*,¶ escaping Jewish refugees would in many cases end up taking the same escape routes used by *fleeing*** German war criminals.

---

*   Roots: Backgrounds and the countries or towns where people come from.

†   Countrymen: People who come from the same town, city or country.

‡   Middle East: The lands south and east of The Mediterranean Sea.

§   Continent: A division of the world by map-making geographers into seven major land masses: Asia, Europe, Africa, North America, South America, Australia and Antarctica.

¶   Ironically: The opposite of what is ordinarily expected.

**   Fleeing: Those running away .

When Matt Hale explained all of this to David that evening over dinner, the boy was even more pleased that his dad and he had stopped SS Colonel Schmidt and his two goons from making a *clean getaway*.* Later, as he lay his head on the pillow, the boy looked up at the Vienna sky and whispered, "Good night, Anne. Good night Margot."

It had been barely five years since the Frank family first had gone into hiding in Amsterdam, Holland. David Hale, for his part, was becoming increasingly aware that there was a lot more work that had to be done—work for spies—work for him. In the face of such evil, he wasn't all that sure that there is a Heaven and a Hell when our life is over. His mom said yes; his dad said he did not know—but he certainly hoped so. David Hale was quickly learning that there certainly can be a *Hell on Earth*[†] for innocent people who fall victim to the Nazis or the Communists—as far as David Hale was concerned, from everything his dad had shared, the two powers were *identical*.[‡]

---

*   Clean getaway: Escaping with no problems of any kind.
†   Hell on Earth: What life is like when so many bad, evil things are happening and life is filled with misery and suffering.
‡   Identical: Exactly the same.

David Approaches Red Storm Hotel

2

*Casing** The Target Hotel

The Date: July 8, 1947
Early Tuesday Morning.

David woke up earlier than usual. The morning sounds of downtown Vienna were different for him than the Hale castle sounds which at dawn included roosters crowing down at the Vogel cottage. Across the castle, each morning David could hear birds chirping high from the parapet while they surveyed the countryside for hawks and other *predators*.[†] Now, awakened by the unfamiliar sounds of the city, the new junior spy was up and out exploring at a time well before the medical conference visitors staying at the nearby hotels. Most of these visitors had spent the previous evening drinking Russia's and Poland's favorite alcoholic drink, *vodka*.[‡] With almost no one out in the streets this early in the day, the boy and dog strolled around the downtown area without ever seeing a single Russian.

David decided, therefore, to take a look at the Red Storm Hotel, where his dad said the Polish delegation was staying. It was within walking distance of the center of the city and just inside the Russian sector. Using the map, David had no

---

*   Casing: Very careful collection of information about a place of interest in an intelligence operation.
†   Predators: Animals hunting and hoping to eat them.
‡   Vodka: A clear white alcoholic drink made from potatoes.

trouble finding the Red Storm Hotel. He took a deep breath and approached the front door, but stopped for a few seconds to look back at Thor. He told his *sidekick** to sit outside while he went in. David had no idea what to expect.

His dad, meanwhile, had gotten off to an even earlier start that morning and had been gone when David awoke. Dr. Hale was at the nearby Rothschild Refugee Hospital which had some new patients who had arrived there in terrible condition. Most had either typhus or typhoid fever. To make matters even worse, the patients were suffering from *starvation*.† Dr. Hale made his *rounds*‡ and had to put aside his thoughts of Russians, Poles and spies for the time being. For the next two hours, he simply was Dr. Hale and the *desperate*§ hospital patients were glad to have him there. When he left the hospital later as the sun was rising, he *converted*¶ back to senior intelligence officer, intent on tracking down Polish Major Gorski for the U.S. Embassy. But, he first had to get back to his hotel and prepare for the rest of the day ahead.

Just a few blocks away, David was walking in the door of the Polish delegates' hotel where he met an elderly man working at the Red Storm Hotel's front desk and who greeted him in German, "Good morning, can I help you, young man? You are out so early."

At this point David decided to answer him in German since

---

* Sidekick: From the world of the American West that David loved so much, it means a cowboy's partner.
† Starvation: Poor diet; not enough food to eat; hunger; malnutrition.
‡ Rounds: The visits to sick patients a doctor makes to see how patients are feeling.
§ Desperate: Just about without hope.
¶ Converted: Changed into or became again.

he had been practicing with Frau Vogel. He replied, "No, I am waiting to see my father downtown. I came in here hoping to get a drink of water." The old man said he would get it for him and be right back.

It was then that David spotted two big, rough-looking men sitting in chairs in a far corner of the *front lobby**. They were guards who looked like they had been up all night. Their clothes were wrinkled and they were unshaven. They were clearly carrying guns as David could tell by the big bulges in their brown overcoats. He knew they were Russian guards, for he had heard enough Russians speaking at the different checkpoints around Vienna and Linz when out with his dad.

The junior spy sat down on an old sofa that looked like it had been through two wars. Its covering was badly worn and *dingy*[†] as was the carpeting on the floor. There was an old iron lamp in the corner. In front of the sofa was a small wooden table on which David spotted two stacks of papers. One stack had a map of downtown Vienna that showed the Conference Center as well as the nearby hotels and restaurants. The other pile of papers displayed an hourly conference schedule for the entire week. *Specifically,*[‡] it was the program for the Polish delegates who were in town attending the medical meetings.

David *assumed*[§] his dad would want to look at both papers, so he moved himself slowly over on the sofa to be within arm's reach of both stacks. The two Russians across the lobby paid no

---

* Front lobby: The entrance way of a hotel where guests wait for visitors.
† Dingy: Dirty.
‡ Specifically: Exactly.
§ Assumed: Thought or believed in advance.

attention to him. After all, their orders for the week did not say anything about being on the lookout for kids. The guards were there to prevent any of the Polish delegates from defecting to The West, period. If anyone did defect, then the guards might as well run away too because they would be in a lot of trouble if they returned to Poland without all of the delegates. Looking at the stacks of paper for a moment, David thought how his dad might act in this situation; he decided to move slowly and stay cool. No, he would not rush things. First, he would try to figure out what was going on. He wanted to see how alert the two Russians really were. And it did not take long for David to realize that they had no interest in him or in the stacks of paper.

Rather, their attention and eyes were on a cleaning girl who was mopping up the lobby. They kept trying to strike up a conversation with her but had no luck. After all the *assaults** on Austrian women by Russian soldiers in the months after the Battle of Vienna, like most Austrian women she had no interest at all even talking to them.

Knowing the guards were distracted, the junior spy made his move. David *casually*† reached out and took one paper from each pile of papers and brought them down to the floor. He then reached down as if he was going to tie his shoes but, instead, quickly folded the papers he had swiped and slid them into his socks. David then reached for the glass of water, took a quick sip, slowly got up and walked to the front desk. He thanked the old gentleman behind the front desk for the drink and then headed out the door.

---

*   Assaults: Physical attacks.
†   Casually: In a slow, natural way that did not draw attention.

Thor stood waiting outside the hotel doing exactly as he had been told. David's heart was beating a little faster than usual but, when he got out on the street and away from the big Russian guards, he quickly relaxed and felt satisfied. Boy and dog then headed back to their hotel. Matt Hale had arrived there some minutes before and was wondering where they had been. "How was your walk, Son? See anything interesting?" The doctor was seated in the lobby which was as clean as a hospital *operating room** compared to the *rundown†* place where the Polish delegates were staying.

The junior spy, before answering, looked around to make sure no one else could hear their conversation. David was sitting across from his dad and this time it was he who asked a question. "Can you guess what I found down at the hotel where the Poles are staying? Two guesses, Dad, go ahead."

Now the dad was at a loss for words as he tried to figure out what made David so *spunky‡* so early in the day. "Okay, son. Before we get to the Red Storm Hotel, I am guessing you found a German Luger below the castle parapet. Herr Vogel said he had seen it but later it was gone. You probably hid it in your closet flooring is my guess. How am I doing, Son? Okay so far?"

Now it was David who was *on the spot§*—he had planned to show the Nazi Colonel's pistol to his dad, but wanted to hold onto it a day or two just for the excitement of finally having a

---

*   Operating room: A special room where they do surgery and must be perfectly clean to avoid infection.
†   Rundown: A place that is worn out from years of use and years without getting fixed, painted, or repaired.
‡   Spunky: In a happy mood.
§   On the spot: In a difficult position or in some trouble.

Luger—hopefully one of his own, that is, if his dad would let him keep it.

But, the senior spy admitted he had no idea what David had found downtown this morning and said so. "David, I don't have a clue what you may have found at the other hotel. Tell me and I will show you how to use and handle the Luger safely—once we get some free time back at the castle. Lugers, after all, are not toys, which I am sure you know very well. So tell me, what did you find this morning that might be so interesting? I have to get going and figure out how, when and where I can get our friend Visitor in contact with the Polish fellow he is after."

'Well, Dad, maybe I have saved you some time!" Reaching down inside his socks, the junior spy pulled out the two papers, unfolded and placed them on the table in front of his dad. "What do you think, Dad? These were just sitting on a table in the lobby at the Red Storm Hotel. They were placed there for the conference delegates most likely by two lazy Russian guards more interested in a young Austrian cleaning girl than in doing their jobs. Looks like they are written in Russian and Polish, which you can read—which you, dad, can understand."

"This is good, but how could you be so sure they would not see—or worse—catch you taking their papers, Son? What made you think it could be done so safely?"

"I am telling you, Dad, I studied the two guards carefully and figured I could have taken their boot laces *unnoticed*.* In the fifteen minutes or so I was in the lobby, these guards never once looked my way—never looked at me—probably would

---

*   Unnoticed: Not having been seen.

not remember I was even there. The two stacks of paper had many copies. I just took one from each stack. As you saw, I had them in my socks. And when I walked towards the door to leave the Red Storm Hotel, the guards were still trying to chat with this Austrian girl who seemed to ignore them the entire time." Matt Hale *skimmed** the papers, smiling and said, "David, you just saved me a half and maybe an entire day of work. Good for you. Now, get something to eat. As for Thor's meal, you will find it is up in our room.

"And two things: Yes, the Luger will be yours some day when I am sure you can handle it safely. The pistol would be perfect for tunnel rats when you are a bit older. But for now, I removed the firing pin so the gun cannot be fired and no one can get hurt. Also, next time, you can take those guards' boot laces, too! You, Son, are getting pretty darn good for a beginner—no, *very good*!"

David tried not to *gloat*,† but was smiling widely as he and Thor started up the stairs to their room.

---

* Skimmed: Read quickly.
† Gloat: To brag or try to show off.

Visitor Contacts the Hales

3

*Ops Planning** with Visitor

Visitor arrived at the hotel room a little later, just as David was taking Thor out for another walk. He greeted the boy, as always, with a warm smile and then proceeded to give Thor a neck and back rub. He knew all about the dog's war record and had a very special fondness for this particular patrol dog. Visitor too had served in combat early in the war, before he was moved into Army Intelligence when it was found that he had spoken Polish since childhood. As far as learning a foreign language goes, Polish is one of the most difficult to learn—more so than Russian or German, neither of which languages is all that easy.

Once David and Thor headed out the door, the two senior spies—Matt Hale and Visitor—*got down to business.*† Matt Hale had spread a map of downtown Vienna on the table and was reading through the information sheets David had brought back from the Red Storm Hotel. Visitor was delighted to learn that David had picked up the papers that could help them *isolate*‡ Major Gorski. This would help Visitor find a time in the conference schedule when he could contact and be alone with Gorski for a few hours. Visitor would need time to *determine*§

---

* Ops Planning: An abbreviation for Operations Planning which is the careful preparation for an intelligence action.
† Got Down to Business: Started working.
‡ Isolate: Get him alone.
§ Determine: Figure out.

whether this Polish Officer was *recruitable** as believed and reported by the earlier Polish defector, Dr. Kaminski. Visitor was fairly confident that, if he could meet with Gorski privately for a few hours, he would be able to *assess†* him and see if he really was the type of man who could live with the risks of spying under the watchful eyes of the Russians. He might well be such a rare individual. After all, he had managed to survive since the war ended without the Communists ever realizing he was not happy with them and their system of government.

Spying inside the *enemy camp‡*—for example, back in Poland—is far more difficult than just trying to survive there. It requires an exceptional kind of courage which even those who are bravely fighting in combat may not possess. In combat, things happen fast and soldiers have *buddies§* fighting alongside of them. War fighters also have the extra boost that comes from their own adrenalin. In spying, by contrast, one is usually alone among enemies, things can move slowly over a long period of time, and there are no buddies around to help deal with the risks and dangers from the Secret Police. Furthermore, a spy's own adrenalin could become his own worst enemy. For, if he got too nervous, the Russians might wonder why Major Gorski suddenly seemed so *agitated.¶* Spies who are able to survive in

---

* Recruitable: Able to be recruited because he is unhappy with the Soviet system.

† Assess: Come to understand all about a person to decide if he can do a certain job, in this case spying.

‡ Enemy Camp: Inside Poland or Russia where the Russian Secret Police control security, telephones, cameras, listening devices and the very life of the citizens.

§ Buddies: Friends and pals, fellow soldiers.

¶ Agitated: Nervous and shaky.

the enemy camp need to possess three C's—they have to be "cool, calm and *collected*."*

Finally, the stress on a spy is made even greater because the Russian Secret Police make sure that everyone knows what happens to enemy spies whom they catch operating *on their turf.*†
They kill them most certainly but, first, they *torture*‡ them in order to learn as much as possible about their enemies before saying, 'Ready-Aim-Fire!'—making them much like the Nazis, after all.

Visitor would have an important initial step to go through with Gorski as part of the *recruitment process.*§ Visitor had to be confident, first of all, that he was not already a spy—for the Russians! There is nothing worse in the world of intelligence operations than making the mistake of letting your enemy put one of their men inside your own *network*§ or organization. Yes, thinking a man is on your side—but having him really working for the enemy—is the greatest mistake an intelligence officer can make. So, how would Visitor make sure Gorski would be on our side and not already working secretly for Moscow?

Well, he would do three things. He would, of course, get to know Gorski in their meetings together and see whether the Polish Officer looks, speaks and acts like a *reliable*** and not a

---

*   Collected: Having control over your emotions. Able to seem relaxed when you are in real danger.
†   On their turf: In their country.
‡   Torture: Hurt someone very badly trying to get information.
§   Recruitment Process: The organized steps that go into getting a person to agree to be a spy.
§   Network: The group of intelligence people working against the Russians.
** Reliable: A person who could be trusted to do what is right and what he has agreed to do.

bad or *unreliable** person. Visitor would ask himself, "Does what Gorski is revealing to us now make sense with everything we already know about him?" Dr. Kaminski, of course, had spoken highly of Piotr Gorski and said he owed the Polish Officer his own freedom. That was a good beginning.

The next thing Visitor would do is get Gorski to tell Visitor about *important, secret things happening in Poland*—things the Russians would not let him expose if he were *under their control.*† The Americans had to be sure, then, this was not a *dangle operation*‡ in which the Russians present a fake possible spy who is entirely under their orders and direction. Dangle operations can make a spy organization waste a great deal of time. It also can expose some of their own secret agents and secret techniques to the enemy. As added protection, Visitor would have Gorski take a *polygraph*§ or *lie-detector*¶ exam. This would be done to see whether Gorski was trying to deceive the Americans on important things such as working secretly for the Russian Secret Police.

Visitor knew that by the time he had spent several hours with Gorski doing all of the above, he would be able to judge very well whether Gorski should be recruited, trained and return to Warsaw as a trusted secret agent. If the answer turned

---

*   Unreliable: A person who cannot be trusted.

†   Under their control: Really working as a spy for the Russian Secret Police.

‡   Dangle Operation: Just as one may hang a shiny object in front of a baby to get its attention, intelligence services sometimes make it look like a person is willing to work for the enemy when, the whole time, he is just fooling or deceiving them.

§   Polygraph: A machine that measures the heart, breathing, skin reaction to test a person for honesty.

¶   Lie-detector: The common name for a polygraph machine and test.

out to be yes, then Visitor would get Gorski trained thoroughly in *secret communications** which is what the Polish Major would require to report on secret things without being caught by the Russians back in Warsaw. After all, once he agreed to spy for America, Gorski's own safety would become the U.S.'s highest responsibility. He would be a member of the American team—an ally—one of the family, so to speak. In sum, Visitor had to be very thorough in *screening*† the Polish Major now so everyone later on was not terribly sorry.

Getting down to business, Matt Hale and Visitor examined the papers David had delivered, which were proving to be quite helpful. To begin with, the papers showed that Major Gorski in his security duties at the Vienna Conference would be busy during the day and occupied watching over the delegates long into the nighttime hours. The papers that David brought back informed the Polish delegates that, if they had any problems, they should contact Polish Major Gorski at his room in the Red Storm Hotel, "room number 7 on the first floor." Delegates were told to contact Russian Major Ivan Volkov in room number 11 on the second floor if they had any problems with Russian officials in Vienna. The schedule showed that the only time Gorski might be safely contacted by Visitor would be after midnight. At other times, Gorski might be spotted with Visitor by other delegates—or even worse, by the Russian, Major Volkov.

---

* Secret Communications: All the things a secret agent might need to be trained in, such as secret writing, clandestine photography, shortwave radio, dead drops or hiding places, and secret signals to be able to report to the American intelligence officer he would be working with inside Poland.

† Screening: Complete and careful examination of a person's background and suitability for a job.

Major Volkov was, in fact, a member of the Russian Secret Police. He had been sent to Vienna from Warsaw to keep an eye on the Polish delegates as well as on Gorski. It was all part of the Russian Secret Police program to tighten its *grip** on the Poles—especially on those working for them in matters of security. So, it was decided in Visitor's discussion with Matt Hale that he would go into the Red Storm Hotel after midnight that night—he would arrive there *in disguise,†* dressed as a plumber repairman. Because most of the old Vienna hotels had problems with their pipes, faucets, and toilets, it would not be cause for surprise that a plumber would show up even at that late hour.

Visitor would knock on Gorski's door at 12:15 am and *address‡* him with a Polish greeting and hand Gorski a handwritten note from the scientist recently rescued by the Hales up in Linz. The note would say that Visitor too is a 'friend of Chopin' who wanted to meet Gorski and say hello. As a Security Officer himself, Gorski would have a pretty good idea almost immediately what Visitor really wanted. The Major would either welcome Visitor or, if he were afraid even to talk, probably say he was busy and not interested. The first contact between the Polish Officer and the American spy would be no more complicated than that.

Visitor was thinking that one of the good things in going after an intelligence or security officer in the spy business is the *efficiency§* of it all: the fellow being contacted *grasps¶* immediately what is happening and has a good idea which intelligence

---

*   Grip: Control over.
†   In disguise: With a change or look or appearance such as wearing a wig or wearing a worker's clothes.
‡   Address: Speak to.
§   Efficiency: Can be done rather quickly.
¶   Grasps: Understands immediately and without explanation.

service is interested in him. This saves time and is quite effi-
cient. So, as he walked out of the Hale hotel, Visitor was feeling
pretty good about things. David and Thor, *coincidentally,** were
arriving back from their walk around town. Visitor told the boy
he had left him something to practice with in the city and that
his dad would tell him all about it.

When David and Thor reached the room, Matt Hale greeted
his son with a big smile and said that the papers David brought
from the Red Storm Hotel were helping Visitor *considerably.*†
They had saved an entire day, at least, which was important
for Visitor who had barely five or six days to carry out an important operation. Matt Hale then told David he had a couple
of neat cameras David might like to use. One, a gift to the boy
from Visitor himself, was the latest 35-millimeter camera—the
Leica 3c. That brought a smile to the boy's face as he picked up
the prized German camera and read the tag—"For DH, Best
Photo Guy in all of Austria."

The junior spy then told his dad that, as he was approaching
their hotel, he saw something odd. A Jeep was parked across
the street—it had soldiers—four in all—each one wearing a
completely different uniform. "The driver was an American—I
could not tell for sure about the others. But one looked like a
Russian!"

Matt Hale explained that these were known as *Four Men in
a Jeep.*‡ Yes, these were all soldiers and there was an American,

---

*   Coincidentally: Just happened to be.
†   Considerably: Very much; a great deal; a lot.
‡   Four Men in a Jeep: To keep peace and quiet in the International
     Zone in downtown Vienna, the Jeep carried four military police of-
     ficers including an American, an Englishman, a Frenchman and a
     Russian.

an Englishman, a Frenchman, and yes even a Russian. They patrolled downtown Vienna—the International Zone—like policemen. How Austria ended up with such an unusual situation—rather than the Viennese running their own city—is quite *complicated.*"*

Four Allied Soldiers in Jeep Policing Central Vienna

---

* Complicated: Not easy to understand.

4

Austria: The *Occupied** Decade

The senior spy went on to explain how it all started in 1943 during World War II when the Allies met in Moscow, Russia in a conference to reach an agreement on how they would manage things across Europe once they had defeated Nazi Germany. Austria presented a *unique*[†] situation. It had been the first country Hitler's Nazi Army invaded when, in March 1938, they marched into the nation and forced the Austrians to give up their independence and become part of Germany. After being *forcibly*[‡] made part of the Nazi Third Reich, a million Austrians went on to fight on the Nazi side in World War II. *Regardless*,[§] because Austria had in fact been invaded in the first place, the Allies decided to treat Austria after the war as the first victim of Nazi Germany—and not the same as they would treat Germany itself. It was agreed, instead, to set up special rules that would help Austria recover from the war and be treated in the future as victims of Nazi Germany, and not enemies of the Allies.

At the same time, back in Moscow, Russian leader Josef Stalin directed his intelligence and security services to go after

---

*   Occupied: When foreign armies are in control of a country, in this case Austria.

†   Unique: Like no other; unusual; one of a kind.

‡   Forcibly: Not freely but, instead, under extreme pressure.

§   Regardless: Even though; despite the fact that.

America which he *declared** was the new MAIN ENEMY of the Communist world. So, at the very time America and Russia were supposed to be Allies and the Americans were sending to Russia hundreds of supply ships loaded with free military materials and food to carry on their fight against Nazi Germany, Communist leader Stalin in fact was himself preparing for post-war conflict against The West.

The practical difficulties in dealing with a false ally like Russia really started to become *crystal clear*[+] two years later, in 1945. This was when the Russian Red Army—the first Allied army to reach Austria—began their bloody assault on Vienna. The Russians, attacking from the east, soon captured the Austrian capital city but only after losing thousands of soldiers in the battle. That was in April. Attacking from the west and north, the American and British Armies reached the northern and western parts of Austria later on. The Americans arrived in July and the British in September. By the time the Americans and British got into Vienna in the east of Austria, the Russians were well *advanced*[‡] in their program to steal and send to Russia everything they could get their hands on—not just in Austria, but in every country they conquered on their way to their final destination, the Nazi Germany capital of Berlin.

The Russians were very *aggressive*[§] and *bullied*[¶] the British to turn over to the Red Army and Russian Secret Police many

---

*   Declared: Strongly said.
†   Crystal Clear: Just as clear as looking through a washed fine glass.
‡   Advanced: Far along.
§   Aggressive: Pushy, forceful.
¶   Bullied: Pushed around and took advantage of them.

thousands of refugees, including *Cossacks** who had fled Russia back in 1918, after fighting the Communists during the Russian Revolution. Knowing the evils of Communist Russia, the Cossacks would later fight on the German side in WWII. Once in Russian hands as prisoners, the Cossacks were murdered in great numbers—especially their leaders. The rest were shipped like cattle to the most *remote⁺* Russian region in the frozen north.

Back in Vienna, the Soviet *replacement⁺* troops, who came into Vienna after the Red Army fighting had ended in April, were out of control—raping Austrian women as well as killing and robbing the local citizens. Because of the *bad conduct§* of their soldiers, the Russian leaders soon realized they could never control the Austrian population as completely as the Red Army and Russian Secret Police had been able to do in the rest of Eastern Europe. This was clearly demonstrated when the Austrians voted in their first free and open election—the Russian-supported Communist Party of Austria won only five percent of the votes. Seeing how much they were despised by the Austrians, Russia's leaders in Moscow finally agreed with America and the British to allow the Austrians to regain their independence after ten years—in 1955.

That agreement required that, after 1955 when the Allied troops all left the country, Austria would thereafter be *neutral⁋*

---

*   Cossacks: A fierce tribe of warriors in Central Europe who were famous for their skill as horsemen and warriors.

†   Remote: Far away from their own lands or the major cities of Russia.

‡   Replacement: Those who took the place of the Battle of Vienna fighting troops.

§   Bad conduct: Terrible behavior and way of acting.

⁋   Neutral: Not on either side; independent.

between Russia and The West. The Russians did not get all that they really wanted—to turn Austria into a Communist nation. Yet, in the end, Moscow came away with billions of dollars' worth of stolen machinery, food and industrial goods. They also got the assurance that Austria would remain neutral and independent in the *Cold War** that began as soon as WWII itself had ended. The Russians knew from 1943 onward that they were going to be in a new kind of war—this was a reality that leaders in The West still had not yet realized or so far figured out.

It would take until 1946—and an important *Telegram†* from the American Embassy in Moscow—to awaken and convince America's political leaders back in Washington that they were indeed in a new kind of struggle, now against Communism— one so serious and dangerous in fact it had to be treated as a war. This life and death *competition‡* would hopefully not become a shooting or a *Hot War§* like the first two World Wars where millions were killed. It would be a *"Cold War"* in which spies would play an important role as The West faced an enemy more dangerous than any they had faced in the past.

An American *diplomat¶* in Moscow, George Kennan, wrote and sent what became famous and known as the "Secret

---

*   Cold War: The strategic struggle between East and West—Russia and America/England—that started in the mid-1940s and lasted till the Soviet Union collapsed in 1991.

†   Telegram: An electronic message more or less like an email.

‡   Competition: Struggle against each other—West against East.

§   Hot War: Where countries and armies fight an enemy using bombs, missiles and guns.

¶   Diplomat: A person sent by the State Department overseas, in this case to Moscow to work in the embassy and deal with the Russians.

Telegram" or "Long Telegram." He had been asked by the Treasury Department in Washington to explain why the Russians had become so opposed to joining America, England and other countries in a partnership to help in the recovery program for nations damaged severely in the war. Kennan wrote back an 8,000 word reply that explained the background and hostility of Stalin's Russia and, in the report, alerted leaders in America that The West indeed had a very serious "Russia problem." In his well-written and *persuasive** report, he succeeded in convincing America to change its ways in dealing with this new and dangerous threat from Communist Russia. Like Nazi Germany back in the 1930s, the Communist Russians were showing they too wanted to take over Western as well as Eastern Europe. Kennan argued that America and its allies in The West had to develop a Policy of Containment to keep Russia from conquering more lands and leading the world into World War III.

Speaking to his son this July day in 1947, Matt Hale predicted that the Cold War in the end will be won or lost—not mainly because of bombs and guns—but because of ideas and the *commitment*† needed to hold back the Russians until their terrible Soviet system collapsed. Matt Hale explained further, "because the Russians use subversion, terror and *deception*‡ as their *principal*§ ways of dealing with other countries, America must use its own secret intelligence operations and spies to make absolutely sure our leaders know what the Russians are

---

*   Persuasive: One that informs and changes minds.
†   Commitment: Strong intention and willingness to fight to remain free.
‡   Deception: Misleading, lying, fooling.
§   Principal: Most important.

doing and be equally sure they do not succeed. And, Son, this means you and I must help Visitor in every way possible—what he is doing is terribly important."

Matt Hale then told David that he should use the afternoon to get to know Vienna better and become familiar with his new camera. "After all, Son, our brain can *record and recall** only so much information—so few images. There is nothing better than black and white *35-millimeter film*[†] to do a spy's job. The new color films give us pictures that are pretty, but they are not nearly as good in our "special work." A black and white photograph has more *detail*[‡] than color photos. Take Thor with you and then you won't have to worry about getting robbed. I know that both his black fur and white teeth look scary to most strangers. Here, use this little carrying bag for the camera and it will be less visible to any thieves and pickpockets in downtown Vienna."

"And look, Son, let's see whether you can become an expert in the downtown area itself. If so, that could be very helpful. How about I test you on this Vienna city map later on? If you impress me with what you have learned, we'll head over to the Sacher Hotel for a slice of 'Sacher Torte.'[§] That hotel is now the headquarters in Austria for our friends, the British. By the way, stay away *altogether*[¶] from the Red Storm Hotel. If you are spotted around there a second time, even those sleepy security

---

*   Record and Recall: Remember later on.
†   35-Millimeter Film: The most common standard film size in the world at that time and for years afterwards.
‡   Detail: Information.
§   Sacher Torte: World famous chocolate cake with a layer of apricot jam in the middle.
¶   Altogether: Entirely, completely.

guards may start wondering about you. See you at 6:00." David listened intently to his dad the whole time he spoke—not saying a word. Trying to become a better listener, he just nodded and gave a *crisp** military response—*"Aye, Aye, Sir."*[†]

Matt Hale smiled while winking at the boy and thought how lucky he was that David had wanted to spend the summer with him. Real lucky. Later on, at 6:00 o'clock *sharp,*[‡] father and son met up and reviewed the city map together. It was clear at this point that David was getting a good grasp of how Vienna had been designed and knew the locations and layouts of the interesting buildings, parks and public gardens, just as his dad had suggested. The two then walked over to the Sacher Hotel and had a small plate of *Hungarian Goulash*[§] followed by a slice of their famous cake. It was such a good meal.

---

*   Crisp: Neat, smooth, fast.

†   Aye, Aye, Sir: In the Navies of both England and America, it means the speaker understands what he has been told to do, and he will do it immediately and exactly as ordered.

‡   Sharp: Exactly.

§   Hungarian Goulash: A beef and vegetable dish of food with a rich gravy. Hungary is on the eastern border of Austria and, like Poland and so many other nations of Eastern Europe back in 1947, would soon find itself under the control of Russia's Secret Police and the Red Army.

Dressed as a Plumber, Visitor Contacts Gorski

5

Visitor Meets Gorski

The Date: July 9, 1947
Early Wednesday, After Midnight

If Visitor's own mother had been standing in front of the Red
Storm Hotel that same evening when the clock struck midnight,
she would not have recognized her very own son walking past
her and *strolling** in the hotel front door that led to the lobby.
He wore the clothes of an Austrian *tradesman*† and carried a
plumber's bag of tools. Wearing both a grey wig and *unkempt*‡
moustache, he looked much older than his thirty-three years.

As he went past the front desk clerk, Visitor spoke just three
words in German: "Toilet, room seven." Visitor then headed
down the *corridor*§ to the right as though he had been there before. The hotel lobby was crowded with drunk or nearly-drunk
conference delegates loudly returning from another night on
the town. Some needed help finding their rooms. The busy
front desk clerk paid no further attention to Visitor; he would
not even recall later on that some old plumber had been there
or where he had gone. At this late hour he just wanted to get

---

*   Strolling: Walking in a calm relaxed way as though he were out for a
    Sunday walk.
†   Tradesman: The working clothes of a man who made or fixed things.
‡   Unkempt: Sloppy looking and not nice and neat.
§   Corridor: A long hallway with many rooms on either side.

all the Russian and Polish drinkers quickly back to their own rooms so none would get sick in the lobby and *puke** all over the place—he was so tired of cleaning up after them.

The hotel guest in Room 7—Major Gorski—was glad it was past midnight. It meant that all or almost all of the Polish delegates were back in their rooms. The chances were good, then, he would get a good night's sleep himself—assuming he could get to sleep. Major Piotr Gorski was a deeply tired man—*physically*[†] and *mentally*.[‡] He was tired of taking care of grown men who did not just get a little drunk—they drank more than they could handle so they would get very drunk. Gorski was sick of many things—from his Polish bosses back in Warsaw to—as he privately called them—'the rotten Russians' who treated him and the other Poles more like prisoners of war than like allies.

And he was *stressed*[§] by his family situation. Since his wife died in the bombing in the war, he had barely managed to care for his two children. He was fortunate that he had the help of his sister who lived outside the city of Krakow in western Poland. This was not far from the border of Czechoslovakia. She had been raising them since he lost his wife, as though they were her very own children. Major Gorski did not want them brought up as little Communists, as he would have been forced to raise them if they were with him. He personally had behaved with the Russians as though he were a loyal Communist—so

---

*   Puke: Throw up, vomit.
†   Physically: In his body and how strong and healthy he felt.
‡   Mentally: In his mind and how rested and clear-headed he was his thinking.
§   Stressed: Pressured, worried, not at peace.

far they seemed to believe this act. After all, to get on better terms with the Russians, he had joined the Polish Communist Party—a move that probably saved his job security, and even his own life.

It was a move that made him feel deeply ashamed whenever he thought of his childhood friends who were murdered by Russian death squads early in the war. Yes, they had been the true Polish heroes and innocent victims. Yet Gorski wanted to believe he had no other choice—he had to stay alive to protect and support his two children. At least that was what he told himself. But, when alone and thinking about his life, about his wife or just saying a prayer, he would occasionally beg for God's forgiveness because he had not fought the Russians as so many of his Polish pals had done.

Without saying a word to anyone, Gorski secretly *mused** that he and his children might someday get away from the Russians—to Austria or Italy or possibly to the American city where so many of his childhood Polish friends had gone— Chicago! That was his dream. For a hobby—and to keep up his own spirits—he had memorized almost all the street names and their locations in the *Windy City*,† as though he would get there—some day—somehow.

And now, just when he was ready to take off his shoes and try to get to sleep, he got a knock at his door. "What a long, long week this is going to be," he thought. He went over, opened the door and found a stranger standing there with some

---

*   Mused: Dreamed or privately wished for in his mind.
†   Windy City: Nickname for Chicago because of the breezes and strong winds that come off Lake Michigan.

kind of workman's bag in hand. Visitor started to enter—Gorski blocked his way. He had learned under the Germans and then from the Russians not to trust anyone. So first he demanded to know exactly who this man was and what he wanted at this late hour of the night. He started speaking to the stranger in German, "Can I help you, Sir?"

But he got a shock when the old man with the bag looked at him, smiled and spoke to him in perfect Polish, "Major Gorski, Piotr, I come as a friend of Chopin. I need to speak with you about the future—Poland's and yours. If necessary, I can return tomorrow night instead." Visitor then handed Gorski a note written in Polish from the Major's old friend, Dr. Kaminski, saying "Thank you, Piotr—all is well."

As much and as long as Major Gorski had been hoping for this day to come, he was *stunned** and too nervous to remain standing. He pulled Visitor in by the arm and quickly shut the door. He felt unsteady and sat on the bed. For a few seconds he could think of nothing to say.

To begin with, he was deeply *concerned*† that Major Volkov, the Russian, might show up at his door and discover this stranger whom Gorski could not explain. As he did his best to calm down the Polish officer, Visitor went into the bathroom and immediately flushed a huge wad of toilet paper and small cloth that clogged the toilet and sent water flowing all over the floor.

Looking at Gorski with a wink and a smile, Visitor said, "Relax, Piotr. A plumber like me only gets called when things

---

*   Stunned: Shocked, bewildered.
†   Concerned: Worried, afraid or fearful.

are messed up. And, right now, Poland is really messed up and you know that as well as anyone. Anyone coming to the door will find me working to unclog things before the entire first floor gets flooded. Even Volkov the *Ruskie** will agree that a clogged toilet calls for a plumber and needs to be fixed. Besides, Piotr, my friends told me before I came here that Volkov tonight looked like he had drunk a great deal of vodka this evening and had to be helped back to his room. So don't worry—he is sleeping like a *detka*† and a danger to no one."

Gorski nodded in agreement, figuring that this guy understood his situation. Meanwhile, water from the overflowing toilet was running all over the room as Visitor flushed the clogged-up toilet for a second and then a third time. Visitor grinned at Gorski and *assured*‡ the Polish officer that he would clean up the mess before he left.

"Right now," Visitor said, "let me tell you why I am here and it has to do with one thing and one thing only—freedom. We know—and by 'we' I mean we Americans—that the Russians are quickly turning your country as well as many others into slave states, *period*.§ If you, Piotr can accept slave states, then I should just clean up the water here, say goodbye and go on my way. But, if you ever want to see a free Poland again, then maybe you can help make that happen by working with us. As you have certainly figured out by now, this—intelligence—is

---

* Ruskie: Nickname for a Russian and, during the Cold War, not a favorable one.

† Detka: "Little baby" in Russian.

‡ Assured: Promised.

§ Period: The end of a sentence usually but in this case it is a way of ending it more strongly.

my business and I will make sure, Piotr, that you are safe. That, Piotr, is what I do."

At this point, Gorski, who thought he already understood what Visitor was going to ask him to do, *blurted out** that he could not *defect*† and stay in The West. He said he had family members back in Poland who needed his support and protection. "Yes, from the rotten Russians. I must go home." As Gorski spoke these words, tears *welled up*‡ in his eyes. He, like so many parents around the world, cared first and foremost about his own son and daughter—his Jan and his Karina—ages 11 and 8. So, Gorski thought to himself, "Although this American might give me a way to escape the Communists, I cannot walk away from my children and leave them there."

Visitor did not respond right away. He could tell that Gorski was having a difficult time *emotionally*§ with all the pressures he was under. Visitor went back to unclogging the toilet, giving the Polish Major some moments to recover so their discussion could continue. Then Visitor walked over to Gorski and put his hand on the man's shoulder, looked him in the eyes and said that they had no *intention*¶ of asking him to not return to Poland. In fact, defecting to The West was the last thing the Americans wanted at this time. "We actually want you to go back to Warsaw, Major Gorski. In Poland you can help not only your country but also the entire world. You can give your

---

*   Blurted Out: Said suddenly and emotionally, with feeling.
†   Defect: Leave the Communist world and live in The West helping the Americans against the Communists.
‡   Welled Up: Flooded his eyes.
§   Emotionally: In his feelings.
¶   Intention: Wish or desire.

children a better future—with our help. Let's calm down a bit and talk. I promise you I will get out of here in the next couple of hours. First, we need you to clear up some things that, at this point, I do not yet fully understand."

Gorski had settled down *enormously** now that he *grasped*[†] that Visitor did not want him to defect alone to The West—as much as the Polish Major wanted someday to get to Chicago. For the next two hours, the men had a thorough discussion. Visitor had to *determine*[‡] two important things—first, whether Gorski really was a reliable person—meaning not working for the Russians—and, second, that he was *solid*[§] enough *mentally*[¶] and emotionally to work as a spy back in Poland where the dangers were enormously great.

Visitor began by asking Gorski to explain why he had joined the Communist Party and how he had been able to get the Russians to trust him—unless of course he was really on Russia's side. The Polish Major spoke freely and made it clear that he joined the Communists because he knew he could be killed if he did not. When he took this step, his wife had already died. He knew that he would be the only one who could protect and support their children—assuming the Russians did not execute him as they were doing to so many Poles under their control.

Visitor told Gorski that he believed him to be a patriotic

---

*   Enormously: Greatly.
†   Grasped: Understood.
‡   Determine: Figure out or clarify.
§   Solid: Strong, steady, stable.
¶   Mentally: In the clarity and common sense of his thinking and in his mind.

Pole. But, because Visitor was working against Communists—
for whom truth is not important—everyone working in their
special work had to be tested thoroughly. That meant he would
have to pass a polygraph exam. The test, said Visitor, would
help prove that Gorski could be trusted to do secret work back
in Warsaw. "In fact," said Visitor, "we have to get that step over
with soon—if at all possible, tomorrow night after midnight."

Gorski agreed to do so. He added, "Tomorrow night will
be fine so long as Volkov has another busy night of drinking
vodka and does not come to my room—drunk or half drunk."

Visitor said his friends would make sure Volkov got a few
free drinks to ensure Gorski's safety. Visitor then said, "Look
Piotr, tell me about the Russians in Warsaw. Who is the head of
Russian Security in Poland? Is he in the *NKVD** or the *GRU*?†
I need the names of the top Russian intelligence and security
operatives in Warsaw. Tell me about the Red Army tank and
troop units in Poland. Tell me about the tanks themselves.
Which model tanks? How many do they have and where are
they located? Which cannons are on the new tanks? Tell me
the names of Russia's key military officers in Poland. Where
are the Red Army military storage areas? Tell me the plans the
Russians in Poland have in case there is a war."

And, so it went—for two hours Gorski answered all of
Visitor's questions one by one while Visitor took extensive
notes. When his watch showed it was three o'clock, Visitor
thanked the Polish Major and said, "I am proud of you, Piotr—
as a man and as a Polish patriot. I hope things will work out.

---

*   NKVD: The Russian civilian spy agency later called the KGB.
†   GRU: The Russian military intelligence agency.

And, Piotr, I hope you know that you can quit working with us at any time that you wish. Unlike the Russians, we are not in the business of *blackmailing** people to help us out. When you work with us, protecting your personal safety and freedom begins immediately—and it will not end. We will talk tomorrow night about your two children—when the polygraph is over—on how we might help them. And Piotr, do not write anything down that we have discussed or you think might be of interest to me. The Russians here in Vienna have very great *capabilities.*[†] They may even go through your room while you are gone for the day. Good night my friend. See you tomorrow night."

---

*   Blackmailing: Forcing a person to do something he does not want to.
†   Capabilities: The ability to do things. Including spying in hotels, following people, listening in on phone calls.

David Enters Red Storm Hotel, Russians in Lobby

6

Recruitment Is a Team Sport

The Date: July 9
Daytime Wednesday

All three of the American players in the Polish Major *recruit-ment activity** were busy this third day of the operation. After leaving the Red Storm Hotel in the early morning hours, Visitor had returned to the Intelligence Group at the Vienna office and wrote his report on the Gorski meeting, as well as relayed the information Gorski had provided on the Russian tanks and battle plans in case of war. He left a copy for the Intelligence Group Chief and sent a copy *electronically†* to Washington. By the time Visitor finished all of this, the sun was rising over Vienna. He drove to the Hale hotel and, although he had not slept, was feeling pretty good. Later, probably around mid-day or early afternoon, he would need to get a couple of hours of *shut-eye‡* if he were going to able *to function§* well with Gorski again after midnight tonight. But, he needed first to meet with Matt Hale and tell him how the meeting with Gorski had gone.

---

* Recruitment Activity: The complete steps being taken to get a person to agree to work as a spy.
† Electronically: By a radio message which was encoded so that the Russians could not read it.
‡ Shut-eye: A slang word or term for sleep.
§ Function: To work well and be awake and alert.

By the time Visitor got to Matt Hale's room, David had already gone out and was taking pictures with his new camera and sack full of new film. Thor went along and provided protection from any early-morning thieves. Yes, it was a new war—a Cold War—a new enemy—the Russians—and Thor was on patrol once again.

So far, in Visitor's mind, things were moving along quite well. But, there was still some work to do to make sure he was not being fooled by the Russians. The polygraph exam tonight would help *confirm** whether Gorski was being entirely honest—or not. Meanwhile, Visitor was somewhat concerned there might not be enough time to train Gorski fully and properly in the various types of *clandestine commo technologies*† that would *enable*‡ the Polish Major to pass secret information to the American contacts when he got back to Warsaw.

Visitor then asked Dr. Hale if he could think of any reasonable medical way that would allow Gorski to remain in Vienna for another week—but be able to do so without placing the Polish Major *under suspicion*§ with the Russians.

"And I do not mean running him down with a car, Matt," joked Visitor. "After all, we aren't the Russians. No, we need him to delay his return to Warsaw, if it is possible—for two reasons. First, the security situation in Warsaw is getting very bad, making our work there highly dangerous. So, Gorski needs to be well trained to survive as a long-term clandestine reporting

---

*   Confirm: Help know for sure.

†   Clandestine Commo Technologies: The many ways for a spy to send and receive messages; for example, radio messages, photographs, secret signals on the streets of Warsaw, dead drops for hidden messages.

‡   Enable: Allow or permit.

§   Under suspicion: Where they do not trust him.

source. Second, Gorski is already showing signs he could very soon become a most valuable secret agent. His *access** to senior officers of the Russian Army in Poland is excellent. Almost none of the Russian colonels and generals speaks Polish— they rely often on Gorski to translate for them. That puts him in a superior position to report to us on Russian *military intelligence.*"[†]

Visitor continued, "Our Intelligence Group here in Vienna, I am sure, will be highly impressed with Gorski's *potential*[‡] and by the information he gave me last night. I am confident we will soon hear back from the *Pentagon*[§] in Washington that the Generals there feel the very same way—that Gorski, in a short period of time, has reported some great stuff."

Dr. Hale sat back in his chair and thought a while before answering. He responded that he might have a way to delay Gorski's departure. He wanted to join Visitor in tonight's meeting—after a successful polygraph test—to examine the Polish Major physically and find out about Gorski's *general health*[¶] and see whether he already had his *appendix*** or *gall bladder*[††] *surgically*[‡‡] removed.

---

*   Access: Ability to meet important people and learn important secrets.
†   Military Intelligence: Secret information about armies and war plans of the enemy—in this case, of the Russians.
‡   Potential: How good he could be as a spy in the future.
§   Pentagon: Is the headquarters for the American Military including Army, Navy, Marines and Air Force. Built during WWII as the largest office building in the world, it is also is where America's top generals work.
¶   General health: For his age, is strong, energetic and free of major medical problems.
**   Appendix: A small organ in the belly area that sometimes gets infected and must be removed.
††   Gall bladder: A small organ in the belly area that helps digest food.
‡‡   Surgically: When a person has an operation where a doctor operates on him and opens up his body.

"I have an idea that could work. But, I would need to examine him myself to be sure he is healthy enough for surgery. I have an Austrian friend, a *surgeon,** who might be able to do the operation; his wife, a nurse, would *assist*† him. This doctor works in the Vienna General Hospital. He and I worked together on some secret operations in the war; I know we can trust him. Dr. Hans Brandt has removed many hundreds of gall bladders. My guess is that it would take about ten days to two weeks after the surgery for Gorski to be okay to travel back to Poland—giving you the time you need to train him. If we are able to operate on him, we will need his *Blood Type*."‡ Good luck tonight. I have to get out to my favorite farm and pick up some supplies that could help—assuming Major Gorski still has a gall bladder. If this is so, there is a pretty good chance we are going to take it out!"

The new day had begun quietly for the Hales who arose much earlier than the *majority*§ of the downtown hotel residents. David awoke first, as usual, and Thor was last. Father and son had a simple breakfast of bread, cheese and cocoa in their *mini-kitchen*.¶ Thor had a large beef bone that he was happy to chew outside on the hotel porch. The clock showed almost six o'clock when the Hales went on their way. David

---

* Surgeon: A medical doctor who operates on people and performs surgery.

† Assist: Help.

‡ Blood Type: The most common blood categories in humans are Type A, Type B, Type AB, or Type O. Your blood type determines which blood types you can receive.

§ More than half of the hotel guests.

¶ Mini-kitchen: A small kitchen inside their hotel room where they could heat up food and simple meals.

Hale decided to use the morning stroll to walk more than a dozen miles around downtown. He and Thor would have covered more ground except there were areas that had blocked streets as the Viennese were still restoring their beloved city from all the bombings of 1945. In Vienna alone, 3,000 bombs fell in the last months of the war—many still lay *unexploded** under shattered buildings and streets. Each such bomb had to be removed carefully so that no one got killed.

The boy and dog started out in the direction of St. Stefan's Cathedral which gave the boy a good *reference point*† so he would know at all times where he was in the city. This *majestic*‡ church and *landmark*§ in the center of Vienna was still severely damaged from the wartime Russian artillery blasts. However, its tall South Tower had not been destroyed and was quite visible from all parts of the city. David had a map—he had his new Leica C camera—he still did not have a precise plan this morning except that his dad had told him to learn what he could generally about the *layout*¶ of Vienna streets, parks and buildings. He also had to practice taking photos with the various camera settings so he would learn how to get good pictures every time—that is, photographs that were not too light or too dark.

Outside photography, after all, is far more complicated than

---

*   Unexploded: Did not blow up but were still very dangerous.
†   Reference point: Something tall and easy to see from anywhere in Vienna to keep from getting lost.
‡   Majestic: Very special and the kind of place that would be suitable for a king or special events.
§   Landmark: A well-known building, hill, monument or place.
¶   Layout: The design of the city and location of the major streets, avenues, and the small stream running through Vienna.

copying travel documents under a steady bright light in his dad's study as David had done during the Nazi gold *caper.**
David wrote down in his small notebook the *camera settings*†
he used so that he could later see how well the camera worked under many different light settings and *shutter speeds.*‡ To be able to compare results *accurately,*§ he took three photos of the same building, bridge, park, or monument at three different camera settings and recorded the numbers in his little book. This system came about when David asked himself before starting out what his dad would do to be sure, at the end of this day or week, that he would have learned as much as possible. He was not of course just another tourist taking photos to show his family and friends. David was becoming a full-fledged junior spy and he had to do his job *just right.*¶

Dr. Hale, for his part, had a busy day as he was juggling his roles as both medical doctor and senior spy. He had started off the day going to the Rothschild Hospital where he worked with refugees who had arrived the previous week from the east. He then had his meeting with Visitor before driving to the countryside where he bought several bags of carrots for use with Major Gorski—assuming that the Polish officer still had his gall bladder. Before going back into Vienna itself, he drove by the Vogels to ask them an important favor: he needed

---

*   Caper: Adventure.
†   Camera settings: Changes that make a camera take lighter, darker or clearer photos.
‡   Shutter speeds: The amount of time the camera eye or lens stays open so the camera can capture the photo.
§   Accurately: Carefully and with precision.
¶   Just right: Exactly and correctly.

them to make a couple of gallons of *concentrated** carrot juice in large milk containers to take with him. It was so *urgent†* he waited until the mixture was ready. Frau Vogel was happy to help. Due to her own military experience in the war, she asked no questions and proceeded to grind up the carrots, adding just enough water to make the juice drinkable. It took over an hour to get it done, so Matt Hale used the time to go up the hill and check out the castle before he headed back into central Vienna.

On his way back to the hotel, Matt Hale dropped by the Vienna General Hospital and had coffee with his friend Dr. Brandt to see whether his Austrian friend could perform the surgery to help keep an "unidentified friend" in Vienna for several days—sufficient time to be trained by Visitor before traveling back to Poland. Dr. Brandt said he would be more than happy to help—he would make sure the patient got treated well and also had plenty of privacy.

So, each of the three—Visitor, Matt Hale and David Hale—had a job to do to help in the recruitment of Major Gorski—to get him ready to return to Warsaw fully prepared to spy and report on the Russians. There were others who would be needed to make this all come together correctly. After midnight tonight, Visitor would bring to Gorski's room the *polygraph operator‡* to conduct that *pivotal§* test. And, because Visitor was the best Polish speaker in the U.S. Intelligence Group, he would assist with the polygraph exam so there would be no room for con-

---

* Concentrated: Very thick pasty mix.
† Urgent: So important it must be done right away.
‡ Polygraph operator: A technical expert who conducts lie detector tests.
§ Pivotal: Absolutely important.

fusion in the polygraph operator asking or in Gorski answering the very important security questions.

Dr. Brandt at Vienna General Hospital would play an essential part by performing the surgery later in the week even though Gorski's gall bladder was most likely working quite well. At this point—with Gorski's own and his children's future freedom and welfare at stake—Dr. Hale was quite prepared to do what he could to get the Polish Major prepared to work safely back in Poland. If Gorski did not want to have the surgery, he would have to return home sooner, but not as fully trained as he should be. Thus, with less than *sufficient** training, he would be under much greater risk of being caught by the Russians and put to death. Gall bladders, after all, are not the most necessary organ—many people have them removed and go on to live long and healthy lives. And that is what Dr. Matt Hale and Visitor wanted for Major Gorski—a long and happy life after he helped the U.S. Government understand what the Russians were doing and planning.

---

*   Sufficient: Enough.

Major Gorski Polygraph

7

Major Gorski on 'The Box'

The Date: July 10, Wednesday night/Thursday Morning

As midnight approached, a slight fog blanketed downtown Vienna and created a perfect setting for the city's spies. Yes, like young David Hale in his castle adventures, spies are primarily nighttime actors—they enjoy the protection they get when *visibility** is poor. While hotel guests stumbled back into the Red Storm Hotel from nearby bars, Visitor and the polygraph operator entered the hotel through a rear door, avoiding the lobby entirely. Gorski had made sure that the rear door was unlocked, as Visitor had asked him the previous night. They went to room seven without seeing or being seen by anyone. As Gorski also had been directed the previous night, he had left the shade in his hotel room window half way up so that Visitor would know—before entering the hotel—whether Gorski had anyone in his room and could therefore not be met this evening.

Gorski's spy training for Warsaw was about to begin. Visitor knocked—Major Gorski let them in—the polygraph operator was introduced simply by the alias '*Marco*.' As he had done the night before, Visitor was dressed as a plumber and, immediately

---

* Visibility: Tells how clearly things can be seen because of the amount of available light or such things as rain, fog and sunshine or darkness.

upon arriving in Gorski's room, clogged the toilet with paper and a cloth. With the second flush, water spilled out onto the floor to give Gorski an innocent *cover story** in case anyone came to his room.

Marco set up his polygraph machine which those who are in the spy business simply *refer to*† as "the box." Visitor and Gorski were doing all the talking—Marco knew some German, but not a word of Polish. Three different devices or gadgets were attached to Gorski, who was told that this really was just another medical exam—they were getting readings on changes in his blood pressure and changes in his breathing. Also, the machine would detect any changes in his *perspiration*‡ when he answered questions. People who are nervous or feel guilty sweat more than usual and their hearts pump faster. The polygraph machine records and *calculates*§ all such changes in the body. Finally, to be certain that Gorski had not taken any drugs to try to appear calm to fool the box, Visitor had Gorski pee in a small cup which he covered and set aside to be tested back at the office—that was to be sure the Polish Major was *clean*¶ and drug free.

The polygraph testing got started around 12:15 am. It was all done by 2:00 am. The questions were read and explained by Visitor who assured Gorski that everyone involved in his case had been tested on the box too—so Gorski should know that

---

* Cover story: The agreed-upon excuse for a meeting or operational action that will seem innocent and reasonable to outsiders who may be interested in spies at work.
† Refer to: Call or name something.
‡ Perspiration: Sweating, which can show whether a person being tested is nervous or not.
§ Calculates: Figures out whether a person is telling the truth, or not.
¶ Clean: Without any drugs in his system to try to fool *the box*.

they were not asking him to do anything that they had not done themselves. The rules and the security requirements were the same for everyone!

The polygraph questions were really of two types—*informational questions** meant to help understand Gorski's life and his security situation so U.S. Intelligence would know how best to support him and keep him safe. And then came *reliability questions*† to help understand his past and present loyalties, and try to figure out how he might act in the future as a secret agent back in Warsaw.

Gorski would be asked whether he had told anyone else that he had been contacted by American Intelligence, that he helped his Polish friend Dr. Kaminski escape from Warsaw, or that his life's dream was *eventually*‡ to get away from Poland with his children and live in The West. It was also important to know what, if anything, he may have told his sister in Krakow. He was asked whether he had ever committed any crimes, stolen any money from his government, from the Russians, or from anyone. Also, had he ever been arrested or put in jail?

The exam went on for close to two hours when, at the end, Marco spoke privately with Visitor and said that there had been no signs of any lying or *deception*§ in the testing: Gorski had passed the polygraph exam so Visitor could now move

---

* Informational questions: Used to find out things about Major Gorski such as family situation, his work, his schooling, his fellow workers and bosses, what his friends knew about his true feelings.

† Reliability questions: These used to make sure the subject was being entirely honest and could be trusted to help learn as much as possible about what the Russian and Polish Communists were doing in Warsaw.

‡ Eventually: At some time in the future.

§ Deception: A sign that the person is being dishonest or hiding something.

forward with the *stay-behind operation.** Visitor went over to Major Gorski, smiled and nodded his head to show that all had gone well. He then gave Gorski a *bear hug*[†] while whispering his congratulations.

"Now, Piotr, we have a lot to discuss to get you back to Warsaw properly trained. We need to discuss ways we might in the future get your children out of Poland—maybe even along with your sister, if that is what you and she want. It might be wise to get your family out of Poland before the Russians shut down the borders in both your country and Czechoslovakia which is the best *pathway*[‡] we can use to get them safely out to Austria before borders are closed. Our Intelligence Group *estimates*[§] that within six months the Russians will make their final move to turn both Poland and Czechoslovakia into Communist-controlled nations. If we get your children and sister out of Poland safely, we would settle them here in Austria until you decide that leaving your country is right for you. Keep in mind, the longer you stay in Warsaw reporting to us, the larger your bank account will be when you do leave Poland for good."

Visitor continued, "You should know by all of this that we highly value both you and the military intelligence reporting you can provide. As we put all of this in motion, we want you to agree to remain in Warsaw for at least two years. During that

---

*   Stay-Behind Operation: When a spy remains in a country controlled by the enemy, in this case Poland under Russian Communist rule.

†   Bear Hug: A really strong hug between very good friends.

‡   Pathway: The route or way that would be used to get them from Poland to Austria.

§   Estimates: Concludes, thinks, figures, or guesses.

time, the United States Government will place each month in a secret U.S. Dollar account—in your *code name**—the salary of a United States Army Lt. Colonel to help you start a new life with your children—when you get out—while they are still young. Finally, if the work we do together in Warsaw is truly successful, we will *resettle*† you and your children in the United States—in Chicago, if you so wish. There, you will be able to work and live your lives in freedom. For now, we desperately need *current*‡ information on the plans and capabilities of the Red Army Forces in Poland as well as in the rest of Eastern Europe.

"Why is all this so important? Because as soon as Germany and Japan were defeated in 1945, America and England immediately—and many believe quite foolishly—returned to their peacetime ways as most of our World War II soldiers became *civilians*§ once again. They became farmers, teachers, truck drivers, factory workers and millions returned to college under a special program that paid their school expenses so they could prepare to work in the *peacetime economy*.¶ We shut down our weapons factories, closed most of our military bases and prepared for peace and not *endless war*.**"

"On the other hand, Russia did not—in 1945–1946 or even now in 1947—do what America and England were doing when

---

*   Code name: A made-up name that is used to protect Gorski from the Russians.

†   Resettle: Move him and his family permanently to Chicago.

‡   Current: Up to date, this week's or this month's.

§   Civilians: Men and women who are not in military service.

¶   Peacetime economy: The factories and businesses that are not working on military products.

**   Endless war: Fighting and battles that never end but go on and on.

peace came at the end of the war. *On the contrary,** Moscow didn't move to a civilian or peacetime economy. Stalin instead kept much of his enormous Red Army in the countries they had captured in the war. To make things worse, he used his Secret Police to put Communists in charge of governments all across Eastern Europe. It took a while for The West to wake up but, Piotr, you should know that we in America and those in England as well as much of Western Europe are now wide awake to the Russia threat. And, fortunately, the picture is not all bad."

"To begin with, we are no longer fooled by Moscow—we are rebuilding our military forces to keep the Russians contained and unable to expand their empire. The Red Army is an enormous and dangerous threat to the parts of Europe they do not yet control. You and I—and our freedom-loving friends—are going to make sure Russia and its Communist empire do not *expand*[†] any further. The contribution you can now make is to keep The Western leaders informed on what the Red Army and Russian Secret Police are doing in and around Poland. We need your help, Major Gorski, because the Poles need ours. Eventually, I am certain, Russian Communism will fail."

Gorski sat silently in deep thought. He was thinking about his children. He also thought about his childhood friends who were murdered by the Russians at Katyn Forest early in WWII. And he thought how he was being given a chance to fix his life and erase the shame he had felt ever since joining the Communist Party and working with the Russians. Then he spoke from his heart.

---

*   On the Contrary: Quite the opposite, quite differently.
†   Expand: Increase, grow larger.

"This is the first in a very long time that I feel truly alive—like a man—like a Polish patriot and not a rat. So, yes, I will help you. Just tell me, my friend, what I can do. I promise you will not *regret** putting your trust in me. From one Pole to another, I give you my sacred word."

Tears of joy welled up in Gorski's eyes; this time the tears were neither from sorrow nor from shame. Visitor smiled, shook the Major's hand and said, "Okay. Time to get to work. I have a doctor *colleague*† we will call Dr. Polo who needs to check you out and see whether we can come up with a medical excuse to delay your return to Warsaw for ten days so we can prepare you to work safely with our people in Poland. Dr. Hale then arrived at Gorski's hotel room after receiving a *pre-arranged signal.*‡

With the polygraph exam completed, the operator gathered his equipment and headed off back to the Intelligence Group office to write his report on the test results and send them off to Washington. Now it was Dr. Matt Hale—using the alias *Dr. Polo*—who took over the meeting. Visitor again served as *translator.*§

Dr. Hale proceeded to ask Major Gorski basic questions about his personal health history. It was he who needed to *determine*¶ whether the Major was a healthy candidate for the gall bladder surgery. Visitor also wanted Dr. Hale's assessment on

---

* Regret: Be sorry for.
† Colleague: A person who works with him in his job.
‡ Pre-Arranged Signal: A sign telling Matt Hale when it is time to come into the Red Storm Hotel.
§ Translator: A person who explains in English, for example, what is being said in Polish.
¶ Determine: Decide.

another important question: whether Major Gorski seemed to have the required intelligence and *strength of character** for the role of secret spy back in Warsaw where the stress and dangers were quite great.

Fortunately, it turned out, Gorski was in excellent health and had never smoked or drunk alcohol. Now in his mid-thirties, he was as healthy as an athlete and Dr. Hale told him so. There was no obvious reason why he would not go through the gall bladder surgery without difficulty. Before leaving, Dr. Hale showed the Polish Major the two *four-liter jugs†* of carrot juice and explained to him why he must drink as much of the liquid as he could *tolerate‡* in the next couple of days. With this drink, his skin would begin to turn a slightly orange color even though the juice in fact was a very healthy drink. Gorski took a small sip and said it tasted pretty good.

After the polygraph and medical exams were finished, Visitor and Polish Major Gorski had some time alone to discuss the *operational climate§* in Warsaw *in some depth.¶* It was Visitor's job to tailor Gorski's training to make him both safe and *productive*** as a reporting source on the Russians in Poland. The

---

*   Strength of Character: The personal toughness, flexibility and
      instincts.
†   Four-Liter Jugs: Each jug is slightly more than a gallon.
‡   Tolerate: Be able to accept or deal with.
§   Operational Climate: From the point of view of security, this covers
      all of the risks and dangers that a spy faces when he is working in a
      particular country or city and trying to keep from getting caught.
      This includes the police checkpoints where people have to present
      their travel documents and there are both patrol dogs and surveillance
      cameras.
¶   In Some Depth: In some detail or completeness.
**   Productive: Able to report on a timely basis to the American
      Government just what the Russians were doing and planning both in
      Poland and the rest of Eastern Europe.

good news for Visitor was that Gorski was not like so many people in his position, who were *inclined** to *underestimate*[†] the spying risks. Instead, Visitor found Gorski *realistic*[‡] in *grasping*[§] that Soviet Secret Police control of his country did not come about by accident. On the contrary, the Russian NKVD in 1947 had been in power and had become very good at catching spies since the Russian Revolution and World War I, back to 1918. The Communists in Russia had remained in power for three decades precisely because they had succeeded in capturing and killing so many of their enemies inside the Soviet Union. With WWII over, they were using these same *techniques*[¶] of terror all across Eastern Europe.

What made the Russians especially dangerous was that they were willing to murder totally innocent people who were no danger to them. The Soviets killed many tens of thousands of innocent people, not for anything they had done but because of each person's family, religion, nationality, or background. So, if a person came from a wealthy family, that was reason enough to arrest them, imprison them in faraway Siberia and simply work them to death in mines and forests without proper food and housing. In Poland and in the other dozen countries Russia had recently conquered, the NKVD was applying all the lessons of counter-intelligence they had learned back in Russia—both during and after the Russian Revolution.

It was well after midnight when the meeting with Major

---

*   Inclined: Having a certain habit.
†   Underestimate: Assuming that things aren't that bad, being too confident and sure of oneself.
‡   Realistic: Having common sense and not a foolish risk-taker.
§   Grasping: Understanding immediately.
¶   Techniques: Tools and practices.

Gorski ended. Visitor had to get back to his office and write his report with the favorable results of Gorski's polygraph and medical examinations. Things were looking really good that the Americans would soon have a new and most valuable spy in Warsaw!

8

*Spycraft** in Vienna

On Thursday morning, David Hale was up early and got ready to do the job his dad had given him: get to know the central zone of Vienna and become skilled in the use of the Leica camera. One thing David would do to avoid attracting any attention would be to sling the camera strap around his neck and let the camera hang down inside his light *windbreaker.†* In this way, the camera would not be visible from the back or from his left and right sides. When anyone walked or stood directly in front of him, the young spy would *refrain‡* from taking photos until that person was out of the way. In sum, the young spy was developing the kind of *street skills§* needed to assist his dad or Visitor in downtown Vienna which was loaded with police, spies, *counter-spies¶* and soldiers who take notice of anything that looks *suspicious.***

---

*   Spycraft: The basic training in the spy world and the ways spies are kept safe from discovery.

†   Windbreaker: A light jacket that one would wear in spring and fall, but not on very hot or cold days.

‡   Refrain: Stop completely until it was safe and no one could see that he was taking pictures.

§   Street Skills: The ability to get his spy tasks done without attracting attention.

¶   Counter-Spies: Police or security officials in a country trying to find foreign spies.

** Suspicious: Things that looked unusual or different than what one normally sees in Vienna.

Thor, for his part, would basically be *along for the stroll*.* The dog had no specific job to do, except one *crucial*[†] one: his duty at all times—both at the castle and on the streets of Vienna—was to protect young David in a city that contained all sorts of criminals and all sorts of risks. These dangers included kidnappers, thieves, murderers and, of course, old Nazis and present-day Communists. Vienna was far more *perilous*[‡] than life had been back in the United States where David, sister, and Mom had lived safely during the war. The good news for David was that, because he had Thor along, he had more freedom to roam around Vienna than other eleven year old boys who did not have the protection and company of a courageous war dog.

By noon, after a few hours of taking snapshots in and around the public parks and monuments, David led Thor back to the hotel where he developed the Leica film to see how well he was doing in shooting photos. Interestingly enough, he was looking forward to his dad's *critique*[§] because he knew it would make him a better photographer and, of course, a more *effective*[¶] junior spy. His dad was waiting in their room. He had just finished writing the medical reports on the morning's hospital visit that included the treatment plan he had to submit on each of the refugees he had examined that day.

Matt Hale looked over each of David's film shots and pointed out which ones were excellent, which ones were only fair and

---

* Along for the stroll: Out for a pleasant walk.
† Crucial: Of great importance.
‡ Perilous: Extremely dangerous.
§ Critique: Evaluation of the boy's photography and suggested improvements for his future photo work.
¶ Effective: Better at doing his work.

which shots would not be very useful because they were *deficient** in some way. Overall, the senior spy was impressed by how the boy had followed his directions and clearly had covered several of the city parks and streets in just a single afternoon. In addition, the boy also had taken good notes. The father explained to David how a photo shot was just right or could be improved by using a different camera setting on the Leica or by maybe taking the shot from a different *vantage point.*[†]

By this time, after casing the central zone of Vienna, the junior spy was becoming quite familiar with the city streets. He also was becoming a *more selective*[‡] camera-man than when he had first started. More importantly, he was enthusiastic about the task because, he figured, his dad or Visitor would soon be using his camera skills, not only in practice exercises but on things that really mattered. When the father and son team had gone through all the Leica 35-millimeter photo shots, the senior spy showed David the second camera Visitor had dropped off earlier.

It was a most-special camera known as the *Minox.*[§] About the size of a cigarette lighter or small box of matches, this especially-small camera could be held unnoticed in the hand. When

---

*   Deficient: Not too good.
†   Vantage Point: The spot where David was standing or should be standing to take a better photo.
‡   More Selective: Careful about which pictures were worth taking and which ones were not.
§   Minox: Developed in Latvia and first manufactured between 1937 and 1943, it soon became the world's best spy camera. Of exceptional quality, it was expensive and used by intelligence services throughout the world.

he saw the Minox, David's eyes lit up right away. Compared to the Leica, this was indeed a *miniature*[*] camera—an *honest-to-goodness*[†] spy camera! To David it looked as *sleek*[‡] as the German Luger he liked so much. With his eyes wide open and his facial expression showing his enthusiasm, David felt *downright*[§] excited as his dad explained that the Minox could do both document photography and take outside shots—the same as the Leica. He was surprised to learn that such a small roll of camera film could capture fifty shots and that the film itself came in a *cartridge*[¶] that was simple to load and unload. His Dad then showed him how to take photos. David was relieved to find out that he would not have to develop the thin ribbon of film that requires special equipment located back at the Intelligence Group Office.

"When can we try it dad? When can I take it out to the parks?" Matt Hale said he would first need to meet with Visitor to get more specific instructions. He did know that Visitor wanted David's help in photographing every park and monument in downtown Vienna—not from a normal distance as a tourist might take a picture. No, Visitor needed very *close-up*[**] shots taken from a distance of just a few feet. His dad and Visitor figured that David could get that done more securely

---

[*]   Miniature: Extremely small, tiny compared to others cameras used in most photography.
[†]   Honest-to-Goodness: The real thing and without any doubt whatsoever.
[‡]   Sleek: A lovely design that showed it had been created by an excellent engineer.
[§]   Downright: Completely and absolutely.
[¶]   Cartridge: Container that held the film.
[**]   Close-up: From a short distance of a couple of feet or less.

than an adult could—after all, a boy out walking with his dog attracts little or no attention.

With some free time on their hands before Visitor was scheduled to arrive, father and son headed over to the Sacher Hotel for a late lunch and a slice of the hotel's Viennese pastry. Returning to their own hotel after lunch, the two were soon joined by Visitor who finally had managed to catch a few hours of sleep. Matt Hale filled in Visitor on how his surgeon friend, Dr. Brandt, was willing to do either gall bladder or appendix surgery—whichever was required.

Visitor addressed David, "How about you and I have a chat about photography in and around Vienna? Your dad tells me you were just given the Minox Camera and have had plenty of practice with the Leica. This special project I want you to do is going to require patience and very *close-up** photography. I do not want you to attract any attention to yourself. We do not want the Russians to notice that you have any special interest in Vienna's parks and its monuments. The Minox, then, is the right camera for certain parts of this task. If you use it carefully, no one should be able to see what you are doing. In fact, it would be good if you bring along the Leica camera as well. Let that one hang around your neck, but just don't use it. Anyone who sees you and Thor will think you are just a kid out with his *pooch*† for a walk. By the way, we will soon go over in detail the special project involving the Vienna Parks. We can do that once it is approved by the American Intelligence Group. I think you will find it quite challenging and interesting. Take care, young man."

---

* Close-up: From very near.
† Pooch: A slang word for a dog.

Then Visitor sat with Matt Hale and went over the next day's operational plan for the Polish Major who had been originally scheduled on the weekend to be taking a train back to Poland. After midnight, Visitor would have another meeting with Gorski to make certain he was ready for the surgery and not *arouse** any suspicion in the Russian Officer's mind. Separately and earlier in the night, Dr. Hale would be having dinner with Dr. Brandt to *coordinate*† the surgery which would take place early on Saturday morning. With Dr. Brandt's wife assisting in this 'emergency surgery,' no one at the Vienna General Hospital would question the surgery itself.

---

*   Arouse: Cause to be noticed or questioned.
†   Coordinate: Making all parts of the operation and surgery come to-
     gether, again without causing any suspicion.

9

Vienna Surgery *With a Twist**

Friday evening at the Red Storm Hotel was more or less a repeat of the first week of the International Conference on Refugee Infectious Disease. The visiting medical delegates from Eastern and Western Europe, including Germany and Austria, had been learning about the latest treatment techniques and medicines that were being used successfully on refugees infected, in many cases, with *multiple*† diseases. Dr. Hale was one of the physicians with the most recent direct experience in treating these refugees; the speech he gave and the medical treatment paper he delivered were warmly received by the attending guests. With millions of homeless refugees roaming around Europe, every country in the region was struggling with the *burden*‡ of feeding, clothing, housing, as well as medically treating, these foreign victims of war. As the Conference concluded, each of the delegates was getting ready to return to his home country better able to deal effectively with the enormous problems in the camps and hospitals where hundreds of thousands of displaced persons still needed help.

Tonight was their last evening in Vienna and the *majority*§ of the conference visitors were mainly interested in finding a bar

---

*   With a Twist: Different from the usual or normal.
†   Multiple: More than one.
‡   Burden: High cost and work caring for displaced persons.
§   Majority: More than half.

or restaurant where they could get a good meal and consume plenty of wine, beer, or vodka. The alcohol, they believed, would help them forget at least briefly their problems and other *depressing** stuff they would have to deal with once they got home. That was especially true for any conference visitors from the Eastern European countries still occupied by the Soviet Red Army and harshly controlled by the Soviet Secret Police. By 1947, all across *war-torn*[†] Eastern Europe, things since the war ended were just getting worse. Why so?

To begin with, across countries to the east of Vienna, the Russians were starting to close down national borders and take control of the local and national governments. In addition, many Eastern Europeans knew friends who had disappeared *without a trace.*[‡] Suddenly one morning, some neighbors were gone—a few may have quietly snuck away to freedom in The West. But, many more had been kidnapped by the Russians and sent deep into Communist Russia—never to be seen or heard from again.

By contrast,[§] one of the conference delegates was eagerly preparing his return home to Poland and was taking extra-ordinary steps to do so. Polish Major Piotr Gorski was *setting in motion*[¶] the plan agreed upon with Visitor from the American Intelligence Group. The Polish recruitment operation, in fact, really got into high gear on Thursday night when Gorski began

---

*   Depressing: Sad, miserable and heartbreaking.
†   War-torn: A region with bomb-damaged buildings, roads, bridges, schools and homes.
‡   Without a trace: Where no one had seen the person or family leave the area.
§   By contrast: Instead, on the other hand.
¶   Setting in motion: Started or began.

drinking carrot juice every half hour to turn his skin an orange color and prepare himself for the required gall bladder surgery.

Early on Friday morning, Gorski contacted the still-sleeping Russian Security Officer, Major Volkov, and told him he was feeling extremely sick and had a deep pain on the right side of his *abdomen*.* Volkov—who had been over-eating and over-drinking all week himself—was not too concerned. He just assumed the Polish Major too was merely dealing with a case of *indigestion*.† All week long, Gorski seemed fine and had been doing most of the security work at the conference. The Russian, on the other hand, had spent much of his week meeting and drinking with Russian military officer friends stationed in Vienna. Realizing that Gorski had done most of the security work all week, Volkov told the Polish Major to take it easy and get some rest.

As it was the last conference day, Volkov contacted each of the delegates from Poland to make sure that none was missing or had disappeared. He was fairly *confident*‡ that all of them would get on the train headed to Warsaw this Saturday because each conference attendee had family members back in Poland who would be *severely*§ punished if a family member defected to The West. Yes, relatives of Poles who traveled abroad were basically *hostages*¶—they were used by the Russian Secret Police

---

* Abdomen: Stomach or belly area.
† Indigestion: Being sick to one's stomach.
‡ Confident: Sure of himself or certain.
§ Severely: Very harshly.
¶ Hostages: People kept prisoner by kidnappers or a police state. In fact, Russians even needed to have and use 'internal passports' in the Soviet Union and had to have government permission to travel from city to city.

to keep these foreign travelers in line and following all the rules. As far as Major Volkov was concerned, things seemed completely normal and under control when he went to his own room and fell fast asleep after midnight.

So, on Saturday morning when he was double-checking to be sure that none of the returning Poles was missing, Volkov went looking for Major Gorski. He asked the two Russian guards in the lobby and learned that Gorski had been taken to the hospital very late on Friday night—but no one had bothered to wake him up and tell him. After he yelled at the guards and threatened to report their failure to advise him, Volkov had the front desk clerk call the Vienna General Hospital. When they finally were able to speak to someone in charge at the hospital, he was told that the Red Storm Hotel guest had gone through emergency surgery in the night and was now resting in the hospital *recovery room*.*

The previous night, as planned, Dr. Brandt had been waiting at the Vienna General Hospital when Major Gorski arrived by ambulance to the Emergency Room. After middle-of-the-night surgery, the Polish Major was transferred to a small clinic across the street in downtown Vienna. By the time Major Volkov even had learned about the surgery, it was time for him to be at the Wien Hauptbahnhof—Vienna's Central Train Station. Volkov, now alone, had to get the all of the Polish conference visitors on the Saturday morning railway car for the 425 mile trip back to Warsaw.

Well, the *deed was done*†—Gorski's gall bladder was *kaput*‡—

---

* Recovery room: Where patients are kept until they have gotten through surgery.
† Deed Was Done: When it is too late to stop something from happening.
‡ Kaput: Gone, broken or disappeared.

and the Polish Major was going to be recovering in Vienna for several days and maybe for as much as a week. At this point, Volkov did not give Gorski another thought. Overall, the Russian was feeling content as he did a final *headcount** of the Polish delegates and found that all 27 of them were at the station and ready to get on the late-morning train back to the east. Later in the day, once the railway car crossed the border back into Poland, Volkov looked out the window, took out a small *flask⁺* of vodka, and drank every last drop. He did not think again about Major Gorski who had helped make Volkov's own stay in Vienna so easy.

For one thing, the Russian was pleased and aware that the Soviet Secret Police and Red Army would soon be imposing very tough rules on the Polish people. The whole idea of *cracking down⁺* on the Poles and other Eastern Europeans resisting Russian rule made the Russian Major very happy indeed. While he had not personally participated in the Katyn Forest *massacre§* of Polish prisoners early in WWII, he would gladly have done so if he had been assigned to that operation. Among the Soviet Secret Police officers in Warsaw, Volkov, after all, was widely known as a *hardline§ enforcer*** of the laws and of punishments—he was, in fact, *enthusiastically⁺⁺* looking forward to the new Soviet policy to crush Polish *resistance.⁺⁺*

---

*   Headcount: Counting systematically ... one, two, three and so on.
†   Flask: A small bottle used for carrying gin, vodka or whisky.
‡   Cracking down: Getting tough with.
§   Massacre: The murder of great numbers of innocent people.
¶   Hardline: Very strict and harsh.
** Enforcer: A person who makes people follow rules and also punishes people who do not.
†† Enthusiastically: With eagerness and spirit.
‡‡ Crushing: Breaking or punishing.

On the other hand, Volkov did not dislike, let alone hate, Major Gorski as he *despised** most other Poles. This was due probably to Gorski's Communist Party membership as well as his natural *survivability trait*[†]—Gorski tended to get along with all people and was not inclined to clash with those different from himself. This, in Visitor's mind, had been one of the *principal*[‡] reasons he was *confident*[§] on the probable success of this operation—to get a spy in Warsaw.

For the first 24 hours after surgery, Major Gorski had been in a very deep sleep in the recovery room clinic across the street from the Vienna General Hospital. Dr. Brandt had chosen this quiet place for recovery because he knew there would be little or no chance the Russians in Central Vienna would know that Gorski was there. Dr. Brandt knew also that his patient would get the rest he needed on the weekend and be available as early as Monday morning to meet with Visitor and begin his operations training.

---

* Despised: Hated or had a terrible, automatic dislike for someone—in this case just about all Poles.
† Survivability Trait: The ability to endure or last when facing difficult or dangerous conditions.
‡ Principal: Main or most important.
§ Confident: Positive or optimistic.

Vienna General Hospital

10

*Stay-Behind Training**

While the Polish Major was recovering from his surgery, and while Russian Major Volkov was traveling back to Warsaw by train, Visitor put together the *covert training program*† for Gorski. Visitor himself would be *conducting*‡ the spy training over the course of the week. The covert training would be conducted in a private wing of the rehabilitation clinic where Major Gorski was recovering from surgery. This was where Dr. Brandt's wife was employed as the senior medical administrator. She would be making sure that the meetings held with Gorski would be done in private. Dr. Matt Hale had not informed his former war-time ally, Dr. Brandt, exactly what was the U.S. Government's interest in Gorski—or even that the Polish Major would be returning to Poland. Nonetheless, by this time in mid-1947, intelligent and *influential*§ Viennese like Dr. Brandt had already made their personal decision to support The West and not the Russians. Dr. Brandt clearly was on the side of The West. By this time in Austria, fortunately, Russian Communists were unpopular as was clearly demonstrated in

---

*   Stay-Behind Training: This is the special preparation given to spies who will be operating inside the enemy camp, or headquarters, and cannot afford to make mistakes that could cost them their lives.
†   Covert Training Program: Secret spy training.
‡   Conducting: Running the training.
§   Influential: Important people with good contacts in Vienna government, politics and police circles.

the country's first post-war election in late 1946 where the non-Communists received over 95% of the Austrian vote.

The five days of training that Visitor planned for Gorski were very *concentrated** because the Polish Major had to be on the train back to Warsaw by the next Saturday morning. It was helpful that Gorski was familiar with the Russians and knew how to avoid problems since he had to deal with them on a regular basis. On Monday, Visitor planned to concentrate on Gorski's own personal safety and security. Now that the Polish Major had shown that he had *indirect access*[†] to Soviet military intelligence on a *strategic level,*[‡] he had to be protected as completely as possible. Because of this, Gorski's personal safety was *foremost*[§] in Visitor's operational planning. *The Pentagon*[¶] in Washington already considered Gorski to have great *potential value*** as an intelligence source. At this point in 1947—after two years of dealing with the Soviets since the war—the U.S. Government's most important unanswered intelligence question was whether the Soviets would attack and make The West end up in another war—this time, one started by the Russians. What made the matter even more important was that the Soviet Red Army—especially its tank forces—far *outnumbered*[††] all

---

*   Concentrated: Given at a rather fast pace.

†   Indirect Access: Which meant that, although he did not get to see important intelligence information of the Red Army, he was in contact with Russian Generals who knew about Soviet war plans and occasionally let him know what was going on.

‡   Strategic Level: In this case, most important intelligence would include war plans of the Soviet Red Army and especially whether they were preparing and taking steps to attack The West.

§   Foremost: The first and most significant step in the training process.

¶   The Pentagon: Built during World War II, the Pentagon is headquarters for all of America's military services.

**   Potential value: What intelligence he could provide in the future.

††   Outnumbered: There were far more Soviet tanks than the Americans had in Poland and Eastern Europe.

the armies in Europe, those from America as well as England. Militarily, things looked rather *grim*.*

As a result, Visitor was *crystal clear*† on the great importance of Gorski's safety—he had to do everything he could possibly do to help make Gorski an effective spy. But, equally important was that the Americans must try to keep Gorski from being caught by the Soviet NKVD. So, the first thing Visitor did was establish a 90-day *cooling-off period*‡ during which Gorski was told that—with one very important exception—he must do absolutely nothing back in Warsaw for the next three months that could possibly call attention to himself or accidentally alert the Russian Secret Police. Visitor discussed with the Polish Major that he needed to behave back in Poland exactly the same as he had acted before coming to Vienna. Therefore, if the Russians were to take an interest in him from the viewpoint of security—maybe because he had just returned from Austria where the American intelligence agents were known to be active—NKVD would see nothing new or unusual in Gorski's behavior that would raise suspicions. Later on, after the cooling-off period was over, a suitable *commo plan*§ would be developed that would both protect Gorski and enable him to send intelligence reports to the American Intelligence Group in Warsaw.

---

* Grim: Not very good; in fact quite unfavorable for the Americans and Western Europe.

† Crystal Clear: As easy to see as looking through a sparkling clean window.

‡ Cooling-Off Period: A period of time he would do no spying and no reporting. This was just in case the Soviet Secret Police investigated him after his Vienna visit as a way to be sure he had not been recruited by Western spy services.

§ Commo Plan: This is what spies call the secret communications plan that protects intelligence operations from being discovered by a foreign government, in this case the Soviet Russians.

What, then, was the exception that Visitor wished to discuss? It was pretty *straightforward**—what should or could Gorski do before the cooling-off period ended if he learned that the Red Army was about to attack The West? Obviously, a war between East and West would be *catastrophic*.† The Red Army in Europe at that time was several times larger and probably too strong to be stopped—especially if they made an unannounced sneak attack, one that came without any warning.

Gorski understood this right away. He knew what had happened to Poland back in 1939 when the Nazis sneak-attacked from the west on the 1st of September and the Russians did the same from the east on the 17th. It was not necessary for Visitor to convince Gorski of the seriousness of such an invasion. The Polish Major enthusiastically told Visitor that he would immediately warn the Americans—assuming he had a safe way to do so.

For a moment, Gorski became quiet as he recalled friends he knew who had been killed fighting both the Germans and the Russians. This discussion reminded him that he not only had not fought the Russians—like other, patriotic Poles—but instead had in fact been working with the Soviets in Warsaw since the War. This was a stain on his *conscience*‡ that Gorski very badly wanted to erase. This led to the subject of clandestine or spy communications including signaling devices and short-wave radios that might be capable of telling the Americans of

---

*   Straightforward: Clear, simple, uncomplicated.
†   Catastrophic: Causing countless deaths and destruction as occurred in World Wars I and II.
‡   Conscience: The inner voice that tells a person whether something is right or wrong.

such an attack. As eager as Gorski was to please Visitor, it was Visitor who insisted that Gorski would not be carrying any obvious spy devices or spy materials when he got off the train in Warsaw. Later on, Visitor assured the Polish Major, he would be given the equipment and materials he needed in his secret work ahead. But that would only happen if it were safe to do so.

The rest of Monday was used to review with Gorski maps of Poland and areas where, as far as Gorski was aware, the Soviet Red Army seemed to be concentrating its military forces. Gorski did mention one region in northwest Poland where, it was rumored, the Red Army Generals had been talking privately among themselves about creating a most secret military base that would be used to attack The West. This base was being kept *Top Secret** by the Russian Generals—in fact, that town and military base had been taken off all maps of Poland. Major Gorski only learned of this when he was helping a senior Russian officer with the travel route he would follow for a military inspection.

Borne Sullinowa was a small village in Western Poland almost 300 miles north of the city of Krakow. Before WWII, the town was part of Germany and the Nazis had built a major Army base there. Hitler visited the base on August 18, 1938 and it was used by the Nazi Army to prepare their invasion of North Africa. After Germany lost the war, a large slice of eastern Germany—including Borne Sullinowa and its secret military base—became part of Poland. During the entire Cold War, however, the town and base were kept hidden and treated not

---

*   Top Secret: The highest or most important intelligence information of the government.

as Polish territory but, instead, as a part of Soviet Russia itself. Poles were not allowed to visit there. Its location and role in Red Army war planning were considered 'Top Secret.'

On Tuesday, Visitor spent a great part of the day discussing with Major Gorski what he could do if he learned that Soviet tank and infantry forces were preparing and taking steps to launch an attack on The West. Obviously, that would be critically important information he would be expected to report. After all, and Gorski agreed, it would do no good if he learned about an upcoming invasion but had no practical way to get that *critical** warning to the Americans.

Wednesday's training was all about clandestine communications and how Gorski might be able to report to the American Intelligence Group in Warsaw as well as receive questions and feedback on his reports. The subject of *dead drops*† was discussed at length as Visitor showed sample materials and photos or sketches so that Gorski would be able to use such strategies safely and effectively. Gorski was not too *confident*‡ that downtown Warsaw was currently a safe place to use dead drops—the streets, alleyways and fields were constantly changing as refugees and school kids were always picking up trash and litter, thinking the materials might be useful at home. Warsaw, after all, had been badly bombed and shelled by *artillery*§ in the war—so, what looked one way today might look entirely different tomorrow.

---

*   Critical: Extremely important.
†   Dead drops: Rocks, tree branches, trash and other secret hiding devices and materials which could be used for Gorski and the Intelligence Group to send messages back and forth with little chance of falling into the wrong hands.
‡   Confident: To be certain or sure of oneself.
§   Artillery: Long guns that shoot explosive shells several miles.

Thursday morning was used to give the Polish Major a course in *Secret Writing** and the use of chemicals to send reports not detectable by postal authorities. If and when the security situation in Poland became clearer—and the Intelligence Group had successfully tested sending secret writing messages out of Poland—Visitor decided it would not be *timely*† enough in Gorski's case, especially if he was trying to send information that the Red Army was getting ready to attack. In this case, Gorski needed to have a practical way to get an *Emergency Signal*‡ to the American Intelligence Group. But how?

As they were chatting during lunch, Visitor asked Gorski whether he had a dog and, if so, did he think he could carry with him to Warsaw a simple dog whistle from Vienna. If he had no dog, could he get one? Gorski said he had no dog but could get one when he returned to Poland—after all, there were *stray dogs*§ everywhere. A dog would give him an excuse to go for walks around the parks and streets of Warsaw—it could be helpful also in finding acceptable dead drop sites.

By Friday, Major Gorski was well trained in the *principles and practices*¶ of clandestine commo even though he had not been able to practice using such tools and techniques on the

---

* Secret Writing: Writing a letter that uses invisible chemicals that are not visible until they are treated with heat or other ways for the hidden message to be read, usually by the spy organization in another country.

† Timely: Rapidly or fast enough.

‡ Emergency Signal: A warning that something terribly important was about to happen—like an invasion.

§ Stray Dogs: Animals that have no owner and are wandering around just trying to stay alive.

¶ Principles and Practices: The rules and the ways of operating secretly and safely (in Poland the Russian Secret Police were everywhere).

streets of Vienna before going home. With so many Soviet intelligence officers in Vienna, and with Gorski just getting over his surgery, it was considered safer to do all the covert training off the streets and *out of the public view.**

It was indeed fortunate that Visitor was there to conduct the training in Polish and to build on the good and growing relationship between them. Why would that be important? Well, the *litmus test*[†] in spy recruitment and spy training takes place later on, after the trained spy is back in his home country. Then—all alone—the new spy has to face the dangers, pressures and risks that would cost him his life if he is caught. Over the decades of the Cold War, many recruited and trained spies returned to their countries and, although having agreed to report secretly to an intelligence service, they were never heard from again. Instead, they simply ditched or threw away their spy gear in a river and quietly disappeared. They just were too afraid to be spies, after all.

Visitor's participation in the training would turn out to be essential to the success of the Gorski spy operation. For one thing—unknown to Major Gorski at this time—Visitor would soon be transferred to Poland where he would be in charge of all of the American covert operations—he would also be providing direct in-country operational support to the Polish Major. In all of Eastern Europe, history would show, Poland would *in the long run*[‡] turn out to be the most important nation in helping stop the *savage*[§] Russian bear from devouring Europe entirely.

---

*   Out of the Public View: Where Gorski would not be seen.

†   Litmus Test: Named after the reliable chemistry test for distinguishing acids and bases using litmus paper, a litmus test is a true test or measure of effectiveness.

‡   In the Long Run: Over the course of many years, in Poland's case four decades during which they were occupied and controlled by Soviet Russia, the Red Army and the Secret Police.

§   Savage: Cruel, brutal, uncivilized and very much like barbarians.

Before Visitor and Gorski finished the training, they spent a couple of hours reviewing options in case the Polish Major had to get an emergency signal to the Americans that the Red Army was preparing an attack from their strong base in Poland. Given the fact that there was no safe or reasonable way for Gorski to meet secretly with the Americans in or around Warsaw, it was decided that the best way would be for Gorski to send a signal that an attack was *imminent** by using the silent dog whistle Visitor had given him and that he would be carrying back to Poland. David had donated Thor's dog whistle for the Gorski operation and delivered it to Visitor using the BMW R75 motor cycle with side car to ferry him and Thor to downtown Vienna on Gorski's last night in town. Such a whistle—invented a hundred years earlier—sends an *ultrasonic signal†* that cannot be heard by humans but can indeed be heard by dogs. It also could possibly be detected by the police or Red Army who

David and Thor Deliver Dog Whistle to Visitor

---

* Imminent: Ready or about to happen.
† Ultrasonic signal: A higher pitch than humans can hear.

might know that an ultrasound signal had been sent somewhere in Warsaw—but they would have no idea precisely where it was sent from or who had sent it.

Gorski was told he should send it in the evening as he walked along the Vistula River in downtown Warsaw. If the Soviet attack was scheduled to begin in less than 72 hours, Gorski should send a second signal three minutes later. In any case—whether he blew the silent whistle once or twice—he should immediately throw the whistle into the river and walk away into the darkness. At this point, he should take a train to Krakow where he would be contacted at his sister's farm by Visitor himself or another *friend of Chopin** to arrange for their evacuation to Austria.

A full week later than originally scheduled, Major Piotr Gorski went to the Vienna railroad station and boarded the train back to Warsaw. It was July 19, 1947 and, *within*,† he seemed to be a changed man He felt he had *vigor*‡ in his walk. He was holding his head high as he took a seat in the section reserved for military officers and senior government officials. He did have some tightness in his bandaged abdomen where once he had *borne*§ a perfectly-healthy gall bladder.

Remembering the advice that Visitor had kept repeating—about not drawing attention to himself—Gorski kept from smiling the smile he was feeling in his heart. After all, he was

---

*   Friend of Chopin: The code name first used by Gorski himself to help the Americans contact Dr. Kaminski in Linz.
†   Within: Inside himself.
‡   Vigor: Energy, strength.
§   Borne: Carried.

returning to Poland to work for peace. So, *consciously** and with *determination*,[†] Major Gorski put on the dour, sour, and humorless face of *Soviet Man*.[‡] In crossing the Polish border, he was starting his new career as a secret American spy in *Soviet-occupied Poland*.[§] And, if the Americans with his help learned what the Red Army and Soviet Russian Secret Police were up to, then maybe war could be avoided and East and West might live in peace. If so, it would in good part be due to American leaders having good intelligence from brave spies such as Major Gorski.

---

*   Consciously: Completely aware of what he was doing.

†   Determination: With the strong intention of hiding his true feelings at that moment.

‡   Soviet Man: An unhappy person beaten down by a heartless Soviet system.

§   Soviet-occupied Poland: From the moment the Red Army came into the country, Poland became a nation totally controlled by the Soviet Russians. In reality, Poland was Poland no longer.

Visitor Trains Gorski in Secret Communications

11

Hide and Seek

As a *wannabe** junior spy, David Hale awoke this late July 1947 morning with his anxiety level climbing again. This was just as it had been right after the Hales had rescued the Polish scientist from the *clutches*† of the Soviet Russian Secret Police (Book I, *Escape to the West*). Now, having dealt effectively with the Nazi goons who had returned to the Hale castle in search of buried loot (Book II, *Nazis on the Run*), David found the morning peace and quiet *unsettling*‡—again, he was fearful that the spy games may have come to an end and that he would be left with little more than memories because the 'Knights' of Hale castle had slain all the local dragons. Yes, as leaders of dozens of nations grappled with the chaos and *turmoil*§ of post-War Europe, including Austria's, David secretly was wishing that things would not settle down completely and get fixed too quickly. After all, the recruitment and training of Polish Major Gorski—though pretty darn good—was not sufficient itself to *turn the tide*⁅ and bring the Cold War to a quick and favorable end. Besides, the boy had another month before school began again—he was in no mood to settle for that.

---

* Wannabe: A person who 'wants to be' just like someone else, in this case David wanted to be like his dad working for the American Intelligence Group in Austria.
† Clutches: Claws or traps.
‡ Unsettling: Disturbing.
§ Turmoil: Chaos or messiness.
⁅ Turn the Tide: Reverse or completely alter, change or fix.

Obviously, David Hale was thinking first about his own situation, not the *overwhelming** struggle between West and East—basically, between the Americans and the Russians. The boy wanted to do things spies do. At eleven years old, he was not always able *to see the big picture*[+] as clearly and as automatically as could Visitor and his dad. He did, however, have *a good itch*[‡] to get back out on the streets and in the parks of Vienna to take spy photos which were of value to Visitor and the American Intelligence Group in Vienna. In sum, he wanted again to experience the fear and then the triumph that comes when he defeated the *genuine*[§] evil knights of his day's world—the Russians—trying to capture Austria which had battled foreign armies for a thousand years. *Fittingly,*[¶] he would soon get his chance. Fortunately, he would not be on his own but instead he would have support and guidance.

On the Friday after Major Gorski went back to Warsaw, Visitor arranged to visit the Hale's castle in the evening. He wanted to discuss downtown Vienna and what David had accomplished so far in the parks within the First or International District at the very heart of historic Vienna. The photos David had taken were proving to be quite valuable to Visitor as he planned future intelligence operations against the Russians who had their Headquarters at Vienna's Imperial Hotel quite close to

---

*   Overwhelming: Massive, enormous.
†   To See the Big Picture: Understand the most important things happening in Austria and across Eastern Europe.
‡   A Good Itch: A very strong desire or hope.
§   Genuine: Real, not imagined.
¶   Fittingly: For good reasons.

the Russian World War II Memorial and nearby *Stadtpark*.* At 8:30 in the evening, Visitor arrived at the Hale castle through the garden after he came up the river by boat—Visitor was clearly determined to protect the operational security and cover of the Hales, even if it meant that getting to the castle for him was a bit damp, as well as *time consuming.*†

Dr. Matt Hale greeted Visitor and suggested they go to the kitchen and have their discussion over a cup of coffee and a slice of strudel that Katrina Vogel had baked in the afternoon. David was upstairs going through his growing collection of photographs and would join them later if Visitor thought that would be useful. Visitor said that would indeed be good because what the Intelligence Group was planning operationally very much concerned the boy. Regardless, Visitor wanted to first bounce off the doctor the operational plan and get his approval even before raising it with Hale's enthusiastic son. As the meeting began, Visitor explained to Matt Hale how the worsening security situation was *altering*‡ the Americans' plan to deal with the growing Soviet Russian threat.

To begin with, Washington was concerned that the Red Army was showing signs of strengthening their forces, possibly to be able to attack the Western Allies as soon as next Spring— maybe even sooner! The military leaders at the Pentagon had decided, therefore, to prepare their military forces in Germany

---

*   Stadtpark: People's park, in German. This is the largest park in the International Zone and quite handy for spies from the Russian Embassy headquarters in the Imperial Hotel. Because the Russians had reached Vienna first, they had chosen the most impressive hotel and occupied it until leaving Austria altogether in 1955.

†   Time Consuming: Slower than simply driving there by car.

‡   Altering: Changing.

and Austria for stay-behind operations that would help slow down and possibly stop the Soviet Red Army before it would be able to push through and conquer all of Western Europe. So, throughout the American Zones in both Germany and Austria, the U.S. Army had secretly started burying military weapons and war-fighting supplies to help defend these countries should the Soviets launch a surprise attack. At the very least, they would be able to slow the Red Army *advance** until the American and British forces in the U.S. and England were able to respond. Because the Soviets had so many *armored tanks*† as the *backbone*‡ of their military power, the Americans were hiding thousands of *bazookas*§ in caves and salt mines as well as burying them in fields throughout Central and Western Austria and Germany.

Visitor then spoke about the reason why he needed to see the Hales *on short notice*.¶ Visitor explained that the American Intelligence Group in Vienna had decided NOT to send the Hale-Castle Nazi Gold bars to the United States. Since the bars had most likely been made from gold the Nazis stole from the Austrians themselves, it would not be right for the U.S. to take it out of the country. Instead, the four gold bars would remain in Austria in case the Red Army invaded—the gold could then be used to buy weapons to help fight off the Communist forces. In fact, Visitor said, the gold bars would be buried in Vienna, probably within the International Zone. But

---

*   Advance: Progress conquered territory.
†   Armored tanks: War machines that have several inches of steel covering.
‡   Backbone: The strongest structure and foundation.
§   Bazookas: Weapons carried by soldiers that fire shells that can destroy a heavy armored steel tank.
¶   On Short Notice: So quickly.

where? Since the Hales had found the gold in the first place, the Intelligence Group wanted their input and suggestions on where to put the gold bars so they would not be *stumbled upon** accidentally.

Matt Hale, at this point, called David to join the men in the kitchen to see if he could think of a safe place for the gold bars. When David heard the call, he set aside his batch of photos and started down the back stairway in his usual acrobatic way. He entered the kitchen and was pleased to find Katrina's strudel and the hot chocolate his dad had prepared. He then got a big surprise that went beyond anything he might have dreamed—Visitor proceeded to ask him where he would bury the four 25 pound gold bars in downtown Vienna if he wanted them never to be found by anyone, accidentally. That's right— for years and years to come! After all, David had become as familiar with the city layout and design as had anyone in the American Intelligence Group. Being such a *precocious*† young boy, David just might come up with the best solution! At this point, David sat there eating his strudel, thought a while, and said he had two questions for Visitor: Should the gold be buried altogether in one location or separately in four—and must it be buried inside or outside?

Visitor was so glad he had the boy on his team because playing hide and seek was something more natural to kids than adults. But, in answer to his first question, Visitor said that each gold bar should be hidden away from and *independent of*‡ the other three. "And, oh, outside, definitely outside!"

---

* Stumbled Upon: Found by a stranger's plain luck.
† Precocious: More alert and capable than most other eleven year olds.
‡ Independent of: Separate or away from.

After talking and speculating for nearly two hours, it was getting late, so Visitor suggested they *call it a night** and meet the following evening to come up with an effective plan that would *practically guarantee*† the gold would remain safe and available to the Austrian Army in case the Russians were to attack. Recently, the American Intelligence Group's own *assessment*‡ was that, because things were getting so bad across Eastern Europe, the chances of a Red Army attack in the next six months was somewhere around *fifty-fifty*.§

Before leaving, Visitor explained the method he would use to bury the gold—David needed this information so he would be able to do his part in the operation. The four gold bars, Visitor explained, had already been *re-cast*⁋ to remove the Nazi Swastika on each bar found in the Hale castle cellar. Instead, each new bar now had *imprinted*** the historic Austrian Black Eagle symbol and weighed almost 25 pounds. Visitor told David his job would be to find four hiding places in the parks of Vienna and mark each burial spot with the railroad spikes Visitor brought with him. Once David selected a site, the boy should use his foot to drive the spike into the ground so Visitor can find it with a magnet that would *assure*†† him he was burying the gold in precisely the right place. Each of the

---

*   Call It a Night: Decide to do no more that day.
†   Practically Guarantee: Make just about certain.
‡   Assessment: Judgment or conclusion.
§   Fifty-Fifty: Just about the same chance that an attack would take place or not (50% to 50%).
⁋   Re-Cast: Melted down and placed in new molds.
**   Imprinted: Printed by force or pressure and therefore a permanent marking deep within each gold bar.
†† Assure: Guarantee or make certain.

four hiding place reports should include a sketch, a photo and a written description of the site.

David then asked Visitor how he would bury the bars so no one else would notice that some recent digging had taken place. Visitor explained that one of his engineers had designed a tool that could drive a pipe deeply underground—the engineer had shown he was able to drill a *vertical hole** three-inches wide and just over 6 feet underground. This tool would be used to drill the hole, then each gold bar would be pushed down deep enough so that anyone doing gardening or planting bushes would not reach the level of the gold—at least six feet underground! Each *insertion*† of a gold bar, and filling the hole with dirt, would take the Visitor team about 20–30 minutes from start to finish.

After Visitor left their meeting by way of the river, father and son chatted for a while longer. David was delighted the gold bars were not being shipped back to Fort Knox in Kentucky where America's golf reserves are *safeguarded*‡ in the country's most heavily-protected fortress. With tons and tons of America's gold bars already buried at Fort Knox in huge underground vaults, the boy figured that 'Thor's gold,' as David called it, belonged and could be more useful right there in Austria. As the clock struck midnight, David headed up to his room. For almost an hour, he lay wide awake as he thought about the dozen or so parks he had visited, most of which were either in the American or International Zone. He then fell into a very deep sleep.

---

*   Vertical hole: Straight down towards the center of the earth.
†   Insertion: Burying or implanting.
‡   Safeguarded: Protected by heavy security.

When the sun came up and David awoke and—for reasons not clear to the junior spy—he thought he had his answer. To make sure the gold would not be discovered accidentally or by chance, he needed hiding places that would never change—not for years, not for decades, and not even for centuries. "The *memorials**" he said out loud, of course, "THE MEMORIALS!"

When the boy got out of bed this Saturday morning, he sat at his desk and began putting together a plan. Ordinarily, he would have started the day by going downstairs looking for his dad to tell him what he was thinking. But, this time, he decided he would, on his own, do some deep thinking and try coming up with a complete solution to 'the gold problem.' This time, he wanted to offer his dad and Visitor not *merely[†]* a general idea without *details.[‡]* Instead, he would think through the entire problem the way his dad and Visitor seemed to do when faced with an important and difficult intelligence matter—they took their time—they made sure they *took everything into account.[§]*

Yes, this time, the plan David offered would be A to Z complete! To be certain he would be proposing a plan of action that was *accurate,[¶]* David decided to go into downtown Vienna for the day and check out the three parks he had in mind. He asked

---

* The Memorials: Statues and monuments built in public parks and along public avenues in remembrance of former battles, victories, heroes and famous leaders and citizens.

† Merely: Only or simply.

‡ Details: The many minor or less important things that go into a plan to build something or solve a problem. David remembered the checklist his father had put together and used when rescuing the Polish scientist in Linz.

§ Took Everything into Account: Made sure they covered all fine points needed for complete planning.

¶ Accurate: Exactly right, correct.

his dad for a ride into the city so he and Thor could spend Saturday morning in the parks before they became too crowded with weekend family visitors. Before leaving the previous day, Visitor said he would probably do the burials of the four gold bars the next weekend, probably at 2:00 in the early morning of August 2nd when that night's full moon would give Visitor enough *luminescence** to see what he was doing. Once he found the railroad spikes David had *implanted,*† Visitor would drill the four holes a couple of yards down into the soil. Fortunately, Vienna's parks were closed at night so Visitor knew he could visit the three parks without being seen and plant the gold bars in total secrecy.

The parks David selected were within walking distance of each other, so he was sure he could scout them out on foot within 2 to 3 hours. He began at Vienna's City Park (called Stadtpark in German) that happened to be the largest public area in the International Zone of Central Vienna. Located near the center of the city, Stadtpark had two monuments that each had a dirt-grass area where a deep but narrow hole could be dug for *inserting*‡ a gold bar. David and Thor walked around Stadtpark for close to an hour and came across two statues that seemed just right for Visitor's purposes. Composer Franz Schubert's statue had been designed and built in 1872, some 75 years earlier than David's and Thor's *expedition*§ in late July 1947. The other statue in Stadtpark David assumed would never be moved was that of Johann Strauss, Jr. His monument showed

---

*   Luminescence: Brightness.
†   Implanted: Buried or placed.
‡   Inserting: Pushing a 2–3 inch gold bar into the ground.
§   Expedition: A trip for exploring.

Monument to Composer Franz Schubert, Vienna

Monument to Composer Johann Strauss, Vienna

the Waltz-King *composer** playing a violin and was coated in a gold-colored metal. It had been erected in 1921 and was possibly the most popular statue in all of Vienna.

The next park where David found a statue he liked for the project was in the People's Garden (Volksgarten in German) which is part of the Hofburg Palace in the center of Vienna. This *majestic†* monument had been built in 1875 in memory of Austria's favorite poet and writer, Franz Grillparzer.

The fourth and final memorial David selected was that of Franz Joseph Haydn who not only composed great music, but had been a *beloved‡* teacher of both Beethoven and Mozart. Haydn died in 1809 and, though his *remains§* had been later moved to another cemetery, the original gravestone stood in Haydnpark, named after him in downtown Vienna.

David and Thor were waiting at the entrance to Stadtpark when his dad drove up. The boy was not surprised to see that so many Viennese families had arrived at the park since much of the city was still recovering from the bombing and families needed to get away from their own badly-bombed homes and get some fresh air. Father and son returned to the castle and David set about writing the plan for his early-Sunday visit to the three parks to plant the four spikes that Visitor would need to put the gold bars where they belonged.

---

*   Composer: Writer of music.
†   Majestic: Spectacular or amazing.
‡   Beloved: Highly respected and
§   Remains: Bones.

Monument to Poet Franz Grillparzer, Vienna

Monument to Composer Joseph Hayden, Vienna

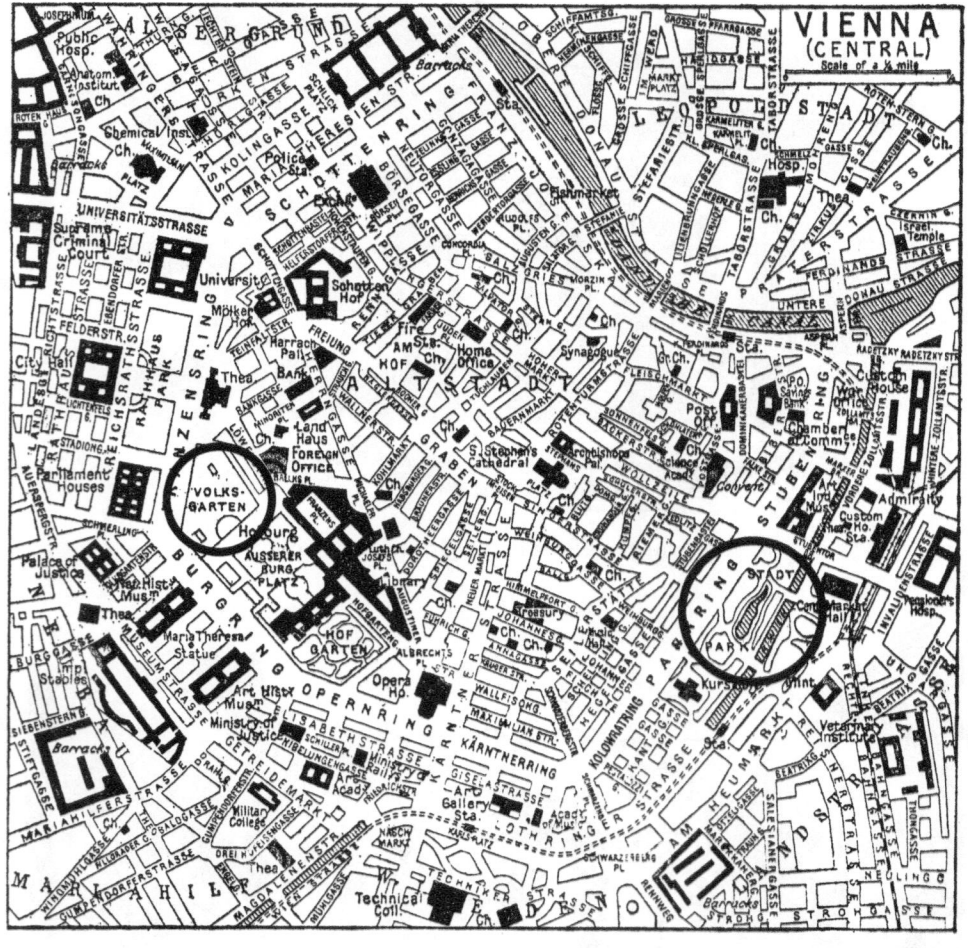

Map of downtown Vienna around the end of WWII, with circles showing
the locations of Volksgarten and Stadtpark. Haydnpark is off the map to
the southwest (near the lower left corner of this page).

12

American Baseball Comes to Vienna

By mid-point in the summer of '47—while Europe and Asia were in growing *turmoil** from the Communist armies of both the Russians and the Chinese—Americans in the States were enjoying their lives as though the end of World War II meant the end also to serious foreign dangers. Families were moving on with their peacetime lives—buying homes and cars, going out to parks, picnics and beaches while baseball continued to be America's favorite sport. The New York Yankees continued in their *dominance*† of the game which began back in 1919 when the Boston Red Sox sold baseball homerun great, Babe Ruth, to the New York Yankees. In 1947, to be precise, the Yankees would win 40 more games than they lost while the Red Sox would end up far behind, in third place, trailing behind both the Yankees and the Detroit Tigers.

So what does Major League baseball in 1947 have to do with the Cold War in Eastern Europe and a boy named David? Well, at the time when Americans were living their lives with a high degree of *normalcy*,‡ the junior spy set aside his baseball concerns and was engaged in the growing battle of America against Soviet Russia. And by the last week of July 1947—some 2,000

---

* Turmoil: Chaos and troubles.
† Dominance: Winning ways in the competition.
‡ Normalcy: The ordinary way things are done when there is not a war or total chaos.

miles to the east of New York and Boston in Vienna—lifelong baseball fan David Hale was preparing a plan to bury gold bars to do battle, not for a baseball trophy or great publicity, but for the quiet satisfaction that comes when freedom itself wins against *tyranny*.*

Accordingly,[†] when the boy got thinking about the parks, he decided to connect his Vienna monuments plan to American baseball in a way that would protect the operation's security in the years ahead—he would create and use a code that would be *unbreakable*[‡] and *enduring*.[§] In fact, even the great Russian chess players, he thought, would not be able to unscramble David's code. It would be powerful and operationally secure. David felt *confident*[¶] it would meet with Visitor's approval.

Before starting to write up his plan, he reviewed the baseball book he had bought in Cooperstown, New York at the National Baseball Hall of Fame. David examined the records of four players who were voted into The Hall in its first two years, back in 1936 and 1937. He chose, from the 1936 group, Ty Cobb and Babe Ruth. From the 1937 group he chose great pitcher Cy Young and great batter Napoleon or 'Nap' LaJoie. In each case, David based his selection on career records that, even ten years later in 1947, were considered long-lasting and probably unbreakable.

Detroit Tigers batter Ty Cobb's Lifetime Batting Average was .366. To come up with a measurement that made sense

---

*   Tyranny: The harsh rule by a cruel leader or group over the lives of simple citizens.

†   Accordingly: Therefore, or as a result.

‡   Unbreakable: A secret code not able to be understood or unraveled.

§   Enduring: Lasts forever, not temporary.

¶   Confident: Sure of himself

and would help Visitor find the railroad spikes in the middle of the night, David decided he would take Cobb's 366 as centimeters—then he would make the 366 a simpler measurement by *converting* it to feet. How would he do that? He remembered his dad's math class where he learned to convert centimeters to feet by dividing the number of centimeters by 30.48. THE FIRST SPIKE IN VOLKSGARTEN PARK WOULD BE PLACED 12 FEET EAST OF THE FRANZ GRILLPARZER MONUMENT. (366 divided by 30.48 equals 12 feet.) Using the centimeters-to-feet conversion method, David did the same conversion to the Hall of Fame career number of the other three American ballplayers.

New York Yankee slugger Babe Ruth, for example, had 714 Career Home Runs. So, David divided Ruth's 714 home runs by 30.48 which meant that THE SECOND SPIKE WOULD BE PLANTED 23.4 FEET FROM THE FRANZ JOSEPH HAYDN MONUMENT IN HAYDN PARK. (714 divided by 30.48 equals 23.4 feet.)

Cleveland pitching great Cy Young had 511 Career Winning Games. THE THIRD SPIKE WOULD BE PLANTED 16.8 FEET FROM THE FRANZ SCHUBERT MONUMENT IN STADTPARK. (511 divided by 30.48 equals 16.8 feet.)

Finally, Nap LaJoie had baseball's Single-Year Highest Batting Average of .426. THE FOURTH SPIKE, then, WOULD BE PLANTED 14 FEET FROM THE JOHANN STRAUSS MONUMENT, ALSO IN STADTPARK. (426 divided by 30.48 equals 14 feet.)

---

* Converting: In Math, one must divide by a conversion factor that is correct. For example, to change feet to inches, one uses a conversion factor of 12 inches being equal to one feet. So, when David needed to change the large centimeter numbers of the four Hall of Fame players to feet, he divided each player's Hall of Fame record number by the correct conversion number—30.48. As a result, Visitor would have a small and simple measurement to find the buried spikes. After all, he would be doing the burying of the gold at night.

In all four cases, a gold bar would be buried directly *due east** of the front left corner of each monument exactly at the distance shown for that particular player and monument. Needless to say, the secret code itself would be explained on an entirely separate paper. The Austrian parks and monuments in David's report to the American Intelligence Group would be re-named "The Ty Cobb," the second would be "The Babe Ruth," the third would be called "The Cy Young," and the last one would be known as "The Nap LaJoie."

To locate the spike he would use in burying the gold, Visitor would be using an American tape measure in feet and inches. He would also be using a *compass*† to find the spikes and be burying the gold bars exactly to the east of each monument. The boy then took a clothesline and cut it to give himself lengths of ropes of 12 feet, 23.4 feet, 16.8 feet and 14 feet that he would use with Thor's help to bury—and Visitor would later use to locate—the railroad spikes that would tell him where each gold bar should be hidden.

On Saturday night, Visitor was back at the castle to review the plan David had been working on and make certain that everyone—Matt Hale, David and Visitor himself—understood how David was going to bury the spikes and how Visitor would later be burying the gold bars.

Needless to say, when David explained his coded system to his dad and to Visitor, each of the men was exceedingly pleased

---

*   Due east: Exactly to the east.

†   Compass: A hand-held instrument with a magnetized needle that points to the North Pole and permits its user to locate North and South, East and West. In this case, David chose to have each gold bar buried east of each monument's front-left base.

that the boy had put so much thought into it. Visitor was especially impressed by the boy's deep interest in operational security. But Visitor wanted to know why David had *devised** a coded system in the first place. After all, the only people who would know anything about the secret gold burial in Vienna would be the Hales and members of Vienna's American Intelligence Group.

The boy explained that in an earlier meeting Visitor had mentioned that the four gold bars were worth around $70,000—in 1947, that was a *great deal of money*.† So, David reasoned, why not try to make certain that no one in the future is tempted to steal the gold bars. After all, they were being hidden to protect Austria and certainly not to enrich a thief—whether Russian, Austrian or American! Visitor and Matt Hale both agreed that the junior spy was correct and his security warning would be followed. Visitor then remarked: "Not everyone is a *saint*,‡ so I agree with you that we must be extra careful. I will make absolutely sure that the secrecy of the 'David Code' and 'Thor's Gold Bars' are protected long into the future—in fact, longer than Russia presents a danger to other nations and people. Knowing the Russians as I do, I imagine that may well turn out to be a very long time."

Visitor left and both Hales went to bed.

---

* Devised: Created.
† Great Deal of Money: By 2023, for example, four gold bars weighing 100 pounds would today be worth Two Million, Eight Hundred Thousand Dollars! (100 pounds = 1600 ounces at $1,750 per ounce = $2,800,000.)
‡ Saint: An honest person who does everything right and would never steal, even a fortune in gold.

On Sunday morning at *sunrise**—5:22 am—father and son headed for downtown Vienna with Thor, as usual, sticking his handsome head out through the Mercedes rear window. They went first to Stadtpark with its Strauss and Schubert monuments, then on to Volksgarten and finally to Haydnpark. David brought along his carrying sack with the four railroad spikes, the four lengths of rope as well as the U.S. Army compass that Visitor had given him the previous week. Around his neck he hung the Leica camera so he looked like a bird watcher out for an early Sunday walk.

When he arrived at the Schubert statue, he took out the 16.8 foot rope and got Thor to hold it in his mouth just above the front left corner of the monument's foundation. David then took the compass and, after watching the needle point to the North, he was able to find the Easterly direction. He then placed one of the spikes on the ground while Thor just stood there seeming to enjoy his part in whatever game David was now playing. At this point, the boy dropped his end of the rope, looked all around to be sure that no one in the area was watching, and then drove the spike down into the soil with his boot. He then covered it with a handful of dirt.

And so it went with the three parks, the four monuments, the four spikes and the four lengths of rope. David also took several photos of each park and monument. The average time spent at each site turned out to be less than fifteen minutes. The entire time spent in downtown Vienna was a little less than two hours. David had some work to do writing his report, developing

---

*   Sunrise: When the sun in the early morning comes over the horizon and gradually brightens the world.

the film as well as drawing his sketches. His dad had a busy morning writing reports on the week's hospital visits. Dr. Hale happened to have a medical meeting scheduled at mid-week in downtown Vienna—he was able to pass David's *casing report** along to Visitor, who planned to bury the golden treasure in the Austrian capital on August's first full-moon night. The burial *phase*† of the operation went smoothly and Visitor was able to get it done with the help of the Intelligence Group's *technical wizard*‡ who had invented and built the *excavation*§ tool.

When Visitor sent a message to the Hales that he had buried the gold bars without difficulty—and especially to thank David—the junior spy sat on the castle wall and reviewed in his mind the previous week's activity. He thought back to the rainy day Thor and he had found the Nazi trunks in the castle north tunnel. He recalled the excitement he felt when he first showed his dad the entire cache of gold, money and documents on Germany's top 100 war criminals. And then he *mulled over*¶ in his mind how the four precious gold bars now lay buried in Vienna's parks when, instead, they could have been caught up in the *Nazi South American ratline*.** "What a different outcome," he thought. "What a great way to be spending my

---

* Casing Report: A report that shows the locations where spy material is buried—in this case, the four spikes.

† Phase: Part.

‡ Technical wizard: One so gifted in working in engineering/ technical things that he seems to be almost a magician.

§ Excavation: Hole digging for building a home, a highway or—as in this case—burying gold bars.

¶ Mulled over: Pondered or was thinking things over.

** Nazi South American Ratline: This was the organized secret operation after WWII to help Nazi war criminals escape Germany and Austria and avoid being punished for the war crimes they had committed during the war.

summer! What a wonderful dog is Thor! Oh my, I wonder—as in Hollywood movies—whether this might be The End."

Visitor and Major Gorski Review Warsaw Map
to Plan Future Clandestine Meetings

Epilogue
The Vienna Trilogy

Escape to the West – Book I
Nazis on the Run – Book II
Stopping the Russian Bear – Book III

The summer of 1947 for junior spy David Hale came to an end, much as the boy feared, without anything spectacular happening in the spy world beyond what had already occurred. The Polish scientist, Dr. Kaminsky, was working in the United States on nuclear safety. The four gold bars were resting peacefully near monuments in three of downtown Vienna's parks. The trio of former Gestapo Nazis were entirely out of the way; in fact, KAPUT! The recruited intelligence and trained spy was back in Poland where he would be supported by Visitor who was transferred to Warsaw in the middle of August. So, the Hale boy, in the course of a single summer, had assembled both great memories and satisfaction that his remaining in Vienna had been worthwhile.

Dr. Matt Hale and David did travel back to the States in late August and joined mother and daughter for two weeks of swimming, fishing, hiking and family conversation. Not discussed were the operational capers that had been the focus of Matt and David's summer. They were, after all, security-classified matters that would be shared only on a need-to-know basis. Mother and Ellie did notice a couple of things about David that caught their attention. To begin with, his German skills had improved greatly over what was the case back in June. The other change that Mom and sister Ellie saw in David was that he seemed more grown up and had become more responsible and serious.

Part of the reason they did not dwell on these changes in David is that they were told that Dr. Hale had been given an offer to take charge of the Refugee and Displaced Persons Medical programs in Germany as well as Austria. The good news for the family was that the Hales took a vote and everyone agreed they should keep the castle. David seemed to perk up when he heard he might get to visit Berlin with his dad in the fall. "Lots of spies in Berlin, Dad?"

"Yes, Son. Lots and lots."